Tillie Cole hails from a small town in northeast England. She grew up on a farm with her family with many rescue animals. After graduating from Newcastle University, Tillie and her husband traveled the world for a decade.

Now in Calgary, Canada, she writes, throwing herself into fantasy worlds and the minds of her characters. She writes Contemporary Romance, Dark Romance, Young Adult and New Adult novels and happily shares her love of alpha-men and strong female characters with her readers. Her books include *Raze*, *Reap* and *Ravage*.

Visit Tillie Cole online at:

www.tilliecole.com
www.facebook.com/tilliecoleauthor
www.facebook.com/groups/tilliecolestreetteam
Instagram: @authortilliecole
Twitter: @tillie_cole

Also by Tillie Cole:

Scarred Souls: Raze & Reap

RAVAGE

A SCARRED SOULS NOVEL

TILLIE COLE

PIATKUS

First published in the US in 2016 by St Martin's Press, New York
First published in Great Britain in 2016 by Piatkus

1 3 5 7 9 10 8 6 4 2

A CIP catalogue record for this book is available from the British Library.

ISBN 978-0-349-41107-1

Printed and bound in Great Britain by
Clays Ltd, St Ives plc

Papers used by Piatkus are from well-managed forests and other responsible sources.

MIX
Paper from
responsible sources
FSC® C104740

For those with a little darkness in their soul

ACKNOWLEDGMENTS

Mam and Dad, thank you for all the support. Thank you to my husband, Stephen, for keeping me sane. Samantha, Marc, Taylor, Isaac, Archie, and Elias, love you all. Thessa, thank you for being the best assistant in the world. Liz, thank you for being my super agent and friend. Eileen and Dom, the best editors a girl could ask for, thank you from the bottom of my heart. Thank you to all the bloggers that have supported my career from the start. And lastly, thank you to the readers. Without you none of this would be possible.

RAVAGE

PROLOGUE

Vladikavkaz,
Republic of North Ossetia–Alania
Russia

House of Abandoned Children
Fifteen years ago . . .
Three hard raps on the door downstairs startled me from my sleep. I squinted my eyes to look at the clock on the wall. The other boys in the room didn't move, but that didn't mean they weren't awake. We all knew what those hard raps meant—*they* were coming for *pickings.*

The Night Wraiths.

My body filled with ice when the long high-pitched creak of the main door's opening sliced through the expectant silence of the house. Then came the boots. Heavy boots pounding on the old wooden floor.

The rooms were pitch-black, as they always were at three o'clock in the morning. They always came at this time. I knew it was so the residents of the small town didn't hear or see *them* coming for us orphans.

Whispering, deep hushed voices seemed to fill every inch of the room; this was the signal that I needed my feet to move. As I pushed the thin blanket back from my bed, my bare feet hit the freezing-cold wood. I froze, not wanting to make a sound. Balling my hands into fists, I took small silent steps toward the back staircase. As I passed the neat rows of small cots, I could hear cries and sniffles from the other boys. They lay paralyzed with fear in the centers of their beds. The stink of urine filled my nostrils, some kids so afraid that they'd instantly wet themselves.

But I kept going. I needed to get to *her*.

My heart raced even though my movements were slow, until I reached the locked door that separated us boys from the girls. Removing the small pin I'd stored in the secret pocket of my pants, I silently inserted it into the lock. I focused on feeling for the lock to snap, while all the time desperately trying to listen for any sound, any sign that the *Noch' Prizrak*—the men known only as Night Wraiths—were heading to this floor.

A bead of sweat formed on my forehead, but I bit my lip to focus on the task. My hand moved slow and steady. With a quick exhale, the lock snapped and the doorknob turned slowly under my hand.

I glanced behind into the darkness, making sure that no one was following me. Sometimes a few of the other boys panicked and tried to follow. But they couldn't. I could only save two. The rest would have to fight for themselves, in this fucked-up house of hell. The house of *pickings* for the Wraiths that came at night.

Sensing that no one was behind, I slipped through the open door and quickly locked it. Returning the pin to my secret pocket, I slunk across the landing to the narrow staircase. Creeping carefully down each step, I came to another small landing. Seeing the door that led to *her* room, I picked the lock and slipped through. The second I entered the girls' dorm, a wave of loud crying hit me, burning my blood and rolling my stomach. These were the young girls. One of them was my sister: my best friend and my only reason for living.

I carefully stepped out fourteen paces, having memorized this short journey over the years of our imprisonment. I remembered everything. My brain never forgot a single thing. As I reached the fourteenth step, I pushed out my hand and immediately felt the small fingers of Inessa, my baby sister.

I smiled a small smile, fighting back tears as her little fingers shook, while gripping mine so impossibly tight. Wordlessly, I pulled her from the bed and lifted her into my arms. Inessa's head tucked into the crook between my neck and shoulder, her thin arms wrapping around my neck like a vise. I allowed myself a moment to squeeze her in return. The sound of a door being opened echoed through the hallways, forcing me into action.

I ran.

I ran as fast as my feet could carry us.

As I ran, screams from the dorms down the hall pierced the stillness of the night. Inessa's breathing grew faster. As I approached the door to the hallway, her cold hands tightened around my neck and she whispered, *"Noch' Prizrak."* The fear lacing her hushed voice almost caused my legs to buckle, but I pushed on through the doorway and into the empty stairwell. This time shouts and screams could be heard from the direction of our secret safe place.

Dread enveloped my body. I rocked on my feet, pure fear taking hold. I tried to think of what to do, where to go, when a crash sounded from the direction of the boys' dorm.

"Valentin?" Inessa sniffled into my neck. I could feel her whole body trembling. Her heartbeat was racing, its vibration pounding against my bare chest. I squeezed my eyes shut, trying desperately to think of another place to hide. The heavy boots of the Wraiths sounded like thunder, no, worse, a stampede of elephants, coming at us from all sides, slowly caging us in.

Then it hit me—the medical room on the floor above. In seconds my feet were sprinting up two flights of stairs. Inessa never made a single sound the entire time I was running. My thighs burned with the effort, until I came to the old door with a red cross painted on its only glass panel. But the sound of boots increased. The *boom boom* of footsteps grew closer still. I sweated. My heart raced. This wasn't going according to plan. The doorknob turned. Just then the loud click hit my ears. It was the boys' dorm door opening.

Rushing through the medical room door, I shut it tight. Moonlight filtered into the room, showing four small beds. There were no closets to hide in, no hidden doors or cupboards to hide behind or climb in.

Loud voices filled the air. Knowing that the Wraiths were coming our way, I ran to the farthest bed and placed Inessa on the floor. Her hand gripped on to mine so tightly, but I couldn't stop to comfort her. I had to get us safe.

Dropping to my knees, I pulled Inessa to the floor and crawled under the bed. Inessa followed—she always followed anything I said or did without question—and we shuffled under the small bed. I made for the corner, making myself as small as I could, and wrapped Inessa in my arms, her little body curled tightly against my chest. We stayed still, very still.

We breathed quietly. Inessa cried silent tears, her small body trembling. I kept tight hold, hoping and praying that the Wraiths wouldn't come our way. That they would pass us by tonight. That they wouldn't load us onto their trucks, headed to God knows where?

Placing my hand on the back on Inessa's head, I brought her

cheek against my chest and closed my eyes as I laid a kiss to the top of her black hair.

There was silence. A silence so heavy I didn't dare breathe for fear of it sounding out. Then a small creak outside of the medical room's door sent white-hot sparks slicing down my spine.

Inessa whimpered against my chest, so I put my finger over her lips, desperate for her to not make a sound.

I watched the floor for any sign of shadows, and my stomach fell when I saw the door open and several boots fill the room. Their voices were low as they talked to one another. They were Georgian, some words in their language unfamiliar. I held Inessa tighter, watching like a hawk as the boots walked around the room, stopping at each bed.

Then on a sharp turn, two sets of boots made their way from the room to the hallway outside. My wide eyes focused on the two pairs of boots left, two pairs of boots that slowly, painstakingly slowly, began approaching this bed.

I held my breath, too scared to even exhale as the boots came to a stop. Tears built in my eyes and I knew this was it.

The Wraiths had found us.

And it all happened so quickly.

In a flash the bed we were hiding under was overturned and the lights were flicked on, blanketing the room in a blinding white light. I flinched as Inessa screamed in my arms, the sudden flare of light blinding her, too.

I blinked, and blinked again, until the faces of the Wraiths came into view. There was a man, a huge dark man, and next to him was a woman. The woman was dressed all in black—as all of the Wraiths did—like a military uniform, her hair tied back in a bun. And her narrowed dark eyes were watching us, mainly focusing on the back of Inessa's head. I tried to keep my sister close, to keep her face hidden, but as if feeling the woman's stare, Inessa lifted her head and looked round. And I watched as the female Wraith smiled. A smile spread on her thin lips. Looking up to the man who stood by her side, she nodded her head.

Immediately understanding what that meant, I jumped to my feet, Inessa still in my arms. I ran. I ran forward as hard as I could, but as I got to the door the two guards I thought had left reached out and grabbed me by my hair. I gritted my teeth as pain shot through my head. Then, as I was unable to keep hold, a huge male Wraith ripped Inessa from my arms. Inessa screamed, her little arms stretching out for me. My body filled with red-hot rage; I punched out, my fist hitting the Wraith in the stomach.

I didn't stop. I kept hitting and hitting until he let go. My eyes were focused on Inessa, who was being backed away farther into the room. I lurched forward, but as I did, a pain slammed across my stomach. My legs gave way at the power of the blow, all breath leaving my body.

But I still didn't stop. Inessa was a statue in the Wraith's arms, her blue eyes wide and watching. As a tear fell down her cheek, I forced myself to move. Using my arms, I dragged myself toward my sister, teeth gritting at the pain in my stomach. Suddenly another blow hit me, this time across my back. My body slumped to the cold floor and blood trickled out of my mouth, the tinny taste coating my lips. But with one look at Inessa, I forced myself forward.

In the back of my mind I could hear the Wraiths talking to one another in hushed tones, but when Inessa reached out her hand I redoubled my efforts. I crawled and crawled toward my sister. Just as I was about to touch her hand, I was whipped off the floor. I fought and fought, struggling to get free, but the man who held me was too strong. My body was too weak from the blows.

"Let me go," I hissed in my native Russian. "You won't take her from me."

The woman moved into my line of sight. Her small dark eyes stared at me, a smirk pulled on her thin lips. My eyes flared and I snapped, "Let me go!"

That smirk then turned into a smile, and a man came over to stand beside her. It was the man who had flipped the bed to find us. His dark eyes watched me, his large arms folded over his chest.

The woman stepped back toward Inessa, her eyes never moving from mine. I watched her all the way. When she reached Inessa, my sister shrank back in fear. The woman lifted her hand, as if to strike.

I thundered out a shout.

I roared. I kicked and punched to get free. The woman dropped her hand, and I could see some kind of understanding flash across her face. She took four steps back to me—I counted each one—before lifting her hand to my face.

"You will do anything to protect this one, won't you?" she said in Russian, her thick Georgian accent coming through with each word.

My jaw clenched, but I said nothing. She laughed and the man next to her tipped his head to the side. The woman looked up at him and said, "We take both. She is a beauty. And he is unlike any other I've ever seen. So loyal and fierce."

The man nodded his head. My blood turned to ice. The woman lifted her hand and snapped her fingers. Immediately the man holding Inessa began carrying her out of the room, the man holding me moving, too. I never took my eyes off my sister as we were carried past the rows of lined-up boys and girls. I didn't move my eyes from my sister as they led us to a van. And I didn't take my eyes off my sister as the female Wraith moved her mouth to my ear and said, "If you want to keep her alive, you will learn to do anything we say. You will become one of us. You will become a Night Wraith, as this place calls us. You will become an unseen killer. You will become one with the night. You will be my prized *Ubiytsa,* my most effective assassin."

And I did.

As the years passed, I became a ghost in the night.

I became the deliverer of death.

I was torture.

I was pain.

I was the fucking nightmare that no one ever saw coming . . .

. . . until it was too late.

1

ZOYA

Manhattan, New York

Present day . . .

"Sykhaara," I murmured in shock, my chest cracking open with hope, a hope that I hadn't dare let myself feel in the twenty years since the massacre. The hope that my brother was alive. Now, after all these years, he was *alive.*

"Miss?" Avto, my protector and minder, pushed, but I was frozen on the spot. My legs were numbed in shock. Zaal, *my Zaal,* was alive.

Water blurred my eyes as I looked to Avto once more. "And Anri? Is there news of Anri?"

Avto's face fell with disappointment. "No, miss. There is no word of Anri. But our source got word of a Kostava arriving in the city. They watched him; they watched him and watched him. And—"

"And what?" I interrupted, hanging on every word Avto said.

"And it is Zaal, miss."

A sob ripped from my throat and my hand covered my mouth. I pictured Zaal in my mind. His eight-year-old face looking at me as he held me in his arms, walking us from our estate's forest toward the house. His smile was wide as he looked at me counting the three moles on his left cheek, *"One, two, three."* I remembered long black hair hanging down his back and his green eyes bright with life. And I remembered Anri walking beside us, his frame and hair the exact replica of Zaal's, but his eyes were a dark brown, like mine.

A hand landed on my shoulder pulling me from the memory. Avto was looking at me in concern.

"Miss, are you okay?"

"Yes," I whispered, then shook my head, "I don't know. It's just all so . . . I had hoped and prayed that he had survived, that both of them had, but when nothing was heard in all of these years, I had lost that hope. It . . . it is all too much to take in."

A sinking feeling hit my stomach. "Are you certain, Avto? I'm not sure I could take it if this was a mistake. My heart has been broken for over twenty years; it cannot take any more pain." Avto's gentle brown eyes softened. "We are sure, miss."

I frowned. "But is he in hiding still? Who has been protecting him all of these years? How has his identity been found out? Is he in danger?"

Avto's soft gaze turned sorrowful. My hand jerked out and wrapped around his arm. "Avto? Tell me. Where has my *sykhaara* been?"

Avto sucked in a long inhale and said quietly, "Miss, the Jakhua took your brothers and used them."

"Used them? How? I don't understand?" I wanted answers.

Avto tensed and said, "Miss, there are things in our world that you are unaware of. People that exist, places that exist, only in the underworld. Only in secret."

My eyebrows pulled down. "Avto, what are you trying to tell me? Where has my Zaal been? What did that man do to my brothers?"

Avto's arm muscle was rigid under my hand. Taking a deep breath, he explained, "Zoya, the Jakhuas were developing drugs."

"What kind of drugs?" I asked.

"Obedience drugs, miss. Drugs that wipe the memories of the victims, coerce them into doing horrific and despicable acts."

I swallowed, my chest tightening. "Like what?" I whispered.

Avto's shoulders slumped. "Killing. Murdering. Doing anything their Master asks of them. And I mean anything. No matter the moral implications."

Bile built in my throat, but I choked it back down. "And Jakhua." I swallowed again when my voice broke. "Jakhua used this drug on my brothers?"

Avto nodded, but his face blanched.

"What?" I probed.

"Miss," Avto rasped, "Masters Zaal and Anri were not simply put under the influence of the drug. It was on your brothers that the drug was developed."

I stared. I stilled. My hands trembled. My throat closed in, but I managed to ask, "He, Jakhua, he used my brothers to test his drug on? He experimented on them like laboratory rats?"

Hot tears streamed down my cheeks when Avto answered, "Yes, miss. Since they were twins he used them to test all the stages of the drug's development. He compared the results."

Jumping to my feet, I ran to the wastebasket and threw up.

Avto followed behind, his old hand gently pressing my back in comfort. But there was no comfort to be found at the thought of my brothers, my strong and brave beloved brothers, being injected with that, that poison, for years and years, until they had no memory—

Gasping, I wiped my mouth and turned to face Avto. "Their memories? Zaal's memories?" Fear filled me as I confronted the possibility that my brother would not know who I was. It had to be the cruelest of God's jokes, my twenty-year wait for their return, only to find one of my brothers, my only family, could be a stranger.

"We have heard that his memories are returning each day, and Zoya, we believe he remembers you, but—"

"But what?" I said almost inaudibly.

"Miss," Avto said, and stepped closer, "he believes you died in the massacre. He has no idea that you survived. He never got word that your body was never found."

My head fell forward at the thought of Zaal remembering his family after all of these years of blackness, only to believe we had all perished. "He is all alone?" I asked, imagining what he must be going through.

Avto did not say anything in response. When I lifted my head, Avto was rigid, his seventy-five-year-old body taut with tension. This time I didn't ask what was wrong. I simply waited.

"He is not alone," Avto admitted, after many strained seconds.

"He has minders that found him? People loyal to our family?"

Avto shook his head, his crepe-thin skin paling. I edged forward and placed my hand on his arm. "Avto?"

But Avto did not say anything; instead he reached into his jacket pocket and pulled put a picture. My heart kicked into a sprint as I stared at the white back of the photograph. Zaal. I knew my Zaal was in that picture.

I reached out my hand, but Avto pulled it back. I met his eyes in annoyance. Avto cleared his throat. "Zaal is not alone, Zoya. We have heard the news that he is recently engaged to be wed."

My lips parted in shock and I shook my head. "Engaged? How is that possible? I thought he had been imprisoned by Jakhua? When did he have time to find a woman? I don't understand how any of this is possible."

Avto stared down at the picture in his hand, then pushed it out for me to take. My hands shook as I reached out and grasped the picture. I brought it to my chest and closed my eyes. I'd always wondered what Zaal would look like older. Would he be as tall and strong as I always thought he would be? Would he still wear his black hair down to the middle of his back, like the Georgian warriors of old? Would he still smile with carefree abandon, yet be quiet and reserved in personality?

The picture against my chest felt like it was burning a hole through my clothes. With a deep breath, I pulled the picture back and dropped my gaze to the two figures captured in the scene.

My heart swelled in my chest as I stared at the man. The hugely built man with tanned olive skin and long black hair that fell to his back. His green eyes were bright, three moles standing proud under his left eye.

And he was smiling.

He was smiling so wide. The smile packed with an abundance of love, as my brother—my now adult and strong brother—stared down at a woman with nothing but adoration.

My eyes drifted across the picture to the woman and a lump clogged my throat. She was beautiful. Long blond hair fell down her back. She was slight of build, utterly captivating, and her deep brown eyes were looking up at Zaal, her lips smiling, too.

It felt surreal. My brother who I thought had died was very much alive. Alive and in love. My heart was full and warm.

Bringing the picture closer to my face, I could see tattoos marring Zaal's skin, and on closer inspection I could see scars littering bare arms revealed under his short-sleeved shirt. I had to close my eyes as a wave of sorrow washed over me. What must he have gone through under the hand of that evil man?

Blinking fast, I glanced to Avto. "Who is the woman?"

Avto did not reply; instead he rocked on his feet, his hands clasping together behind his back.

"Avto?"

Shaking his head, Avto said, "I can scarcely believe it to be true, but his fiancée is . . ." Avto trailed off, his jaw clenching.

"Who is she?" I demanded, injecting an urgent tone into my voice.

Without lifting his head, he revealed, "Talia Tolstaia."

I was sure the walls and floor of the apartment were falling down around me at the mention of *that* name. I shook my head, convinced I had misheard. "Can you repeat what you said?" I asked.

Avto shook his head. "You heard me perfectly, miss. Zaal, our new *Lideri,* our leader, he is betrothed to Talia Tolstaia, daughter to Ivan Tolstoi, one of the Volkov Bratva Red Kings."

My legs weakened so much that Avto reached forward and guided me to the nearest couch. Once I sat down, I studied this picture with new eyes. This woman, this blonde, was the daughter of the family that betrayed my father. The family my brothers, the Kostava Clan, were set to hate, to inflict their revenge upon.

"I don't understand, Avto. How could he do this to our family? How could he disgrace us and dishonor our Kostava name by being with this woman?"

"Miss Zoya, our source informed us that although he does not know the whys—no one can infiltrate their inner circle—the Volkov Bratva were responsible for the rescue of your brother. They found him in the clutches of Jakhua. They somehow freed him. It was under their protection that he fell in love with the Tolstaia girl."

I stared and stared at the picture, and a war broke out inside my heart. My brother was alive, yet he had fallen for our greatest enemy. I could barely wrap my head around this impossible truth.

Avto placed an arm around my shoulders offering comfort. I melted into his side, and just as I had began to relax Avto added, "Lideri Zaal killed Levan Jakhua. With the help of the Volkov *knyaz,* Luka Tolstoi, he killed the man that massacred your family. The Jakhuas are no longer a threat, miss. We are no longer in hiding. Our people, *you,* are free."

Startled by Avto's words, I straightened and absorbed them.

"Did you hear me, miss? We are no longer in hiding."

"You mean I can leave this apartment?" I whispered, not saying the words aloud, fearing they were false.

"Yes. And our people, miss. All of our people that have been in hiding—the lieutenants, the guards—every one, they are beginning to hear of the news as well. The fact that our *Lideri* is alive, in your brother, is traveling like wildfire among those in hiding." Avto smiled and said excitedly, "Our clan can rise again. The Kostavas can take their place here in New York—at long last!"

My eyes dropped to the picture of Zaal and his Tolstaia love, and my heart fell. "What if he does not want to be *Lideri*? What if everything he has gone through under Jakhua has scarred his soul too much? What if he wants a life with his woman, and not to be leading our people?"

Avto's smile faded. "He is Zaal Kostava, of the famous and noble Kostava Clan. He was born for this role."

"Yet you said he has spent his days as a killer created by an evil man." Avto's mouth hung at my words, but I shook my head. "None of us are the people we were born to be. I have been in hiding all my life. Zaal has been fighting for his life since he was eight. And Anri? Where is he? What I do know is that none of us are the same. How can we be? All we knew was taken from us and destroyed."

Avto reached for my hand and squeezed. "Our people have been hiding from Jakhua for over twenty years, some found and killed in the most horrific of ways. Our people need this; they need us to be strong again. They need Master Zaal to be our *Lideri*."

Silence stretched out as I replayed Avto's words over and over in my head. But he was correct. Our people had lived in fear for over two decades. Only the hope of my brothers' survival kept their days filled with optimism.

"I have to see him," I said, and felt the tension seep from Avto's body. "I have to tell my brother I am alive. I have to know where

Anri is." My eyes filled with tears and I sniffed. "I need to have my family again. I need to see my *sykhaara*."

"I understand, miss," Avto said. Reaching into his pocket, he pulled out a piece of paper. He handed it to me and nodded his head. "Zaal's home address is on there, as well as the Tolstois'. Every Tuesday and Thursday night, he goes to the Tolstoi household in Brighton Beach, Brooklyn. We will decide on a day and take you there, soon." Avto squeezed my hands tighter as I realized today was a Tuesday. "He will not be able to believe it. His sister, his bloodline, is still alive."

Nodding my head, I leaned into Avto and kissed his cheek. "You're a good man, Avto. Now go home and celebrate this news with your family. If all you have said is true, I am finally safe on my own. That is a blessing."

Avto looked to me as a father would to a daughter, then got to his feet. "I'll come by tomorrow evening. I'll arrange a car to take us to Brooklyn, to the apartment Zaal shares with his fiancée."

I smiled at Avto, and nodded my head as he left the apartment. I heard the door locks snap shut and I flopped back against the couch. When Avto and his family found me as a child, on the brink of death, under my deceased family's bodies, our people had rejoiced. I was alive. The Kostava Clan, who had been a royal family of sorts to the people of Georgia, had a living heir. And Anri and Zaal were missing. Not dead, but missing. A hope that was diminished was suddenly reborn.

Like the proverbial princess locked in the tower, I had been hidden and treated like a goddess my entire life. We had moved around a lot, until I feared I would go crazy from the suffocating seclusion my life had become. I was treated more like a prized jewel than a human, too precious to lose to our enemy. The last pillar of hope for the Tbilisi Kostava dynasty.

Until now.

Jumping to my feet, I rushed to the heavy black curtains that were always drawn in my apartment. Pushing the curtains aside just a fraction, I stared out into the cold dark night, searching for any signs of life. People were walking past, going about their business, but other than that, I could see no danger.

Dropping the curtains, I closed my eyes. "There is no more danger," I said aloud, convincing myself that the threat to my life was no longer there.

Moving to the closet, I took out my long hooded dark coat and slipped it over my black slacks and black silk blouse. Tucking my long black hair down my back, I clutched the paper with the addresses on and headed toward the door. I needed to do this, alone. And after twenty years of waiting for this news, I could not wait one more second to see my brother.

I rarely left the apartment, yet I knew the territory like the back of my hand. Years ago, when Avto brought me to New York, he had made sure I memorized every road, every subway station. I had to be prepared, in case I had to flee alone. I was trained to sink into the shadows.

Opening the door to the Manhattan street, the snow falling down painting the darkened concrete roads in white, I pulled my hood up, and made my way down the steps of my apartment building, immediately becoming one of the people on the street. With my head down, I arrived at the subway and entered the busy station. Sitting down on a spare seat, I allowed myself to pull out the photo and stare at the happy couple.

The long journey to Brighton Beach was much quicker than I imagined it would be. My focus was on the brother I'd thought I'd lost forever, mixed with the heady anticipation that within the hour I would meet him again.

The train pulled to a stop, and I hurried out of the station. I had never been to Brighton Beach before, and when I stepped out onto the street I gasped at my surroundings. I felt like I was in another world. The gray buildings were empty and falling apart. The streets were dark and dingy. Cold wind whistled through the boarded-up houses and half-standing restaurants and shops. It was nothing when compared to the opulence and beauty of Manhattan.

Ignoring the icy chill racing down my spine, I forced my feet to move, the soles of my black boots crunching on the snow beneath. I stayed in the dark of the unlit streets, becoming one with the night, until I arrived at a row of brownstones. The center house stood proudly in this place of dilapidation. Its upkeep clearly showing the owners had money.

My heart raced.

The House of Tolstoi.

The windows were high and wide, and anyone could see that the people residing in this house were a cut above the rest. Then my heart stilled when shadows moved past the window. I squinted my eyes, focusing through the petals of falling snow. There was a tall man, with a broad chest, holding on to a woman with long brown hair. I held my breath when a blond woman moved into center stage. Her hands were on her hips as she joked and laughed with the brunette.

Talia Tolstaia.

I searched for lost breath as I stared at my brother's fiancée; then I ceased to breathe at all when two large arms threaded around her shoulders from behind. The arms were olive skinned and tattooed, and I knew I was staring at Zaal.

I prayed for him to move into the view of the window, but his face never came into view.

I needed to see him.

Wrapping my arms around my waist, my hood firmly in place, I took a deep breath and stepped out onto the silent street.

It was time he knew I was here.

That his bloodline had survived.

2

194

"Get up."

Coldness ripped me from my sleep. My body was drenched with ice-cold water and shot off the floor where I was laid. I roared as I lurched to my feet, my naked body jerking at the feel of the cold air lapping my skin.

My hands tightened as I turned to the *Gvardii,* the Georgian guard of my cage. He was nothing more than *svin'ya* to me, a pig. All of them were pathetic pigs dressed in Wraith uniforms, trying to act tough. One strike from me would bring them nothing but death.

They acted like death.

I *was* death.

The guard backed away from the metal bars of the cage when I approached. "Stand to attention, *Beast!*" he ordered, trying to act tough. "She'll be here soon."

Then he smiled at me, and I braced for the serum. He pressed the button on his remote; the metal collar around my neck immediately tightened, the needles inside the collar slicing into my neck. My teeth gritted with the pain of the serum injecting into my veins.

Then came the heat. The serum burned as it ran through my

muscles, my head snapping back as the poison took its hold. Like being ripped back from my body, a bystander forced to watch, I felt my free will drift away. The need to kill soon became the only thing in my head. The only thing I could feel. The only thing I was—a killer.

Footsteps sounded on the long corridor, the sound of those feet taking me back to before, to that night, the night when they took me.

When they took her.

In a flash the memory left and I shouted, rage pulsing from within. Seeing the guard smiling from behind the bars, I charged forward, slamming my shoulder into the metal. The cage door creaked; he stepped back in fear. The collar tightened even more, my veins throbbing with the pressure.

I stood back, then braced myself to charge again. Just as I moved my feet to charge, a voice made me freeze where I stood.

"Halt!" the female voice snapped, the serum in my body caused my body to stiffen at the voice of my Mistress.

My Mistress that I had to obey.

My eyes stayed focused on the floor and I watched her black boots come into view. My skin pricked as her hand lifted through the cage bars and ran down my chest.

"Leave!" Mistress ordered the guard. I heard him scurry away, leaving us alone. Mistress opened the cage door, and I felt her step inside, slamming the cage door shut behind her.

Her fingers landed on my arm and ran up until they drifted over the black metal collar I forever had to wear. "194," she whispered, and her fingers ran to my cheek. I wanted to rip her arms from her sockets, snap her thin neck, but the serum kept me still; the serum kept me from disobeying Mistress.

"Lift your eyes and look at me!" she ordered in Russian, and on command my eyes snapped up. I watched her. My eyes bored into hers. Her dark hair was slicked back in a tight bun, and her hard face glared at mine.

Then she smirked. That same smirk I hated so much.

"You have been out for a few days, 194. We had to move locations. You have a new hit." My blood pumped faster as I knew I was to kill. The serum made me want to kill. When I killed I'd get relief. She wouldn't know I got relief. This bitch would never know that for me the serum only worked temporarily. She would never know I didn't become 100 percent obedient, like some of the other test subjects had.

Mistress moved in closer, her tits pressing up against my bare chest. Her mouth went to my ear, as her hand drifted down my stomach, to land on my cock, her warm hand wrapping around my flesh. She began stroking me, my dick hardening with the serum. "You will kill, 194, you will kill, or *she* will pay."

My teeth gritted together in anger at her threat. Mistress moved back and, staring at my expression, began to laugh. But her hand never left my cock, her tight grasp hard and increasing in speed, causing my breath to come in short hard pants.

Mistress watched me, her eyes shining with power, until she edged closer still and whispered, "Fuck me. Hard. Take me like the beast that you are." Her tongue licked around the shell of my ear. "Take me like the ugly beast I *made* you into!"

Sheer anger washed over me as I practically felt the long scars on my face and head burning from her words, but her command saw my body lurching forward and grabbing Mistress by her hair. Using my strength, I slammed her front against the wall and wrenched up her dress. She wasn't wearing anything underneath—she never did—so I kicked her legs apart and slammed myself inside.

I was as rough and as hard as I could be—I wanted her to suffer—but the scream from Mistress's mouth wasn't from pain. The bitch loved it. She loved pain. Torture. She loved making me bend to her will. She loved to own me.

Mistress'd trained me well. This was what I did. I killed. I fucked. I could make any bastard talk.

Gripping her hair tighter, her head snapping back, I placed my other hand on her hip and repeatedly pounded inside.

I wanted to hurt her, but the harder I tried, the more she got off on my savageness. Her pussy was dripping wet, the sounds of her juices in her channel slapping against my dick.

I grunted at the effort. Mistress's cunt began to tighten around my shaft. I wanted this to last. I wanted to make her bleed, rip out her hair, and bite the flesh off her neck, but she'd only ordered me to fuck, so all I could do was fuck this evil bitch.

My thighs began to tingle, the pressure of my release racing up my back. Sensing I needed to come, Mistress ordered, "Do not come until I say so, *Beast*!" My jaw clenched at her command, but my body obeyed, my balls full and painful with the need to come. I thrust into her harder, Mistress's breath coming faster and faster. Agony surged through groin and prick with the inability to find release, but I took it. This pain would fuel my revenge when the time came.

Because it would come.

Mistress began to moan, moan louder and louder until her cunt gripped my cock like a vise and she screamed a command. "194, come now!"

My head whipped back with the pain of my release—like razor blades were being ripped from my flesh.

Mistress loved this. She loved to torture me, to mess with my head. I roared with each new spurt of release. Roared until Mistress turned, ripping herself from my length, her back pressing against the wall.

My hands balled into fists, eager to wrap my fingers around her neck. But Mistress smirked that rage-inducing smirk and pushed her black skirt down to her knees. She fixed her hair with her hands, then, moving closer, aggressively slapped her hand across my face, before softly holding my cheeks in her hands.

"Next time, you give it to me harder. I made you into a savage." She leaned in closer and whispered, "So damn well act like one."

My lip curled with the warning growl leaving my throat. She walked round me without fear, my eyes tracking her every move, until she reached into her jacket and pulled out the rectangular device she always brought to me.

My heartbeat raced with a mixture of relief and dread, as the screen came to life. There was 152. She was asleep, curled up on the floor of her cage, her thin body draped in the white see-through gown they always made her wear.

I controlled my breathing as I watched her deep in slumber, her curly dark hair falling down her back. Then Mistress closed in the screen on 152's bare legs and every part of me froze. Bruises. Hand-print bruises all up her legs. Scratches and more black bruises on her hips.

"Can you see them, 194? Can you see what the latest male did to her?"

Who? I snapped inside my head, my eyes unmoving from the screen. But Mistress pulled the screen from my eyes and placed it back inside her jacket.

Several seconds went by in silence, until Mistress stood before me. "Your hit is a man that lives here in New York. The stupid prick messed with a very important associate of ours." Mistress ran her fingers over my collar as she said those words. "He killed and murdered a man that was extremely important to us, to *me*. And I made him a promise. I made him a promise that if this man killed the one who was so important to me he would die, too. He would die slowly, painfully, and under the hands of my most prized, sadistic, and lethal *Ubiytsa*." She smirked and her fingertips ran over my lips. "That, 194, is you. You will be the one to deliver his death."

Mistress sighed and backed away. "It seems my brother has seen your 152. And I'm afraid to say, 194, that he is very much interested in calling her to him to have as his own. And we know that anything he demands he gets. He is the Master of our people after all."

My eyes flared at the thought of 152 being ordered to the Master, being taken away from me, and I wanted to hit something, kill something *quick*. Mistress knew how I would feel, and crossing her arms, she said, "If you can kill the hit effectively, and . . . *creatively,* I will make sure your precious 152 will stay close by. I will make sure she is not sent away."

I tracked Mistress, feeling my chest lighten with her promise. A promise she made with every hit. There was always a next time before 152 would be returned to me, but I couldn't give up because *next* time could be *the* time—then I would strike.

Mistress moved to the cage door and reached out for something on the floor. She walked back toward me holding clothes in her hands, along with a notebook and a key. Placing them on the floor at my feet, she said, "You have ten minutes before a van will take you to the drop-off point. The address of the chamber you will use is in the notebook. As is the address for your hit." Mistress moved until she was flush against my chest and lifted to her tiptoes. Her lips brushed against mine. "Kill him slowly, 194. You have weeks to make him pay, precious time, and you will need it. He is very well protected, protected by a powerful family that can never know of our existence. So use anything and anyone in his circle against him. Use and interrogate anyone you need to to get closer to him. Do you understand? You use any means possible." She paused and smiled against my mouth. "Then kill them all. Make these assholes pay in blood."

"Yes, Mistress," I replied automatically. Mistress pressed her lips against mine, but I did not move mine back. With all the fucked-up things Mistress made me do to her, the feeling of her thin lips on mine was the worst. I never knew why. I just knew she, this close, was repulsive to me.

Mistress moved back with a laugh and sounded a buzzer to call a guard forward. When the guard reached the cage, she turned to him and said, "Fill his collar with new serum pellets I specially ordered, enough to last, and program it to dispense a dose twice a day. We need him to be at his most impressive."

"Yes, Mistress," the guard said obediently.

Mistress loitered by the cage door, then said, "I will miss our time together while you are gone, 194. Maybe I shall pay 152 a visit in your absence, see if she can be as effective in my pleasure as you. You share the same blood, after all."

As I lost grip of my control, my head snapped in her direction, body braced to strike. Mistress frowned, and I forced myself to pretend that the serum still had me in its clutches. In truth it only ever lasted a little while on these pellets. I could eventually fight the fog they brought.

My eyes dropped to focus on the floor, and I heard Mistress finally walk off.

The guard held his picana—a form of cattle prod—in his hand and ordered, "Dress; we have to leave!"

Still picturing 152 on the floor, the bruises on her thighs, the broken position she was in, I dressed quickly, vowing to do my worst to this hit.

As I followed the guard down the hallway of my new prison, I opened the notebook and read out the name of the man who would soon be screaming in pain.

Zaal Kostava.
Brooklyn.
New York.

★ ★ ★

I'd never been to this place before. New York. Brooklyn. Brighton Beach. My days had been spent around the world, where the Master had his businesses *and* enemies. That was where I came in. Master always wanted his best man for the job—I was always it. But this was different. This was Mistress's hit. A *personal* hit. Now personal to me, too, since it secured 152's safety.

Master wanted her. I couldn't let that happen.

152 was beautiful. It was the reason Mistress had taken us all those years ago. Even when 152 was a child Mistress could see the potential 152 had as a *mona*. And Mistress had used her for years. Abused her and made her life hell.

A hell I intended to stop.

Slinking into the shadows, I made my way toward one of the addresses I'd been given for the hit. When I approached the street, I noted that every fifteen minutes a car went by. It was slow in speed and had blacked-out windows. This hit was clearly important in this community. His house was well protected.

It would be a waiting game. A waiting game until one of his people made a mistake and I could take him, or someone close to him.

Leverage.

Standing in an alleyway opposite a brownstone house, I watched in silence as a car pulled up and a large male with fair hair got out of the backseat, holding his hand out to someone inside. I squinted my eyes to better focus on his features, but this male was too light in coloring to be my target. A female slipped out of the car next; she had long brown hair and blue eyes.

I committed these people to memory and waited. Fifteen minutes later another car pulled up. And exiting from the backseat was a tall dark male with black hair down to his mid-back. My nostrils flared when he turned and his stern face came into view, green eyes looking down at someone else leaving the car.

Him.

The hit.

Zaal Kostava.

Careful not to move, relying on all the years of training, I was as still as the night. But I watched. I saw there were three guards surrounding the car. Then a female was by his side. Blond. Brown eyes. A ring on her left hand.

His wife? His fiancée?

My eyes tracked them walking up stairs and entering the house. The windows were large, and I concentrated on the shadows, tilting my head as I studied the movements.

The guards in the cars continued for the next two hours, men casually dressed in everyday clothes walking in circles around the block, their hands in their pockets—holding on to guns, no doubt.

In two hours I never moved an inch. This was why I was the head assassin, the *bringer of death.* I never failed. And I never failed in making my victims scream out in pain. Only after they'd screamed at the sight of my disfigured face. I was their every nightmare come to life.

Movement from my left suddenly caught my eye. A figure dressed in all black was approaching the side of the street where I was hidden. I watched with focused eyes, seeing that it was a female.

Her arms were wrapped around her waist, a large hood covering her face. Her steps were quiet as she rushed down the street. I never took my eyes from her as she slipped into the darkness. She wanted to keep concealed from view.

She kept approaching until she stopped, mere feet from me. She didn't sense me lurking at her back. They never did.

I watched. I watched her breathing increase and heard the heavy exhale leave her mouth. Flakes of snow landed on her black coat, but the female kept completely still.

Her attention was on the house I was stalking. But she made no effort to move. I watched as her hand reached into her pocket. But what I noticed more was that it was shaking.

A photograph was pulled out of her pocket. Just as she lifted it to view, I caught sight of the image—my hit and his female.

The side of my lip curled up in satisfaction. This female was *someone* to the hit. And she'd just made herself my prey.

Suddenly the female's breathing hitched, and when I glanced to the house I could see the people I'd watched entering the front door move in clear view of the windows. This female's grip was iron tight on the photo, and I could see her holding her breath.

She was waiting to see the dark male.

A sudden tightness gripped around my neck, my body jerking in shock. My jaw tensed and I shut my eyes as my collar tightened, the functions inside the metal brace moving to inject into my neck. My teeth slammed together as needles slowly pushed into my skin. And then it came. The burning of the serum flooding into my veins.

While I still had time before my triggered rage took hold, I pulled out my notebook and memorized the name of the chamber. Then I looked to the female in black and I knew what I was about to do.

The needles pulled out of my skin, and then it came. A red mist curtained over my eyes. My muscles strained as the venom filled my every vein. Rage. Uncontrollable rage took its hold, bringing with it the need to deliver pain. To hear screams. To draw blood.

To obey Mistress and all that she'd commanded.

Just before I became lost to the darkness, the bringer of death role I knew I would embrace, my gaze darted to the female dressed in black once more. I crouched, bracing to strike.

Just as the female took a deep breath and stepped out onto the road to cross the street, the venom finally peaked. My eyes widened as I felt my free will fade to nothing—my body was reacting worse than normal, submitting to the drug like Mistress had intended.

The beast inside was freed.

And I attacked.

I attacked the female before me.

Hooking my arm around her neck, I slammed my hand over her mouth. She fought to get free, her voice trying to break from my hand and scream. Dragging her back into the shadows, I tightened my arm around her neck. She fought me all the way, her legs kicking and her fingernails scratching at my hand over her mouth.

My muscles burned at the fear taking hold of her body, my heart beating fast, enjoying the life leaving her body. When the female's body began to lose fight, I slackened my arm. She flopped in my arms, unconscious. The picture fell from her hand onto the ground. I looked at the picture, my hit's face staring up at me.

And I smiled.

I smiled, holding this female in my arms.

Because she would pay.

She would pay in pain and blood . . . then I'd be coming straight for him.

3

LUKA

"Any thoughts to where you'll marry, Tal?" Kisa asked my sister as we all sat in my parents' house.

Talia moved closer into Zaal's side and laid her head on his huge bicep. "Maybe just here at the house. Something small." Talia's face fell and she shrugged. "I only have you guys and"—she cleared her throat when Zaal got tense, his face sharp and unmoving—"and, you know, Zaal is on his own."

Zaal's posture was rigid, his long dark hair falling over his face. Talia pushed back his hair and put her palm on his face. Zaal turned into her hand and she kissed him. All the tension immediately left his body.

He was struggling. Struggling as I had.

My stomach tightened, because at least I'd had my family. He had no one outside of us. We weren't his blood. It wasn't the same.

A hand ran across my chest, and when I glanced down Kisa was smiling up at me. Leaning forward, I kissed my wife on her head and moved my hand down to her stomach, which now held our baby. Kisa laid her head against my shoulder. I'd never felt so content in all my life.

"Still not finding out if I'm having a niece or nephew?" I looked up to Talia, who was smiling at me.

"No, we want it to be a surprise," Kisa answered, just as my father and Kirill entered the room. Kirill was dressed in a three-piece black designer suit as always. His sharp eyes met mine, and he flicked his head in the direction of my father's office.

Kirill next turned to face Zaal. "Study."

Dropping one more kiss on Kisa's head, I stood and followed my father and the Pakhan into the office with Zaal, my, the *knyaz's*, number two, on my heels. As we entered the room, the Pakhan dropped behind the desk and we sat on the chairs opposite.

Zaal sat to my right, my father to my left. Over the last few months Zaal had slowly adjusted to his new role as a sworn member of our Bratva. I took him with me everywhere, showing our people that a new king had joined the Volkovs. Zaal's sheer size and strength ensured that everyone knew we were growing stronger by the day. And I felt stronger with him by my side.

My father, though suspicious of Zaal for a while, had slowly come round to allowing a Kostava into the ranks. And I couldn't be happier. The Volkov Bratva had always had three kings; with Zaal's admission, the thought of assuming the Pakhan mantle no longer filled me with dread—I would have a trustworthy brother to help me lead when it was my time to take the Pakhan seat.

Kirill pulled out a bottle of vodka from behind his desk and poured four glasses. We each drank the shot, and Kirill refilled the glasses.

Pushing the glasses back in our direction, he lay back in his chair and said, "There was an unregistered small private aircraft that arrived yesterday. Our man from the airfield put himself in the re-fueling center when the aircraft arrived."

"And no one cleared it with you?" my father asked, eyebrows pulled down.

Kirill flicked his hand and downed his shot before shaking his head. "No permission was sought, but then again, people have no respect anymore for the way things are done in my territory. No respect for the old ways." He clasped his hands over his stomach and added, "But that does not mean they will not pay for their lack of respect and honor."

Frowning, I asked, "Who was it?"

Kirill sat forward, meeting my eyes, and said, "Ah. But that is the mystery, Luka. It seems that no one knows or remembers."

"Then we make those that allowed the plane into our airspace remember. Whatever that takes." My hands fisted on the arms of my chair. The thought of bringing violence to our enemies making my blood burn with excitement.

Kirill smiled coldly at my reaction and refilled my glass. I knocked back the shot to keep calm and to keep from imagining spilling blood.

"Thinking just like a pakhan, Luka. And as any good pakhan should, I already ordered my head *Pytki*—my torturer—to 'speak' to the men who allowed the landing."

"And?" my father pushed.

Kirill sat back and replied, "No names were given, so those men were quickly disposed of for the traitorous rats they were, but we did get one piece of information I found particularly interesting."

My body was tense with the knowledge that a new threat could be in town. Kirill was calm. Always calm. But I'd learned that the calmer he seemed, the more rage he was feeling inside.

Kirill's eyes drifted toward Zaal, who had been silent and still beside me. Zaal was always silent. He absorbed everything that was said but rarely spoke.

Zaal tensed as the Pakhan's eyes landed on him. Kirill tilted his head to the side and stated, "The plane came direct from Georgia."

Zaal's eyes flared. Kirill's lip curled in amusement. "My question is, why would a Georgian dare undermine my authority? Why would a Georgian pay my men off, under my nose, to enter my city?" Kirill sat back in his chair, yet his eyes never left Zaal.

The room filled with tension, until I said, "There's no fucking way Zaal organized this, if that's what you're implying. He's sworn into the Bratva. He's pledged himself to you, life for life, blood for blood."

Kirill flicked a glance to my father, who was rigid in his seat. I knew that they both had to be doubting Zaal's loyalty, but I was absolutely sure he would never cross us. Even if that loyalty was solely based on his love and devotion to my sister.

Which it wasn't.

I had opened my mouth to say as much when Zaal said slowly and with force, "I would not betray this family. I am a warrior; if I were to cross your rule, I would face you head-on, not hide in the shadows."

I sat back in my chair and watched the Pakhan's eyes narrow. Eventually he sat forward and pushed a glass of vodka at Zaal. "Now that is clear, I believe there could be another theory."

"What?" my father asked, but Kirill was still boring his gaze into Zaal, waiting for my brother to take the drink. Zaal sat straight in his seat, his huge size dwarfing the chair. His fingers were gripping the wooden arms and I could see the anger in his face. But he forced himself to push out his hand, and without dropping his gaze on Kirill he took the shot.

As the glass slammed on the desk, Kirill turned to my father to answer his question. "I have been thinking. Does it not seem strange to you that we"—he pointed at himself, then Zaal—"or Mr. Kostava has received no payback for Jakhua's death?"

The temperature in the room seemed to drop at the mention of that man, the Georgian cunt who had used Zaal as his personal puppet for twenty years, the man who beat my sister and took her love from her.

Kirill continued, "The Jakhuas, though they had little presence here in New York, are a large clan. They are powerful in many places, and no doubt have 'associates' that would be disappointed their supplier of the obedience drugs was disposed of by us." Kirill held out his hand and began counting off. "Sex traffickers, underground fight rings, black-market slave traders, and any other undesirables that wanted to bring people under their control. Is it not strange that Jakhua was killed by our hand, yet not one strike against us has been taken in the months since his death?"

"And now a Georgian plane has landed in New York, landed without our permission."

Kirill raised his eyebrow in response and said, "If I die through an enemy's attack, I have deals with the Italians, the Irish, and the Jews to respond on my behalf. Hell, I even have the British mob on hand too, should my potential killer's reach stretch that far."

"You're questioning who Jakhua had in his pocket?" my father finished for the Pakhan.

"Exactly," the Pakhan replied. "Jakhua was not a stupid man. He will have had all his cards in a row before coming to New York. He knew what his appearance here would mean to us. So, if he was even half the man I think he was, he will not have failed in securing his revenge, should the event of his death occur."

I inhaled a deep breath when my father looked across me to Zaal and asked, "Can you remember any of the men you demonstrated the drug for? Any of the men that watched you kill for Jakhua? His closest associates?"

Zaal dropped his head, his eyes closing as he racked his brain. His knuckles turned white and his fingers shook as he tried to remember. I watched as his back bunched with tension, until he released a defeated breath and shook his head. "I remember nothing but nameless faces. The drugs, the drugs wiped my mind until I awoke in the basement of the house in the Hamptons with Talia. But there were many people Mast—" Zaal shook his head and corrected, "*Jakhua* traded with."

"It would make sense that his closest ally was a Georgian. Question is, beyond the Jakhuas and Kostavas, who is there that is strong enough to threaten the Volkovs?" my father asked, his unapologetic disdain for the Georgians lacing his voice.

"That is the question," Kirill responded. "Which Georgian group has managed to remain unseen? What Georgian organization has lived so far underground that we, the greatest crime family in the world, have no reference for it?"

I sat listening to the conversation, then said, "Jakhua's generals, his guards, his top men, should have come after us, but no one did." I could feel all eyes on me when I snapped my head up and said, "Unless they were assimilated into another brotherhood."

Kirill this time smiled wide at me and nodded his head. A wash of pride ran through me at the Pakhan's obvious praise. "Exactly, Luka. The Jakhuas must now belong to someone else. But who?"

A memory of Anri suddenly came to mind. "Anri, just before we fought, told me that he had been picked up by a Georgian mob. They captured him and made him fight." My mind raced as another realization hit. "And they must have known about the gulag Anri and I were kept in. They came for him after the escape. They knew he was a death-match fighter."

Kirill looked to my father, who nodded his head. "I think Luka could be right."

I turned to Zaal to hear his thoughts, but his head had dropped. I knew it was because I had talked about his brother. The brother he still had little memory of.

"So," Kirill said, clearly bringing the meeting to a close, "it looks like we have a new Georgian threat on our hands. Which means heightened security for us all. Because make no mistake, if these Georgians have made it into New York *unseen,* have kept their existence a secret, they most certainly pose a real threat."

Kirill ran his hand over his face and addressed Zaal. "Maybe it is time that the Georgians were made aware that the heir of the Kostava Clan is alive. Maybe those that pledged loyalty to your father should be told you have survived, survived and killed the man that massacred your family."

Kirill rose from his chair and walked round his desk, to stand before Zaal. Zaal kept his head down, and Kirill added, "Survived and are ready to take your rightful place as the Kostava *Lideri.* As a joint venture with the Volkovs, of course. The Georgian underground is not so large that whisperings among your people have not mentioned this other mob. If we show the people their king has risen from death, the hidden peasants that worked under your father will flock to us, and, in turn, so will this mob's identity."

Kirill leaned back against the edge of his desk and folded his arms. I glared at the Pakhan. There was no way Zaal would be ready for this. No one knew what it was like for us to suddenly have to live in this free world. And what was done to Zaal in his captivity was the worst of all.

I had moved my mouth to say so when Zaal rasped, "I am not *Lideri.* I was born to lead with my brother, together; without him I will not take the seat of my house. I am not the man I was destined to be. My people deserve more than me."

Zaal kept his head lowered, his long black hair hiding his face, when my father said in an authoritative, but fatherly, voice, "You *have* a brother, Zaal. He sits beside you, ready to take on this family's seat, too. You are a Kostava, but you are soon to be joined to my daughter. I would say that even with what you have both gone through—Luka and yourself—you are exactly where you were meant to be."

Zaal slowly lifted his head and stared at my father. I could see the disbelief on his face that my father had said such words. Zaal didn't say anything in response.

Seeing him struggling, I sat forward and said, "Let him think on it. In the meantime we can use our resources to find out what we can about these intruders of our territory."

Kirill nodded his head and stood from his desk. "Then let us go eat; I can smell the dinner drifting in through the door." Kirill walked out of the office without any other word, my father following behind.

I stood from my chair, but Zaal's elbows were leaning on his knees, his head cast down. Reaching out, I laid my hand on his shoulder and said, "It may be hard now, but things will get better in time."

Zaal lifted his head, pushing his long hair from his face. "I feel rage, Luka. I have a rage that sits within me all day and all night. My head is fucked up; faces and images from memories I can't place keep me up at night. But worse than that, every time I think of my name, of my family's legacy, I see them all piled up dead against the wall of the house. I see the river of blood running from beneath them as I'm dragged away screaming for my family." Zaal took a deep breath to calm down and said, "I cannot live with these memories, which being the *Lideri* would bring. All the Kostavas have died but for me. It is time the Clan dies, too." Zaal rose to his feet and put his hand on my shoulder. "I am your brother; of that I am sure. And I will stand by your side when you are Pakhan, and now as *knyaz*. I will honor this family who have saved my life, who took me in and gave me my Talia, and I will move past my old life." His hand dropped and he turned to leave, but just as he did he looked back and said, "Anri was always the true leader out of us both; you knew him, so I suspect you see this, too. And it is not cowardice that makes me refuse this title of Kostava *Lideri,* but acceptance of the man Jakhua made me into." Zaal's green eyes met mine when he added, "I know you understand this, too. We are both no longer the boys we were when our people knew us. We are freaks, Luka. Freaks."

Zaal left the room, and I slumped against the desk. I ran my hand through my hair just as the door creaked open. Lifting my eyes, I couldn't help but smile as my Kisa stood in the doorway, her long skintight black dress showcasing her swollen stomach.

Tilting my head to the side, I smiled at my wife, getting a blinding smile in return. Kisa shut the door and walked forward until she stood before me. My hands immediately went to her hips, and I pulled her close to my chest. Kisa ran her hands through my hair, and she pressed a kiss to my forehead. Pulling back, she said, "My papa is talking about you out there. You have definitely pleased him in your meeting."

Wrapping my arms around Kisa's waist, I lifted my head for her to press her lips against mine. Kisa didn't hesitate and crushed her mouth to mine. Lifting my hand, I wrapped it in her hair and pulled her closer still. Kisa broke away on a gasp, and I whispered, "I love you, *solnyshko.*"

"And I you," Kisa replied, then added, "You are happier, *lyubov moya.* You are happier in yourself."

Nodding my head, I replied, "Because of you. Because you took me as the man I am now." I dropped my mouth to her bump and kissed her raised stomach. "And because of our baby. I'm gonna be a papa, because of you. The girl I've always loved."

Kisa smiled, but it soon faded. "But Zaal is not happy like us?" I raised my head. "That is why you're worrying, and pursing your lips in that delicious way that I love."

My chest warmed as her finger ran across my lips, but I replied, "He is without family."

"We are his family now," Kisa said.

I stood, taking her hand. "True, and we need to make sure he knows it," I said firmly.

Kisa laid her head on my arm. "Spoken like a Pakhan."

As I led Kisa from the office, I said, "No. That was said as his brother."

4

ZOYA

The sensation of flying was what hit me first. The pain around my neck was what hit me next. I tried to open my eyes, but when I did I was met only with darkness. Disorientated, I tried to remember what had just happened. Flashes of me standing in front of a house filtered into my mind. A house in Brooklyn. A house that held Zaal—

I gasped when I remembered someone grabbing me from behind and dragging me into the shadows. I'd fought, but he'd choked me. A cough ripped from my throat when I tried to inhale.

Suddenly arms I hadn't even realized were holding me tightened and a hand slapped over my mouth. My heart pounded in fear. Avto had gotten it wrong. I hadn't been safe. Our enemy was very much alive and must have followed me to the house that held Zaal.

Dread raced through me. I had led our enemy to my brother. Would they be going there next?

Even though I was terrified, instinct took over and I thrashed to get free. It was in vain, because as soon as the captor felt me try to get free the arm that was still around my neck tightened until my body went limp. As my consciousness began to fade again, I realized my captor was running with me in his arms. My hood was pulled over my head so I couldn't see a thing, but I heard my captor. And I was sure it was a man. His breathing was low and heavy. His arm around my neck was thick and unyielding.

His scent filled my nose: spice and musk. I remembered the dark spicy scent enveloping me as my eyes fluttered shut, then everything went dark once again.

I woke with cold against my cheek. Instinctively I knew I was in trouble. Something in the back of mind told me that I was in danger. Avto had tried to school me in how to react if I was ever abducted. With my eyes still closed and my body unmoving, I tried desperately to remember those lessons.

Nothing came to mind, save the drive to resist telling anyone anything about who I was. To anyone outside of my people, I was Elene Melua, a poor farm girl from Kazreti, Georgia.

I controlled my breathing when I realized that my hands were shaking like a leaf. I focused on keeping calm. Counting to ten, I slowly opened my eyes. I was met with a dark, black wall.

Taking another breath, I counted a second set of ten and cautiously rolled onto my other side. I studied my surroundings: black walls, black ceilings. No amount of counting could calm me as I realized what type of room I was in.

My lips parted to release a shocked gasp as my wide eyes drank in the contraptions in the room. I could barely understand what they were, but I saw chains hanging from the walls, the ropes suspended from wooden blocks in the ceiling, and there was a metal bed, a crucifix, and masses and masses of other machines littering the black tiled floor. They looked like medieval torture devices, and bile rose in my throat as I lay on the floor of what appeared to be a large metal cage. Thick bars imprisoned me on all sides.

I closed my eyes again and wrapped my coat around my freezing body. The temperature in this torture chamber was colder than outside. If I couldn't have seen the room under the red dimmed lights, I'd assume I was in a freezer of some description.

I shuffled my body back into the farthest corner when footsteps began approaching from what looked to be a narrow hallway to my left. My body shook with a mixture of cold and fear, and my eyes never left that direction.

I held my breath as the footsteps closed in. Then he appeared. I assumed it was the same man who captured me. My attention remained on the floor, on his bare feet. I did not dare look up. His feet were rough, but I could see by the shape of his legs underneath his black sweatpants that he was huge. The sweatpants were loose, but I could see the definition of his thighs; they were thick and muscled.

The room was deathly silent, my warm breath misting before me due to the low temperature in the room. I could hear his breathing as he stood beside the cage. Heavy breathing, slow, a low rasp in its sound. I kept my head down, waiting for what he would do next. But he didn't move.

Minutes and minutes passed in strained silence. I kept huddled in my corner, and he stayed exactly where he was, next to my cage. His feet were pointing in, and even without lifting my head I knew that he was staring at me. I could feel the weight of his intense glare bearing down.

The longer we stayed still, the more the dank coldness seeped into my bones. My lips became numb and my teeth began to chatter, the clattering of their touch sounding deafening in this dimly lit hell.

Then he moved.

It was simply a flicker of a movement, but it was enough to make me stiffen in anticipation of what he would do next. Was he just going to kill me? Was he going to take me into the mouth of the chamber and torture me? My head ached as my mind raced with the fear of what was about to transpire.

The sound of metal clanging against metal forced me to look up. I instantly regretted what I had done. It was what he wanted. He'd wanted me to break.

A callused hand was holding a black metal rod, a metal rod that was pressed against a metal bar of the cage. I froze as my eyes stayed on that metal rod as it focused on that hand. It was large and scarred, and my gaze traveled up the muscled bare arm holding the rod like it was an extension of his arm. His skin was fair in tone, the complete opposite of mine, but it was covered in a mass of dark tattoos. They were muddled writings etched in black ink. They appeared to be a swirling, disorganized list of names brandished on his skin.

I swallowed, my mouth becoming incredibly dry. I tried to make out the names, and when I did my stomach dropped again. Most were Eastern European: Russian, Ukrainian, Serbian. But what scared me most was the appearance of the Georgian.

Georgian.

My pulse pounded in my neck so fast I was sure it was protruding out of my skin. *Georgian,* I thought again. My mind raced with what these names meant. Were they people he had killed? Were they people he knew? Were they the people he worked for?

The rod suddenly moved. My eyes couldn't help but follow the tip of the rod to the top of the metal bar, and when I did it brought with it the view of my captor's chest. My nostrils flared as I studied his bare broad chest. A large tattoo reading "194" was the centerpiece, and the swirl of names continued over his thick muscled chest and torso. But that's not what had me losing control of composure, panic and anxiety setting in. No, that belonged to a black metal collar sitting tightly around my captor's neck. A wide neck with muscles stacking high on his bare shoulders.

My heart thundered when I wondered what the collar was for. Who had put it on him? What did it do?

The captor jerked the rod to the top of the cage, but I kept my eyes from meeting his. I did not want to look into his eyes; I did not want to see his face. In my head that made this all too real. But then a buzzing sound came from the tip of the rod, an electric sound traveling through the metal cage. A shock sparked against the part of my back that was leaning against the bar. I jumped forward, crying out in pain. The electric shock had burned my skin.

And then I did look up. My gaze slammed to meet his and all the blood drained from my face.

Dilated eyes stared at me from a sternly featured face—a heavily *scarred* face, deep scars like road maps over his cheeks and forehead. His pupils were so large and black, I could barely make out the color of his irises, the appearance of the blown pupils only adding to his menacing visage. The scars continued off his face and ran up over his shaven head.

My God, I thought; he looked like a monster. I continued to study his face, unable to look away. Under the scars, high cheekbones covered in dark stubble framed his face along with his strong jaw and broad forehead. His lips were full, his bottom lip slightly fuller than the top. Jet-black eyebrows arched perfectly over his predatory eyes. His right cheek was marked with a prominent long scar that started at his temple and ran down his cheek, cutting through the dark stubble, cutting under the metal collar, and traveling low to his defined right pectoral muscle.

As I looked up, I swallowed, my hands trembling even more as his eyes remained fixed on mine. Those penetrating dilated eyes the only unscarred or undamaged part of his entire face. The only human part of him.

Sucking in a shuddering inhale, I waited for him to speak. With a slam of the metal rod against the metal bars, a jolt of electricity sang as it traveled through the metal bars. I scurried farther into the center of the small cage, only bringing me closer to my captor's dominating presence. From what I'd seen from Zaal's picture, this man could surely rival him in height and width.

My eyes were wide, my arms holding my coat tightly around my waist, when my captor struck the bars one again and aggressively commanded, *"Davdget'!"*

I flinched at the guttural, harsh sound of his voice. Then ice ran through my veins. It had nothing to do with the temperature of the room. The man had spoken to me in Georgian. He commanded me to stand. Though it was clear from his accent that he was Russian.

He knew I was Georgian.

My eyes closed while I debated the probability that he knew who I was. But I steeled my nerves and resolved to deny my true name.

I was Elene Melua, a poor farm girl from Kazreti, Georgia. And I knew nothing of the Kostava Clan. I knew nothing of Zaal.

The rod striking the bars with an incredible force caused me to jump in shock. My captor screamed, "I said *stand*!" in his heavily accented Georgian.

Fear alone had me lurching to my feet, the ceiling of the cage now only a few feet above my head. I suddenly felt closed in and claustrophobic. I was terrified. As weak as I know that makes me sound, when my family had been known for their strength, I was terrified of this man.

This monster.

My captor stepped closer to the cage, the metal prod slipping through the gap in between the bars until it stopped just inches from my chest. I remained absolutely still. I could hear the electricity building at the end of the metal rod. I prayed he wouldn't push it against my chest.

My eyes remained downcast, until he ordered, "Look up!"

I flinched at the venom in his voice, his harsh and scathing voice. But too afraid to disobey, I snapped my eyes to meet his. The moment our gazes clashed, I felt seared on the spot. There was nothing but contempt and hatred in his piercing stare. His nostrils flared as he watched me, and his scarred top lip curled as if in disgust.

He rolled his neck, a gesture that looked impossible under the tightness of the metal collar and with the thickness of his muscles. Then he closed in, his heavily built chest pushing against the bars. As his skin connected with the metal, I could see the electrical current hit his scarred tattooed skin, volts of electricity shooting through his bones. But this man didn't even flinch. His arm holding the electric rod didn't even move. His eyes not once flickered away from mine.

If I had felt fear before, it was nothing to the pure terror I felt under this man's hateful, penetrating stare. This man felt no pain. This man who clearly wanted to hurt me.

As my desperate situation began to hit home, he raised his chin and coldly ordered, "Strip."

My face blanched. I didn't move, paralyzed by fright. But he shook his head and snarled, "Strip!" He paused and leaned his head forward to hiss menacingly, *"Suka."*

Bitch. He'd called me a bitch in Russian.

He pressed something on the top of the black metal rod that caused sparks to hiss from the tip. Forced into action, my trembling hands lifted to my coat. It took longer than I meant to push my heavy coat from my body. My arms were numb with cold and distress.

All the time the scarred man watched me, the terrifying buzzing from the rod mere inches away. Tears built in my eyes as my fingers next fumbled with the buttons on my blouse. The minutes that I undressed felt like hours, my clothes dropping to the floor. The slap of the harsh cold air almost brought me to my knees. But I willed myself to be strong. My tears didn't escape even though they built like a wave. I would not fall to the floor in fear, even though my legs warred with my quest to remain standing tall.

As my pants fell to the floor, my underwear the only remaining garments, I pictured Zaal and Anri in my mind. I pictured Zaal's suffering for years under the torture of Jakhua. And I pictured Zaal in the photograph, smiling and in love.

Zaal had survived.

I was Kostava. I had the strong soul of our family line.

I could survive this, too.

Inhaling deep, I gritted my teeth at the humiliation of being naked in front of a man. I had never been with a man. I had never been naked and exposed, and now this man was forcing me to bare all to him.

My hands shook profusely as I fought to free the clasp of my bra. I winced as the lace bra fell free, cold air biting at the flesh of my breasts.

I fought back the need to cover myself; instead I forced my hands to lower to my panties. I pushed them down my ice-burned red legs. When I was free of my clothes, I straightened, keeping my eyes downcast.

"Push them out of the cage," the man said, withdrawing the rod from before my chest. Bending down, I gathered my clothes and pushed them out of the cage as ordered. Backing away, I took my place again in the center of the cage.

I waited.

And I waited.

It felt like at least an hour passed as I stood in the middle of the cage, my captor standing before me, glaring. The whole time glaring. I did not need to look up to see this.

Suddenly, when I feared I would fall to the floor through exhaustion and cold, my captor turned and walked away down the narrow hallway, leaving me alone.

I remained standing for a long time afterward in case this was some test I was meant to pass. But when my knees finally buckled I had no choice but to lie on the floor.

The black tiles were so cold beneath my skin that I felt like I was lying upon a block of ice. But I stayed strong. I didn't let the fear take control. I didn't let my despair make me cry. And even when the temperature in the room abruptly switched from Arctic cold to tropical heat, I didn't scream out in pain. My too-cold muscles throbbed and my skin felt like it was being sliced apart with razors. I closed my eyes and breathed through my nose.

And I pictured Zaal. I memorized his face, because as I lay on this floor, now too hot, sweating on account of the burning air, I became sure we would never be reunited after all.

I [illegible] nothing [illegible] appetite [illegible] But when [illegible] finally ended I had need [illegible] in the food.

In [illegible] could [illegible] that I [illegible] make [illegible] I [illegible] through [illegible]

[illegible] me sure [illegible] all.

5

194

I woke, slumped in the corner of a small room. I blinked and blinked as I drank in the dark space. There was nothing in here but a screen on a desk and the picana resting against it.

My eyes narrowed as I stared at the picana; then I glanced at the screen. Distant images began playing like a reel in my head as I stared at the dark-haired female, lying unconscious in the center of the cage. I struggled to know who she was. I struggled to remember how we got here.

The serum had taken hold and brought severe memory loss. Mistress must have loaded my collar with double-dose serum pellets—she did that from time to time when the hit was of great importance. The serum didn't work on me like they thought it did under the usual dose. I was meant to be completely under Mistress's control, all day, every day—but I wasn't. Instead, with this bastard collar, with this double dose the guard had put in, I had blacked out when it injected me. I didn't even know how long I'd been out.

My lip curled. Truth was, Mistress didn't need to drug me at all. They had all the control they needed. I would do anything they said to keep 152 alive.

Anything. Pain and killing meant nothing to me. I'd done it for so long, the screams of my victims had faded to vapor in my head. The men who had died under my hands were nothing to me but one step closer to 152's freedom.

I squeezed my eyes shut and, as though watching from a distance, I recalled everything I'd done under the drug's influence. I saw myself carrying a dark-haired female in the cage to this chamber. I'd turned the temperature of the room to a freezing degree. I'd made her strip. I saw myself hitting the bars of the cage, the electrical currents arcing to shock her flesh. And I saw myself returning to this room and turning the heat up to the highest point. Yet the female seemed untouched by the sudden change in temperature.

Pushing myself to my feet, I staggered across the room, my neck burning and raw under the collar. Reaching the desk, I stared at the screen, the single camera in the room focused on the female.

I swallowed as I watched her. She was slight in build with long black hair that ran to her lower back. Her skin was tanned, and disgust fused in my veins when I recognized her features: Georgian. I hated Georgians. Mistress's face flashed in my mind and I snarled aloud. I especially hated Georgian females. *Suka.* They were all *suka* whores.

Then my skin pricked when the female in the cage moved. A pool of sweat lay below her and her dark hair was slick to her damp naked skin. Moaning in her sleep, she rolled onto her back, her arms stretched out at her sides. My breathing paused when her full tits came into view, her pussy only slightly showing because of a bent leg. Her stomach was flat and dripping with droplets of sweat. Her arms and legs were slight but toned. My head dropped to the side as I studied her.

Mistress didn't look like this. Mistress was harder, more muscled. There was nothing about Mistress that I liked, but this Georgian female . . .

As she lay on that floor, my breathing paused. Images of 152 unconscious and broken—used and abused—on her bed flashed through my head. I shook my head trying to push them away, but a sick feeling burned in my chest seeing this dark-haired female like this. Broken. Helpless.

A sudden rage consumed me. I wouldn't let myself do this. *Couldn't. You hate all Georgians,* I reminded myself. *No matter how broken and helpless they look.*

The female's face was turned away from the camera; then on another groan she turned and her face came fully into view. I stilled again. I stilled and I stared. She had smooth skin on her face. A small nose that was slightly upturned at the end. Her lips were big and pursed. Her black eyebrows were pulled down, and I knew she was in pain.

I smirked.

I smirked seeing how easily she was breaking.

"Suffer, *suka,*" I whispered to myself, my voice raspy from the needles in my collar. But that smirk faded when a small whimper left her lips.

Her pretty face screwed up in pain, and I felt a foreign ache in my chest. 152's screaming face came to mind. Her screaming out in pain when she was being abused by the guards under Mistress's orders. Ordered to keep me under her control.

This female in the cage sounded just like 152.

Chasing the ache away, I let the ice fill my veins. I had to cause her pain. I had no choice.

The beast would bring her pain like nothing before. She'd be terrified of me like they all were. I would torture her until she told me who she was to my hit, the Kostava male. Until she told me how to get past his army of protectors. Until she told me a way I could capture my prey and bring him to this chamber, to unleash on him hell in her place.

Only then Mistress would keep 152 from being sent to Master. Only then Mistress would keep 152 from being sent away from me.

Once more my eyes drifted to the Georgian female. I closed my eyes and pictured the bruises on 152's skin. On her legs and hips. Any empathy for this dark-haired female was gone.

There was no choice. No room for weakness.

Snapping my eyes open, I walked to the thermostat and dropped the temperature back to a minus degree setting. The vents sounded beyond the door that led to the chamber. I watched as the cold air began circulating around her. My eyes flared when another moan ripped from between her full lips, and her body curled in. White puffs of mist shot out of her mouth, as her breathing increased to short pained pants.

Reaching for the picana, I had gone to leave when I heard a muffled scream. I looked back to the screen. The Georgian was on her back. Her eyes were screwed shut. Then, mouth silently dropping open, her eyes sprang open, staring straight down the lens of the camera.

A rush of breath escaped my lips. Her eyes were as dark as the paint on the chamber's walls. They were huge. I urged my feet to move, my grip tightened on the prod in my hand, but I couldn't fucking move.

The female rolled onto her stomach and tried to push herself up off the floor of the cage. My teeth scraped across my bottom lip as her ass slowly lifted. Like everything else about this female, it was nothing like Mistress. The little Georgian's ass was firm and round. It was smooth and soft. It stirred life in my dick.

A growl built in my chest as my cock ached with its growing hardness. Forcing my eyes from the screen, I allowed myself one last lingering glance. The female had managed to sit, arms wrapped around her legs. Her huge eyes were darting around the chamber.

Something warm built in my chest as I watched her. She looked a little older than 152, but not by much.

And with the thought of 152, any warmth building inside morphed into ice. *This* suka *is Georgian,* I told myself. It was the Georgians who took us away. And it was a Georgian bitch who had ruined my life. Fucked with my head. Hurt 152.

Georgian, I thought. *I make Georgians pay. I bring them pain. I collect their screams. I bring them nothing but death.*

Surging with the focus of causing pain, I opened the door to the chamber, not even flinching at the blast of freezing air smacking against my skin. Gripping the picana tighter, I walked slowly down the hallway, my feet heavy on the tiled floor. Every few steps I stopped and waited, knowing the female would hear my approach. I wanted to mess with her mind. Have her so scared of me that she'd give up anything I asked.

Casting my head down, I could hear her heavy breathing. Her breathing was shaky. She was terrified of me.

Terrified of the ugly beast.

Walking again, I slammed my eyes to hers as I rounded the corner of the cage. The female's skin paled as she held my gaze. A stab of something strange and unknown sliced through my stomach as her lips parted and started trembling. But I sucked it up and braced myself against the front of the cage.

She didn't say anything. For one so small, I was impressed at her silent strength. She didn't cower or shrink away when she saw my face. Some of the biggest men I'd been forced to kill—slowly, very slowly—had cried and begged for their lives just at one glance at me. But this Georgian was silent, looking me straight in the eyes.

Twirling the metal picana in my hand, I pressed the button on the handle. The electric current sparked, the crackling sound booming in the silent room. She flinched, but she didn't cry out.

Stepping closer to the bars, I stood erect and asked coldly in Georgian, "What's your name?"

I studied every inch of her body, especially her face. She blinked a second too long, and swallowed deep, before whispering, "Elene." My jaw tightened at the sound of her voice. Her accent was strong. Her repulsive *Georgian* accent.

But that was forgotten when I let her response sink in. She was brave to try to lie. Because she *was* lying. Whoever had trained her had trained her well. But she was exhausted—*my doing*—and she couldn't control her body well enough to disguise the deception.

She was staring at me, masking her features, her lies. As I rolled my neck from side to side, it cracked. I pushed the button of the prod against the bar, the current sweeping through the cage. The female flinched and curled up in the center of the floor.

When the current faded, I slammed the handle of the prod against the cage and barked, "Tell me your name!"

She sucked in a sharp breath and whispered shakily, "Elene. Elene Melua."

My body tensed. She had lied to me again. I stared at her. She stared right back. But she didn't crack, not even under my rage-filled glare. Females especially hated my face—Mistress made sure of it. They caved as soon as they saw the scarred, ugly *beast*—but not this female.

It made me stop and watch her closer. *Why wasn't she disgusted? Why wasn't she cowering back in fear?*

Challenge, and a morbid hatred of my victim's disobedience, surged through me. Flicking my chin, I ordered, "Get up!"

The female's muscles tensed but for a second; then, pushing off the floor, she got to her feet. My nostrils flared as I drank in her naked body, her full tits and her nipples rock hard due to the cold. Her cheeks flushed red as I stared. She immediately tried to cover herself with her arms.

Slamming the handle against the bars, I ordered, "Keep your arms at your sides!"

She did as instructed. Her long wet hair hung in clumps over her chest, covering all but her tits. Discreetly slipping my thumb over the off button on the prod, I slowly, painstakingly, pushed the prod through the bars toward where she stood.

She stiffened as the tip of the prod hovered just an inch from her skin. Holding it exactly where it was and trying a new tactic, I repeated less harshly, "What is your name?"

She didn't even pause for breath. "Elene Melua."

Her soft voice was strong and steady. But she was lying. I could sense it. The little female was hiding who she was. My head tilted to the side in reflection. *Who the hell was she? Why was she protecting my hit?*

Her dark eyes tracked me. Suddenly I lunged the prod forward. Her eyes snapped shut as she braced for the shock. As the tip touched her skin, the expected shock didn't come. She gasped and opened her eyes. She was breathing hard as the tip of the prod pressed against the bottom of her throat.

She never moved, her body as still as rock as I pushed the tip harder against her skin. She began breathing slowly through her nostrils as I started to drag the prod over her skin. I kept her focus, my hard stare coldly capturing hers, as I continued my journey with the metal tip.

I moved the prod slowly down her chest until it lay over her sternum. I applied a little pressure, the tip slightly pushing into her smooth skin, until a tiny spot of blood began to sprout underneath. The female's face contorted into a pained expression. The ache of seeing her in such agony returned to my chest, but I forced it aside.

There was no room for sympathy in this chamber.

Just as I gauged the pressure was becoming too much, I eased off and dragged the tip over to her breast. She gasped as I ran it lightly over full flesh. Her cheeks, despite the cold, flushed bright red, her lips parting in shock when I gently circled the hard red nipple.

She watched me in fear. My eyes stayed locked on hers as I moved from that breast and traced along her tan skin, over her wet hair, to the other breast. The female's white mists of breath increased in speed as I gave her right breast the same attention as the left. Her skin erupted with millions of tiny bumps. Yet she still didn't break. Her body didn't move even though I could shock her at any moment. And her strong gaze never swayed from mine.

Alight with challenge, I moved the prod to her sternum again. But this time, I began steering it south. I ran the prod down her torso, over her stomach, and stopped just above her pussy. Her hands flexed at her sides. Once more I cocked my head to the side in interest.

It was the first time she'd moved since I'd begun my exploration. Her steely dark eyes didn't drop from mine, but they began to fill with water. Glancing down to where the picana had stopped, I forced myself to ignore the ache in my stomach as I looked at the short black hair on her pussy. Meeting her gaze again, I lowered the prod until the tip of metal ran through the top of her short hair. Her lips trembled. Then I knew. I read her perfectly: she had never been touched by a male.

Excitement surged through me—her weakness had been found.

Dipping the prod lower, I ran the metal over the apex of her thighs, and the bitch's breathing changed. It was shaky, and her hands were fisted at her sides. I stopped moving the prod and demanded, "Your name. What is your name?"

She swallowed. She opened her mouth and tried to speak, but nothing came out. I moved the prod's tip toward her folds and she cried out. She didn't like it; that I could tell. Now she was scared. Fear was spreading all over her pretty Georgian face.

But then she shocked me again. "Elene Melua!" she managed

to call out through a thick throat. Her voice was weak, yet determined not to give in.

But with that final lie, I broke.

Ripping the picana back, I pointed it to the left corner of the cage. "Stand against the bars."

The female sucked in a breath and flicked her gaze behind her, then back on me. I tilted my head just daring her to defy me. Her self-preservation won out, and she scurried to the corner as ordered. I slammed the picana against the bars. The loud clang of metal on metal rung through the bars. I watched as the female braced for the expected electric shock. Her body froze, her muscles tensed, but the shock never came. When the sound calmed, I coldly smiled into her terrified eyes.

Pressing the button to ignite the picana's current, I moved to send it through the bars but then at the last minute pulled it back. And I did it over and over and over again, over hours, toying with her mind. The female panted harshly as she braced each time for the pain. But it didn't come; instead her exhaustion from the anticipation finally brought her to her knees.

"Get up!" I ordered. The female was panting on the floor, her skin paling, but she pushed herself to her feet. Her body was swaying from side to side with tiredness, but her sunken large eyes defiantly met mine.

The challenge was set.

Snapping the lock on the cage, I wrenched open the door. Fisting the picana at my side, I ordered, "Get out!"

The female dropped her head. Her shoulders sagged slightly, but she put one shaky foot in front of the other and stopped beside me. This close, I towered over her. She was smaller than Mistress, at least half her size. Her skin was dark against my pale form. It was soft against my ink and rough scars.

My jaw clenched as I fought the need to touch her. Fought

against the urge to stop her pain. But I couldn't; 152's face in my mind forced me to keep going.

Pointing the picana to the upright metal slab in the center of the room, I growled, "Stand against it." She glanced up at me, anxiety racking her now-pale face. I stepped closer, so close that my hard chest brushed up against the cold skin of her arm. I caught her sharp intake of breath at the contact, and a jolt of fire raced down my spine. I schooled my confusion as to why.

Her skin bumped again. My muscles jerked at how affected she had become in my proximity. Leaning down, catching her stiffen, I placed my mouth at her ear and whispered threateningly, "I said. Fucking. Move. Georgian." I leaned back just a fraction, my powerful, scarred body looming over her.

I knew I had her now. I could practically feel her fear filling the room. This would be where she cracked. This would be where she spoke.

Then, shocking me to hell, her tiny foot took a step toward the metal slab. Frustration immediately swept through me. And just as she took another slow step, I threw my arm out in front of her face, my hand gripping one of the metal bars of the cage. The female gasped in shock, grinding to a halt. Leaning down, I ran my nose along the curve of her neck over her damp hair, feeling her trembling where she stood.

There, I thought. I'd found another weakness.

Me.

This ugly beast's unwanted touch.

My nose ran up and down, up and down. Her breathing was ragged; her body shook. My closeness was tearing down the walls of her bravado. But as I inhaled, I fumed when I responded to her scent—sweet and addictive.

Attractive.

Without letting myself think, I pressed my body against her

side. My chest brushed against her arm, and my hips set against her hip. The female suddenly froze, and when I glanced down my long hard cock was pressing against her side. As I saw the flush race up her cheeks, my teeth scraped over my bottom lip. Then my hips pushed forward, my dick under my sweatpants now flush against her thigh. My hand tightened against the bar at the feel of her against me, and I leaned down to her ear once more and repeated, "Your name?"

Her body jumped, trapped between the cage and me. Yet, even wrapped in nothing but fear, she opened those big lips and stuttered, "E—Elene M—Melua."

I stilled, and the iron bar creaked under my equally iron grip. Blinking, I snapped out of the feeling of her body up against mine and wrenched back my arm. The female flinched at my sudden movement. My jaw clenched and, taking the prod, I hammered it against the bars and barked, "Move!"

She rushed forward. She didn't look back as she kept her head down and hurried to the metal slab.

I watched her go, my gaze drifting down to her round ass. My muscles stiffened at the sight and I forced myself to lift my head. The female stopped just beside the slab. Rolling my shoulders, I took the prod and approached where she stood. Standing directly in front of her, I placed the prod on her stomach. She flinched. She still expected to be shocked. That was what I wanted—to completely fuck with her mind. I wanted her guessing when the next jolt of pain would strike. I pushed the tip of the prod against her skin and commanded, "Step back four paces!"

The female did exactly as I said. Looking up, I saw she was directly under the showerhead above. Reaching out to the lever on the wall at her side, I yanked it down, and a spray of ice-cold water covered her tiny frame.

She cried out and gasped for air as the water drenched her skin.

Waiting until she was fully immersed, I pulled the lever and moved forward until I could slam my hand down on the hard metal slab behind her.

I waited for her to react, but when she tried to lift a foot she fell to the floor, the cold seizing her muscles. I tensed as she fought to get back on her feet, her long hair draping over her face so much that I couldn't see her expression. Her body convulsed at the cold. I watched her put a trembling hand on the floor, trying to move, but her body simply wouldn't work.

A slice of pain slammed through my chest. Coughing, I tried to clear the ache that had taken hold of me. My hand clenched at my side as I fought against the need to help her. The need to lift her and save her—like I wanted to save 152.

Then came the following rush of anger, anger that I'd felt anything for this little Georgian at all. I was trained to resist empathy. I was trained to switch off from feeling anything at all.

Right now that training was failing.

Don't feel sorry for her, I told myself. *She's a Georgian* suka. *This* suka *stands between you and your kill. This* suka, *alive and surviving, sends 152 away to Master. No one else matters but 152. Nothing else matters but setting her free.*

Clinging to that thought, I bent down, wrapping my hand around her arm. She tensed under my hold, but I picked her up and held her against the slab. Stowing the picana to the side, I shackled her wrists and ankles to the attached metal cuffs. Standing back, I stared down at her strapped to the slab. Her thick long hair was still covering her face and chest. Moving forward, I brushed the wet hair back until all of her body was exposed. As her chest was revealed up close for the first time, I let my eyes roam.

When they abruptly stopped.

Three wide scars, looking like patched-up holes, stood proud on her skin—one under her shoulder, one on her left waist, and one just above her left hip. The female's stomach was quickly rising and falling, drops of water turning to ice on her skin. When I looked up to her face, the skin was pale and her lips were turning blue, with the skin beginning to crack.

But those eyes, those fucking dark eyes of hers, were still watching me. Only this time there was no water filling them. They were staring straight through me, glazed.

Knowing she was at the brink of collapse, I moved to the opposite side of the bed and took hold of the fan and heater, positioning them at the front of her wet naked body. Flexing my wrist, as I held my hand over the cold-air fan's switch, I asked, "Tell me your name."

She stared at me blankly. She didn't react. After several seconds, her mouth dropped open and with her eyes still glazed she managed to whisper, "Elene Melua. Kazreti, Georgia."

Closing my eyes, and with that traitorous sympathetic ache flaring back in my chest, I switched on the fan and smothered her smooth wet skin with the coldest of air.

6

ZOYA

I didn't think it was possible to feel any more pain. My skin had gone from feeling on fire, to as if it were being ripped apart by razor blades, to nothing but numbness with the deliberately changed temperatures I'd endured over the last couple of hours—torturous heat, swiftly followed by unbearable cold. I tried to wrench my arms and legs free as the pain ripped through me, but the cuffs wrapped around them made that impossible.

I gritted my teeth, suppressing the scream in my throat from slipping out of my lips. My back arched. My fingers and toes became rigid. But my eyes never moved from the man who stood before me. The monster who had returned today with piercing crystal blue eyes. Gone were dilated black eyes, and in their place were intense blue pools. A deceivingly beautiful feature on a man so cruel.

He watched me now as the heat caused my skin to sweat, and I could see in his blank stare that my pain and my suffering made no impact on his heart. He was huge, severely scarred and muscled, and the most frightening thing I had ever seen.

My body continued to jerk and jump as the effects of the

changing temperatures. But I watched my captor. I never removed my arms, suddenly confused when, on occasion, his eyes would tighten in the corners as though he felt discomfort in causing me pain. His hands would ball at his sides, as though they were fighting the urge to turn off the heater or cold-air fan.

As the hours rolled on, I wondered if I was simply imagining it, but it was there: an element of empathy or remorse.

Maybe this heavily scarred monster had feelings after all.

Since I had arrived in this chamber of hell, since this man had made me strip, I felt my innocence tearing to shreds. I had never been with a man. But he had bared me. He had touched my naked skin, he had run his nose along my neck, and he had pressed himself against my naked flesh.

Yet something was different between this man and the one from last night. Last night, his blue eyes were dilated and blown. His body was taut, as if filled with anger and rage. Last night, the man was coldly cruel and violent. He gave his instructions like he had no choice. Like something deep inside was making him do these despicable things.

This version of the man had knowing eyes. His movements were not so strained, definitely more fluid. And his eyes? His eyes today were bright and filled with the most amazing blue color. And he knew exactly what he was doing. The way he watched me. The way he smelled me. He teased and tested my endurance. It was all him. This version of the monster was very much in charge of his own actions.

This version of the man terrified me like I'd never been terrified before—he knowingly made me scream. Yet despite this, I could see a flare of humanity in his stare.

Last night, there had been none.

The monster turned off the heater, my head dropping with exhaustion. He stepped closer and leaned down, his musky scent of dark spices blanketing my face. As before, his nose tucked into the crook of my neck, the tip of his nose dusting below my ear. It ran down and back up my tender skin, until his warm breath stopped at my ear and he whispered, "How do you know Zaal Kostava?" His voice was soft, almost convincing me into thinking he felt a morsel of regret. Then I remembered his balled fists and tight eyes and wondered if he did.

He repeated the question again and made all the blood drain from my face. My eyes slammed shut. Whether I wanted to or not, a tear escaped the corner of my eye. I knew he had felt the droplet. When my eyes reopened, I saw he had captured the droplet on the pad of his finger.

I kept my mouth closed, holding back the answer to his question. He lifted the finger holding the drop. Making sure I tracked his movements, he brought the droplet to his mouth, and flicking out his tongue, he then wrapped his lips around the digit.

Slowly, he pulled his finger from his mouth and lowered it, until it landed on my chest. Even the featherlight touch of his finger felt like the stab of a dagger to my sensitive skin. But he kept it moving, until it ran over my breast and circled the wet tip around my nipple.

My breathing hitched at the fear of not being able to move, at the fear of what he would do next. I knew he was pushing me for an answer, testing my resolve. Avto had told me what torturers could do. However, learning of such acts and enduring them were not even comparable.

Fluttering my eyes closed, I tried to take myself away from the here and now. I instead pictured the meadow when I was a child. I remembered Zaal and Anri walking side by side as I hid behind a tree, watching my two brothers smiling as they talked. I remembered my grandmama rocking me in her arms as she sang me her favorite song. I remembered my papa buying me whatever it was that I asked for. I remembered lying with my mama, her stroking my hair as my baby brother and sister slept in their cribs. And I pictured Zaal, my *sykhaara* now. I held the image of his photograph, smiling and in love.

Inhaling through my nose, I finally pictured Zaal's fiancée in the window of the house in Brighton Beach. I saw his hands wrapped around her waist. And she was happy. The house seemed full of such happiness. My *sykhaara,* after a life of pain, had finally found happiness. He had found another family. That was all that mattered.

Steely resolve settled over my soul; I vowed to never betray him. I would not heel to this monster. No matter what he tried.

Then when I opened my eyes, I took in the size of my captor, the scars, the tattoos, the collar around his neck . . . the collar resembling that of a slave, and my face blanched. I replayed what Avto had told me about Zaal and Anri, that they had been captured and drugged. Experimented upon until they were like beasts, monsters, ghosts of who they once were. Forced to kill and fight for Jakhua. Then I pictured Zaal's tattoos on his arms, tattoos not too dissimilar from this man's, and I wondered if he was the same. He wanted my brother. My brother who had recently killed the man who had experimented on him as a child.

A man whose people could still want revenge. A man who might have had more than just my brothers under his control.

What if . . . ?

As I lifted my eyes to meet his, my captor was waiting for my answer. Swallowing, I shook my head, ignoring the headache pounding in my skull. The man froze, his jaw clenching in frustration.

He stepped back to stand by my side. I braced my body for what I knew would come next. His free hand took hold of my face, lightly gripping my cheeks. He pulled my face to the side until it was facing his, mere *inches* from his, and he said, "You may believe you are strong, little Georgian, but I have barely begun. You will not be able to take what I can deliver if you force my hand. In the end you will break." Flexing his arm, the inked names littering his skin protruding with the movement, he added, "You all do. I'm the fucking *Smert' Kosoy.* Designed to do only one thing—kill."

My heart missed a beat as his words drifted into my ears, and I whispered, "*The bringer of death.*"

My blood ran cold when this man, this scarred Russian *bringer of death,* smiled. Two rows of straight white teeth gleamed under his full lips, the top marred by a red scar, and his smile brought fear to my core. Because I knew he spoke the truth. Nothing on this man screamed, *Safe!* In fact, it was the opposite: his appearance, his very presence, screamed, *Danger!*

Yet, even as he reached over to switch on the cold fan, all I could think of was how he had said *designed to do only one thing. Designed.* Not born, not chose to, *designed.*

Like Zaal and Anri had been designed to kill too, by Jakhua.

Zaal who had been turned into a killer, now a man at peace and free.

Perhaps like this man could be. My stomach clenched as I stared at his scarred body and face, those tortured blue eyes. Suddenly all I saw was my twin brothers standing before me. My brothers forced into brutal slavery. My brothers, who had once been pure and good men.

And like Zaal, my captor too could have once been a good man.

It was the last thought I had as I lost consciousness . . . that maybe this man could be saved like Zaal, too.

I wasn't sure how long the punishment had lasted. When I first passed out, I woke alone. But then he did return, because he *always* returned. He would come back, and every time he would douse me in water and both heat and cool me until I lost consciousness again. When I awoke, his questions were endless. He would demand to know my name. He would demand to know who I was to Zaal. He would demand to know who protected my brother—their names—and how he could get to Zaal.

But pride filled my chest that even in my time of weakness, even in my disorientated state, I stayed true to my blood.

I was Elene Melua from Kazreti, Georgia, and I knew nothing of a Zaal Kostava.

I stayed shackled to the slab, fighting to keep my eyes open, when the man appeared once again. This time, his presence didn't cause a reaction within me. I wouldn't allow it. I had to be strong to endure his torture.

My eyes drunkenly traced his every step. Suddenly he stopped, and the collar around his neck seemed to tighten. I watched in rapt attention as he threw back his head. The corded muscles in his chest, torso, and arms tensed and protruded with thick veins. But his neck, the collar was doing something to his neck. I watched as his teeth gritted together and his body shook with rage. He released a deafening roar and promptly dropped to the floor.

My racing heart pumped the blood around my body so quickly that I could hear the rush of liquid flowing through my ears. But as tired as my eyes were, they never once strayed from the man on the floor, seemingly now broken. Minutes and minutes passed, yet he didn't move. His head dropped forward and his torso was slumped over.

The collar. The collar was doing something to him.

Drugs? I thought, my heart breaking. Because if this man had been captured and hurt like my brothers . . . what was his life? What had he endured?

As I watched him lying still on the floor, I couldn't help but see my brothers before me. In my exhausted, pained mind, all I could see was my childhood heroes. Like this man, only filled with the need to kill.

That thought brought a new kind of fear to my heart. Because if he was being drugged, if the man last night was drugged, I knew the monster he would be when he awoke.

I frantically pulled on the cuffs, trying to break free, but as I heard a low growl I whipped my eyes to the floor. Staring at me was the captor from last night. His eyes were dilated to black and he stared at me like he wanted to rip me apart.

I froze. Sweat broke out on the man's body, his scarred skin glistening with damp. Then he pushed off the floor, the veins in his bulging muscles so pronounced that they appeared unnatural.

The man approached, and his darkened eyes roved over my prone body. With a fury-ridden face, he reached for the cuffs at my wrists and snapped them undone. He then moved to my feet, repeating the action, all the time panting in harsh heavy breaths—as if something inside was burning him alive.

As the shackle was ripped from my ankle, I moved my numb limbs. I cried out at the molten pain coursing through my tired muscles. I gritted my teeth through the pain, praying to find some relief as I dropped to the floor, the man releasing me from his hold.

A noise from in front of me caught my attention. When I followed the direction of the sound, it was to see my captor pacing the tiled floor. His hands were balled, and his face was severe in expression. Every inch of his sweating ripped body broadcast the purest and most terrifying level of ferociousness. His entire soul seemed ravaged; by what, I did not know.

His gaze flicked to me, and without pausing his frantic movements he snarled, "Name. I need your fucking name!" His deep voice was urgent and dripping with venom.

I opened my mouth and rasped, "Elene—," but before I had chance to finish my rehearsed response the man swung my way and he hammered his fist on the metal slab above me.

Glaring down, he roared, "You lying Georgian *suka*! Tell me your fucking name!" The pupils of his eyes were so large his eyes were two blazing coals.

Lips trembling, I replied, "That is my name."

His neck tensed, and he hissed, "Lies. Georgians lie. Georgians only ever lie!"

Jerking himself away from me, he took himself to a lever on the wall and pulled it down. The sound of metal against metal echoed from the ceiling. As I lifted my head, a large hook was lowering down toward me held by a thick chain.

Suddenly he was at my side, holding yards and yards of thick rope. I swallowed on seeing the rope, my stomach coiled with apprehension. As he approached, loosening the rope in his hand, he murmured, "Pain to the Georgian whore. Nothing but pain to the one that took her away from me."

At that point I knew this man was not seeing me. Whatever was being pumped into his veins by his collar caused him to be somewhere else in his head.

To his eyes there was someone else sitting here on this floor.

Someone he wanted to see hurt.

Someone else's torture was about to be delivered to me.

7

194

I woke in the back room of the chamber.

A blinding pain shot through my head, and my muscles ached. As always, I felt the burning sensation in my neck first, then I tried to crack open my eyes. The dim light hanging from the ceiling felt like a flame scalding my eyes. Lifting my hands, I ran them over my eyelids, where I felt rough and broken skin. Pushing myself to sit up, I squinted and focused on the palms of my hands. Red rope burns were sliced across the skin, my fingers split and covered in dried blood.

My mouth was dry. I crawled forward and took a bottle of water from the desk. I emptied it in one gulp. The screen on the desk was black. When I focused on the picture, I realized the lights in the chamber were out. The whole place was in darkness.

Leaning on the desk, I pressed the heels of my hands against my eyes and tried to remember what I'd done last night. My mind was like a fog. Rage swept over me when I remembered that the pellets in my collar were stronger than normal. Mistress must have known my tolerance to the serum was strengthening. And she'd known these new pellets would black me the hell out. They'd ensure I got her her kill.

She wanted Zaal Kostava to be punished by me in the worst possible manner. She wanted the Georgian male to suffer.

At last the fog on my mind cleared. I watched the images when I was under the serum play out in my mind's eye. I'd taken a thick rope and tied the little Georgian up until she couldn't even move. Lifting her limp body in my arms, I attached the back of the rope to the butcher's hook hanging from the ceiling. She had moaned at the rope cutting into her skin. I'd asked her question after question: What was her name? Who was she to Zaal Kostava? What were his weaknesses? But she didn't answer. I tightened the rope, her limbs reddening at the pressure, but she still didn't talk.

I'd forced water down her throat, food into her mouth, and let her use the bathroom, but soon after, she'd slipped into unconsciousness. I'd walked back to this room and plunged the chamber into darkness. Light deprivation had a way of breaking my subjects down.

Staring at the screen, I flicked on the switch to the chamber; the little female's body hung limply from the ceiling. Her head snapped up when the light came on. I watched her eyes flinch at the flaring light. I watched as she winced in pain at being held suspended midair and wrapped up tightly by the rope. But she remained still. A warm feeling spread through my chest as I watched her very obvious show of strength.

She was resilient. Resilient and determined.

But if I was to save 152 this female *had* to crack.

Taking a protein bar from the desk, I forced myself to eat the damn thing. *What would break her?* Days had drifted by. Even with all the pain, and the fear, she hadn't cracked.

I paused eating when I recalled the only time she'd reacted. It was when I pushed against her naked body. It was when my nose ran along her neck. It was when my cock pushed against her side.

I froze when I realized what would work. I had to change tactics with her. My stomach clenched at the thought of having to get that close to a Georgian, to another female. But as my eyes strayed to the screen, to the female tied up, my tension drained away. She was nothing like Mistress. She was soft. She was young and, even if I hated the Georgian for *being* Georgian, she was beautiful.

My skin bumped as I remembered smelling the sweetness of her skin, feeling her silky long neck under my nose. My muscles tensed at the thought of her brown eyes looking into mine. That one time she had looked at me not in hate. Like she was seeing something different in me from a fucked-up ugly beast. That she was seeing who I used to be underneath.

Just *more* than what I was now.

I quickly chased that image away.

Straightening my body, I cracked my neck and opened the door to the chamber. Just before I left I turned the temperature of the chamber to sixty-eight degrees. The first part of this plan was to take away her fear. Food, drink, and warmth. Then spend hours and hours with her under the ministrations of my hands.

She would be repulsed by the ugliness of my face, but there was no way, with my training, she could resist the pleasure of my hands. Even if she was previously untouched.

Walking into the bright room, I kept my eyes forward. My teeth were gritting and my hands fisting at what I would have to do. Mistress had trained me to be an expert in sexual torture, but never before had I the opportunity to practice it. Most of my hits were males. There were only ever two females I was sent to torture—they buckled as soon as they woke up in a chamber. Their deaths were quick, as a reward for their useful information. Nothing like this little Georgian female.

As I entered the main room of the chamber, her eyes lifted to greet me. They widened, and her lips parted. It was in fear. She watched me close in, her chest rising and falling, her full tits pushing through gaps in the rope.

Standing before her, I stared straight into her eyes. Her face subtly relaxed when she studied my eyes—I had no idea why.

As her body jerked from being tied too long, I walked to the lever on the wall and pulled it down. The sound of the mechanism grinding into action rattled up above. After a few seconds the butcher's hook began to lower her to the bed in the center of the room. She landed on the surface, the rope unrelenting.

Moving to the bed, I slid the hook from its rope catch then and flicked the lever to withdraw it to the ceiling. Not once did the female flinch as I moved around her. Returning to the bed, I lifted my hands and began to slowly untie the rope. A rush of breath came from her mouth. Her freezing body remained motionless as yard by yard I unwrapped the thick rope.

Minutes later when she had been freed, I dropped the rope to the floor. As I turned my attention to the female, I noted the rope burns on her skin, her limbs marked with delves and indents from the tightness of the rope.

Unconsciously, my hands moved. I snapped to attention as I saw them hovering above her back. Clenching my jaw, I ripped them back.

Pulling my shit together, I ordered, "Stretch!"

Her back tensed at the command. Due to the cold, the Georgian's body was curled in and distorted. To make my new plan work, she had to get back to how she looked before. Felt before I had hurt her.

I hurt her . . . , the errant thought circled in my head, pulling the ache back to my chest. For a brief second I allowed myself to dislike that I had hurt her, before I pushed it back away.

I hovered behind, but she didn't move. Leaning forward, I brushed back the long hair from her face, placing my mouth at her ear. Bumps broke out over her rope-burned skin. I felt a flood of warmth inside, knowing my closeness affected her. I knew it wasn't in attraction, but she didn't need to find me attractive to come. "Stretch!" I commanded once more.

A low moan sounded from the female's mouth. Her body shook, but she forced her legs currently curled into her chest to straighten out. Her arms, wrapped awkwardly around her chest, slipped to her sides, her head flopped back on the bed, and her back flattened out on the surface. Eyes closed, she panted through the pain. Though the room remained cold, sweat beaded on her forehead. I knew what her pain felt like.

When Mistress trained me to be her most effective assassin, she made sure that I also experienced suffering through torture. She told me that I needed to know how this felt: the pain, the suffering, and the complete fucking with the subject's mind. She got off on seeing me in pain. Got off the same way she did when she slashed and tore up my face.

The little Georgian's rough breathing slowed down. My eyes traveled the length of her beautiful body. Rope burns tracked over the skin, showing exactly where I had caused her the most pain. Leaning over the bed, I noticed that her hands were bent on the surface, fingernails trying to dig into the bed below. But all I could see was soft skin underneath the marks, her full tits, and, of course, her pussy.

Reaching out, I pressed my fingertips lightly on her calf. She jumped under my touch. Her breathing quickened as I swirled my fingertips up over her knee and along the outside of her thigh.

The female, completely still before my exploration, began moving slightly. Her knee bent as I ran my fingertips along her inner thigh and around the side of her cunt. A breathy moan slipped from her mouth and her stomach tensed at the feeling.

I knew it wasn't pleasure . . . *yet;* I knew it was from the unfamiliar touch of a male. I continued my journey over her stomach until I reached the bottom of her tits. I paused, and flicked my gaze to her face. Her cheeks were flushed. Her previously dull eyes were bright with fear.

Poking out my tongue, I ran the tip along the seam of my lips, slow and wet, watching as she watched me with those wide, virgin eyes. The female's breathing hitched. Resisting the victorious pleasure I was feeling at how quickly she was reacting to my touch, I ghosted my fingertips over the plump flesh of her left breast. Her red nipple hardened into a small firm point. I circled my finger around and around the nipple, watching as pink skin produced bumps and shivered in my wake.

And I couldn't look away. Her body was tight and lean. Her tits were full and firm. Her skin was so soft. But it was the look on her face that had my balls aching and my cock rock hard. There was no doubt this female was terrified, but there was something else in her eyes, too. Something yet to be named, as I explored her body with an eager hand. It confused me, because whatever it was, it wasn't disgust. She wasn't looking at my messed-up face and overscarred inked body and hiding away—it was fucking with my mind. It was tightening my damn chest.

My fingers reluctantly abandoned her tit to run up her neck. She froze, her limbs straightening, breathing paused. Suddenly she swallowed as my fingertips walked onto her cheek. Then my fingers stopped. Huge dark eyes were staring at me, long black eyelashes fluttering against her cheek. My stomach tensed. The female's full lips parted and her warm breath drifted over my hand. Something within me held me captive, as her dark eyes bored into mine.

We stayed that way for a few minutes. Then Mistress's face flashed in my mind. She was the only female I'd ever touched. And I'd relished every minute of causing the sadistic bitch pain. But not once had I touched her face. Her ugly, poisonous face.

As I ripped back my hand, my eyebrows pulled down in anger. I backed up three steps. I backed up farther, then turned and walked to the room at the back. The minute I was through the door, I growled low in my chest and hit at my head. Reaching into my sweatpants, I gripped my balls tightly, my cock instantly softening with the pain.

Five minutes later, I'd placed food and water on a tray and headed back into the chamber. The Georgian was still on the bed, but her head tipped up and her eyes found me as I walked toward where she lay.

"Sit up!" I ordered. She pressed her palms against the bed and sat up. My nostrils flared as her legs swung over the side, and her thighs fell slightly apart. I forced my eyes up. They narrowed when I saw her body. She'd lost weight.

The female eventually lifted her head. Stepping forward, I placed the tray on the bed. "Eat. Drink!" I ordered.

The female's eyes flicked down to the tray. I folded my arms across my chest. "Eat. Now!" I ordered loudly. She reached out a shaky hand and picked up the sandwich. She slowly brought the sandwich to her mouth, and all the time I watched her. I never moved. I stayed right in front of her until the sandwich had disappeared and the bottle of water had been drunk.

The female wiped her mouth as I stepped forward and removed the tray. I placed the tray on the floor, then stretched out my arms. The female never took her attention off me.

Inhaling deeply, ready to begin, I edged forward until I was standing in front of her legs. A long strand of her dark hair had fallen over her shoulder. With controlled gentleness, I brushed it back, drifting my finger over her cheek as I did so.

The female stiffened and sucked in a sharp breath. Very slowly, I put a hand on the bed at each side of her body. My face invaded her personal space. This close, I could detect the stuttered breathing struggling to pass her pursed lips. I placed my nose against the length of her neck and ran it upward until my mouth was at her ear. "Tell me your name, *kotyonok*." My voice was graveled and low and I ran my nose back down her neck, only after I'd called her kitten in my native Russian tongue.

The female whipped her face toward mine, her full lips brushing across my cheek. As soon as her lips pressed against my stubbled skin, she dropped her head and whispered, "Elene."

Rage burned inside as she continued to lie, but I didn't allow my face to change. "Elene," I murmured, my hand lifted to wrap into her hair. She jumped, and I added, "Elene. Elene Melua from Kazreti, Georgia."

"Yes," she replied breathlessly. Moving back an inch, I could see the pulse in her neck pounding hard. A bead of sweat dropped from behind her ear as the room temperature began to rise to a bearable heat. Seeing it run over her beating pulse, I flicked out my tongue and lapped it into my mouth.

Her shocked reaction emerged as a confused whimper. And I smirked into her hair, moving my chest closer to hers.

"Elene Melua," I murmured again into her ear. "So beautiful. Too beautiful for me to hurt anymore. Too beautiful for me to make scream"—I paused, then added, "in pain." My fingers pressed against the front of her throat as she sucked in a gasp at my words; then they drifted down to her chest.

The female completely stilled. Rubbing my chest against her tits, I eventually moved back and held out my hand. She looked down at my hand and shook her head in resistance. Stepping closer still, my heavily muscled legs pushed between hers. She fought to refuse my entrance, but combating her strength was like swatting a fly—she was nothing to me.

I moved forward. As my thigh pushed against her heat, her back lowered toward the bed. Planting my hands on either side of her body, I crawled over where she lay, my chest scraping against her own. Her flat stomach met mine. Her breathing became erratic. I pressed my body down, watching a deep flush coat her skin. A timid cry slipped from her lips, the sound of her discomfort stimulating my muscles to burn in victory. She may have been strong in the face of pain, but me, like this? Close and touching her body? She was helpless and unable to quell her fear.

Pushing my hands higher until my top half completely covered hers, I placed my cheek against her cheek and dragged my mouth to her ear, her hands lifting to grab at my sides in response. She pushed hard against my chest. My cock filled with blood as she tried to fight me back. I laughed low and deep into her ear, pressing down harder until she couldn't move beneath me. As my mouth hovered beside her ear, I flicked out my tongue and, with painstaking slowness, licked along the outside shell of her ear.

Her skin burned against mine, and with one last lap of her earlobe I growled, "In this chamber, you're mine. What I want you do, your body I own, until you tell me what I want to know."

She inhaled a shaky breath. Turning her head until her mouth was at my ear, she whimpered, "No. I beg you . . ."

She'd barely made a sound, but excitement raced through my veins as that plea filled the quiet room.

"You beg me what?" I probed.

Turning my head, I watched as her eyes squeezed shut and she simply repeated, "I beg you . . . no." Her face contorted.

The ache built back in my chest and swelled to take root in my stomach when her hand suddenly ran down my chest. Slowly. Softly. My breathing paused as I searched her eyes wondering why. But I couldn't read her. Couldn't read her as tears filled her eyes and her finger ran just underneath my collar. The collar that now had her attention.

I frowned as that unknown feeling almost had me jumping back off the bed. She was touching me softly. *Me,* the Mistress's ugly beast. *Me,* the Russian bringer of death. It was impossible; Mistress made this face to keep all females but her away, so she would own me completely. But that fucking ache wouldn't go at the thought that the little Georgian wasn't seeing the scars. She was somehow seeing the forgotten *me* living underneath the beast's scars.

No! I snapped at myself. *You're wrong. You've hurt her. She only sees you as you are—an evil killer. This isn't real. This is only her fear taking hold. You're her torturer.*

I gritted my teeth, pissed at my stupid thoughts, and pushed myself to keep going with the plan. Rearing my face back until it was hovering above hers, I asked, "Who is Zaal Kostava to you?"

A single tear slipped out of the corner of her eye, but steeling her expression, she said, "I know no one by that name."

Her dark eyes pierced through me as I studied her pretty, delicate face. Nodding my head, I slid down her body, my lips dragging along her flesh. Stopping just before I met her pussy, I lifted off her body. I couldn't help but lick my lips and plant my palms on her tiny waist, then run my hands along her silky skin.

She was too fucking beautiful.

Lifting my hands, I held one out to her and with a harsh glare silently commanded her to do as ordered. She lifted herself from the bed and, trembling, placed her tiny hand in mine. For a second I stared at the sight of her palm on my palm. Her thin fingers looked lost in my rough and callused hand; the feel of a warm hand shot a slice of pain through my stomach.

Her hand flinched, bringing me back to my plan. Wrapping my fingers around hers, I pulled her from the bed and guided her to the wall.

Turning round, I placed my hands on her shoulders and guided her back against the wall. Her face wore a nervous expression as I ordered, "Do not move!" The female stood against the wall, her small frame looking lost against the matte black background. Moving to a chest in the corner of the room, I opened the top and pulled out the leather padded cuffs. Carrying them back to where she waited, I bent down. Taking the ankle cuffs, I gently wrapped one around each ankle. Standing up, I took the wrist cuffs and did exactly the same with her wrists.

Gathering both of her wrists in one of my hands, I guided them above her head, and with my free hand I ran my finger slowly down her waist, leaning in to ask, "Do they hurt, *kotyonok*?"

At that name—kitten—slipping from my lips, she winced, but when I tilted my head to the side, waiting for her answer, she shook her head.

I caught her briefly staring intently at my identity number on my chest. When she realized I was watching her, she tore her gaze away. I frowned but kept going.

152 *needed* me to keep going.

Placing my finger and thumb on her chin, I bent my legs until my gaze poured into hers and instructed, "You answer me from now on, *kotyonok*."

The little Georgian nodded her head obediently. My eyes narrowed in confusion at her sudden compliance. When I let my confusion show in my expression, she nodded and answered, "Yes. I'll answer you."

Shock rushed through me. I didn't understand why she was suddenly agreeing to my commands when she had resisted my every move up until now. I also couldn't work out the look on her face. The sadness etched in her features. Like she was suddenly seeing me differently. Like something had made her see me as someone new.

She watched me, waiting for my response. I pushed away my inner thoughts and pressed my forehead against hers. "Good little Georgian *kotyonok*."

She inhaled a long breath and closed her eyes. Stepping back, I reached up and snapped the cuff's hook into the chains hanging from above. Her arms hung in the air, her firm tits pushing out from her arched chest.

I repeated the action with the ankle shackles, then moved to the pulley farther along the wall. I held the lever until her arms and legs were pulled tight. A small surprised cry left her lips as her body spread against the wall.

Locking the pulley in place, I walked slowly back in front of her and, making sure her eyes were on me, hooked my hands in the sides of my sweatpants. I inched them down my hips, all the time scorching her with my glare. Her eyelids fluttered and her hands balled into fists above the tight cuffs.

My cock twitched under that unknown attentive stare. Muscles tensing, I lowered the sweatpants to the floor and kicked them away.

Straightening up, I met her stare again and rolled my neck. I could feel the tip of my cock hitting my lower torso. More important, I could see the red flush covering the female's body. As I edged closer, her breathing became erratic. Running my hand through my hair, purposely flexing my broad chest, I landed right in front of her.

Her mouth was parted as I stared. Her arms pulled on the chains, and her legs shook. Reaching up, I tugged on a chain and, with my face just inches from hers, whispered, "You're trapped, *kotyonok*. You're all mine." A small breath of air fell from her lips.

Pushing my torso against hers, the hard bullets of her nipples scraped across my chest. I brushed her long hair from her face and asked, "Have you ever been touched?" She shook under my hand, and I added, "Have you ever been touched by a male?"

Nothing was forthcoming, so I dropped my hand until it landed on her nipple, where I rolled it between my finger and thumb. She cried out, her voice breaking with the shock. Releasing the nipple,

I softly massaged her tit. As I slipped my thigh in between her legs, my cock pulsed when she gasped.

"*Kotyonok,* do you remember what I said about answering me?"

She wordlessly nodded. I pushed my thigh forward, brushing the hard muscle up against her clit. The Georgian cried out, her back arching off the wall. I momentarily gritted my teeth at the feel of her on my thigh. It felt so different from Mistress. It felt good.

"I said, do you remember what I said about answering me?"

I lifted my thigh, building pressure on her clit, when she cried out, "Yes! I remember." She breathed hard and fought to look me in the eyes, "I remember," she affirmed.

Withdrawing my thigh, I palmed her tit in my hand, and said, "Then tell me, my *kotyonok,* who is Zaal Kostava to you?"

Her body stilled and her face blanked. "Nothing. That name means nothing to me."

My hand froze as yet another lie came from her lips, yet my nostrils flared.

Flared because I knew the little Georgian's body was now mine.

8

ZOYA

It's to help him, I told myself. I was letting him. I was submitting to him to help him.

It was clear to me now that something or someone was driving him to do this to me. Just like my brothers had had someone controlling them. As he fed me, as he brought me down from the ropes, I saw the regret in his eyes. I saw a brief flash of tenderness in his gaze.

And all I could think of was my brothers. How I hadn't been able to save them. How they may have been forced to do something like this man was being forced with me. And because of that, something inside of me called me to save him.

Save him like I couldn't save my brothers.

The tattoo on his chest kept pulling my attention. It was numerical, like an ID. That, with the collar, made my veins fill with ice. I didn't know what was happening, who he was, who he worked for, but I knew it couldn't be good.

And I couldn't help but wonder why he was so scarred. The slices across his face and head were clearly made from knives, like he had been savagely attacked. But who could have done it? And why? Those scars took away any typical attractiveness, but his eyes . . . his blue eyes were so striking, so expressive. And I, unbeknownst to him, when I looked closely enough, could see every emotion he felt in those eyes.

Including the nervous bewilderment he had obviously felt when I had placed my hand on his massive chest. The flare in his eyes of the unknown, and, sadder still, the flash of fear in their depths. This man, this torturer, had felt fear at my simple touch. I knew in an instant that he had never been touched softly, affectionately, before. It filled me with such sadness that my throat closed with emotion.

Zaal and Anri had probably been the same, too.

So, foolishly or not, I had resolved to let him do what he must. I planned to wait for a moment to ask *him* questions, find out who had sent him and why. But I hadn't expected this new development. I had been prepared for more pain, more sadistic torture. But not this. I wasn't skilled in seduction, completely unprepared for sexual acts.

The man pushed forward again, and with one glimpse into his eyes I saw the vulnerability from before staring back at me. I realized quickly that although this was coming from a place of torture, a quest for answers, I could see in his eyes that he was seeking what I had given him before—a small amount of acceptance.

Of affection.

I realized the torturer had a weakness after all—a need for someone to see the him trapped underneath the monster on the outside. And yearning to be touched.

I knew I had to be that person for him. I had to try. Something inside me made me need to try.

His hand on my breast moved again, and I shifted under his touch.

He repeated the action, the pad of his thumb slipping over my raised nipple. I closed my eyes, trying to break the hold of his intense crystal gaze. And I closed my eyes in confusion when a jolt of heat darted between my legs.

I held back a cry at this unfamiliar sensation, held back a whimper as his hot breath washed over my face. As I fluttered my eyes back open, the man's beautifully scarred face was the only thing I could see. He was so close that I couldn't escape his attention—his light eyes, his fair skin, jet-black shaven hair, and angular face. But his lips? My eyes could not resist slipping back to stare at those lips. They were full and thick, despite the small upper scar, yet looked so soft to the touch. I idly wondered, *Whoever sent this man to kill my brother chose him well.* Not only because of his effectiveness in torture, but also for his terrifying looks, which were somehow, to me, both savage and divine.

The man's body displayed no trace of fat. As he pulled the sweatpants from his body, my face blazed at the sight of this naked man. I had no reference, no sexual experience with men, not even platonic.

He had kidnapped me.

He had hurt me

He had tortured me.

But now I was seeing another side of him. The one who called me kitten in his native Russian and now raked back my hair, whose eyes flared and mouth hissed when he stroked his rough hand—intimately—over my naked skin.

My mind was a mixture of confusion. I was constantly on edge, wondering if the next touch would bring me pain or would whatever was in the man's collar change him back into the bringer of torture and pain? Yet under his current ministrations, a strange sense of safety had washed through me. I was more convinced than not that he wouldn't hurt me.

I didn't understand any of it.

He moved in, lifting his hands to brush back hair from my face.

I felt so small as his large frame towered over me. It seemed to consume me.

One hand drifted down to hold on to my jaw. He twisted my head, until my neck and cheek were open to his attentions. He inched in, his lips ghosting along my cheek, but not kissing the skin, just brushing all along the side of my face. His breath tickled my ear. Hot shivers bolted down my spine.

Wordlessly, the man's lips moved down to my neck and followed the same path as his tongue had previously made. A low rumble sounded from his chest. In my hair his hand was still. He inhaled a long breath. "You smell so sweet, *kotyonok*." My legs weakened as his hoarse voice rasped in my ear. His hand released my face, and as he turned his hand the backs of his fingers began running down the side of my neck, slowly and featherlight. Goose bumps emerged in their wake. When his hand landed just above my breast, my breathing paused. I waited for his next touch with bated breath.

Suddenly, hearing him releasing a frustrated strained groan, I felt a press of warmth against my neck. I was shocked to stillness wondering what he was doing. Then his mouth moved down my throat just a fraction and the feeling of warmth hit me again. Realization hit hard—he was kissing my neck.

In this moment I was glad my arms and legs were restrained. With his touch, this man's whispered gentle touch, I feared I would have fallen to the floor.

I had never been kissed.

I had never felt a man press his lips against mine. I had never felt this before, soft strong lips caressing the skin on my neck. Part of me didn't want it. I wanted to push him off my body, punish him for taking away a first that I'd dreamed of having with a man I loved. But at the same time I strangely didn't want him to stop. This feeling, this strange feeling for the savage but mysterious man, was engulfing me.

My back arched as his lips continued to caress my neck. The feeling intensified when the hand on my chest cupped my breast.

Against my will, a moan slipped from my throat and my eyes rolled at the forbidden feel of his hot mouth on my skin. "Mmm," he murmured as his teeth scraped slowly to the edge of my shoulder. "So sweet."

An ache hit me between my legs. I tried to push the feeling away. But as I glanced down and saw his glittering blue eyes looking back up at me, the tip of his tongue laving my skin, my heart pounded and the ache built higher still.

He traveled farther down my body, until his knees hit the floor and his mouth was level with my breasts.

Both of his hands fell to grip the sides of my waist. His chin flicked up so his face was angled toward mine. His thumbs stroked along my hips, slowly, teasing. I held my breath; then he parted his mouth and asked, "What is your name, *kotyonok*?"

Exhaling deep, I whispered, "Elene."

He froze, his thumbs stilling on my ribs. His head tipped to the side, and without taking his eyes off mine he moved his mouth forward until he stopped just a fraction from the tip of my nipple. My body tensed when he licked his lips and, leaning the final inch forward, his tongue flicked against my hard flesh. I cried out at the sensation, my fingers wrapping around the chain suspending my arms.

The monster hummed as he swallowed down my taste. His eyes closed, and when they opened again they were alight with hunger.

Shuffling closer, I almost whimpered seeing his naked length hard and aroused. And he was huge. I had nothing to compare it to, but I instinctively knew he was larger than most. The intense ache between my legs vied with intense trepidation. Would he take me?

My pulse raced with fear at the thought, but all those thoughts dissipated as his tongue once again licked at my nipple. Only this time it was not a flick; the flat of his wet tongue laved over me. He licked and licked until I feared my chains would snap under the strain of my fisting hands. My skin was on fire. It flushed. A bead of sweat trickled down my spine.

His hand moved to palm my flesh, and with a soft growl his mouth swallowed the flesh of my breast, before sucking it back, his teeth rolling the nipple in its grip.

My head snapped back, and I emitted a muffled cry. My legs strained and pulled at my ankle shackles. It felt too good, my body bending at the heat of pleasure coursing through my veins.

Glancing down, my eyes widened as he watched me. But that was not what had me entranced; that honor belonged to his free hand, which palmed his length. His gaze held mine captive as his hand roughly, but slowly, stroked up and down the flesh of his hard shaft.

Knowing he had my breathless attention, the monster moved in again. He repeated the action—sucking, licking, and palming my breast until I fought to gain my breath, fought to maintain composure.

Pressure began building between my legs. I fought to close my thighs, to relieve the ache, the pleasurable pain throbbing in my core, but the shackles held tight.

As something big, something so intense, built between my legs, the man pulled back. I gasped for breath as the sensation began to fade; then a wave of frustration swept in and I regained control.

"No," I protested almost silently, most certainly reluctantly.

The man's hands still roamed over my body. I heard his sharp exhale of breath. Glancing down, I saw his face was upturned. I stilled at the strange expression on his damaged face. I could not read what he was thinking. His scarred cheeks were flushed, his nostrils flared, and his eyes were so bright that I felt they could see into my soul.

Shaking his head, he clenched his jaw, then demanded, "Name."

My body was taut, in need of something, *reaching* for something I didn't understand, but I let my head drop as I answered, "Elene."

His bright eyes frosted, and he dived for my other breast, sucking the plump flesh into his mouth, his hot tongue lapping at the raised bud. I moaned; then the noise got trapped in my mouth as his hand journeyed south. With his mouth occupied at my breast and his hand dragging down the center of my torso, my senses overloaded. I tried to bend my knees to relieve the ache, but no matter how hard I tried I couldn't move.

Removing himself from my breast, he focused his attention on my eyes as his hand drifted lower still. His roving fingers stopped as the hair between my legs began. My heart thundered so hard in my chest that I could hear its heavy beat pounding in my ears. I studied every inch of his face; heat pooled at my core when his teeth ran over his full bottom lip. A frustrated groan rumbled from deep inside when the pad of his index finger began tracing the perimeter of my triangle. Heat sliced up my spine. But this did not compare to how my body burned when the man flicked out his tongue and lapped around my belly button.

"I'm begging you," I found myself confessing.

Crystal blue eyes looked up at me, and he asked, "What, *Elene*?" while sliding his free hand around my back until his rough palm landed on the flesh of my behind. I yelped as his hand met the flesh.

Unconsciously my body jerked. "I'm begging you . . . I don't know!"

The man stopped, and lowering his head to the lowest part of my stomach, he sighed. "Then give me your name, *kotyonok*. Your real name, and this all can end."

I squeezed my eyes shut, but tears tumbled down my cheeks. His hand squeezed my behind again, and his finger slipped low, stroking toward my core. Lips parting, my eyes flew open and I released a strangled moan. My body shook with the unfamiliarity of my most private place being caressed, so freely and unbidden. Yet, darkly and treacherously, I wanted that finger to travel lower. I wanted the spring, currently wound so tightly, to be released. I wanted that something I just knew was out of reach.

In my inner turmoil, I had not seen him rise to his feet. One of his hands was still at my behind, the other still skirting just above my core, but now his face, his flushed and hungry scarred face, was directly before mine.

"Please," I begged again, looking beyond the three harsh scars to see patches of smooth and milky skin.

He shook his head, his long black eyelashes fluttering as he blinked. "Shh," he whispered, pressing his forehead against mine. I felt the finger now playing at the top of my pubic hair move down to the crease of my thigh. I caught an apprehensive moan in my throat. I was confused at my breasts aching for his callused touch and my nipples hardening against the monster's naked broad chest.

"Tell me, *kotyonok,*" he whispered, and pressed his lips against my cheek, "have you ever been touched?"

I dragged in a quick breath when he slipped the finger at my behind lower toward my core. "Answer me," he said roughly.

"No," I admitted, voice trembling. "I have never been touched."

His head reared back slightly. The hunger in his expression intensified tenfold. Lips parted, his pupils dilated and his bare shoulders rose and fell in quick and exaggerated movements. His breathing was erratic and the truth struck home.

He liked that I was untouched. This man relished that I was a virgin.

At this moment, lust blatantly pulsed from him in waves, and I felt it, too. Clearly seeing something in my eyes or the heavy blush of my skin, he pressed his chest against mine. Then he raised the hand that had been caressing my behind to cage me in and rest above my head. The finger running along the apex of my thighs continued onward. He pressed his lips to the corner of my lips and murmured, "You are so beautiful."

For a moment I hated myself. I hated what hearing him call me beautiful did to the rhythm of my heart. I had liked it. I had liked this man calling me beautiful.

Another press of his lips on the corner of mine came next; then he asked coldly, "Do you find me beautiful? Do you find this fucked-up beast beautiful, too?" Pushing his hand off the wall above me, he leaned back until his body came into full view—a plethora of name tattoos, a smattering of scars, and that black inked "194" dominating the center of his chest. As always, my focus dwelled upon the collar fixed around his neck. There was a seam at the side, heavy metal hinges keeping it tightly in place. His face was hard, his expression, as well as his voice, mocking. But before I could help it, an answer poured from my mouth. "Yes," I said shockingly but honestly, "you are beautiful to me."

He stilled as though he did not expect my answer, his black eyebrows pulling down in a threatening frown. I kept the truth in my expression when I caught the briefest flash of vulnerability in his gaze again. That flash immediately unlocked something inside me, that one-second lapse of control striking something in my heart.

The man's heavy muscles bunched, the raised muscles on top of his shoulders twitched, but I could see that my reply had unnerved him. His jaw clenched and his eyes narrowed. His head tilted to the side, scrutinizing every part of my face. When, abruptly, his expression changed, losing its harshness.

Groaning, he flew at me, causing me to brace. For a moment I feared he was about to strike me, that I'd read him all wrong. I feared that the man who had caused me pain for days and days had returned. But, instead, his hand threaded through my hair and his lips pressed to the corner of mine. His touch was warm and I could feel that warmth travel from my head to my toes.

Pulling back, he ran his finger down my cheek and rasped, "You did not lie, *kotyonok*. You think *me* . . . beautiful. *Me?*" His eyes flared and his head shook as though in disbelief. His hand left my face to take its place at the apex of my thighs once again. I cried out as his finger traveled lower this time, and he added, "It is the first time since I stole you that you did not lie. I am an ugly beast, yet you did not lie."

Tears fell again. A part of me didn't want his touch, but at the same time I wanted it more than anything else in my life. It was that tone of disbelief in his deep voice, the tone of vulnerable disbelief, that made me want to know him more. Made me want his touch more. To show him he wasn't just the monster he believed himself to be.

The finger, just centimeters from my core, was lighting me with fire. His reaction to my truthful admission encouraged me to tell him everything he wanted to know, just to have his fingers on me. Just to have his fingers relieve my ache.

But I knew I would not betray Zaal. I knew I had to stay strong.

"Do you want me?" he asked, causing my hands to flex and curl.

"No," I whispered, unable to meet his eyes. I didn't want him to know how much it was true.

A smirk spread on his mouth, and putting his lips at my ear he said, "You lie. I know when you lie, *Elene*. I can see the deception on your beautiful face, can hear it in your soft voice." He stepped back and truly met my eyes. "I know your body now, little Georgian. I can see that you want me." He stepped closer. "Like I want you."

Fire and ice struggled for supremacy. But as his finger slipped into the seams of my core, its tip tracing along my entrance, fire was victorious.

He growled as I cried out at the feel, yet he pulled his finger immediately away and brought it to his mouth. I fought for composure as he ran the finger around his lips, before pushing it into his mouth and sucking on it hard. His eyes blazed as he withdrew his finger and ran the pad around my lips, too. He watched his finger in rapt attention, before leaning in and saying, "If you do not want me, *kotyonok,* then why is your pussy so fucking wet?"

Tremors racked my body at his crude words and gruff tone. I stayed silent, knowing not what to say in response. Then he smiled wide. My lungs seized at the stunning sight of his damaged face looking so bright, then his hand slipped back between my legs. My hips instinctively pushed forward, chasing his touch.

He only smiled more.

He traced his tongue along my cheek as his finger began flicking back and forth along my seam. I tried to keep my eyes open. I tried to show the strength of my resistance to his intimate touch, but my eyes closed on feeling the heady sensation.

"You are drenched, *kotyonok,*" he murmured, his Russian accent thick and fueled with lust. "Have you ever come before? Have you ever touched yourself and made yourself come?"

I managed to shake my head, whimpering as he ran his finger over my bud of nerves. His finger froze, and I bucked trying to feel the sensation it brought. When I opened my eyes, I saw him waiting impatiently for an answer.

"No," I confessed, "I have never touched myself before."

Air swooshed out of his mouth, and he moved closer against me. His hot chest grazed my breasts. His finger slipped from me. I almost screamed in protest at the loss. The pressure in my stomach was too strong to stand. Then his face hardened with determination and the pad of his finger slipped to land back on my clit.

I jerked with the surge of pleasure that rushed through my body. My muscles grew so taut that I feared they might snap. My mouth fell open in ecstasy.

His chest was scalding against my breasts. His mouth dragged along my cheek as his finger pressed harder against me, beginning to move in small slow circles. I pulled and pulled on my arms and legs, my body desperately needing to move, but the shackles held me tight. The man's free hand pressed on the front of my throat. His firm yet gentle grip pushed my back against the wall.

His finger worked faster at my clit. The hand on my throat asserted his strength, domination, and complete control. His forehead pressed against mine, his breath panting as fast as my own.

I moaned loudly as a wave of pleasure pulsed through my weakened legs. His lips rolled together, his cheeks flushing with red. Edging closer until we breathed the same air, he said, "You like that, *kotyonok*? You like the feel of my hand on and in your cunt?" My body jerked as his illicit words added to the pressure building in my core. I tried to obey his command. I tried to answer. But when the hand on my face moved to my behind, a cry was the only response I could offer.

His finger on my clit circled faster and faster; then suddenly the hand on my behind slipped through to approach my core. My eyes snapped open when his finger traced around my entrance. Two hands, two of his long fingers placed at the wet center of my spread legs.

Warm breath drifted over my face, and as our gazes collided he said, "I am taking this hot cunt, *kotyonok*." I cried out when his finger took hold. A light began building behind my eyes. His breath mingled with my cries, and he added, "I'll own you."

I cried out as my legs began to tremble, something beginning to build at the bottom of my spine.

"What is your name?" he pushed, the touch of his two talented fingers seeming to be everywhere—in my body, my mind, and my soul.

Seizing upon a morsel of sensibility, I rasped, "Elene . . . Melua."

His chest pinned me against the wall, his fingers increasing in speed, round and round, in and out. A high-pitched moan clawed up from my chest.

He pushed again, "Who is Zaal Kostava to you?"

Squeezing my eyes shut, I fought the all-consuming sensations inspired by the orchestrations of his fingers and breathlessly answered, "No one. I don't know him."

The fingers increased in speed until I feared the bolts of pleasure shooting up my spine would tear free and consume my entire body. Then suddenly my muscles tensed, my heart slammed fast, and a brilliant light burst behind my eyes. I resisted the combustible tingling between my legs, but the man's face closed in and he ordered dominantly, "Come!"

Screaming at the crash of bliss taking my body hostage, my lungs burned and my skin dripped with dampness.

He growled before me, and I felt his rock-hard length pressing against my thigh, its wet tip coating my skin. But his fingers didn't stop; they circled and circled against my clit until I began to convulse. My core was too sensitive. I couldn't stand his touch. My muscles tensed, testing the strength of the shackles.

My eyes rolled open. On seeing him watching me with a blazing expression, I begged, "Please," in a ragged voice, "it's too much. I can't take it."

But he didn't stop; instead he worked his fingers faster and asked, "What's your name?"

"Elene," I choked, gasping for breath.

His fingers moved faster still until I could feel the pressure rebuilding in my spine. "No," I begged, "not again. I can't—"

But he kept on driving his hands, punishing me with the overwhelming sensations.

"Who is Zaal Kostava to you?" he asked again.

I shook my head, tears slipping down my cheeks. "No one. I don't know him!"

I choked on a sob as the pressure built again. Just as the blinding light behind my eyes splintered into a million shards, he asked, "Who is your family? Where is your family, little Georgian? Tell me!"

Pain sliced me in half at the mention of my family, more than any dagger ever could. As the torturous bliss burst inside of my tired body, I released two decades' worth of pain and screamed, "They're dead! They were massacred right before my eyes! Are you happy?" I coughed on my harsh words and croaked, "Are you happy now that you've made me break?"

My heart raced in the aftermath, a mixture of the intense pleasure coming down and the devastating memory of that day now in full view of my mind's eye.

Sobs racked my body. It took me a moment to realize that the man had removed his fingers from me. His chest no longer pressed against my skin. Instantly I felt cold, my body hanging limply supported only by the chains. Blurry-eyed, I lifted my head to see him frozen before me, watching me, scarred face stern and muscles tense. A sense of incredible embarrassment consumed me when I thought of what he had just done.

But the sorrow it gave way to forced me to whisper, "I am alone. I have always been alone. They were all killed—parents, grandmama, my younger siblings, and my brothers that I adored. *I* survived." I steeled my gaze. Without a single tremble in my voice, I said, "Most days I wish to all hell that I had died, too."

The man seemed to flinch at my words, but his hand lifted. For a split second I wondered if he was going to offer me comfort, to try to touch my face. No sooner had he lifted his hand than he snapped it back to place it at his side.

His mouth opened as if wanting to speak, but with a swift turn of his heel he pounded out of the room. I watched him go. Left alone, hanging from these chains, I replayed the image of his bunched muscles as he left, and his fingers as they alternated from fisted to rigid by his sides. When he'd pushed me for that answer, when I'd screamed how I'd been so alone, something within him snapped. I saw it in his face. I saw it in his stance.

I saw it clearly in his expressive blue eyes.

I now knew he really wasn't a monster at all. I knew he had no choice in performing these horrible acts. I knew his life had been as impossible as mine.

Knew he wasn't truly as evil as he seemed.

He was just like my Anri and Zaal. Like me.

Broken.

9

LUKA

A fist of iron slammed into my jaw, snapping my head back on impact. The taste of copper filled my mouth. I spat the blood out onto the floor.

Nodding, I looked at my opponent who was pacing the cage. His eyes were lit with rage, with the fire that I too had burning inside me. Catching him off guard, I ran at full tilt, slamming into his body and tackling him to the floor. Rolling to straddle his waist, I sent two swift punches straight into his face, blood spraying on my chest, before he bucked his hips and I jumped to my feet.

My opponent pushed off the floor. The whole place fell silent as other fighters gathered round to watch. We circled and circled, panting hard, dripping with sweat, both braced to strike. Then a gunshot rang in the air, signaling the end of the match.

I didn't move. I didn't take my eyes off my opponent. Neither did he with me. I crouched low, ready to strike again. Then someone stood between us. My blood haze ebbed away, ushering my return to the here and now.

"Break it up, boys," Viktor called. I took three steps back as I worked on calming down. I glanced across the cage and caught my opponent doing the same. Closing my eyes, I breathed in and out ten times. I thought of Kisa, my wife, and my unborn baby. I thought of our home and my position as *knyaz*. I had to. I had to remind myself that I was no longer in the gulag. I was no longer a death fighter, a prisoner in the cage.

Feeling a hand hit my arm, I opened my eyes to see Viktor staring at me with a raised eyebrow. I nodded my head, letting my trainer know that I was back. Luka was back. The bloodlust of my alter ego, Raze, had been assuaged, if only for today.

Viktor moved aside and I walked to my opponent, Zaal, whose eyes were closed as he too centered himself.

I waited until his eyes opened and he looked over his shoulder at me. As I held out my hand, Zaal took a deep breath and clasped his hand in mine. I shook it once and released his grip. Zaal's chest was still pumping fast when he said, "It will take some getting used to, this"—he gestured between the two of us—"resisting the urge to kill. Not drawing out your last breath. Pulling my killer instinct back at the last second."

My jaw clenched as I instantly related to his feeling. "One day it'll come."

Zaal stared for a second too long, then asked, "You, too?"

Dropping my eyes, I nodded and replied, "I pray that one day in the future I will wake up no longer harboring the urge to kill or draw blood."

Zaal closed his eyes, then, glancing to the locked office door—the locked door of the office holding our females—said, "Then I will pray for that day also." Grabbing his towel from the floor, Zaal wiped the blood off his chest and face and said, "I want to be a stronger, more normal male for my Talia. Not this version of me who dreams of stopping hearts and cracking skulls. I still do not understand this life. At times, it becomes too much for me to take." He tapped at his head. "It gives me pain, in here."

Looking over my brother's shoulder to make sure the office door was shut, I closed in and said, "We're different, Zaal. We were conditioned all of our lives to be like this. Our females know this."

A pained expression crossed Zaal's face, and he asked, "Then why do they stay locked away when we spar? Why do her brown eyes get sad when she sees us fight and draw blood?"

I sighed and ran my own towel over my face. But I had shit to say. Kisa accepted that I would never be the boy she used to read to when we were kids. But Zaal was right. The women might have accepted it as part of who we are—the monsters we'd become—but I knew they both struggled to see us like this, choosing rather to ignore the violence within. Like Zaal, I pray for the day we don't wake up in a cold sweat, programmed to kill merely to survive.

Turning to survey the gym, I found it was teeming with fighters, all training under the watchful eyes of their coaches. Viktor, our newly appointed Dungeon Manager, walked among the fighter scum, checking all was well.

Dropping the towel into the cage-side basket, I had started to move toward the showers when I heard my Mikhail, my head *byki,* barking in Russian for someone to shut up.

Snapping my head toward the entrance, I stood next to Zaal, who was also staring in that direction. Both of us were ready for the fight. My heart pumped in my chest at the thought of someone coming to attack. Then Mikhail entered the lower level of the gym, dragging an old gray-haired man behind him.

I straightened from preparing to fight and narrowed my eyes on whom he held in his hands. I noticed the office door open. Talia walked out. I watched as my sister looked at Zaal beside me. Her face dropped. Zaal's face was bruised and his lip was split. I knew she hated seeing him hurt.

I held out my hand to my sister, signaling for her to stay put. I saw Kisa appear beside her, her big blue eyes immediately searching for me. I tensed as she did, but my wife just smiled and nodded her head—she'd accepted that I had to do this.

The man in Mikhail's grip shouted out when Mikhail brought him to stand before us.

"*Knyaz,*" Mikhail announced as the old man kept his head down, "caught this fucking *krysa* hiding upstairs. He was looking for a way in."

Striding forward, I crossed my arms over my bare chest and peered down at the man. "Who are you?" I asked coldly in Russian, and saw him tense as he absorbed the question.

He said nothing in reply. Mikhail lifted the old man's head up by his hair and advised, "You answer the *knyaz* when he asks you a question."

The man slowly lifted his eyes, but when he did they didn't stay on me for long. Instead they landed on Zaal and remained there. I watched Zaal tense and narrow his eyes. The old man paled.

Clearly feeling my stare, Zaal flicked a glance to me. I could see discomfort in his expression. When I looked again to the old man, something in his stare made me seek out Viktor. I found him by the far wall, watching us, not the fighters. Flicking my chin, I waved my hand and signaled for Viktor to clear out the gym.

I didn't know why, but the way the old man was staring at Zaal made ice shoot up my spine. Five minutes later the gym was cleared and the old man was still fixed on Zaal.

Zaal folded his arms across his chest. I could see confusion in his face. Taking the lead as *knyaz,* I approached the man and asked, "Why were you outside this gym?"

I'd spoken in Russian again and I knew he understood me. Clearing his throat, the old man opened his mouth but stopped himself from speaking. Mikhail tightened his grip on the man's hair and neck. When I nodded to my head *byki,* Mikhail let the old man go.

As soon as he was free, the old man turned toward Zaal and

bowed his head. My eyebrows pulled down and I saw Talia and Kisa step farther out of the office toward us, Talia taking the lead. My sister looked from the old man to Zaal and back again; then her worried face turned to me.

I had opened my mouth to say something else when the old man whispered, "*Lideri,* it *is* you." I stilled. My heart pounded when the man spoke in Georgian. Kisa, Talia, and my *byki* all wore expressions of confusion—none of them spoke Georgian—but I did from years in the gulag, and of course Zaal did, too.

Zaal rocked on his feet and he drew in a long breath.

The man had called Zaal *Lideri.* The man knew who Zaal was. He knew he was looking at a Kostava.

"Name?" I asked the old man, and his head lifted. He forced himself to address me and said coldly, "Avto Oniani."

The more I watched him, the colder the man's attitude became toward me. Stepping next to Zaal, I saw the man watching me like a hawk. As I stopped, I asked, "You know this man?" I pointed to Zaal.

Avto nodded his head, and water filled his eyes. Zaal had been silent and absolutely still since the man turned up, but something caused him to snap out of his trance and ask, "How? And who do you think I am?"

Zaal had spoken in Russian, and I knew it was so Talia could understand. There wasn't anything Zaal did that Talia wasn't involved in.

The man frowned but answered in like manner. "You are Zaal Kostava, from Tbilisi, Georgia." He put his hand on his chest. "I am Avto; I was a servant to your family, when you were a boy."

I heard Talia gasp, but before Zaal could say anything else the man stepped forward with urgency. "*Lideri,* the night your family was killed I had just lost my mother. I had been at her funeral when the attack happened, but I returned *that* night to return to my duties to find . . . to find . . . ," the man trailed off as emotion clogged his throat. Reaching up, he wiped away his tears.

Zaal was a statue as the man spoke of his family. I could see Talia about to move to her man, but I shook my head in her direction, demanding that she stop. Kisa placed her hand on Talia's arm and spoke into her ear. Talia was angry at whatever my wife said, but she did as I had signaled.

Avto wiped his face and, stepping yet closer to Zaal, continued, "I found them, sir. I saw the blood." Avto's eyes closed as though he was reliving the tragedy. "All the servants had been slain; the guards that had stayed loyal were slain, but for one. He was injured, but not badly enough. He told me what had happened." Avto lifted a shaky hand to Zaal. "That you and your brother had been taken by *that* man."

Zaal was gritting his teeth so tightly I thought his jaw might break. Avto glanced around the room, and his hands started to shake. My eyes narrowed seeing his anxiousness, his sudden change. "*Lideri,*" Avto properly addressed Zaal, "I, along with my wife, we buried your family—your parents, your grandmama." Avto shook his head. "The little ones—your youngest brother and sister." Zaal's breathing deepened and quickened in pace. His nostrils were flaring. The effect Avto's storytelling had on Zaal was there for all to see.

Avto bowed his head. When he looked back up his eyes were red. "I couldn't believe it, sir. All that life, gone; left to die like animals." He wiped at his damp cheeks, then said, "We buried all of your family, *Lideri,* on the hill on your property, in case you ever go back." I could hear the grinding of Zaal's teeth, but everything went silent when Avto informed, "All except one."

The room temperature seemed to drop, and Zaal growled, "Explain," his deep rough voice betraying how painful all of this was to him.

Avto swallowed and continued, "When we were lifting the

bodies, we thought they were all dead." He took a deep breath and added, "But when we reached the bottom, we noticed that someone was breathing. Hurt, severely wounded, but there was still life."

"Who?" Zaal demanded, the veins cording in his neck.

"Zoya, *Lideri*. Little Zoya was alive."

A soft cry came from across the room. Talia had her hand over her mouth and her eyes staring at her man. "Baby. Your Zoya."

Zaal's body began shaking. Every part of him shook, until he managed to ask, "She was breathing? She was alive?"

Avto's face fell, and he said quietly, "Yes, *Lideri*. She had been shot three times. She was bleeding badly, and I feared she would die before we could get her help." Avto ran his hand across the back of his neck. His face had turned ghostly white. After several seconds, he continued, "We managed to get her to a family member of mine. My wife—" His voice broke, but he coughed and said, "My wife held her tiny body in her arms. There was blood everywhere, and the little one was so pale. My wife stroked through her hair, and rubbed at her arms to keep her warm until we got to my cousin's house."

A tear ran down Avto's cheek; this time he didn't even wipe it away. His old eyes were lost in the memory, his aged hands clasping together so hard that his knuckles were bone white.

"My cousin had to work hard, *Lideri,* but he managed to extract the bullets." He shook his head as if ridding something from memory. "She lost so much blood that my wife and I were covered. But she fought so hard to stay alive. Her little five-year-old body would not give up. She was so strong, so brave."

This time sniffing came from both Kisa and Talia and when I looked to my friend he was practically unchanged, but his cheeks were wet with tears, his green eyes haunted. I closed my eyes, feeling the hurt in my chest. Hurt that this new brother of mine had thought everyone was dead, only now to be told he had blood left alive.

"She was brave?" Zaal asked in a broken voice, pride filling every word. Avto nodded and Zaal's lip twitched. "She always was. A true little warrior."

Avto's attention fell to the floor at Zaal's words. "Day by day she grew stronger, until the day she finally woke up." More tears fell down Avto's cheeks. "She was so scared. So frightened. At first she did not remember; then, gradually, the memories returned in her dreams and she screamed." Avto sighed sadly. "My wife tried to give Zoya comfort, but she wanted her mama and papa." Avto's sad gaze lifted to Zaal. "She wanted her *sykhaara*. She wanted *you*."

A pained sound came from Zaal's mouth and his head fell forward. "Where is she?" he asked roughly, "Where is my little Zoya?"

Although it seemed impossible, Avto paled even more. He said quickly and shakily, "We fled Tbilisi. We found a way to get into America and brought her here. But the guard that had been left alive at your home had told the Jakhuas that Zoya had survived. He joined their organization to save his own life." Avto swallowed. "They knew we had fled to the United States, so Zoya's hiding began. To protect her."

Avto stepped forward to Zaal's huge frame. "We kept her hidden, fearing that the Jakhuas would come for her if they knew where we lived. Then. Not long ago, we heard Jakhua had been killed."

Avto stared off to the side and inhaled deep. "I went to her days ago to tell her the news." Avto wiped his sleeve across his face. "And I told her . . . I told her even better news."

"Which was?" I pushed when the old man didn't continue.

Avto shook his head and looked at Zaal. "*Lideri*, our people, the clan that survived Jakhua, most moved here to New York. We are not the army we once were, but there are loyal men, many of whom have gone on to have sons. They have stayed close to Zoya, to honor the sole survivor of our family."

Zaal shifted on his feet and tipped his chin for Avto to continue. Avto bowed his head and did as commanded. "Some of our men had heard rumors that Jakhua had you and Lideri Anri held captive." Avto darted his eyes to me, then immediately looked back to Zaal. "They had heard that the Volkovs, the Tolstois, had captured you."

"They saved me," Zaal corrected sharply.

Avto froze. The old man quickly held up his hand. "Yes, *Lideri*. That became known when the men began tailing the Russians." Avto looked over his shoulder to Talia. I could see the anger in his eyes. "And we saw that you were engaged to a Tolstoi."

The air around us seemed to turn ice cold as I, Talia, my men, and, more important, Zaal took real fucking offense at his shitty looks. I had shifted to move when Zaal pushed me back and barked, "Talia will soon be my wife. And the Volkovs, the *Tolstois,* are my family. You do not look at any of them with disgust!"

Avto shuffled back in fear of Zaal. Mikhail caught him by the neck and threw him forward until he fell to his knees. Zaal cracked his knuckles, his expression livid. He bit out, "Where is my sister?"

Zaal walked over to tower above Avto and repeated, "Where is my sister?"

Avto shook his head. "I do not know." Avto reached into his pocket and nervously held out something in his hand. I frowned, wondering what it was. When Zaal took it and lifted it, I saw it was a photograph. Zaal studied the picture and said, "It's me and Talia."

I peered over Zaal's shoulder to see Zaal and Talia laughing in the shot. Zaal wiped at the picture, dried dirt coming off on his hands.

I frowned and, finally losing my patience, said to Avto, "You need to start speaking, because I'm starting to lose my shit with you."

Avto's lips trembled, and he confessed to Zaal, "I told your sister we had found you." Zaal froze; then Avto continued, "She fell to the floor, the shock too much after all of these years alone." Avto began to cry, his voice growing thick. "She asked about you, where you had been, what had happened to her brothers. I told her we had only found you." Avto paused, then added, "I told her what Jakhua had done to you."

"No," Zaal hissed, and shook his head.

"She was so hurt," Avto continued. "She asked where you were, what you looked like, if you were safe." Avto pointed at the picture. "I gave her that picture. One of our men took it to verify you were alive."

"What did she do?" Zaal asked roughly. I could hear him working hard to keep his emotions under control. He stared down at the picture. "When she saw this." His thumb ran over Talia's face. "When she saw me and my Talia?"

Avto blinked away his tears. "She cried." Avto flicked a worried glance to me, then said to Zaal, "She asked who the woman was."

Zaal maintained a stony silence as he waited for the man to continue.

Avto sighed. "I told her she was a Tolstoi."

Zaal stiffened and I saw him wince. "What did she say?" he prompted cautiously.

Avto's face filled with redness, and his head fell. "She did not understand how you could be with a Tolstoi."

Zaal's shoulders dropped, and he turned away.

"But she also loved how you looked happy," Avto said quickly, making Zaal freeze mid-stride. He didn't turn. Avto shifted on the floor and said, "We told her how they rescued you, and any dishonor she felt seemed to fade away." Zaal still didn't move. Avto looked around the room and slowly pushed to his feet. Swaying nervously on the spot, he said, "*Lideri,* I have watched her grow for over twenty years. Most days she was silent and sad." Zaal's hand fisted at his side, but Avto finished, "Until the day she found out you were alive. Until the day she saw your face. Your older face."

Zaal turned his head and looked over his shoulder. "Where is she?" he whispered, defeated.

"She was meant to wait for me. We were to come to you in a couple of days when I had things in place, but she must have changed her mind when I left. I returned to find her gone." Zaal turned, and Avto bowed his head. "I went to the Tolstoi residence where she knew you would be. And in the alley opposite was this picture . . . along with marks on the ground that looked like dragged feet."

I tipped my head back and blew out a breath.

"I think someone has taken her, *Lideri*." Avto's voice broke and his tears came thick and fast. "We thought the Jakhuas were gone. We thought there were no more threats." His pause thickened the tension in the room. "I must have been wrong. I told her she would be safe. After all of these years keeping her safe, I told her there was no danger and she ran out to the waiting wolves."

"She came to see me," Zaal stated. I watched his back as it started to shake. "She came to see me," he muttered, but this time pure rage tinged his voice.

Talia edged forward, then forward again, until a deafening roar burst from Zaal. Lurching forward, Zaal kicked over the stacks of free weights racked up beside the training ring. Balling his hand into a fist, he slammed it into the wall. A dull thud echoed through the room.

Zaal staggered back and dropped to his knees. "Zaal!" Talia called out, and ran to her man from across the room. My sister slumped to her feet and sat before Zaal, whose head was cast downward.

"Baby," Talia whispered, and pressed the palm of her hand on Zaal's cheek. I felt someone stand beside me. Kisa's arm then wrapped in mine and she dropped her head to rest on my biceps. Leaning down, I kissed her head. Seeing my brother so broken reminded me just how far I'd come since getting my female back.

"Look at me," Talia told Zaal. Her fiancé lifted his head. "I love you," Talia said softly, and leaned in to kiss Zaal on his lips.

Avto coughed from behind. He turned his head as if he couldn't stand to see them together. Anger wrapped around me. It was clear the Georgians held as strong as a grudge against us as my father did against them.

"My sister," Zaal said in a hushed voice. "My sister, Talia. She survived. All these years . . . she survived, and I did not know."

Talia squeezed her eyes shut and nodded her head. Moving in, she wrapped Zaal in her arms, but her eyes met mine as her head tucked into his shoulder. I could see the fear in her eyes, and I knew I had to do something, not only as Talia's brother but also as the Volkov Bratva *knyaz*.

Someone was fucking with my city, and that shit just wasn't going to happen.

"How long has Zoya been missing?" I asked Avto.

His old eyes fell on me. "A while."

Zaal must have heard the conversation. Taking Talia's hand, he rose from the floor. He took a deep breath, his back still turned; then he faced us. And his face was stern. And set with fierce determination.

It was the first time since Zaal had killed Jakhua that I'd seen this look on his face. Stepping forward with Talia by his side, Zaal spoke to me. "The Georgian plan" was all he said. I nodded my head. "The Pakhan was right. They're here for me, for us. My . . . sister."

Kisa looked up at me with a frown on her beautiful face. "There's danger, again?"

I pressed another kiss on Kisa's head and gave her a look that told her it was Mafia business. Sliding my arm around her shoulders, I kept her at my side and regarded Zaal.

"Well, what are you wanting to do? You know it's your call. You have the backing of the Bratva." I tipped my head at Talia and said, "We know where your loyalty lies. But I know more than anyone what it feels like to have this inheritance in your blood." Zaal ran a hand down his face. "It's who you are, Zaal." I cleared my throat, fighting the sadness, and said, "Anri would want this for you. Even without the memories, he knew something back in Georgia was calling him home." Zaal wrenched Talia to his side and held her close. "I think his soul told him he was coming back for you. Coming back to restore your family's legacy."

"*Lideri* Anri has died?" Avto's weak voice drifted from the side. Zaal's forehead fell into Talia's hair, so I nodded my head at the old man. Avto's shoulders dropped in sorrow.

"Zaal," I called. Zaal lifted his head. "You're not alone. Our families will unite. You and I will rule together, just like the Bratva always has. A brotherhood. A family."

"Zaal?" Talia called.

Zaal looked down at his fiancée. "You want this for me?" Zaal asked doubtfully.

Talia sighed. I could see that she had no desire to be a mob leader's wife, but she made me proud when she replied, "I want you happy, *zolotse*. And I want you to find your sister." Talia smiled and said, "I want to meet her so badly, too."

Zaal was still for what felt like an age. Then, releasing Talia, he approached Avto, who straightened where he stood. "I have few memories from my life. I regret that I do not remember you."

Avto nodded his head slowly but hung on Zaal's every word. "Firstly, I want to thank you"—Zaal's voice was thick as he said this—"for saving my sister when I could not. You have my gratitude, and I am in your debt."

"*Lideri,* no—" Avto went to argue, but Zaal held up his hand. "You told me I have clan men here in New York?"

Avto nodded. "Many, *Lideri,* and more throughout the United States. They are good loyal men. Many were guards or advisors to your father."

Zaal nodded again, then held out his hand. Talia walked over to stand beside him. Zaal brought Talia's hand to his mouth, then puffed out his chest. "This is my Talia. She is a Tolstaia. I know that our families have a bitter history, but our coming marriage turns that into a bond. An alliance. If you have been living in New York, you will understand that the Bratva run this place. And now I am one of them."

Avto swallowed but bowed his head. "You will get word to our people that I live and I am ready to take my place as the Kostava *Lideri.*" Avto smiled, but Zaal added, "You will let them know that we will work beside the Volkovs, and that any threat against them will be dealt with as though they had turned coat on a Kostava."

"Yes, *Lideri,*" Avto said, then fidgeted with his hands. "But what about Zoya?" His eyes shone with fear. "We have no idea who took her, or what they may be doing to her."

Zaal reached out and laid his large hand on Avto's small shoulder. "We have an idea," he said, "and they are Georgian." Avto stiffened, but Zaal added, "Our people will be integral to rescuing her, Avto. To returning our Kostava daughter."

Avto paused, then put his hand on Zaal's arms. "Our people will die to save Miss Zoya, *Lideri.*"

Zaal dropped his hand, then let Talia cup his face with her hands. "We'll find her, *zolotse.* My father"—Talia looked to me just for a second before looking back at Zaal—"and my brother will not rest until you see your sweet Zoya again."

Zaal brought Talia into his chest as Kisa squeezed my hand and said, "*Lyubov moya,* you must do this for Zaal. You must give him the peace his sister will bring to his soul."

Pressing a kiss to Kisa's soft lips, I promised, "It's just a matter of time, *solnyshko.* With Zaal inheriting the Kostava *Lideri* seat, the Volkov Bratva have just become the strongest underground crime family on the continental U.S."

"So you're saying you'll get Zoya back?"

"I'm saying it's just a matter of fucking time."

10

194

I entered the back room, then slammed the door shut, snapping the metal locks tightly into place. My back hit the door and my legs became weak. I lifted my hand and stared at my rigid fingers. I'd almost touched her. A hollow feeling built in my chest, and I squeezed my eyes shut. *I am alone. I have always been alone. They were all killed—parents, grandmama, my younger siblings, and my brothers who I adored. I survived. . . . Most days I wish that I had died, too.*

My heart beat rapidly against my ribs. Her voice, her voice was broken and cut. I could hear the devastation in her every word.

She felt just like me.

She felt like *me.*

Fisting the hand that was still raised, I moved off the door. I walked to the desk, and my eyes immediately fixed on the screen. The female was crying, her head down and her body shaking with sobs. My stomach tightened, and without my meaning to my finger lifted to touch the screen. My index finger traced the outline of her face and naked body.

She was so beautiful as she hung off that wall. I gritted my teeth as the thought ran through my mind. She was a Georgian. I hated all Georgians. They'd brought nothing but pain into my life. Mistress was Georgian. The Wraiths that would come to the orphanage, stealing kids, were Georgian.

But no matter how hard I wanted to hate this *suka,* seeing her like this, broken over her dead family, made it impossible. And . . . *Yes, I think you're beautiful, too. . . .*

She didn't lie. She looked at my fucked-up face and didn't lie. She thought me beautiful. No one ever looked beyond my scars. I was Mistress's ugly beast, a killer, nothing more.

But this little Georgian's eyes. Those huge dark eyes. Her lips, her tits, her body, that long dark hair. My chest warmed and I smirked—her refusal to break under my questions. Her strength and iron will.

I'd never met anyone like her.

I stared and I stared at the screen. And I watched as the female lifted her head and drew in a deep breath. As if feeling the weight of my stare, her dark eyes peered down the camera lens.

My heart pumped fast, blood soaring through my veins. My hand ran down my face. As I still watched her like she was right in front of me, my finger landed on my lips. Freezing. Remembering that my finger had been on her pussy, I slipped it into my mouth, my dick hardening until it was painful. I sucked and sucked on my finger, tasting the sweetness of her juices.

Moving my hand down, I gripped my dick—picturing her lean body twitching, tensing, and moaning as my fingers circled her clit.

She'd been wet for me.

My hand worked faster, my dick leaking with my just seeing her panting. Her brown eyes shone and her olive skin flushed red, her nipples hardening like bullets. She may have been untouched, she may not have wanted it to be me who made her come for the first time in her life, but she had mewled and moaned, until she'd screamed out her release.

My jaw clenched and my head threw back as I came all over my hand. I stroked my release along my prick, coating the skin. My body jerked and I fought to catch my breath.

And the female still looked up at the screen, like she knew what the thought of her pussy had just made me do. My nostrils flared, as I imagined I was hovering above her, sinking my cock into her tight hole, but then just as my cock began to harden once more a buzz from within the desk drawer snapped me back to reality.

My heart dropped when I knew what it was.

Straightening, fighting back the rage that was already engulfing my body from the toes up, I slowly opened the drawer and pulled out the device Mistress always made sure was in the chambers I used.

Laying the device on the desktop, I pressed the button, the small screen immediately coming to life.

I wanted to look away. Then I wanted to reach into the screen and rip this prick apart. The prick who had pinned my sister down as she writhed on the bed. The Type B drug. The Type B drug that Mistress infused in my sister's body from when she was a child. The one that took my sister away from me as a child. The drug that held her captive, held her body captive, internally writhing in pain until she was taken. Until some Wraith asshole—like the one that was slamming inside of her right now—took the pain away by fucking her into peace.

Mistress. It was all Mistress. Promising she'd give me my sister back after the next hit, the next kill, the next torture. But there was always a next time. Never the reward of freeing my baby sister, now twenty-two, from this hell.

Fury built inside me when the screen clicked to black. Just as I was about to throw the device against the wall, I forced myself to back up three steps. Lowering my head, I breathed and breathed, pushing the image of my sister being taken against her will from my mind.

When my head lifted, it was to stare into the small mirror on the wall. I glared at my reflection, not even recognizing the ugly beast I was now. My hair was shaved, scars and tattoos covering every inch of my skin. A scar on my right cheek, my left, my head, and my lip—the right cheek scar trailing from my temple to my chest—that I'd gotten when I spat in Mistress's face as a child. The scar she'd caused by having a Wraith pin me down as she ran her switchblade through my flesh, narrowly avoiding my eye, all to teach me that I was her property. All so I'd look like a fucking nightmare. All so no other female would ever want me but her.

My body was over-muscled, years and years of Type A drug use the cause. And I hated it. But the collar, the damn collar around my neck, controlling my life. The clear sign to everyone in the Wraiths that I was Mistress's dog, her pet whom she controlled to exact her revenge on anyone who pissed her off. The pet whom Master, Mistress's brother, let her have, to keep her the hell away from him and his enterprises.

The bitch was poison. A poison that someday I'd destroy.

I wasn't sure how long I stood in the center of the room, but when I was sure no more rage could flow through my veins I looked over my shoulder and to the little Georgian on the TV screen.

My eyes narrowed. She knew something about Kostava. My mind raced, and my head tilted to the side. She said all her family had died, been massacred, but as I thought of her screams, of her cries, I detected a shake in her voice as she'd mentioned her brothers.

I didn't doubt that her family had died. But my little *kotyonok* was lying about *who* had actually died.

I stepped forward, ready to reenter the chamber. As I did, my body came to a stop. My heart began to pound and my stomach fell.

Realization hit. I didn't want to hurt the little Georgian anymore; I wanted to be inside her. I wanted to hear her moan as I took her over the edge. I wanted her to suck my dick as I gripped on to her hair. I wanted her to look up at me with those brown eyes and not to see them filled with hate.

I wanted to feel her small hand back on my chest.

Shaking my head, I tried to refocus, but all I could see was her dark eyes, her pink lips.

Suddenly the image of my sister being fucked like an animal sprang into my mind. My hot blood cooled rapidly.

Keep focus, I told myself. *Get the information from this* suka, *dispose of her body, and then kill Kostava.*

Running that thought repeatedly through my head, I unlocked the door to the chamber and walked down the narrow hallway to come face-to-face with the female who had gotten under my skin.

Hundreds of kills and she was the first to have any effect on me.

Her eyes immediately bored into mine. Nothing was said for minutes as we stared each other down. And all thoughts of my sister fled my head, only to be replaced by the little *kotyonok*.

Forcing myself to move, I approached her and held her head in my hand. Her cheeks were heated, but our eyes met. As they did, that strange feeling once again broke out in my stomach.

She thought me beautiful. She didn't lie.

The female licked along her lips and whispered, "Water."

Mistress had taught me to use victims' wants against them. But as *Kotyonok*'s beautiful face stared up at me in desperation I wanted nothing more than to get her a damn drink.

Propping her head on my shoulder, her chest against my chest, I reached up to the cuffs on her wrists and unlocked each one. *Kotyonok*'s limp arms fell down beside her body. Bending down, one of my arms now wrapped around her pinched-in waist, I freed her feet, the heavy chain swinging to the side, the cuffs now lying on the floor.

A strange warm feeling entered my body as I held her in my arms. Her hot breath blew against my neck, and lifting my hand I found myself running it through her long dark hair. The feel of her hot skin rubbing against mine caused a low growl to build in my chest. A wave of possessiveness took root.

Leaning down to the floor, I picked up a bottle of water and watched as she drank the liquid down. Her lips were glistening wet, and I threw the empty bottle to the floor.

Moving to the bare wall at the rear of the room, I walked to the long piece of material hanging to the side and pulled it down. The bed built into the wall immediately fell, its small mattress covered in a white sheet. Pushing the bed to the floor, clicking it in place, I slumped down taking the female with me. As I backed up until I was sitting on the mattress, my back against the wall, she lifted her head.

Her eyes met mine, until they dropped as she inhaled softly. Her legs were apart and straddled over my waist; the feel of her warm heat caused my dick to twitch.

I watched her in fascination as she blinked in the room and the mattress we were sitting on. Licking her lips, she faced me and, without meeting my gaze, said. "We are on a real bed."

My hand was still in her hair. As she spoke, my hand trailed down over her neck, then down over her shoulder. Once I'd reached the end of her arm, my eyes were drawn to her hard nipples. Gripping on tightly to her waist, I dragged her slight body farther up my torso, until her hard buds were in front of my mouth. My hips rolled, my balls aching, as I leaned forward and flicked the tip of my tongue over the red flesh. The female's breath hitched and then became heavy. The flesh around the nipple bumped and hardened. On a low groan, I wrapped my mouth around the mound and lapped at the nipple.

She froze, and when I looked up she winced. Releasing her tit from my mouth, I reared back and studied her body. Seeing me watching her, the female bowed her head and whispered, "I am aching. My body feels . . . strange."

This breathy timid admission made my heart swell in my chest. She was hurting. I knew from personal experience what the body felt like after being tied up for hours at a time.

Without noticing, my hands had lifted to her arms and begun massaging the aching muscles. When she released a pained moan, my attention snapped to what I was doing and I pulled back my hands. Anger swept through me. I was meant to be torturing her, making her reveal what she knew about Zaal Kostava. Instead I was trying to make her feel good.

My arms had locked at my sides as I fought to calm down when a shaking hand landed on my cheek. Every part of me stilled, and when I looked up it was the little Georgian's hand. Her eyes were shining, her lips were trembling, but she didn't say anything.

The way she was looking at me, the closeness of her body, unnerved me. No one but Mistress had ever gotten this close. I had seen no one but Mistress and the *Gvardii* since I was captured at the age of twelve. Mistress told me I was thirty now. I had seen no one but Mistress and the *Gvardii* for eighteen years.

The female sat on my lap, her legs wrapped around me. Her naked beautiful unmarked skin pressed up against mine felt better than anything I'd touched in my life before.

But her hand on my cheek was fucking with my mind. Her touch, her soft touch on my face, was bringing me to my knees.

Her throat moved as she swallowed. I waited. I waited, holding my breath, for her to speak. With another lick of her lips, she finally said, "That felt good."

My stomach flipped, shots of fire traveling down my legs.

Unclenching a hand by my side, I brought it forward to land on her free arm. The fingers on my face clasped my skin harder as my fingers wrapped around her biceps and began massaging the skin. The female groaned deeply. Her eyes rolled back in her head. Her lips parted and I watched as an expression of relief spread across her face. At the noises slipping from her mouth, I worked harder on her muscles. Her small body bowed forward, and as it did her hand stroked forward, until it clasped the back of my head. Taking my other hand, I placed it on her other arm and worked that muscle, too. The female's eyes fluttered shut. As more noises slipped from her mouth, my hips began to roll, the feel of her hot pussy growing wetter by the second pressing on my skin. My cock began to throb.

"That feels so good," she murmured.

I squeezed my eyes shut briefly, fighting back the pressure building in my balls. Her fingers dug into my head. As another groan left her mouth, I gripped her arms and turned her round. The female stiffened in fear, but I planted her over my dick, my hard flesh slipping between the crack of her ass, sliding forward to be coated with her wetness.

I wrapped my arm around her waist, pulling her back against my chest. Once her body relaxed, I kicked her legs open, my legs bending, caging them on either side. I paused at the feel of my body pressed against hers; she stilled, breathing deep.

I closed my eyes, trying to fight how good she felt against me, but as her ass shifted and dragged along my cock I knew I wouldn't move, *couldn't* move. I wanted her, Georgian or not, flush against my body. I needed it. I wanted my dick sliding in her wetness, and I wanted to feel her moans coming deep and strong as I massaged her limbs.

The female sighed, causing me to still, but then she leaned back against me, her head dropping to lean on my shoulder. Every part of me was frozen. This close, I could feel her breathing. This close, I could feel her racing heartbeat. This close, I could smell her sweet-tasting skin. Unable to stop myself, I pushed her hair over one shoulder and licked over her racing pulse—she tasted perfect.

The female shifted in front of me, her ass rubbing against my hard cock. A rumble built in my chest. My eyes rolled as heat built in my veins.

I placed my hands on her arms and began circling the muscles, bringing the blood back to her starved limbs. Her body sunk farther against mine. My hands explored her body, up and down her arms, until they moved to her waist. I didn't stop. I continued kneading at her flesh—over her stomach, her torso, until my hands came to her tits.

My hips rolled when the *kotyonok*'s back arched. Her pussy slid along my dick, and I groaned at the feel. I palmed her tits harder, until the Georgian's breath stuttered and strained.

Her feet planted next to mine in the mattress and, with her eyes closed, her hips rolled some more. Unable to stop myself from groaning, I grazed my teeth against the crook of her neck, before biting down and sucking her sweet skin into my mouth.

Needing to feel more of her body, I dropped my hands from her tits and moved them down to her thighs. My hands spread on the outer muscle and massaged in. She turned her face into my neck, her warm breath washing over my face. Shivers darted down my back at having her face so close to mine. For a second I entertained the thought of turning my face into hers. But I stopped myself. I stopped myself from giving that much to the victim in my arms.

She was the gateway to my hit. I knew she could never be anything more. My stomach tightened as I considered those words. As my hands explored her silky skin, a deep need inside wanted me to possess her and take her as my own.

I'd never had anything of my own. Even my sister wasn't mine anymore, ripped from my arms when I was twelve, never to be held again.

This female writhing in my arms was bringing warmth to my cold dead heart. Her strength and courage as she took both pain and pleasure, destroyed the hatred I had of Georgian females. She was nothing like Mistress. *This* Georgian was a warrior queen compared to that sadistic whore.

Kotyonok suddenly moaned. I realized my hands had moved to her inner thighs. Now aware of how my touch was making her react, I closed in farther to her pussy, the heat of her skin showing me the way.

Flicking out my finger, I brushed it over her clit—it was swollen and ready. As I touched the raised nub, the female shuddered and cried out. Her hands, previously lying to the sides, slammed to land on my forearms. Her fingers gripped deeply into my skin, her fingernails breaking open my flesh.

Flames soared in my body, an intense heat, an unbearable need, commanding me to take her. Leading by feel and need alone, I wrenched apart her legs and pushed my dick through her pussy lips, her hot cream wrapping me in its heat. Using the grip on her thighs, I powered forward until the tip of my dick dragged against her swollen clit.

She moaned in my arms, her head rolling from side to side against my shoulder. But my vision blurred, and a single-minded determination took hold of my body—to make us both come like this.

Just like this.

Pulling her legs even farther apart, I thrust faster and faster, until a pressure built in my thighs. The female's breathing labored, her skin scalding to the touch. Unable to resist, I turned my head toward hers until my cheek lay across her forehead. Her skin was damp. I pressed my lips to her face. Her head pulled back, and wide shocked brown eyes slammed into mine. I was locked in. Couldn't look away as my dick pushed against her harder.

Then the female's eyes fluttered. She choked in a breath as her body stilled. A deep red flush ambushed her cheeks and chest. A loud cry ripped from her throat. As I felt the entrance of her pussy clenching, searching for my dick, a rush of heat took me captive until I roared out in release. Light burst behind my eyes as I came harder than I'd ever come under Mistress's commands. I fought for breath as, darting my gaze down between the little Georgian's legs, I saw my release coating her inner thighs. I stared and stared at the sight. A wave of possession rippled through my body.

I stayed still, unsure if I could ever move again, when I felt a hand stroke along the long scar on my right cheek. I threw back my head. Even with this sharp movement the female's hand never moved. I swallowed and watched as her finger began to move again, down my face, following the path of the scar to its end point, on my chest.

I loosened the grip on her thighs, grunting when she sat on my softening dick. My heart beat faster than ever as she reached down to cover my hand with her own. My eyebrows pulled down in confusion when, taking her small hand, she lifted my hand and brought it to the center of her chest. Her eyes never left mine as she took control of my index finger and ran it over her skin until it stopped on her shoulder.

The female blinked, and blinked again, until she pressed the pad of my finger farther down her skin and silently began to move my finger in circles. My breathing paused when I knew I was feeling the rough skin of the scar on her shoulder. I exhaled deeply and she moved my finger across to her other shoulder, repeating the action.

She watched me like she wanted to speak, but her mouth stayed closed, her lips unmoving. Finally, she journeyed our joined hands to the third scar I knew she had on her hip.

This time, as my finger ran over the skin, she whispered, "We both have scars."

My skin pricked at the understanding in her voice. She'd spoken to me. She hadn't talked at me or through me or commanded me. She'd *talked* to me. Like I was someone worth talking to.

Like I was *human*. Not a killer beast.

She waited for my answer, her skin gradually returning to its olive tone from the flushed red. Unsure what to say, I nodded my head.

A flicker of a smile hooked on her upper lip, and the coil that was wound tight in my chest began to loosen.

Ducking her eyes, she peered up at me through long black lashes to say, "We are both damaged." My nostrils flared and my pulse raced when she added, "I think we are not so dissimilar, you and I."

My lips parted as she uttered those words and a rush of air escaped my mouth. Her finger moved again, tracing back up the scar, when it suddenly took a detour, to move across my identity tattoo.

Her black eyebrows pulled together as she traced every number. When she reached the end of number "4," she looked up at me, sadness in her expression. Then she asked, "What is your name?" Only this time, she hadn't spoken in Georgian. Instead she had spoken in perfect Russian.

Questions circled my head as she spoke to me in my native Russian. Mistress and the *Gvardii* never spoke to me anymore in my mother tongue. Without my sister, I had no other to speak to in my language.

Kotyonok was Georgian, yet she spoke to me in my language and as if she saw me as a human.

I had no idea what to do next. Her red lips rolled together and I saw the pulse beating fast in her neck. She was nervous. As I remained silent and unmoving, she asked, still in Russian, "Where you are from, do they call you by this number?"

I could hear the sound of my teeth grinding together echoing in my ears, but I found myself nodding my head. The female's eyes filled with sadness, and she whispered, "One, nine, four."

As my number was read aloud in Russian, something inside of me snapped. Lurching forward, I gripped at the female's arms and flipped her until her back hit the mattress and my body hovered over hers. Shifting my grip until I held her wrists, I pulled her arms above her head and straddled her waist.

My face lowered until it was merely an inch above hers. *"Pozhaluysta,"* she whispered, begging "please" in Russian.

My heart missed a beat at the fear in my throat, and I hissed, "Don't ever call me by that number again, *Georgian bitch*."

Her eyes widened, then filled with water, and she said, "I'm sorry. I didn't know. I—" I increased the grip I had on her wrists, but she asked, "What is your name? Please, tell me your name?"

Inching closer, until my forehead pressed against hers, I replied, "What is yours, little *kotyonok*? And don't lie. I'm getting tired of your lies."

Swallowing, she opened her mouth, then with sagging shoulders whispered, "Zoya. My name is Zoya."

The pads of my thumbs pressed on the pulse of her wrist to detect the lie. But her pulse never changed—she was telling me the truth. Loosening my hands around her wrists, I pulled back and questioned, "You tell the truth?"

Face paling, she whispered, "Yes."

"Why?" I snapped. My muscles bunched at why this little *kotyonok,* this little warrior who had resisted that question for days, gave it up so freely.

Inhaling, she slipped her hand through my loose grip and laid the shaking hand on my right cheek. Her thumb gently ran over the bump of my scars. She said, "When you took me, when you brought me to this hell, I believed you to be a monster." Her eyes lowered, but she blinked away her fear and stared once again at her thumb on my scars. "When you hurt me, when you asked me questions, I did not want to give you the victory of breaking me. But now . . . ," she trailed off.

"But now what?" I pushed, my voice rough and low.

Skin flushing once more, the female dropped her thumb to run along my lips and added, "But now I see you are just like me." She ran her fingers under my eyes, only to drop them and run them over the collar around my neck, and said, "You are in pain. Your life has not been your own, is still *not* your own." She sighed sadly. "Just like mine."

Ice-cold chills ran through my body as I stared at this little soldier beneath me, slight but with a heart of steel. Lifting her head, she pressed her forehead to mine and said, "We are different. Me weak and you strong. Me a Georgian and you Russian, but our broken hearts are tired and old. Our spirits are low, though not broken. But our souls, though thoroughly tested and hardened through pain, are resilient." Her lips twitched, and she added, "They are the same."

Her head fell back to the mattress. "That is why I give you my truth. It is why I give you my real name."

The female wrapped herself around my heart like a warm blanket. It beat with the hope, with the surreal feeling, that she knew what it felt like to be me. She knew loss and grief.

She too harbored a scarred soul.

My hand lifted, and I lowered myself farther against her body. I groaned as my naked flesh met hers. I ran the back of my hand down her cheek and murmured, *"Zoya."*

Zoya's cheek flushed and she smiled. Catching my hand in hers, she asked, "Can I know your name? Do you . . . do you know your name?"

I frowned. I hadn't been asked my name since I was twelve. But I remembered it. I remembered everything; my mind never forgot even when the drugs made everything hazy. I had seen many men brought in and out of Mistress's prisons throughout the years. But where they had fallen prey to the drug Mistress forced us to take, I had fought it with every ounce of my being. I had pretended. I'd played my part, but I kept hold of my memories. My name was locked in my heart.

"Valentin," I found myself admitting in a quiet, raspy voice. "I am Valentin." I rolled my tongue in my mouth, the name so unfamiliar on my lips.

"Valentin," Zoya whispered, her voice like a balm to my inner rage, and whether I wanted to or not, I failed to control myself.

In two seconds flat, I'd crushed my lips against hers.

It was my very first kiss.

11

ZOYA

It was working. I was getting through to him. What I wanted was going according to plan. Or it had been, until hearing how broken he was turned all my planning to dust.

I had let him touch me. I had given in to his every whim. As I hung from the shackles, I decided to let him have me in any way he had wanted. To weaken his resolve.

I had not expected my resolve to weaken to this extent, too.

I'd found myself a slave to his touch, moaning and surrendering to the pleasure he was wringing from my flesh.

When he returned from the chamber, something in him was different. He appeared defeated. His proud hulking shoulders were low and slumped.

When he'd come back for me, uncuffing me from the shackles, bringing me to a real bed he'd pulled from the wall, then holding me in his arms, his eyes had found a new state—compassionate.

My head ached as I wondered if this was yet another trick, but something in my gut told me it was real. I had broken through his high wall.

He was gentle yet firm. When he brought himself to pleasure

in tandem with my own, I knew something was different. The air had charged with static, and there was something new in his touch—tenderness and exploration—that had calmed and soothed my heated blood.

Valentin. His name was Valentin. Such a beautiful name for one so brutal and scarred. For one so vicious. Yet, even though it was dangerous, I felt compelled to reveal my true name.

I knew there was a better man deep inside. Irrationally, I wanted him to know my true name. Because the next time he brought me to pleasure, I wanted it to be my name that rolled from his soft lips.

And then he kissed me.

His lips were soft but firm as they pressed against mine. My heart fired like a cannon as his hard chest grazed mine, every part of my body alight with life and sensation.

Our lips at first were still and afraid, but Valentin slowly parted his lips and began caressing them against mine. I moaned as I tasted his dark spice scent on my lips. Spurred on by my groan, his large hands wrapped into my hair, forcing me closer to him still. Valentin paused, his warm breath filling my mouth, until my hands threaded behind his head and our lips fused. His mouth was hot as we explored, then, to my surprise, his tongue pushed between the seam of my lips, meeting and immediately dueling with my own.

Valentin groaned, his rumbling chest causing my breasts to ache. He kissed and kissed my mouth until my lips felt swollen and tender.

Withdrawing his tongue, Valentin broke from the kiss, his blue eyes bright once again. He hovered above me, his lips just as reddened as my own. My hand left the nape of his neck, and I brought it to my mouth. I ran my fingertip over my overly sensitive lips, then mirrored the action against Valentin's.

He watched me, his breathing heavy and strained, when I whispered, "You have stolen my first kiss." A flurry of feelings swarmed in my stomach. Loss and pain warring with delight and lust.

I didn't know what to feel, I didn't know whether to feel happiness or betrayal, until Valentin threaded his fingers between mine and countered in a hushed voice, "And you have stolen mine."

My eyes widened at this simple confession. Valentin inched closer, his nose running down my cheek and along to the nape of my neck. My eyes fluttered to a close at the feel of his dominating frame pressing over mine. Then he whispered, "I have lived eighteen years not as my own. I have had no choices, no free will. I have tortured, and I have been tortured in return. I have given pain, and I have had pain thrust upon me." He paused, then added, "I have been fucked, and I have been forced to fuck until I could barely stand. But I have never given a kiss, nor had a kiss given to me."

I didn't know why, perhaps the sad cadence to his rough voice, but my eyes pricked with tears. None fell, but my throat clogged and an ache constricted my chest. Sighing deeply, Valentin raised his head and confessed, "I have never before been free to choose." He paused; then, with a deep flush to the apples of his cheeks, he added, "But I chose to share my very first kiss with you."

I had nothing to say in response. I was sure no words from me could be worthy to match his confession. Draping my arms around his neck, I drew him close. At first his taut and stiff body refused the contact, but with a sigh Valentin's huge body pressed against mine, his arms lifting over my head to cage me in.

I let my eyes drift to view the pulley hanging from the ceiling, directly above the bed, as I held my enemy—my torturer—in my arms. His body was too big, his skin and demeanor too rough, yet I felt strangely safe.

I had thought this man a monster, heavily scarred and violently cruel. Thought him an evil and unfeeling torturer from hell. My eyes tightly shut as my mind drifted back to a story my grandmama would tell, of the folktale monster that lived in the woods behind our Tbilisi estate. A monster so big and so fierce, it was told to children that once captured they would never escape. I remembered sitting on my grandmama's knee as she told me the tale and asking why the monster wanted to hurt people.

"Because he is a monster," my grandmama said. "He just likes to hurt people. There is no rhyme or reason."

"But why?" I asked.

"Why what?" Grandmama replied in confusion.

I folded my arms across my chest. "There has to be a reason. Nobody, not even the biggest and scariest of monsters, hurts people for fun. Something must have happened to make him so mad."

My grandmama shook her head, smiling, and pressed a kiss on my head. "You are thinking too much, my love."

"No," I argued. "He must have been hurt, too." My eyes widened. "Did the people hurt him first? Did they not like him because he was different? Maybe that's why he's so mad. Maybe someone hurt him first and he just wants to be loved."

Grandmama stared at me and, hugging me to her chest, said, "I love the way you think, my love, but sometimes, people who are bad are simply bad."

"I don't believe that," I whispered into Grandmama's shoulder, "monsters are just looking for love, too. I know it deep down inside. . . ."

"*Kotyonok*, why are you crying?" Valentin's voice pulled me from my memory. I blinked when his face was blurred. A thumb wiped at my cheeks, and it was then I realized I was crying. I wiped at my eyes with my hands, only to see Valentin staring down. My memory came slamming back when I looked up at this Russian *monster*—his scar, his tattoos, his metal collar—my stomach dropped.

What had happened to him to make him this way? Like the monster of Tbilisi, had he too been hurt and never loved?

"Where have you come from?" I found myself asking, my quest for understanding trumping self-preservation.

Valentin's eyes narrowed, and he froze as my hand lifted to run along the metal collar. My eyes focused on the seam at the side of collar, the small lock that kept the collar in place.

"Hell," Valentin whispered almost inaudibly, "held by the Wraiths of evil."

My lungs constricted at the pain threaded in his voice, his words too cryptic for me to understand. Placing my hand on his face, I tilted his head until his gaze fell upon me. Swallowing, I said, "I am surprised I have not seen you before." Lines marred Valentin's forehead and his face showed nothing but confusion. Pulling his head down closer to mine, I finished, "I am surprised I have not seen you before, since I too have been a resident of hell for quite some time."

Valentin's face lost its tension, and my heart swelled when he whispered, "Zoya." He pressed the sweetest kisses to my mouth. My name on his lips sounded like heaven. It sounded utterly divine.

Valentin shifted over my body, his thick thighs parting my legs. My heart pounded like a chorus of drums at the determined look on his face.

A sweeping heat enveloped my body, as I suspected what was coming next. Just as Valentin inched his mouth toward mine, a hissing sound echoed through the silent room.

In seconds, the veins in Valentin's neck corded so tightly I feared they would break. His body froze, eerily still. Then I saw the collar contracting around his neck.

"No," Valentin cried. He launched himself from my body. Icicles of fear spiked in my veins as he jumped to his feet, his large hands gripping the sides of his neck tightly. Another hiss sounded from the collar, the sound now sinister to my ears. Valentin's fingers fought at the collar, but his fingertips failed.

I watched from against the wall, huddled at the top of the bed as Valentin's neck bulged at the tightness of the metal choking his neck. My body trembled. Then with a loud roar, Valentin's head snapped back and his muscled body corded, veins and muscles strained to their limit.

His body shook. I swallowed when his length hardened and slapped against his torso. His hands balled into fists; then, with a quick pained exhale, he lowered his head.

Dread infused my body when those dilated almost-black eyes set on me. I curled up in fear on the bed.

The drugs had set in. The torturer had returned. No matter how hard Valentin tried to pretend he was not a vicious killer, this version of him, the man with black eyes, was the demon that kidnapped me.

And it was that collar. It was something in that collar that forced him to be this, this . . . *thing.*

Then he approached. He loomed before me and cracked the knuckles on his hand. "No," I begged when he came closer. He stopped. My heart raced at the possibility that I'd gotten through to him.

Shuffling farther forward, I said, "Valentin? Valentin? Can you hear me?" His head tilted to the side. A vain thread of hope took root in my chest.

Then he looked up. When I followed what he was looking at, all blood drained from my body. The pulley. The pulley fixed to the ceiling above the bed.

Suddenly he lurched forward, slamming me onto the bed, knocking the air from my lungs. In seconds, the pulley from above began to lower. Then he was at my side, rope in his hands.

My body shook, my lip quivered, but *this* man didn't care. He reached forward and gripped the ankle of my leg. His breathing was heavy, sweat coating his skin. Whatever the collar was injecting into his body caused his skin to bump and grow damp.

Pulling me to a sitting position, he spread my knees apart with his hand. Grabbing both wrists, he pulled my arms behind my back. I screamed out in pain at the unnatural position, but he ignored my cries. He wrapped the rope around my chest, just above my breasts. Next, with the rope around my chest, he tied my wrists and attached them to the pulley. He yanked on my arms, to check it was in place. I bit on my tongue to stop a cry leaving my mouth.

I couldn't move. I was stuck.

This monster next wrapped rope around my thighs, tying it around the two posts on either side of the bed. Next came my ankles. He pushed them together, securing them to a post on the wall.

I tried to move, but I could barely even flinch.

He walked before me and, kneeling on the bed, harshly gripped my cheeks with his hand. Whipping my head to face him, he barked, "Who is Zaal Kostava to you?"

Staring in his dead eyes, I steeled myself. This wasn't Valentin anymore. This thing could not be bargained with. Could not be beat. I knew from recent experience that this version of Valentin hung around for an hour, two at most.

I would have to endure his wrath.

Taking a deep inhale, I closed my eyes and said, "I know no one by that name."

As I sensed his body moving closer to mine, I felt fingers palming my breasts. I prayed that the hour or two would go quickly. I prayed that Valentin would fight whatever control he was under.

My teeth gritted as I fought for breath. His hands roamed everywhere. His touch was rough and unpleasant.

There was no pleasure in this touch; pleasure wasn't his intention.

A strangled moan came from my mouth and another tore from my chest as his nose ran along the side of my neck. Then the monster knelt before me. I choked on a sob when his teeth dragged over my skin, down over my chest to my breasts. At my loud cry, he looked up. Reaching out his hand, he pushed the hair back from my face. When I pulled away, his grip fisted my hair, wrenching my head back. His face closed in, hovering an inch from my face. He demanded, "Who is Zaal Kostava?"

I didn't speak and he let my head drop.

"Who is Zaal Kostava?" the monster asked again. I closed my eyes, refusing to speak at all. Then I felt him standing in front of me. "Open your eyes!" he ordered harshly. I did as he asked. I caught sight of his hard body before me, his manhood mere inches from my face. I lost all fight.

The monster began palming his length, bringing himself closer to me with each stroke. When it was in line with my mouth, I fluttered my eyes to look up and almost sobbed at the determined expression on his face. His dilated eyes glittered in the dim light and he reached out to grip the back of my head.

"Please, Valentin," I said loudly, trying to break through whatever had him in its control. "Fight it. Don't do this to me. Don't hurt me. You don't want to hurt me anymore."

His hand on his manhood stopped, and his head dropped to the side watching me. His darkened eyes studied me curiously. My heart beat faster. "Valentin?" I tried again. "Fight it. For me . . . *Zoya*."

The monster's entire body suddenly stilled and I thought I caught a flash of recognition in his stare. But he took a step forward, gripping my hair in his hands. Tears fell down my cheeks and I closed my eyes. I didn't want to see his face as he took my mouth against my will.

Then, on an abrupt deafening roar, the monster threw my head back, his hands falling away.

Opening my eyes, I shook my head, trying to clear the water from my eyes, when I saw him stumbling back. My heart beat furiously as I watched him gripping his head. Pained groans and growls emanated from his lips; then his hands moved to his collar.

Hope soared within me as his fingers dipped below the slackening metal and he began to pull. The monster's face reddened until his entire body shook at his attempt to free himself from his collar. But no sooner had he attempted to rip off the collar than he gripped his head again, the pain obvious as he hit the side of his skull with a balled fist.

He fell to the floor, and I waited expectantly to discover what he would do next. I prayed that when he eventually lifted his head I'd see bright blue eyes. But I wasn't so fortunate. When the monster did raise his head, his pupils were still full and bleeding into the crystal blue irises. With fisted hands he pushed himself from the floor and approached.

I swallowed at the expression of pure hate on his face and cried out when his hand slipped and slammed on the rope above me. His hand then dropped to my stomach and made its way to between my legs.

"No," I whispered.

The monster's fingers ran along the top of my pubic hair and he hissed, "Name."

It was strange, because even terrified, I noticed the difference between Valentin's voice and the monster's. The monster's was colder, no feeling in its timbre. In contrast, in Valentin's, his subtle notes would change, the tone expressing his change in mood, his feelings, his regret.

No sooner had those thoughts entered my mind than the monster pushed his fingers closer to my folds. I squeezed my eyes shut, praying whatever he would do next would be over quick. Then suddenly the monster's hand stopped before he broached me. My eyes snapped open. I fought for breath as I panted through the fear. My attention was solely fixed on the monster, once again gripping his head, falling to the floor.

His body jerked. Pained groans wrenched from his throat. Sweat poured from his body. Just like before, his hands lifted to the collar around his neck. His hands pulled and pulled at the metal ring caging his neck, until every muscle in his arms shook with the effort.

He panted and panted, until his head lifted. Staring through me were crystal blue eyes. My heart pounded in relief, and managing to find my voice, I rasped, "Valentin."

Valentin shook his head. Then his unfocused eyes fixed on mine. I saw him drink me in. I saw his face contort on seeing me tied up. I winced when I imagined how I looked, strung up this way.

A sudden gut-wrenching roar came from Valentin's mouth and he jumped to his feet. He released his grip on the collar and walked to the chest at the side of the room. I held my breath, praying that the monster hadn't regained control. When Valentin stood back up, he held a knife in his hand. My stomach fell as he approached, but when I saw his eyes were still crystal blue my heart jumped in relief.

Valentin winced with every step he took toward me. I could see blood forming beneath the metal collar. Fear took hold of me when I realized the skin underneath was torn.

"Valentin," I whispered when he was just feet away. Valentin's jaw tensed, and lifting his arm high, he sliced at the rope above me. I cried out as the rope holding me captive jerked my body, the pain blanching my skin. But Valentin kept hacking at the rope; he hacked until, with a final strike, he cut through the rope and I fell to the bed. Finding strength through a desperate need to be free from my restraints, I unraveled the rope from my chest and arms and bit my lips at the pain of blood refilling my muscles.

Seeing the knife abandoned on the bed, I reached forward and, with shaky arms, cut through the rope at my ankles. As soon as the rope snapped in two, I kicked it off my legs.

Bending over the side of the bed, I vomited on the floor. Feeling light-headed from the fear I had felt, I rolled onto my side. When I looked up it was to see Valentin, back leaning against the nearby wall. His blue eyes were haunted and his arms shaking as he looked upon me.

Zoya, he mouthed, shame shining in his now-clear eyes. I tried to speak, I wanted to, but his massive body began to shake. I watched as his lips thinned and his hands lifted to his collar. It was strange, but as Valentin began pulling at the metal collar, trying his best to rip it apart, his eyes were focused on my breasts. Not understanding what he was staring at, I managed to look down, only to see my skin covered in red teeth marks.

A frustrated groan came from Valentin. He pulled at his collar, legs weakening with every attempt. Spatters of blood began spilling from under the restricting metal. As the collar pulled off his skin, inch by painful inch, I could see needles inserted into it.

Seeing Valentin fall to his knees, the metal collar half hanging from his neck, I forced myself to move to the edge of the bed. I needed him to stop. His face was bright red with the effort to remove the collar, and capillaries were bursting in the whites of his eyes, red replacing the bright white.

I had opened my mouth to shout for him to stop when, with a final broken bellow, the metal collar fell to the floor with a thud. I stared at the metal collar on the floor, the inner band of the device the most horrific thing I had ever seen. Tens of needles were standing, equally spaced around the edges. Beside them were small plastic pellets filled with liquid. Half were empty, but half were still full.

I breathed a sigh of relief when it hit me that Valentin had removed the collar. When I glanced up, Valentin was slumped against the wall, his hands holding the skin around his neck. His face had paled, but what had me pushing my bruised body from the bed was the blood pouring down his chest.

Frantic in my movements, I staggered to where Valentin slumped. As I fell to my knees by his side, his dull eyes found mine. He moved his mouth to speak, but I shook my head.

"No," I whispered, "don't try to speak."

Reaching up, I pulled at his hand, and when it dropped free I swallowed hard. The needle holes around his neck were bleeding badly. A thick red scar appeared soldered onto his skin from where the metal collar had been. I knew that he must have been wearing that collar for years, Lord knows how long. Valentin opened his mouth to speak.

"No," I pushed firmly.

Closing his eyes in obvious exasperation, he lifted his weak hand and pointed to a place in the wall. At first I couldn't see what he was seeing. On closer inspection I glimpsed the outline of a door. Getting to my feet, I slowly made my way to the door and pressed on the shape. The door clicked open. Inside was a small bathroom. I nodded my head when I realized it was the bathroom he'd let me use since I'd been here. He'd always blindfolded me before I used the toilet, to add to the torture. So I didn't know where I could go to relieve myself unless he took me there.

My eyes had scanned the shower, the toilet, the basin, when they landed on a small closet door at the end of the room. I walked toward it, flinching as I saw my reflection in the bathroom mirror. When I opened the door towels were piled high. Bottles of hydrogen peroxide were there, along with other medications I didn't recognize.

I grabbed some towels and peroxide and hurried as fast as I could out of the bathroom. As soon as I entered the chamber, I found Valentin's eyes already watching me, his broad and bulking chest awash with blood.

Getting on the floor, I immediately took a towel and pressed the soft fabric around his neck, trying to soak up as much of the blood as I possibly could. Valentin didn't even flinch; instead he stared down at my breasts, his nostrils flared and his lips thinned.

"I am fine," I said.

His eyes met mine. Nothing was said. I wasn't convinced he could speak now anyway.

Removing the towel, I took the bottle of peroxide and pressed my hand to his cheek. When he looked to me, I said, "This will sting, but we need to close up the holes around your neck. We need to stop the blood." Valentin's lifeless eyes never moved, even when I poured the peroxide over his cut and all around his neck.

I winced, knowing how it must have felt. I re-covered the holes with a clean towel. I moved closer, my heart as bruised as my body, to take in the broken expression on his face.

Valentin tracked me the entire way, but I could see his eyes closing. Dread and fear filled my aching bones. Touching his face, I said, "It's gone, Valentin. You removed the collar from around your neck."

The black stubble on his face stood in stark contrast to the paling sallow skin beneath. My heart surged when his lips twitched, then pulled into a ghost of a smile. A strange feeling washed over my soul as I saw that smile on his savagely scarred and brutal face, but it quickly faded when Valentin's eyes closed and his body grew frighteningly still.

12

VALENTIN

"Where are they taking us?"

I gripped Inessa tighter as the truck we had been thrown into started to move, taking us away from the orphanage that had been our home for the past two years.

"I don't know, dorogaya moya.*"*

I blinked, trying to see something in the darkness of the truck, but I couldn't make anything out. I could hear the cries of the other children the Night Wraiths had chosen, whom she *had chosen. I could hear their sniffles and fast breathing.*

I closed my eyes, pulling my little sister toward me, stroking through her hair. I rocked her back and forth, sighing when her little body stopped shaking and she slumped against my chest.

I worked on keeping still; I worked on breathing in slow and steady breaths. But the truth was, I was terrified. The woman who dressed all in black had ordered the Wraiths to bring us out to the truck. When the door opened, the back of the truck was filled with small cages.

The blood drained from my face. I looked over to Inessa, who was being held by a Wraith. As he went to throw my sister in the back, she started screaming for me, holding out her hands.

As I rammed my elbow into the Wraith that held me his hand released my neck, and I climbed in the van after my sister. The Wraith turned when he saw me running and held out his gun. It didn't stop me. I kept going, seeing the Wraith remove the safety, when a cracking sound hit the wall of the van and the woman commanded, "Stop!" The Wraith holding my sister froze at the woman's command. Heels clicked on the floor behind me, and something ran over my neck and into my long messy black hair.

"Interesting reaction, don't you think?" the woman said to the guard holding my sister.

I suddenly saw what had been running through my hair when the woman hit out a whip toward the guard's still-raised gun. The gun fell to the floor. Inessa cried out and tucked her head in the Wraith's shoulder. My hands balled at my sides and my teeth gritted together as I saw my sister looking so small in that bastard's arms.

The woman then turned to me and ran the edge of the whip down my face. Her dark eyes were bright, and she leaned in, using the end of the whip under my chin to force my head up. "You're going to be an interesting one, I can tell." Her voice was as sharp as a knife, and my skin broke out in shivers at the way she watched me.

She stared at me in silence, but my eyes drifted over her shoulder to check on Inessa. Inessa's blue eyes were watching me, her bottom lip trembling. My stomach roiled at seeing her so upset. I wanted nothing more than to take her in my arms and tell her everything was going to be okay.

The woman followed my gaze; then as she snapped her head back to me she cracked her whip across my cheek. I staggered back as blistering pain sliced across my face. My hand lifted over my cheek, and when I pulled it back blood was on my palm.

I looked up at the woman, rage building in my veins. When my rage-filled eyes met hers, her eyes flared and her thin lips spread into a wide smile. Without turning to the male Wraith, she ordered, "Put them in the same cage! One last ride will not make a difference." My shoulders sagged in relief as the male walked to a cage and put my sister inside. My heart squeezed as I looked at Inessa so small in the metal cage. Her dark hair fell down her back and her blue eyes were so big they almost appeared unreal.

The guard snapped his fingers and I rushed forward, but not before the woman gripped my arm bringing me to a halt. Her long fingers dug into my biceps as her mouth leaned down until it met my ear. I shivered again, something in my soul warning me to pull away.

"I see the fury in your eyes, little boy," the woman said coolly. I saw her mouth break into a smile, and she added, "Good. Keep it. Fuel it. It will become essential for what I have planned . . ."—she looked over her shoulder to my sister, then turned back to finish—"for you and your little angel there."

I wanted to argue, I wanted to hit her in the face, but my body was frozen to the spot. The female didn't release my arm for several seconds, until she pushed me toward the cage. I stumbled but rushed into the cage with Inessa. As soon as I was in the cage, Inessa crawled onto my lap. She threaded her arms around my neck and whispered, "I am scared, Valentin. That woman scares me."

"Shh," I soothed, and held her close. "She won't hurt you."

Inessa exhaled and whispered, "Big Brother Promise?"

Tears pricked my eyes, and I nodded my head. "Big Brother Promise."

"Then I'll be safe," she said softly.

As I glanced up, I heard the other children being loaded into the other cages. But as I did, I met the dark gaze of the woman, now standing before our cage. My body stilled when I saw the look on her face. My stomach turned in dread when I knew she'd heard everything I'd just promised Inessa.

A promise I knew I wouldn't be able to keep, but one I would die trying to honor.

Days and days seemed to pass, the truck stinking of piss and shit. The Wraiths threw us bread and water but never stopped to give us fresh air or clean clothes. And they never once stopped to let us use a toilet. Instead we soiled ourselves. We had to sit and sleep in shit.

I'd stopped smelling the stench after a day or so.

Suddenly the truck pulled to a stop. Low voices sounded outside, but the sound of crying and fear clogged up the back of the truck.

The locks on the rolling door of the truck bed rattled, and in seconds the door rolled open, blinding light replacing darkness. I flinched as the light burned my eyes. I wrapped Inessa in my arms to shield her from the pain.

Male Wraiths dressed all in black flooded into the back of the truck, the metal batons in their hands slamming against the steel cages. The noise was deafening after days and days of painful silence.

A shadow reached our cage and snapped the lock. Tucking my nose into Inessa's hair, I ordered, "Keep hold of me, dorogaya moya*! I'll keep you safe."*

I felt her little head nod and I crawled from the cage just as the male Wraith hit the cage again and ordered, "Get out!"

My legs were weak when I stood. I fought to keep hold of my sister. I gripped on tight, my heart increasing in speed the closer I got to the outside. My breath misted into white puffs as we hit a wall of cold. It was freezing outside; snow covered the ground.

I climbed down the steps, only for the Wraith to point me toward the end of a line. The place was silent as I walked down the line. I stared at the children's faces, recognizing some from my dorm or from the canteen.

My eyebrows pulled down when I saw that all the children in the line were boys. A flicker of movement caught my eye on the other side. When I turned my head, a line exactly like the one I was in stood opposite. Except they were all girls.

A whoosh of breath left my chest when I saw the Wraiths were splitting us up. My body tensed and I felt sick at the thought of my little Inessa being taken from me. I held her tight, and I fought back tears at the thought of her being on her own, of her not having me to protect her.

The warmth of her breath drifted down my neck. I took my place at the end of the line. I stared before me at the long row of young girls, all crying or deathly still, all still dressed in their nightgowns, just like my Inessa.

Then I heard it. I heard the sound of heels on the ground, and I knew it was her. *I focused on the ground, never lifting my eyes, when I saw her feet come into view. Inessa must have felt my body freeze, as she whimpered into my neck. She could sense my fear.*

The familiar end of a whip landed under my chin, lifting my head. My eyes met the cruel eyes of the female Wraith. She stared and she stared, until her whip moved to run down Inessa's back. My sister jumped at the feel, but her grip tightened around my neck.

Next, everything seemed to run in slow motion. The woman snapped her fingers and a Wraith began to approach. When he arrived at where we stood, he reached out and wrapped his hands around Inessa's waist. Inessa screamed, but I held on tight. I fought and fought to keep hold, but as the woman's whip came cracking down on my back Inessa slipped from my arms. Her pretty face was red and streaming with tears as the Wraith took her away. I pushed forward to run after her, but I was kicked to the ground and whipped across my body until I couldn't feel my arms and legs.

My head rolled, pain pounding through my skull. My eyes stung with the cold, but I forced them open to search for Inessa. I screamed a silent scream as I saw the line of girls being led away through a wide arch. I tried to push myself to run after her, but another blow came down, pinning me on the snow-covered ground. I watched through blurred eyes as the girls faded from view. But at the last minute, the girl at the end turned, her dark hair in the bright rising dawn looking like a halo on her head. My breath was lost as I realized it was Inessa. I cleared my eyes, reaching out my hand. Just as she disappeared through the arch, she lifted her hand in a small wave.

She was saying good-bye.

Pain overwhelmed me, burning me from the inside. A sense of failure wrapped me in its embrace and I curled in on the floor. The sound of feet moving, crunching on the snow, hit my ears, but I didn't move.

A pair of black boots came into view, and I heard the woman order, "Get him up!"

Someone grabbed my arm and wrenched me to my feet. My head hung, defeated; then that fucking whip lifted my chin. The woman shook her head, then flicked her chin to a Wraith behind that pushed me into line along with the other boys.

We walked through the same arch, until a huge field came into view. Metal towers and fences topped with razor wire stretched as far as the eye could see. But there were no buildings. I wondered if it was a military base, until we came to a sudden stop. The line started to move again, but I couldn't see where the boys in front were walking. Night Wraith guards surrounded us on either side, and when it was my time to walk my eyes widened at a set of stairs in a field, leading down.

The place we were being taken was underground.

My feet were heavy as I descended the stairs. We walked through a maze of corridors, until we came to a large room. "Sit down!" the Wraith guards ordered in Russian, so we would understand. The guard behind me pushed me into a chair. A man appeared behind me. There was a buzzing sound; then a razor was taken to my head, my messy black hair falling onto the floor around me.

In minutes my head was shaved. The Wraith guarding me pulled me to my feet. He pushed me into step behind the other boys. The line slowed down. When I got to the front there was a man behind a desk handing out black sweatpants.

The line stopped as I was handed my pair, and the Wraith walked before us. "Strip, leave your old clothes on the floor, and put on your new pants."

We did as commanded, and once we were all in the black sweatpants, heads shaved, the line started to move again. Feeling a trickle down my chest, I looked down only to see lashes and blood from the whipping I'd taken outside. I didn't care. They'd taken my Inessa. I wasn't going to feel anything.

We walked and walked deeper into the darkened corridors, until the sound of buzzing and screaming drifted down the halls. The boys in front of me began swaying on their feet, sweat dripping down their backs. And one by one we approached the room of screams.

When it was my turn to enter, a man standing at the door handed me a piece of paper. When I looked up, there were rows and rows of flat beds. The boys were being forced down and a man took a buzzing needle to their chests. As I walked through the mass of beds to the free one at the end, I saw that numbers were being tattooed on their chests. I frowned, until I remembered the paper in my hand. Glancing down, I saw the number "194" staring up at me. I was pushed from behind, and a man next to the free bed took my number and pointed to the bed.

I lay down, and in seconds the man pushed the buzzing needle into my skin. My mouth clenched at the pain and my body tensed. But I didn't cry out like the other boys. I refused to let these Georgians see me break.

It was excruciating. Almost unbearable. But I never moved. I didn't move until the man with the needle stepped back and wiped at my chest with a wet rag. The wet rag felt like a hundred bees stinging my flesh.

Yet I still didn't flinch.

The Wraith guard pulled me from the bed and walked me down a hall. Dull thuds, screams, and shouts came from the room at the end of the hallway. I took a deep breath, bracing for what I would see next, but, honestly, nothing could have prepared me.

A room, bigger than I'd ever seen in my life, was filled with boys of all ages. And they were fighting. Some with weapons, some without. My eyes roved over the huge room, watching the boys hitting and drawing blood. I swallowed. I knew I was looking at my future.

The Wraith guards ahead pushed some of the boys into a pit and stood around them with folded arms. A guard lifted up his hand and ordered, "Fight!"

The boys stood, all fearfully staring at the Wraith guards. A guard lunged out and hit one across the face. The boys backed away as the guard repeated, "Fight!"

Fists and arms suddenly went flying, and the boys fought. They fought until blood was spilled.

The guard beside me pushed me into a pit to my left. I stumbled onto the sandy surface; then other boys were pushed in with me, too. A guard moved toward us when from the corner of my eye I saw the woman watching me. A man was beside her and she pointed into the pit.

The Wraith guard lifted his hand. As he did, rage swept through me, my blood boiling from the anger swirling inside. "Fight!" the guard shouted, and my legs moved toward the nearest boy. My fists flew; my legs kicked at anyone in my path. I bit, I clawed, and I kept going until the guard pulled me back.

"Stop," he hissed into my ear. When I looked around, the boys I'd beaten were lying on the ground. But the anger still built as I stared at the female.

The boys who could still walk were led out of the room. The ones on the ground were dragged out by the guards. The guard holding me put me on the ground, when the woman called out something in Georgian.

Suddenly the guard began leading me down another hallway. This one was quieter than before. When I came out at the end, it was a smaller room with cages along the back wall, a pit in the center, and on the opposite side a door that obviously led somewhere else.

The door at the back of the room opened. The woman and the man she had been standing with walked through. A guard followed behind, pushing two boys into the room. I stared at the boys. They were twins. They were darker in skin, with long black hair that ran down their backs. They were identical, but one had green eyes and the other had brown. The one with green eyes stared straight ahead, as if he was looking at nothing, but the one with brown eyes looked straight across at me.

The twins were pushed across the room, and as they passed me I read the numbers on their chests: 362 and 221. They were locked up in separate cages, but they were next to each other.

The one with brown eyes, 362, sat close to the bars and tried to talk to the one with green eyes, 221. But 221 stared straight ahead, like he couldn't even hear his brother talk.

I swallowed, and this time real fear ran through my veins. The guard pushed me into a cage beside 362. The woman and the man with her left the room, left the three of us alone.

Hours and hours passed in silence, until 362 moved closer and asked me something in Georgian. I didn't know what he said. Then his eyes traveled down my body and he said in perfect Russian, "You're new?"

I nodded my head.

362 sighed and asked, "Do you remember your name?"

I frowned and said, "My name? Of course I do."

362's head hit the back wall and he closed his eyes. "Good; remind yourself of it every single day. Burn it into your fucking brain. Never let it fade."

I was even more confused. I had opened my mouth to speak when he said, "I'm 362. I have no name, or at least I don't now. I have no memory of it." His eyes opened and he rolled his head toward his brother—he was still facing forward, focused on nothing. "Nor does he."

"Why?" I asked, seeing the pain in 362's eyes as he looked at his twin. "How have you forgotten?"

362 faced me again, his forehead lined with confusion. "Drugs. If you're in this room, you're going to be given drugs. That's why we're kept separate." He sighed and, clenching his fists, said, "And they'll make you forget. The drugs will make you forget your name. Your family. Where you are from. Everything. If you're lucky you'll be able to resist the drugs for some of the time; if not . . ." He trailed off and he looked back to his brother. I got the message. If not, you'd be like 221.

The room was abruptly plunged into darkness. I lay on the floor and closed my eyes. My sister's last wave filled my mind. My stomach tightened at the thought of her words to me in the cage. "Big Brother Promise?" *Our thing. When our junkie mother died and we were sent into that hell of a group home, she made me promise to never let anything bad happen to Inessa.*

And I had. Because if this was what was happening to me, what the hell was happening to her?

Tears dripped on the floor, and as I curled my body in I heard 362, say, "That." I tensed, and he continued, "Whatever has you upset, focus on them or that. Hold on to that person in your head. Maybe the drugs won't break through if you have something to live for."

Wiping my eyes, I replied, "It didn't work with you. It hasn't worked with him."

"True," 362 admitted in a rough voice. "But we were the first. We didn't know what these drugs would do." I nodded into the darkness when he said, "He may not remember me, but he's my brother, my blood, and I'll keep him in my head for as long as I can. Then one day, when I get out of this place, and off these fucking drugs, I'll find him again. I'll find him again and kill all the people in this blood pit. I'll kill anyone that tried to rip my best friend from my heart."

Nothing else was said. When I awoke, I was in a room with the woman. The man from the pits was by her side. He had a syringe in his hand. I tried to move, but my hands and feet were strapped down to the bed.

I pulled and pulled as the man approached. Then the woman stood beside me with something in her hand. "Stop!" she ordered, and held out a small screen. My heartbeat that seemed to have been absent from my chest since I'd arrived began to beat again.

"Inessa," I whispered. My newly beating heart now tore into shreds. My baby sister was huddled in the corner of a cell, just like mine. Her blue eyes were huge as she watched the other girls in the room. But my chest warmed with pride when I saw she wasn't crying.

The woman pulled the screen away. "No!" I called out. She shook her head, her ugly face blazing with happiness. "Let me see her again!" I barked.

Her eyes narrowed, and her finger stroked across my forehead. "If you want to see her again, 194, you'll have to earn it."

My muscles tensed. "My name is Valentin," I bit back.

The woman then said, "No, here in the Blood Pit it's 194. You have no name, boy." She leaned in closer, her strong perfume stinging my nose.

"Here you will call me Mistress. Do you understand, 194?"

The man beside me pushed the needle in my arm. A searing heat immediately chased through my veins, my back bowing with pain as my mind filled with a thick fog.

I didn't remember much after that, but I fought to keep my memories. I fought to remember that I was Valentin Belrov from Russia. My sister was called Inessa, and the first chance I got I would slit the throat of the Georgian bitch I'd been forced to call Mistress. . . .

13
VALENTIN

A wet rag dragged across my chest. My mind filled with the man who had given me the number tattoo. Reaching out, I grabbed his wrist, using brute strength to throw him on his back. I wrapped my free hand around his throat, squeezing the thin neck.

I frowned as the sweet smell of sugar drifted up my nose, and when a high-pitched whimper hit my ears I blinked my eyes open, the picture slowly coming into view.

Below me on a black tiled floor was a dark-haired female. Her big brown eyes were huge as they looked up at me. Her small hands were wrapped around my wrist, pushing me to get off. I blinked, and blinked again, trying to push the fog from my mind. Images flashed across my eyes: her lying in the cage, her tied to the wall, wrapped in ropes, her on a bed, being tortured and hurt.

Zoya, she had said. *My name is Zoya.*

Jerking my hands free, my neck throbbing with pain, I pulled back. My legs were straddling her thighs. Zoya coughed and spluttered as she rubbed at the skin of her neck.

I slid back against the wall, still feeling the wetness over my chest. I ran my hand over the damp skin, only to see a bloodied towel lying beside me. I squeezed my eyes shut, trying to clear the blur. When I opened them, the chamber came into view. I breathed hard, relieved that I wasn't back in that hell—the Blood Pit.

Seeing movement from beside me, I rolled my head to the side, wincing at the pain in my neck.

Zoya. Zoya shuffling away from me.

"No," I rasped, my voice barely a whisper. My throat feeling like razor blades as I tried to push out the word.

Zoya stilled and deliberately met my eyes. Swallowing, she asked, "Valentin?"

My heart beat fast as she spoke my name. Unable to talk, I put my hand over my chest and briefly closed my eyes to tell her yes.

Relief washed over her face and she came closer. The closer she got, the more I noticed that her long black hair was wet and her skin had been cleaned. She was still naked. As I looked down her lean body, my nostrils flared as I saw red teeth marks covering her chest and rope burns over her wrists and ankles.

I swallowed as images of me doing these things sailed through my brain. I saw myself tying her up, biting her, about to force my cock into her mouth.

Regret and shame burned like fire in my heart.

Needing to get the fuck away from what I'd done, I tried to move. As I fought to get to my feet, a hand landed on my bare chest. I froze, and when I looked up Zoya was peering down at me. She sucked in a breath and said, "It was the monster, not you. And you stopped him before you . . ."

I frowned, not understanding her meaning. Zoya sat back on her ankles, then pointed to the broken metal collar on the floor. My stomach flipped. I instinctively reached up to my neck, hissing when my hands landed on bare neck.

My bare neck. I hadn't had a bare neck since I was twelve.

I turned to Zoya for answers. Anticipating my question, she explained, "You fought its control over you. You saw what you had done, were about to do, under its influence, and you forced it from your neck." Zoya shuffled forward and ran her finger under my neck. "It made you bleed and pass out. You have been asleep, I think, for many hours." She pointed at the wet rag. "I was cleaning you when you awoke. I think you were having a nightmare; you were restless, and tried to call out."

I stared at her as she spoke. As she was about to withdraw her hand, I gripped her wrist and kept her finger on my chest.

A flush crept up her skin. As I watched her olive skin blush with red, I remembered my lips pressing against hers. I remembered her touch on my face. I remembered her smiling at me when I told her my name.

"Are you tired?" she asked softly.

I closed my eyes again to say yes. Zoya looked over to the bed and said, "Can you get up to sleep on the bed?"

Wanting to get on the bed with her, I forced myself to get off this floor. Planting my palms on the hard tile, I pushed off the floor, my feet staggering when I stood up.

Zoya stayed at my side. Her face was down, as though she was concentrating. Accompanied with a deep breath, she wrapped her arm around my waist, then guided me to the bed. With every step, my heart swelled at the sweet feeling of Zoya's arms around my waist.

"Lie down," Zoya instructed when we reached the edge of the bed.

Doing as she said, I lay down on the mattress, until I was on my back. Zoya stood at the side, rocking on her feet. I patted the mattress beside me. Zoya looked at me through long lashes. Doing as indicated, she crawled onto the bed. She curled beside me, lying on her side. Her hand was tucked under her face. She looked so beautiful. So beautiful that I pushed out my hand and ran the back of it down her cheek.

"Beautiful," I murmured, watching the shock ripple over her face. My raw throat burned in pain, but I pressed my free hand against my throat to numb it and finished, "I have hated . . . all . . . Georgian bitch females . . . my whole life." I swallowed to wet my throat, then scratched out, "But I . . . cannot hate . . . you."

Zoya's eyes dipped; then, without looking at me again, she slid from the bed. My heart sank as she disappeared into the small bathroom, but she appeared again with a bottle of water. Nervously she moved to my side. Kneeling on the bed, she brought the bottle of water to my lips and poured some of the cold liquid down my throat. She repeated the action until the bottle was drained; then, as before, she lay down on the bed beside me.

I cleared my throat, the burning sensation already dulled.

My hand was lying on the mattress between us. Zoya's fingers went rigid, and with a sigh her small hand covered mine. My eyes snapped to hers. Soon her warmth seeped into mine, and she licked along her lips.

"Valentin," she said in the thick Georgian accent I used to despise but now had learned to adore. "You are not a bad man."

My eyebrows pulled down. Those images of what I was about to do to her raced through my head. As if sensing what was happening, Zoya squeezed my hand. "I know what you are thinking," she said softly. I focused on the rope burns on her body.

"Look at me!" Zoya said. My nostrils flared on hearing a command from her mouth. Zoya's face softened and she added, "Please."

Forcing my body to not respond to a strict female voice, I sank farther into the mattress and met Zoya's eyes, as requested, not commanded.

Her fingers began stroking across my own. "When you first touched me, you terrified me." I stayed still, just listening. Zoya's face paled and she said, "The things you did to me when you first brought me to this chamber"—she shook her head—"I could not have even dreamed of in my worst nightmare. The electric shocks, the hot and cold, then the way you used my body and its centers of pleasure against me. It was barbaric, cruelty at its very worst." My jaw clenched at the hurt lacing her voice, but I didn't react. I had committed these acts. I'd done what I'd been commanded by Mistress.

Zoya smiled, but it wasn't a happy smile. "At first, I thought you were coldhearted, a *monster.* But then I realized what the collar around your neck was doing to your body. I knew when it took you in its hold. Your blue eyes would turn black, fully dilated. It still didn't explain the hours when your eyes were blue, yet you still caused me pain. But you began to slip, and I glimpsed fleeting moments of compassion sneaking through." Zoya's head tipped to the side. "And even though you had me held captive, even though you had hurt me, had brought me to a torturous level of pleasure, I worked out that you were doing all of this because you *had* to, not because you *wanted* to."

I rolled my lips together; that feeling again burst within me. I stared at this female. I questioned how she could be speaking to me this way. How could she care for me, after all that I had done to her?

"As I said before, Valentin, we are not dissimilar. And believe it or not"—she tipped her head forward—"you and your chamber are not the most horrific of things that have happened in my life. You see, I think in that respect we are alike." Her hand squeezed mine and she added, "Except the people who found me and took me in were good and honest people. They protected me and kept me safe." Zoya lifted our joined hands and brought them to her lips. As her lips brushed the back of my hand, a blanket of heat covered my body.

"Where I believe the people that found you caused you nothing but pain and sorrow. I believe that had you not been forced to have this life, you would have been a very different man. Do you agree?" she asked, her question hanging thick and heavy in the air.

I shrugged and whispered, "I do not know. I have caused others pain. I have killed and tortured since I was a child."

Zoya's face fell and she asked, "By choice?"

I closed my eyes and slightly shook my head. "No," I admitted, "made to. Forced to."

I heard Zoya sigh. I felt her warm breath on my face. My answer rewarded me with another kiss on my hand. As if some invisible barrier had been torn down between us, Zoya shifted closer until I could feel the heat of her body seeping into mine. A deep blush ran up her neck to fill her cheeks and face. I decided at that moment that she was the most beautiful female that could have ever existed. She, a Georgian, of an enemy race I had vowed to always hate. But with that flush, brown eyes, compassion, and tender grace all the hatred fell away.

Zoya lifted her leg to place it over mine, moving closer until her head lay next to me. "I know you do not like Georgians, Valentin, but my grandmama would tell me the story of the Tbilisi monster. Have you heard of it?" she asked. My lips curled up at her Georgian accent fluidly wrapping around the Russian words.

"No," I replied.

Her brown eyes became lost as she explained, "I was only five years old when my family was killed." My eyes dropped to the scars on her shoulders and hip. Seeing my attention focus on these, she stroked along my face and said, "The day I too should have died." My stomach dropped just at the thought of Zoya being dead. But I refocused on her words as she carried on, "I have no more memories, I believe, from that age. I think it is because I lost them all to trauma. I think when a horrific event has tarnished your soul all the lighter days prior to that event are the brighter for it."

Zoya's eyes dulled for a moment but brightened when her lips pulled into a small smile. "My grandmama loved to tell me stories. And I loved to hear them. She knew this, so she would often tell me stories. But there was one she would tell me over and over again. Every time she told it, I would always find fault."

I listened to her talk of her family with such happiness. At that moment I could have listened to her always. Her voice changed as she recalled her family. I never had that. Even with Inessa, I was always fighting for us to survive, stealing to help us eat.

"Valentin?" Zoya pushed. I snapped back to the present. "Are you okay?" she asked. I pressed my cheek to the hand she had left under my face. "Tell me about the monster," I asked.

She smiled again. "Legend has it that the monster, who is as tall as the trees and as broad as an ox, lived in the deepest parts of the Tbilisi forest. For years he had been spotted by the children in the town. He would live on his own in peace, but the children all wanted to see him. But when they saw him, they would laugh at him and make fun of him, call him ugly. They prodded him with sticks, hit him with rocks, and ran screaming past where he slept to keep him awake.

"Then one day everything changed. The monster fought back. The monster waited and waited in hiding for nasty children to run by. As they passed his hiding place, he jumped out and caught them, bringing them back to his house. In his house he had a cauldron. The captured children were placed inside and cooked alive, into a hot monster's stew."

A laugh came from her throat, instantly seizing my fucking heart. She shook her head. I could see the water glistening in her eyes. "My bedroom overlooked the Tbilisi forest. At night I would search and search for the monster in the woods. I never saw him of course, but I didn't know that as a child. He was my obsession. I thought of him day and night." Zoya's eyes dipped, and she said, "I wanted to see the monster. I wanted to speak to him. I wanted to ask him why he'd done such an awful thing. I wanted to speak to him to ask if somebody had hurt him, and inquire why he was so angry and sad. I wanted to tell him that if he tried to be nice, if he didn't hurt and eat the children, then people might come to like him, that he could make friends. I wanted to tell him that even if he didn't look like the rest of us, even though some found him ugly, he wasn't. He was just different. But of course, I never did see him."

Zoya dabbed at the corners of her eyes with her thumb and laughed again. "My family laughed at me as I searched the edge of the forest, shouting for the monster day and night. My brothers would often hide behind the trees and jump out, making me scream as they chased me over the lawn." Zoya paused.

Zoya edged closer, until her forehead pressed against mine. Her fingers traced over my scars that ruined my face. "Valentin, to me, you are the monster of Tbilisi Forest. You have done cruel things. But just by looking at you, at that collar on your neck, the scars on this face, I could see it was because horrid things had first been done to you. Someone had you under her control; she had the means to make you act so cruelly, to hurt you and believe you were a beast." Her hand pressed over my heart. "I believe it goes against the grain of who you truly are, in here."

"Zoya," I murmured, and she smiled.

Swallowing, I pressed my hand against her cheek and whispered, "Do you realize how much you've just fucked up?"

Zoya froze and paled. I held her head tightly in place and stated, "You are really from Tbilisi, not Kazreti, as you have argued for many days."

Zoya exhaled a shaky breath. Her hand on my face began to shake. Her skin turned cold when I said, "Zaal Kostava is from Tbilisi, Georgia. His family was killed; all the bodies were accounted for but one." Her head flinched as she tried to move away, but I held it still in my large hands. Taking a deep breath, I rasped, "All but a younger little girl, a younger girl called Zoya."

Zoya's eyes closed. My eyes closed, too.

She was Zaal's sister.

The man I was commanded by Mistress to kill.

14

ZOYA

I had never ever felt my heart beat so fast. As I lay here, trapped in the grip of the man I thought I had grown to understand, my heart beat too fast and too strong.

I could feel my body shaking. I could feel my blood turning to ice as it sluggishly tried to infuse my muscles with strength.

Crystal blue eyes watched me, like a hawk watches its prey. I chastised myself for my emotional naivety, for my abandonment of logic and my seriously misplaced trust.

I tried to pull back, but Valentin's grip was too strong. *Please,* I tried to say, but no words fell from my mouth. I had been so wrong. It wasn't the collar. This man *was* a heartless monster. Whatever had been in the collar only heightened the blackness scarring his soul.

I gave up the fight, lying as still as I could. I closed my eyes, seeing Zaal's happy face in my head—the brother I'd just condemned to death.

My breathing quickened in sorrow, then my world was blown apart when the monster said, "Her name is Inessa." I held my breath, my mind confused. Who was Inessa? What was he referring to?

Then he continued, "She is my sister, though she hasn't remembered that fact, or even her own name, since she was four." I blew out a breath, slow and controlled, shock filling every cell of my body. My frantic heart began to slow when I realized, I realized he was confiding in me. He was telling me about himself.

"Valentin," I said softly, my near whisper sounding like a scream in the deathly quiet room.

Valentin's hands ran to the back of my head as though he was trying to bring me as close as possible. I let him take comfort from my proximity. But when I saw a tear roll down his stubbled cheek, my heart broke in two.

"Valentin" was all I could say. I swallowed at the grief in that single solitary tear tumbling to the mattress. "Where is she now, your Inessa?"

Valentin's hold became rigid, but he managed to explain, "I do not even know how to make you understand. She is being held captive, like we all were. But where the men were trained as fighters or, worse, killers—"

"Like you?" I asked, the question tumbling from my lips without thought.

Valentin's eyes shut painfully, but he nodded his head. "Yes. Like me."

"But your sister?" I pushed.

Valentin edged back, his hands sliding from behind my head. He took a grip of my hand, though, like before. No, not this time. When I saw his eyes, they were like nothing he'd shown me before. Vulnerability and despair shone in their depths, and absolute defeat.

"The females are taken down a different path. They are drugged with a serum that makes them sexually subservient. They are driven mad from within, if a man doesn't fuck them like an animal."

Bile rose in my throat. "Your sister? As a child . . . ?" I trailed off, not wishing to hear the answer to my question.

Valentin shook his head. "Not as a four-year-old. As a four-year-old she began to be raised to clean and to cook under a different type of obedience drug. It took away her personality, anything about who she was. Mistress would show me Inessa on a screen every night, 152 as the tattoo on her back said—they didn't tattoo females' chests because it would spoil their looks. Mistress knew that I would never leave the Blood Pit without her. She also knew that I'd do anything to get my sister back, so she personally trained me to be an *Ubiytsa*."

"An assassin," I countered.

Valentin nodded his head. "For years Mistress held me in her personal chamber." He pointed around the room, "This is a replica of her chamber. She keeps it the same wherever we go to find and make the hit, so I know where everything is, to make the torture more painful." Valentin's face, which was pale from his injury, began to redden with the anger thoughts of his "Mistress" were stimulating. "I was twelve when they took me and Inessa from our orphanage. Mistress immediately saw the bond we had. She's a sick twisted whore who knew she could control me using Inessa's safety—and she has; she still does."

Valentin's hands were shaking. I knew it was in fury, not fear. Shuffling closer, I ran the pad of my thumb over the racing pulse in his wrist and said, "Shh, calm. Take your time."

Valentin, to my surprise, leaned forward and pressed a kiss on my cheek. Heat ghosted over my skin at the gesture. I saw his top lip curl, which melted my heart.

"She'd torture me. She separated me from the other boys from age twelve. She had a male there for a time, a male she was screwing. I hated him about as much as I hated her. He had a couple of boys caged in the room too, his own personal playthings, whom he would torture and exploit. But Mistress still took me in her chamber every day, and 'demonstrated' how to torture a captive. The first year was pain." Valentin ducked his head and said, "What I did to you." He swallowed and said, "Fuck, Zoya, how can you forgive me for that?"

I shivered, remembering the prod and the pain that spouted from its tip. But I kept my composure. "Perspective," I replied. "My life has been one of hardship. When you too have walked through a thunderstorm you understand, through perspective, how another soaked by familiar gray skies can feel desperate, too. Desperate people do desperate things."

I drank in her soft skin and beautiful face. I asked, "Are you real?"

Zoya dipped her eyes in embarrassment, then huffed a laugh. "That depends on who you ask. Zoya Kostava is a myth, the famed daughter of the Kostava Clan whose body was never found. It seems I am more of a ghost than flesh and blood, if you are minded to ask the people of Georgia about my name."

Valentin dragged the hand that was on my face down over my neck to skirt over my waist and said, "You're real to me."

I sobered. I felt static energy crackle between us. The tension was high, but both of us were sore and fragile. This was close enough.

For now.

"Tell me more," I said, to continue the conversation.

"She hurt me. She taught me pain. Then she turned the training on its head and I became the one to administer pain. I was happy at first. I got to torture the Georgian bitch who had ruined my life. But as I administered the torture the bitch loved it, stealing any pleasure I could take from those messed-up days."

Valentin reached up and pushed his hand through his hair. "Then, when I was fourteen, I began a new form of torture training. Sexual torture." Valentin's face paled. "I won't go into it, but that fucking bitch raped me. She took everything from my body. She must be at least twenty years older than me; she just lapped it up."

His skin turned a sickly shade of green when he explained, "Then, just like with the pain, she flipped the lesson. She made me touch her. Made me make her come, over and over. Made me stick my dick in her dirty fucking mouth. Then she made me fuck her. Fuck her until I couldn't stand."

"Shh. Calm down," I soothed. Valentin's body tensed so much on replaying these memories that the holes in his neck began to erupt. But he gripped on to my wrists. "She still makes me take her like that. She triggers the serum in the collar until I'm not myself, then orders me to fuck her. But when the serum fades, I still remember everything she forces me to do." Valentin's eyes squeezed shut. "And I hate it. She tears off another piece of my soul every time she makes me fuck her."

I could see that Valentin was about to lose it, so I pushed him onto his back and straddled his waist. His hands instinctively landed on the backs of my thighs, and drifted upward until they stopped on my behind. Valentin gasped as I shifted to lie over his chest, my flesh to his flesh.

I felt him harden underneath me, and heat pooled between my thighs. Valentin sucked in a sharp breath. "Zoya," he moaned as I laid my cheek on his chest.

My arms wrapped around his thick and toned waist, and I listened for minutes as his heartbeat decelerated from fast to slow. When he had calmed, his hand ran through my hair and he said quietly, "I never knew touching a female could be enjoyed, until I touched you. I never knew if I could ever block out that bitch's schoolings, until I touched you."

Lifting my head, I traced my finger over my lips and said, "I never knew a kiss could be stolen, until you."

Valentin's eyes flared, and stroking my cheek with his finger he said, "I never thought I could be a thief of the first kiss, until you."

I stilled. Among all the heavy and sad talk, a laugh burst from my lips. Valentin watched me; then, unable to resist, a gruff rumble came from his chest.

"Come here!" he ordered. Doing as he bid, I climbed up his body. He cupped my cheeks and said, "Soon, I will steal another kiss."

Dropping my smile, I tipped my head to the side and said, "I think I would be happy if you stole all of my kisses."

"You don't mean that," Valentin said sharply, his humor evaporating and a darkness taking hold.

"I do mean that," I argued. "I mean it with everything I am."

"I am your torturer. I have brought you pain."

"Yet here I am, revealing exactly who I am. And you are still here, too."

Valentin studied my face, then threatened, "I could still use the knowledge I have gained to complete my hit." His hands ran down to my neck and held it in his hands. "I could still kill you. My orders are to kill you before I leave this chamber. Did you guess that, little Georgian?"

A moment of fear held me in its grip. But confident in my instincts, I said, "But you will not." I left Valentin's hands wrapped around my neck. With a pained sigh, he released his hands and looked away. I could sense the war he was fighting deep inside. "Talk to me. What is it?" I pushed.

Without looking my way, he said, "I have to complete the hit, I have to return, or Mistress will harm Inessa. Master, Mistress's brother and the man that runs the Blood Pit—controls all of us. He wants my sister for himself."

Ice coated my heart. "Wants her for what?"

Defeat leaked from Valentin's rigid posture, and he said, "When Inessa reached the age of fourteen, things changed too for her. At fourteen her lessons changed from domestic to something much worse. They began giving her different drugs, the drugs that made her sexually dependent. Mistress made me watch her being trained by older women in ways to pleasure men. Then she made me sit and watch my sister's innocence being taken by that male who had given me the drugs. After that, it became my sister's life—a sexual slave to anyone Mistress wanted to grant favors to, or who paid her for my sister's time. At times, even Mistress would take her, to ensure I remained obedient."

"Valentin," I whispered, and hugged him tightly.

"I am to bring your brother back after torturing him, so Mistress can claim the kill. If I don't, Mistress will send Inessa back to Georgia, back to the Blood Pit, straight into Master's arms."

"What is the Blood Pit?" I asked in trepidation. "What happens there, besides rearing children to be monsters?"

"Fighting. Death-match fighting. It is the ultimate death ring. Master makes his money through the gambling. He runs secret underground gulags all over the world. Every few months he brings the champions to the Blood Pit to check who is the most brutal death-match fighter."

I sat up, a sickening feeling stirring in my stomach. Valentin saw me move. Looking into his eyes, I said, "You can't take Zaal from me. I live to find him, once more to be with him. I was about to knock on his door when you stole me off the street."

I heard the trembling of my voice. But I was desperate.

"Shh." This time Valentin soothed me and, with his hand on my wrists, brought my chest back to his. He wrapped me in his arms and said, "I will not kill your brother. He is your Inessa."

My body melted against Valentin's and my eyes began to close. I never spoke anymore, nor did he. What else was there to say? He needed to save his sister and I needed to save my brother. I had no idea how we would progress from this mess, but right now we both needed rest. I was content to lie in his arms.

I was content to comfort the monster.

Because this monster deserved my care.

He needed to be loved.

By me.

I was ripped from Zaal's arms by the guard. I screamed and held out my arms for my sykhaara *to save me. But a guard was holding him back. He was shouting, his green eyes wide as he tried to get back to me. I looked to Anri, who also was fighting to get back, but neither could get free.*

The guard put me on the floor. I tried to run, but my grandmama kept hold of my shoulder. I stopped when I felt her cold hand shaking. I glanced up at her. Grandmama's face was white.

Hearing a scream, I turned my head and saw the man, Levan Jakhua, forcing my twin brothers to face us. I sought out the rest of my family. We were lined up against the wall.

I frowned, but I didn't know what was happening. Then I heard my mama sniff. My papa put his hand on her shoulder. I heard her whisper, "They are going to kill us all, but my boys. Baby, they're going to kill us all." My papa didn't say anything in response, but I was scared. I was so scared.

I looked back to the Jakhua man. I wanted Zaal; I knew he would save me. I moved my foot to run toward him. Just as I did, loud noises filled the air like cracks of thunder. I screamed at the sound; then something hit me in my shoulder. I tried to cry out as hot pain sliced down my arm. Then something else hit my waist, and something else went into my hip. My vision blurred and blurred, until I fell to the floor. I tried to get up, I tried to scream, but someone fell on top of me. I couldn't move, I was cold, so so cold, then something choked my lungs, and everything faded to black—

I gasped awake, but someone was holding me in his arms. Cold was seeping into my bones, but strong arms were warming me up. They rocked me back and forth, and the scent of dark spices filled my nostrils, adding to the warmth. Painful memories began to fade, then completely disappeared when a soft pair of crystal blue eyes moved before me.

"Valentin," I said through a tight throat.

"You were sleeping," he said, and rubbed at my arms. "You were screaming. You were screaming for someone to save you, then saying you couldn't breathe."

Water filled my eyes, like it always did when this nightmare struck. I went to lift my hand to wipe the tears away, but Valentin beat me to it. We had been resting and healing for four days. And every day, we would tell each other a little more about ourselves. He told me of his life with a drug-addicted mother, then his and Inessa's life in the orphanage. My blood chilled when he spoke of the Night Wraiths that would come every few months for the children—the Georgians that bought the children from the orphanage to add to their death-match or sex slave pits.

I told him about my years in hiding. My years of never leaving my house. My days reading and learning how to fight torture if our enemies ever found me.

Valentin told me he was proud of me. He called me his kitten, his little *kotyonok*. It never failed to make me feel safe.

"*Kotyonok,* are you okay?" Valentin pushed, but I wasn't. My body needed to feel alive. After remembering the thick scent and heavy feel of death, I needed him in my arms more than ever.

I wanted him to take me. I wanted him to make me his, all his.

Valentin's hands were still on my arms. I glanced up at his neck. The holes from the collar were closed. The skin was still sore and tender, but he was healing, and he was strong. Since he removed the collar from his neck, since the drugs had left his system, the color of his skin had returned to a natural tone. And his ripped and broad body was fit and strong.

I needed him more than I needed to breathe.

I saw no reason for us to wait.

"Kotyonok?" Valentin asked again. Looking into his concerned blue eyes, I lifted my hand and ran it down his chest, straight to the bottom of his abdominals. My skin flushed as I felt the hard muscle ripple beneath my touch. An involuntary hiss escaped through his clenched teeth.

Valentin's hands dropped from my arms, and he sat back on his haunches. He watched as I rose to my knees, edging closer, to slowly lean in and press my lips to the center of his chest.

"Zoya," he said through a thick tight throat. But I stayed silent. I moved up his body, my warm breath causing his fair skin to bump in my wake. Reaching the bottom of his neck, I glanced down to see his manhood hard and stiff against his stomach. Heat built in my core. Feeling overcome with the need for this man, I leaned in and licked under the permanent scar on Valentin's neck, the scar that years and years of wearing the metal collar had caused.

Valentin's body stilled. I heard him trying to control his hard breathing. I saw his hands clench into fists by his sides. But as I laid a final kiss on the side of his neck I heard a strangled groan rip from his throat as he pushed me back on the mattress.

In seconds, Valentin was crawling over my body, towering over me with his huge size. His eyes were lit with hunger as he stared at my lips. I licked along the seams of my lips as my hands lifted to lightly stroke down his waist. Valentin's neck tensed, and he said roughly, "I'm going to steal another kiss."

A wave of heat crashed over me and I replied, "Good." Valentin went to move in when I stopped him with a hand on his chest.

He immediately stilled and frowned. "Zoya?" he questioned.

Swallowing back any nerves trying to creep into my heart, I said, "I want this with you." Lifting my head to move into his personal space, I added, "I want you, Valentin, to steal the rest of me."

The muscles on Valentin's shoulders bunched, and on a loud roar he crushed his lips to mine. His mouth was hot and searing, and I gripped the hard muscles of his back with my desperate hands.

He groaned low as he pushed his tongue between my lips, immediately dueling against mine. My hand lifted from his back and wrapped around his neck, trying to pull him even closer. I needed him as close as he could get. I wanted him to feel wanted. I wanted him to feel loved.

Valentin's hard body pressed down on mine. As we did not once break from the kiss his thick thigh nudged my legs apart.

My head snapped back at the feel of his length running against my core. My nails dug into the hard flesh of his shoulders. But Valentin's attention never wavered. His mouth pressed kiss after kiss to my cheek and jaw. His hips rolled, pushing himself farther between my legs. A deep flush overtook my body. Valentin's tongue slipped from between his lips, and he began licking at my neck, a hungry rumble echoing in his chest.

Shivers ran down my spine, before splintering apart and chasing through my veins. My hands moved to hold on to his shaven head, the rough feel of his black stubble tickling my palm.

His mouth ravaged my neck, nipping and grazing his teeth against my flushed skin. "Valentin," I cried, my hips beginning to roll in search of the release that was building in my thighs.

Valentin broke from my neck and dragged the tip of his nose over my cheek, until he hovered just above me. His blue eyes were sparkling in need. As our gazes met, we stilled, suspended, just staring at each other.

Valentin's hot breath blew in short pants over my face. My hand fell to cup his beautifully scarred face. "You are so beautiful," I found myself confessing.

Valentin's nostrils flared and he leaned down to press three sweet soft kisses on my cheek. "I am not beautiful," he replied. "I am scarred and worn. An ugly beast."

Turning my face to his cheek, I kissed the skin just below his ear, watching as the skin grew bumps at my touch. "I decide who and what I think holds beauty, and Valentin, you do in my eyes." Valentin's body was still with tension, so I brushed my mouth past his ear and declared, "My beautiful monster."

I had licked over the curve of Valentin's ear when, on a strained moan, he placed his hand on my jaw and turned my face to meet his. Full lips kissed mine in quick and ravaging caresses; then he moved down my neck until he reached my chest. Valentin shifted down my body, his strong rough hands heating my skin. He palmed my breasts and licked at my nipples as their flesh hardened, yearning for his touch.

My eyes fluttered shut, and I pulled on the back of Valentin's head, wanting him to take me harder and faster, the feel of his mouth on me reaching every cell. He was possessing me, owning me, and I had never felt more alive.

His teeth pulled at my nipple, the sensation shooting straight between my legs. His mouth moved to the next breast, and my head rolled on the mattress. It was too much, the feel of this rough and dangerous man, this born killer, this assassin, taking my body as his own.

Then he dipped lower.

Valentin's tongue traced down over my torso, until it reached the bottom of my stomach. Valentin ran the tip of his tongue back and forth over where my short hairs began. I writhed on the bed, and cried out in shock when I felt the wetness of his tongue dip to the creases of my thighs.

Valentin growled and, lifting his head, his eyes intent on mine, asked, "Are you sure?" My heart melted, knowing he didn't want to push me.

"Yes."

Valentin licked along his lips, never breaking his gaze, then with his hands on my inner thighs pushed them apart. I shivered in anticipation of him touching me so intimately. Touching me so intimately with my consent, not as my torturer, but as the man who understood my soul.

Then, to my shock, Valentin lowered until his broad shoulders were between my thighs, the hot breath from his mouth washing over my most sensitive part. My eyelids fluttered, trying to shut at the feel of him so close to me, but I fought to make them stay open, to watch him making me his.

Valentin's attention was solely on my core. His teeth had gritted together as though he was fighting hard to hold back. My chest tightened when I saw his hips pushing into the mattress.

He was as lost to this moment as I.

Valentin moved his hand, and I cried out as his finger ran through my folds. He teased and teased until I squirmed for him to touch me more. "Valentin," I whispered as he kissed the inside of my thigh.

"You're so wet," he said, his voice low and husky with need. "So fucking beautiful." He laid another kiss to my inner thigh, only closer to my center this time, the feeling causing my skin to blaze with fire.

"Valentin, please," I begged, unsure what I was asking for. Instinct was driving me, pleading for this man to touch me.

My hips lifted, and as they did, Valentin groaned, slipping his hands below to grip my behind, and he smashed his mouth against my core. I screamed, my back arching off the mattress as his hot tongue circled my entrance.

My fingers searched to find purchase, but his hair was too short. Instead my nails scraped across his scalp, the action causing Valentin's hands to grip my behind even harder, pushing me farther into his mouth.

I moaned and moaned at the new sensation wrapping me in its

hold, but nothing prepared me for the feel of Valentin's tongue flicking over me. As his tongue brushed past the bundle of nerves, I jerked and my back lifted off the mattress.

My hands fought to push Valentin away, the feel of him licking me there too much to stand. But the killer within him rose from the ashes. The assassin, the dominant monster, took control and with a strong hand pressed on my chest. The strength of his hand pushed me back to the mattress, the action keeping me pinned to the bed as the flat of his tongue slowly and teasingly lapped against me.

My arms spread out, my hands gripping the edges of the bed just for something to hold on to. My body was alight. He was setting me on fire.

Then his tongue moved faster, his hand on my chest gaining in strength, pinning me down. Moan after long moan issued from my lips as his mouth devoured my core. Valentin shifted his body, his wide shoulders keeping my legs spread apart. His tongue never paused as he moved his position. He withdrew his hands from my behind, and I screamed when I felt his finger circle my entrance, before slowly pushing inside.

"Valentin!" I screamed, and fought for breath at the dual sensation of his tongue and finger working in tandem, lifting me higher and higher.

Lights flashed behind my closed eyes. Like lightning, I felt a burst of heat shoot through my veins, bringing with it the most intense heat. And I burst apart; I screamed as pleasure filled my every part, my chest pushing against Valentin's rigid hold. My body bucked and strained until I couldn't take any more. But Valentin never stopped. He groaned as he lapped at my flesh, but I was too sensitive, my body needing a break.

"Valentin," I whispered, my thighs shaking against his shoulder as my body struggled to calm down. "Valentin," I pushed again, and laid my hand over his on my chest. I squeezed at his hand and felt his tongue slow. He lapped at and circled my clit, then slowly pulled his finger from my channel. I gasped for breath as the sensations heating me from within began to cool. But Valentin's thorough tongue lazily licked at my wetness, his soft lips kissing at my core, filling my heart with light.

Minutes and minutes passed by as he caressed my center. My back flattened against the mattress as my hand held on to his, still on my chest. My legs fell to the side, too weak to move. My eyes were closed, and I was sure I could stay like this forever. This, the aftermath of the pleasure, the man I craved most bringing me down and worshipping me. Making me feel alive.

I had survived the massacre that took my family, but lying here, I realized that the years spent away in hiding I was simply existing.

And it took a monster to revive my heart. It took a killer to touch my soul.

Peppering kisses along my folds, Valentin then turned his face to my thighs before finally lifting his head. As his eyes met mine, my heart lurched and my face flushed. Valentin sat back on his ankles, and my attention dropped to his hard long length jutting against his stomach. The tip glistened.

Valentin wiped across his mouth with his arm, then moved forward, planting his hands at my sides. Valentin crawled forward, looking every inch the dark, dangerous predator he was. His muscled inked body, spattered with scars and marks, engulfed mine. I tried to control my breathing. As he stalked me, I tried to cool my blood. But this man hovered over me in silence, hunting his prey. My heart raced and my chest seized with anticipation.

His expression had changed. I could see that taking me in his mouth had triggered something carnal and dark within him. Yet I wasn't afraid. I wanted him like this.

I liked him needing me like this.

Valentin's hands stopped beside my head. Still he remained

silent. The air in the room was still and heavy as he stared down at me. His cut and ripped muscles tensed and rippled as he held his large frame over me. I shivered and shook under his scrutiny, yet my skin burned with need.

My lips parted and I released a pent-up breath, Valentin's jaw clenching as I did so. The static pulsed and crackled between us; then, as he lowered his torso, his heavily muscled thighs pushed mine open until I could not spread them anymore.

Valentin's chest met mine, and his arms caged my head on the mattress.

I was trapped.

I was held captive.

I was *alive.*

Reaching down, Valentin's warm breath ghosting over my skin, I suddenly felt him at my entrance. My heart kicked into a sprint as he ran his broad wet tip up and down my folds. I swallowed at the sheer size of him. I wasn't sure I could take him.

The silence of the room, and the lack of words coming from Valentin, only added to the nerves, topping up the tension. My chest was coiled as I waited for him to push forward. Just as I feared I could not do this, Valentin suddenly lowered his mouth to mine, and he pressed a soft and gentle kiss to my lips.

I whimpered. Just like that, I was calmed. Valentin reared back, but only by an inch. His eyes still bored into mine and no words were spoken, but he moved forward, the head of his hardness pushing into me.

I sucked in a sharp breath at this new feeling. My hands slapped against the heavily defined biceps on Valentin's arms. His jaw was tense, and he scarcely breathed as he slowly pushed forward again.

Air whooshed from my lungs as he pushed farther inside. Pain began to build, and as he continued to move I was sure he could not fit. I wasn't sure I could take him . . . the pain.

I squeezed my eyes shut as he filled me, and filled me, my nails digging into the skin on his arms. Then they snapped back open when, on a long thrust, he filled me to the hilt. I cried out. Valentin's strong arms shook as he held up his torso.

A fast burst of breath rushed from his mouth, an echo of a growl in his throat. My forehead was damp as I tried to bear the pain. Then Valentin moved, his hips pulling back until only the tip of his length remained within me. I froze as he began pushing forward once again, only this time, as Valentin pushed himself within me, the pain dulled and, in its place, a shiver of pleasure ran through my veins.

A surprised moan left my lips. My eyes that were fixed like glue on Valentin's then dropped down between us, and I could feel myself get wet at the sight that greeted me. Valentin's stomach rolled with the movement of his hips, and every time it did I caught sight of him pushing within my core, my skin flushing at this erotic sight.

Valentin's breathing suddenly changed. His long controlled breaths quickened in pace. His fair skin flushed under the dark stubble coating his face. His eyes became leaden as his hips began to thrust faster and faster.

"Valentin," I whispered almost inaudibly. Valentin hissed at his name on my lips. His large arms caging my head closed in, until he was all I could see, all I could feel—within me, around me. The warmth from his skin scalded my flesh, and the low raspy groans beginning to claw from his throat ignited a fire in my blood.

Valentin thrust harder. At the heady feel of his length dragging against something within my channel, something that I knew on instinct I craved, my hips moved too, rolling in conjunction with his.

A loud moan poured from Valentin and his body jerked. "Fuck," he bit, and lowered his mouth until his lips brushed against mine. He never kissed me, just left his soft mouth teasing me. But at the same time my heart stuttered at his closeness.

That now-familiar pressure of pleasure began to build inside me, traveling down to my thighs. My eyes widened at the feel, and I realized it was nothing like the pleasure Valentin had given me before. This was different; this felt very different.

Valentin's thrusts were fast and strong, the pace of him pushing inside of me bringing me to the brink of an unknown precipice. Moving my hands, I wrapped them around Valentin's neck and felt every second of our joining, of our hips fighting for the pleasure that was now within sight. Hot shivers accosted my skin and my heart beat too fast. Crying out as a spark of intense heat spiked within me, I pressed my forehead against Valentin's forehead and whispered his name.

A choked groan was my response and Valentin held me closer, his hips now frantic and out of control as he slammed within me. "Valentin," I whispered again, and again, and again, until a wave crested within me, suspending me in the moment, before crashing through my body holding me captive to the pleasure possessing me. I distantly heard myself screaming out, clutching on to Valentin as if my body feared I would fall were I not to hold him close.

Valentin stiffened. With a thunderous cry, he came within me, the feeling of his seed filling my channel, causing yet another moan to escape my mouth. Glancing up, I watched Valentin's face. His eyes were squeezed shut, his lips were pulled tight, and his jaw was clenched shut. His fair skin was flushed with the force of his release. As if feeling my stare, he snapped his eyes open and set free his held breath.

Panting, his hot skin glistening with sweat, he fell forward, tucking his face into the crook of my neck. Tipping my head back, to allow myself to breathe, my hands ran down to Valentin's broad back, my palm and fingers sliding on his slick skin.

At my touch, his length jerked within me, his skin twitching as it did.

I felt full. I felt so full and complete. So complete that tears burned in my eyes. This man above me. This man, inhaling my scent and possessing my body, was also possessing my heart.

I relaxed into the mattress, just holding Valentin close. Eventually, when he lifted his head, his dark features appeared sinful against his flushed skin. But his crystal blue eyes stood out like stars in a night sky.

And he watched me.

He never took his intense gaze off me.

I blushed under his attention, until he lowered his hand to run his fingers down my cheek. I waited for him to speak, I waited for him to say something, but he didn't. Instead, with his finger under my chin, he tipped my head up and fused his lips to mine.

This kiss was slow and unhurried. This kiss was soft and consuming. And this kiss told me without words how this beautiful monster was feeling inside—content.

His tongue invaded my mouth, and as it gently slipped against mine I tasted myself. My body simmered in the aftermath, at the effect of this sweet kiss. We kissed and kissed for I don't know how long. When Valentin finally broke away, I knew something between us had switched.

He was no longer the torturer.

I was no longer his victim.

Valentin's forehead rested against mine, and inhaling a shaky breath he confessed, "I feel alive." I stilled at these heartbreaking words; then he added, "I feel like yours."

My eyes pricked with water and I encased him in my embrace. "Valentin," I said in a hushed voice. "Not only have you claimed my first kiss; you have claimed my innocence." I took a deep breath knowing I needed to say the words waiting on the tip of my tongue and whispered directly into his ear, "And you have claimed my soul."

"Zoya," Valentin groaned in response, and reared back to look at my face. There was a momentary expression of happiness; then it faded, to be defeated by an expression of pain. "I'm not worthy of this. I'm a killer."

As I tilted my head, my heart sank at these expressions of self-deprecation. "No, Valentin, you're simply . . . you," I countered.

Valentin pushed his lips against mine in a searing kiss, then slid to the side, his length falling from within me. I gasped at the sudden loss of fullness but felt replete when Valentin scooped me into his strong arms and pulled me to his chest.

A happy silence passed between us, until my finger traced the tattooed "194" emblazoned on his chest. I stared at the tattoo, and our reality came crashing back. Feeling a stab of dread piercing through my heart, I said, "As much as I hate this chamber of hell, right now I think I would trade my soul if we could stay in here forever."

Valentin stiffened beside me and, holding me closer to his side, confided, "For the first time in my life, I have no idea what to do next. I've wished to never be commanded again. Now I have freedom, I have no idea what to do with it."

Sadness filled me when I knew he was thinking about the safety of his sister. About what would be her fate if he didn't capture my brother. Throat tightening, I said, "I cannot let you hurt Zaal. But by the same token, I cannot bear for you to lose your Inessa."

A pained sound came from Valentin, and holding me close, he replied, "I do not know what to do, *kotyonok*. My entire existence has been to save my sister, but now . . . ," he trailed off.

"But now there is me," I finished for him. I felt him nod and said, "My entire life, I have waited to see my brothers again . . ." This time I trailed off my sentence.

"And now there is me," Valentin finished for me.

"Yes."

Shifting on the bed, I lifted to lie over Valentin's huge body and glanced at the floor, lost in thought. But then my eyes found the collar, still abandoned on the black tiled floor. I saw Zaal in my mind. I saw him smiling with the Tolstaia girl and hope sprang in my chest.

"Valentin," I said, the names *Tolstaia* and *Volkov* circling my head. When I looked back to Valentin, he was waiting for me to speak. Pushing my hair back from my face, I said, "My brother, Zaal." I paused, staring into Valentin's blue eyes, searching for the reassurance that I could tell him this in his face. All I saw was sincerity and his heart staring back. Edging closer, I said, "My brother, Zaal Kostava, is marrying a Tolstaia. My brother, the *Lideri* of the Kostava Clan, is marrying into the Volkov Bratva."

Valentin's eyes flared; then his eyebrows pulled down in confusion. His lips pulled tight, and when he looked at me again he said, "I think I know this name, Volkov. They are Russian? The crime family?"

I nodded and sat up further, excitement taking hold. "My brother, my *sykhaara,* he could help us. With the collar no longer causing you to black out if we left this place, he could help us. They could help us rescue your Inessa."

Valentin's expression didn't change, until he exhaled a breath and asked dubiously, "You think he *would* help us?"

Taking hold of Valentin's hand, I said, "I know he will. He is a good man, and he is living among the most powerful family on the East Coast."

I paused and asked, "Is your Mistress here in New York? Is Inessa here, too?"

Valentin nodded. "Mistress brings her everywhere with us but keeps her separate from me. The only time Inessa was away was this past year when Mistress gave her to the man that she was a slave to for years. They had a strange relationship. Mistress would fuck me and he wouldn't care. He would fuck my sister; she wouldn't care.

Mistress would tie me to a chair and make me watch. That is why we are here in New York. He was recently killed. Mistress ordered a hit on Zaal Kostava in revenge for her losing her true love."

I frowned. "Why would she want revenge on my brother?"

"I don't know. I just get ordered to kill."

Squeezing Valentin's hand, I said, "We must go."

Valentin didn't move, and I worried that he would refuse. But he sat up from the mattress and pulled me from the bed. "We must cleanse; then I have your clothes. We can be at the house I took you from in less than an hour."

My heart raced in excitement as we showered. When we were both clean, Valentin led me to a back room and handed me my clothes. We dressed quickly, Valentin all in black. His hood pulled over his head made him look every inch the thief I knew him to be.

Reaching down, Valentin took my hand and paused to say, "You believe this can work?" His voice cracked when he added, "I cannot have Inessa suffer for my weakness."

Stepping closer, I rose to my tiptoes and gave him a kiss on his cheek. "It will work, Valentin. My brother was an honorable boy, I have no doubt he is an honorable man."

Valentin nodded his head. He guided us to a large steel door. I nervously rocked on my feet as I waited for the damn thing to open. When the last lock unlatched, Valentin swung open the door and pulled us forward, only to be halted in his tracks when someone stood in his path.

Jarred by the sudden stop, I felt Valentin stiffen, all his muscles tense. I peeked around his shoulder, and all the blood ran from my body when I noticed an older woman dressed all in black, her face stern and cold. Behind her were several large men, all dressed in black. In an instant I knew it was the Wraiths, Valentin's Georgian captors. They were as frightening as their name suggested.

My eyes fell to the woman once more. She was glaring at me. My skin chilled, and pushing me behind him Valentin gritted his teeth and hissed out . . .

"Mistress."

15

LUKA

"You look so handsome, *lyubov moya*."

I smiled at my wife as she stood before me tying my tie, then straightening out my suit. She had gone to move from the view of the mirror when I stopped her with my hand. Kisa dropped her head, and my head tipped to the side. "You are worried?" I asked. No question was really needed; I knew my *solnyshko* more than I knew myself.

Kisa gazed off across the room. "They hate us." Her light blue eyes met mine. "They will especially hate you. You're a Tolstoi. Your name alone brings instant disrespect and possibly violence to tonight."

Cupping Kisa's face, I said, "I understand why you're worried, *solnyshko,* but I won't be hurt tonight. Besides, if one of the fuckers tried, I'd kill them where they stood."

Kisa sighed and gripped my wrists. "I know; it's just . . . ," she trailed off.

Moving her head forward, I made her meet my eyes. "It's just what?"

Kisa's hand dropped to her growing stomach, and she said,

"I understand you're the *knyaz*. Believe me, as daughter of the Pakhan, I know this. And I know you're Raze also. This is our life, and I have been bred for it. But when I got you back, I did not expect all of this." Kisa sighed, then continued, "I love Zaal. I would even if it was for no other reason than to make Talia happy. But now Zaal's sister has been taken. It's just that I have this awful feeling there is more still to come. Nothing about this entire situation feels right. And, well—" Kisa's face paled, but she said, "I feel like I've just gotten you back, and now we're having a baby." She took a deep breath. "I cannot imagine my life without you, *lyubov moya*. I have lived through losing you once; there is no way I could survive it twice."

Feeling my heart fucking swell, I took Kisa in my arms and pulled her to my chest. Kisa tried to pull away. "Luka, your suit."

I kept her close. "I couldn't give a fuck about my suit. I do give a shit about my wife, my pregnant wife, being upset." Kisa melted into my chest, and her arms wrapped around my waist.

I kissed her on her head and said, "I can tell you right now, *solnyshko*. Nothing, not even hell itself, will take me from you." I kissed her again and added, "All of this, I'm doing it so our life can be good. And I'm doing this for Zaal, so he can find his sister and get someone from his family back in his life." Bringing Kisa back so I could see her face, I said, "And I'm doing this so that when I inherit the role of Pakhan we are strong, and we have the right people around us. My life is you. My entire life is you and our baby. And I'm going to do everything I can to make this Bratva, this family, the best thing I've ever done." Kisa nodded. "*Solnyshko,* no one will touch me tonight. Our *byki* will be there in force, and even if they weren't, I can handle myself."

Kisa inhaled, then looked up at me through her fucking doe eyes, her mouth spreading into a huge smile. The air was knocked out of my lungs at how fucking beautiful she was. Edging closer, she re-straightened the lapels on my suit and moved aside to stand behind me. My reflection stared back at me. I was dressed head to toe in a black suit, my white shirt and red tie perfectly in place thanks to my wife.

Kisa disappeared. When she reappeared, she was holding out my cashmere long coat. She held it out and slipped it on my shoulders, and when it was on she slipped something heavy in each pocket.

I kept her eyes trapped in the reflection of the mirror and reached into my pocket. I smirked and pulled out my bladed knuckle-dusters. I raised my eyebrows at my wife and she shrugged. "Take them for me, baby. I've seen what you can do with those things. It would make me feel better if I knew you had them at the ready."

Laughing, I turned to my wife and crashed my lips to hers. Pulling back, fighting my cock hardening in my pants, I said, "When I'm back, you're mine."

Kisa brushed my hair back from my forehead and whispered into my ear, "I'm always yours."

My lips found hers again. Groaning, I carefully pushed Kisa back against the wall, capturing her moan in my mouth. My hands reached down and lifted up her dress, just as a voice called from downstairs, "Mr. Tolstoi, Mr. Kostava is here."

As I sagged against Kisa's shoulder, she pushed me back. My jaw had clenched at being interrupted when my wife laughed and kissed me on the cheek. She had moved toward the bedroom when I ordered roughly, "Be ready for me when I get back!"

Kisa's face flushed red, and she said, "Always, *lyubov moya*."

I raced down the stairs and out into the cold night air. The driver held open the back door of the limo, and when I slipped in Zaal was already sitting opposite me, dressed in a monkey suit like me, his long hair tied back in a bun. The brother had been a nuclear bomb since we heard his sister had been taken.

As the car began to roll away, I asked, "You ready for this?"

Zaal exhaled and replied, "It is who I am. I am the Kostava *Lideri*. It is time my people had their dignity restored."

The isolated warehouse at the Brooklyn docks was surrounded by our *byki,* hidden away in the shadows. Zaal and I got out of the car, Mikhail, my head *byki,* and Otto, Zaal's, falling into step at our sides.

We approached the rear of the metal building; the area around us was derelict and run-down, a wasteland of dirt and filth.

As we reached the doors, a small man came running from the old wooden entrance. Avto. The old man scurried forward, holding his flat cap in his hands. Part of me wanted to allow Zaal to take the lead, but whether Zaal liked it or not, he was part of the Bratva now. The people inside, and any man who followed Zaal's leadership, had to know that the *knyaz* and Pakhan would be in every part of their lives.

"Avto," I greeted. Avto's eyes left Zaal and focused on me. *"Knyaz,"* he replied coldly, then focused back on Zaal.

"*Lideri*"—Avto swallowed, and shook his head—"I'm sorry, but as you stand here, you look just like your father." Avto had spoken in Georgian.

Zaal tensed but then asked, "Are they all here?"

Avto nodded his head. "Yes, *Lideri.* Just under two hundred men."

I nodded my head and said to Zaal, "That shows loyalty." Avto swallowed when I too spoke in Georgian. I glared at the little man, and in that same Georgian I said, "Lead the way."

Avto turned and hurried toward the entrance. As we walked through the doors and down a dusty hallway, I said, "Remember the housing offer. We will need your men close. It will give you time and a chance to see who is most loyal. Who to bring into your inner circle."

Zaal nodded his head, then smirked my way. "You are sounding very much like Kirill, Luka. If I had closed my eyes, I think you could have fooled me into thinking he was beside me."

I smiled and hit Zaal on the back. Holding out his hand, he stopped me and, only to me, said, "I was trained for the role, just as you were. I will never break my loyalty to the Bratva. I love my Talia too much to ever do that—"

"But?" I interrupted.

Zaal shook his head, smiling again. "But I am the Kostava *Lideri*. I will lead my people. Just as you will lead yours. And we make the decisions for our people together."

Narrowing my eyes, I held out my hand. Zaal immediately shook it, and we commenced walking. We had only moved a few steps before I said, "You just sounded very much like Anri. If I had closed my eyes, you could've fooled me into thinking he was back beside me."

Zaal sighed, but I saw the flash of pain in his eyes. "He was my brother. My twin. As much as I, he was meant for this moment."

We walked together in silence. We stopped as Avto slipped through the archway into the main body of the warehouse. Zaal squared his shoulders, and with a firm nod to me and the *byki* he entered the warehouse.

I followed close behind Zaal. I watched with assessing eyes as his people came into view. Many older men stood in the abandoned space, but there were also a lot of younger men, young strong men who had been brought up well by their fathers. In seconds Zaal rounded the corner; their faces expressed their shock at seeing their *Lideri*. I stopped, Mikhail standing beside me, and let Zaal take the floor. He walked past his people, his huge frame towering above them.

My gaze wandered to Avto, who was standing back, watching Zaal take his place at the front of the crowd. Avto's eyes were filled with tears, and even though he hated me, I felt sorry for the man.

From what I could gather, Zoya, Zaal's sister, was important to Avto. His entire life had been pledged to her protection.

A protection that had now failed.

The men all stared at Zaal. Many of the men bowing their heads in a show of respect. Zaal took a deep breath and, raising his head high, said, "Thank you for attending this meeting tonight." He spoke in Georgian, and the people all began to smile. Finally, they knew their *Lideri* had returned.

Murmurs swept the group, many of the men expressing their happiness at him being alive.

Zaal held up his hand, and the men stopped talking. "As you can see, I, Zaal Kostava, of the Kostava Clan, am alive. Levan Jakhua took my twin brother and me captive years ago. I am sorry to say that Anri did not survive." The men all bowed their heads in disappointment and respect for Anri's memory.

"In fact," Zaal continued, "up until this week I believed I was the only survivor of my family. I now know that is not true. My sister, Zoya, will be known to many of you. Many of you will have helped her escape with Avto as a child, and I know many of you have followed her to New York to continue her protection. For that you have my utmost gratitude."

Zaal ran a hand down his face. "Many of you already know that Zoya has been taken, and as yet we have no leads as to who did this. We do, however, know there are Georgians in this city that shouldn't be here. Right now, we suspect they have my sister, and we must get her back."

The men began murmuring to one another, stirred by Zaal's words. My brother glanced back at me, and I nodded my head. Mikhail talked into the communication device on his suit, preparing the *byki* to move in if anything went down.

"I am the Kostava *Lideri*. I intend to lead you once again. If you pledge your loyalty to me, there is housing waiting for you and jobs for you to take up immediately. You will no longer have to live in hiding. And you will all become rich men."

Smiles broke out on the men's faces, but Zaal held up his hand. "What many of you do not know, however, is that I am engaged to be married." Zaal paused at mention of his engagement. I watched Avto, who was fiddling with his cap. I straightened, pushing my hands into my pockets, slipping the cold steel of my knuckle-dusters over my fingers. I braced, ready for trouble, should trouble arise.

"I am engaged to a female called Talia Tolstaia." Zaal spoke my sister's name proudly. I smiled, knowing that the brother would put her before anyone else. This time, no smiles greeted his words. Instead the men began to look at one another, many showing anger on their faces.

"Talia is the daughter of Ivan Tolstoi, granddaughter of Matvei Tolstoi, of the Russian Bratva kings. They are our long-standing enemy. I understand that many of you will not understand how I could marry the granddaughter of the man our people were conditioned to hate. But know this: The Tolstois saved me from Jakhua." Zaal looked to me and flicked his chin. I walked forward, pulling the attention of the crowd. With my head held high, I stood by Zaal's side.

"This is Luka Tolstoi. He is the *knyaz* of the Bratva, and the brother of my fiancée." Zaal dropped his hand, and added. "He too is now my brother." My hands curled in my pockets as some of the men shook their heads.

"Luka Tolstoi saved my life, and thus I have pledged my loyalty to the Bratva. If you pledge to me, know that you also will be pledging yourselves to the Bratva. It is they who are providing the housing at Brighton Beach, and it is they who will help us find Zoya, and bring our *dis,* our taken sister, safely back home."

Zaal stepped forward. With arms folded, he said, "If you cannot join me and make peace with the fact that our grudge against the Bratva has ended, then you are not welcome here. If you cannot live under my new ways, then you can leave, right now."

The room was silent as the men looked to one another. One by one the men knelt, showing their allegiance to Zaal. When all the men, bar two, had expressed their loyalty, Zaal stepped forward. Otto rushed forward and took the men by the arms, lining them up against the wall.

They held their heads high as Zaal stopped before them. "You will not pledge?" Zaal asked. As he finished, one of the two older men spat at his feet.

"You disgrace your father's name marrying that Russian whore! It is because of them that your family was killed. The Bratva cast us aside and let Jakhua destroy us." He leaned forward. "You will never be the *Lideri* your father was."

Blood boiled in my veins as that fucker called Talia a whore, but just as I fought to rein in my anger Zaal lunged forward, snapping each of the men's necks in seconds. The dead bodies fell to the floor. Breathing hard, Zaal faced the gathering. "Anyone else feel this way? Does anyone else dare to call my Talia a whore!"

The men stayed bowed on the floor, none of them moving. My muscles jumped at seeing Zaal kill the men. My instinct to shed blood was hard to taper down.

I worked on breathing, releasing the knuckle-dusters from my hands. Zaal walked back through his men. Avto rushed forward, and with Zaal standing at the front each of the men, one by one, came forward and kissed Zaal's hand to pledge his loyalty.

When the last man had bowed at Zaal's feet, Zaal ordered them to gather around closely. I moved beside him. Zaal's body was still tense when he said, "You will have two days to gather your things and move to Brighton Beach. Avto will be given the assignment of houses and place you in your positions of work." The men all nodded.

"Then our priority will be finding my sister. Starting with any information we can find about the Georgians that have recently moved into town."

Zaal had opened his mouth to speak again when a male, about thirty years old, raised his hand. "*Lideri,*" he said timidly, "I currently work here on the docks. My father, who has not long passed, placed us here years ago to watch out for any signs of our enemies. The Jakhuas."

"And?" Zaal pushed.

"I saw Jakhua when he came back last year. He stayed in a house not too far from the docks. I didn't see you, *Lideri,* but I saw him. My cousin"—he pointed to a man across the room—"my cousin works at the airfield, refueling the planes. He was there weeks ago when a private plane landed."

I focused on the cousin and asked, "Who was in it?"

I'd spoken to him in Georgian, and stepping forward the male said, "There was a woman that dressed in all black, with what looked like a private protection of men, dressed in black, too." He shook his head. "But there was also someone else. A hugely built man that was dressed all in black, a hood covering his head. But it was strange. He looked like he was their captive. The men were pushing him by his arms, his wrists cuffed behind his back."

The male shook his head and raised his hand to his throat. "I saw a quick glimpse of his face when he passed. He didn't look Georgian." The male pointed at me. "He looked more Russian, like the *knyaz*. But what was strange was that he had a metal collar around his neck. He had a number of scars that were slashed down and across his face. He was the scariest motherfucker I've ever seen in my life." The male looked to his cousin, then back to us. "His sweatshirt was open, and across his chest he had a tattoo. It was a number, one nine . . . something else. It just all seemed really weird."

My eyes snapped to Zaal, but Zaal was already watching me. I knew what he was thinking. Who the hell was the male? If he had a tattoo, he was a slave to someone. He was one of us. Ice filled my veins when Kisa's words from earlier circled my head: *I have this awful feeling that there is more still to come. Nothing about this entire situation feels right.* Right now I was having the same damn feeling.

Zaal looked to the male who'd first spoken, and said, "Why did you mention Jakhua to me?"

The male's eyes widened, but he explained, "My cousin, before he worked at the airfield, worked with me at the docks. He recognized the woman from the plane, as the woman that would frequently visit Jakhua at the docks."

Zaal's hands balled at his sides. Seeing the brother about to lose it, I flicked my chin to Avto and said, "Take the men away. Have them moved to Brighton Beach as soon as possible."

The men looked confused but left the room following behind Avto. When the door shut, Zaal threw his head back and screamed out. I stood beside him, waiting for him to calm down. Instead he paced.

"A female that knew Jakhua!" he spat, his voice low and rough. "The Pakhan was right. The Jakhuas had someone coming for me, and instead they have taken Zoya. They've taken my fucking sister!" Zaal panted, and his hands ripped open his jacket and he threw it to the floor. He loosened his tie and, turning to the nearest wall, sent his hand plowing through the wood.

"Even from death that cunt is destroying my family!" He stopped, then faced me. "And the slave with a tattooed number across his chest? Who the hell is that? Did Jakhua have more than me? Or does he belong to this female that dresses in black?"

I shrugged. "Jakhua only had you that I knew of. But I didn't know you even existed until months after I was freed. It makes sense that there's more of us still out there in the world."

"And he has Zoya? A trained killer like you and me has my sister!"

Walking forward, I took Zaal by his arms. He stopped, and I said, "We have a lead. We have a description. We have a link to Jakhua. That's something. We take this information. We take my men and your men, and we get our ears to the ground."

Zaal's face contorted, and he said, "She is my little sister. All the blood I have left. Blood I thought I had lost forever."

"I know," I said, and stepped away. "So use that fuel to find this bitch that's taken her from you. Use that anger and fury to tear these newcomers apart."

A cold, dark look spread across Zaal's face, and he held out his hand. "We take them down," he said. "When we find them, it is you and I against them, killing them in the only way we know how."

My blood spiked with fire, and slapping my palm against Zaal's I nodded my head. "We'll slaughter, we'll maim—"

"And we'll fucking kill," Zaal added with a cold smile.

We shook our hands, cementing the deal.

Then we got to work.

16

VALENTIN

I blinked, and blinked again, as Mistress's face snapped away from glaring at Zoya and focused back on mine. Her look at my *kotyonok* sent a wave of possessiveness flooding through my body. I moved directly in her path, blocking Zoya from sight.

Mistress's dark eyes blazed with anger, and her gaze dropped to my neck. Her lips twitched and she lifted her hand to the Wraiths standing behind. "Take him and his whore to the van."

Fear for Zoya took hold as a Wraith reached forward for her and gripped her by the arm. Raising my hand, I balled it into a fist and hit the Wraith's arm. He bit out in pain and withdrew his arm just as Mistress stepped forward with a Taser and slammed it into my neck.

I heard Zoya crying out as I dropped to the ground, my body writhing wildly from the electrical current coursing through it. Fighting to stand, I saw a Wraith take hold of Zoya and easily wrap his arms around her slight waist.

Her fearful face was looking down at me. "Valentin," she cried, only for Mistress to turn in Zoya's direction. Mistress lifted her hand

and sliced it across Zoya's cheek. Pride filled my chest as Zoya didn't cry out; instead she stared Mistress straight in the eyes.

Mistress closed in, and gripping Zoya's face in her gloved hands she hissed, "His name is 194." Mistress's head tipped to the side as she studied Zoya's face.

"So, the Kostava mystery princess has landed in my *Ubiytsa's* chamber?" Mistress smiled and, dropping Zoya's face, said, "My dead lover would be thrilled if he had seen you for himself. He spent years searching for where your father's men had hidden you."

Inhaling a deep breath, I pushed off the cold ground and staggered to my feet. Mistress turned just as I was about to strike. She held the Taser next to Zoya's throat and said, "You move and I'll hurt your little *kotyonok*."

Blood drained from my face.

"What?" Mistress said, and shook her head. "You think I don't have a live feed on you at all times? You don't think I can hear everything you say to your hits in the chambers? I watch you, 194. I watch you closely."

"You fucking bitch!" I snarled. Mistress never even flinched. Turning to the Wraiths, she withdrew the Taser from Zoya's neck and ordered, "Take her to the van!" Mistress glanced back to me. "If this one attacks me, shoot his Kostava whore in the head."

Everything inside of me fought to snap Mistress's neck, but when my eyes tracked the Wraiths carrying a struggling Zoya away, I brushed past the Mistress and followed. Her hand landed on my arm, stopping me dead. She looked at Zoya and at the Wraith carrying her away, then said, "This scene seems familiar, doesn't it, 194? Another female you love being carried away by my men, and you, being forced to watch and let it happen?"

Turning my head to look at her haggard face, I bit, "One day, I'll kill you, and stare into your fucking dead eyes as your rancid face welcomes death."

The Mistress swallowed hard. My body warmed when I realized that I'd scared the bitch. Snapping herself round, she stepped closer and said, "Follow your *little Georgian,* 194. Follow her before the Wraiths hurt her pretty Kostava face."

Rushing forward, I ran up the stairs that led to the van that stood in the middle of a fallow field. Mistress's chambers were always built under farmlands. Out of sight where no one would ever find them.

The back of the van door was open and I jumped inside; a Wraith stood in front of a single cage. Zoya was already huddled in the corner. Without hesitation I jumped in and pulled Zoya into my arms. Her body was shaking. When I pulled her head around to face me, blood was trickling from a cut on her lip.

"I hate that bitch," I growled, but Zoya shook her head.

"Look at me," she whispered. "Don't give her the satisfaction. Just"—Zoya's eyes dropped, and I could see she was fighting back her obvious fear—"just hold me. Hold me close."

The back door of the van slammed closed, plunging us into darkness. I wrapped my arms tighter around Zoya and pulled her into my chest. "I'm sorry," I whispered, and felt Zoya's head tilt up.

"This is not your fault," she replied, making me feel even worse.

"I took you. If I hadn't done that, Mistress wouldn't have even known you were alive. She *knew* you, *kotyonok*. I could see it in her eyes; she knew who you were as soon as she saw you."

Zoya laid her head in the crook between my shoulder and neck, but nothing else was said. Mistress had gotten me back in her clutches. Only this time, she not only had Inessa to make me do her will, but now she also had the female I had fallen in love with.

Because I had. I had fallen in love with the little Georgian, when I didn't think I'd ever even understand what this kind of love was.

She saw beyond the tattoos and scars. She found the real me

underneath. I closed my eyes as the van began to move. I closed my eyes and held on tight, knowing it would probably be the last time I ever got to hold my *kotyonok* like this.

I knew when we arrived back at Mistress's house she'd take Zoya away. I'd been here before. I knew exactly how this scene would play out.

The back door to the van opened and a Wraith hit the side of the van with his fist. "Get out!" he ordered. He snapped the lock on the cage, and I crawled out first. I held my hand to Zoya, and she followed me out of the van toward the secluded country mansion.

Mistress was nowhere to be seen. The Wraith walked ahead of us, and I pulled Zoya along. She clung to my side, and needing to have her close, I wrapped my arm around her shoulders and pulled her into my side.

The Wraith led us to the back of the house and through a small door. A narrow hallway led down to a lower floor. A long hallway followed after that, several doors leading off to different rooms. The Wraith stopped at one and ordered, "Get inside!"

Resisting the urge to kill him where he stood, I ducked into the room first, Zoya following behind. The room was dark, with no windows. There wasn't any furniture in the room, only a small dull light fixed to the far wall. The door to the room slammed shut, and Zoya jumped. I listened hard trying to detect sounds outside. I heard the Wraith walking away, another door slamming shut and locks bolting, trapping us down here.

Alone.

Exhaling, I turned and found Zoya's face in the low light. Her brown eyes were huge as she stared up at me, and I could feel her legs shaking.

My heart sank on my seeing her so afraid.

"Come," I said, and led her to the corner of the room, the

corner farthest from light. I sat on the floor resting my back against the wall and pulled Zoya down to sit upon my lap.

She followed without argument and rested her head against my shoulder. Squinting my eyes, I searched the room for any cameras or microphones. I couldn't see any obvious signs and relaxed some against the wall.

We stayed this way, silent and still, for a long time before Zoya asked, "Valentin?"

"Yes?"

"What will happen now?"

I closed my eyes and I could feel my heart racing in my chest. Truth was, I didn't know. But I had an idea. Mistress would punish me for my failure. The female in my arms was the easiest means she had available.

I opened my mouth to say I didn't know, but Zoya spoke up first. "She'll drug you again, won't she? She'll drug me too, do to me what she did to Inessa. She'll use me to force you to kill for her, won't she?"

I didn't give a response. I didn't need to. Zoya wasn't stupid. Her entire life had been devoted to anticipating what her enemies might do.

She sighed and her small hands fisted in my sweatshirt. "I hate that woman," she said. I felt her body shaking in rage. "My mama used to tell me you could see if someone had a dark soul just by looking into their eyes. I looked into hers, and I could tell that she was rotten to the core. Owned one of the darkest black souls I've ever come across."

My teeth gritted together. I was too angry to respond.

Zoya leaned back into my chest. Minutes and minutes passed; nothing happened. I kept listening for the sound of Mistress's heels on the hard floor outside, for the bolts of the door upstairs to unlock, but the place was deathly quiet.

When too much time had passed, I raised my hand and stroked it through Zoya's long black hair. Lifting the soft strands to my nose, I breathed deep. I closed my eyes and committed her scent to memory.

Zoya shifted in my lap, and she lifted her head. "What are you doing?" she asked, her voice quiet and timid.

Taking advantage of studying her beautiful face, I ran the pads of my fingers down her soft cheek, committing how she felt to memory. "I am remembering you. I am remembering how you feel, how you smell, how you look, so when I don't have you anymore I can still remember it all. So I don't confuse it with a dream."

Zoya stared at me, then stared at me some more, until I saw her eyes glistening with tears. "Shh," I rasped. But I was too late; big tears began rolling down her cheeks.

Using my thumbs, I wiped them away. Zoya grabbed my wrist, pushing my hand to cup her cheek, and she said, "I've just found you, and now she will take you away from me, won't she?"

"Zoya—" I tried to soothe her, but she cut me off.

"Won't she?" she pushed harder.

Sagging in defeat, I answered honestly, "Yes. She takes everything from me. It's all she's ever done. She lives to see me suffer." Zoya's head dropped and she stared at her lap.

I watched her, knowing I couldn't offer any words of comfort. But then Zoya lifted her head and suddenly moved her legs to straddle my thighs.

I drew in a breath. "*Kotyonok?* What are you doing?"

Lifting her hand, she ran it over my head, my cheeks, and my neck, following the action with her gaze. "If this is all we have, if all we have is right now, then I want to explore you one final time. I want my memories of you to be as strong as the ones you will have of me."

My heart kicked into a fast sprint at the flush building up Zoya's neck. Unable to resist, I cupped the back of her neck and brought her to my lips.

Zoya moaned into my mouth, quiet and reserved, but it didn't make the kiss any less intense. I told her how I felt in this kiss. I poured myself into this kiss, all of me, everything she had made me feel.

My tongue pushed through her lips to meet Zoya's, and as I drank in her sweet taste Zoya's hips rolled, her hot pussy pressing along my hardening dick.

Gasping at the feel, I broke away.

I tried to breathe, to calm myself down. But Zoya leaned forward and began kissing every inch of my face, my heart swelling when she began tracing the length of my longest scar with her soft mouth. She ran her lips down from my temple to my neck, only going off the scar's path to kiss along the red band of leftover scarred tissue from my collar. I groaned and ran my hands over her thighs, trying to stop myself from doing what I was picturing in my mind. But then Zoya's small hands landed on the zipper of my sweatshirt and she pulled it down.

Once my sweatshirt was open, she shifted down my legs and commenced kissing my scar from the bottom of my neck to my pecs. When she reached the end of the scar, she lifted her face, her cheeks red and her skin flushed with need.

"Zoya," I whispered; then she rose from my lap and got to her feet. Never breaking my gaze, she kicked off her boots and snapped open the button of her black pants.

Reaching down into my sweatpants, I grabbed my hard cock and began stroking along the length. And I watched; I watched Zoya as she slowly pulled her pants down and kicked them to the floor. She wore no panties, and as she stepped closer her pussy came into view.

Pre-come leaked from the tip of my cock at the sight. Bending down, Zoya pushed the material of the sweatshirt from my shoulders. Releasing my cock, I shrugged it to the floor just as Zoya unbuttoned her blouse, her tits bared as the material parted.

She stood before me, unmoving, until I held out my hand. Zoya walked forward, and as she stood over my legs I ran my hands down over her chest, my fingers running over her hard nipples and down to just above her pussy.

Zoya's breathing was labored at my touch. She lowered down until she was on her knees and, pushing her hand into my pants, pulled out my cock, pushing the material farther down my legs. My head tipped back at the feel of her soft small hands stroking up and down my dick, her thumb rubbing over the head, spreading the wetness.

Zoya stood up and, as she pressed a kiss to my lips, she guided my cock toward her, the both of us groaning low as she pushed herself down. Her tight cunt fisted my cock, and needing to touch her, I slid my hands round to grip her ass. Zoya moaned again when I palmed her flesh, and she dropped down until I was completely inside her.

We both stilled, and Zoya's hands threaded around my neck, her tits that were peeking out of her shirt close enough to scrape against my hard chest.

Using my hands as a guide on her ass, I lifted her up, her tight pussy strangling my dick as I pulled it out, leaving only the tip inside. Then I guided her back down, the feel of her tight wet heat driving me insane.

Zoya's head rolled back as she sat right down; then it fell forward as I lifted her again. Her forehead pressed to mine, and her hips began to move, slowly rocking back and forth.

"Valentin," she called as her arms tightened around my neck. "My Valentin," she added with a strained sad whisper.

My heart almost stopped in my chest as she called me hers. Unable to hold back, I released a long groan and used the grip on her ass to build the speed of my thrusts.

Zoya whimpered as I increased my speed. I could feel her skin heating to the same scalding temperature as my own. And I could see the same pleasure on her face as the pleasure ripping through my every cell.

Her small body pumped up and down, and with every soft thrust a flush built more and more on her face.

My breathing lowered as my balls began to tighten. Small moans began slipping from Zoya's mouth. Her pussy started squeezing at my dick, and taking one of my hands from her ass, I brought it round to press against her clit. Zoya fell forward, her body jumping at the feel.

"Valentin," she whispered, and ground herself harder against my hand. Her lean thighs tensed as she rocked even harder.

"Kotyonok," I groaned as pressure built in my groin. Then I pumped, I pumped into her harder and harder, until a soft cry tore from her throat. Zoya stilled, and in the dull light I saw her mouth drop slightly open. At the sight of her beautiful face, caught in pleasure, I came. My head fell against her neck as I roared out my release, possessing this little Georgian with it.

My body jerked as my prick released the last of my seed. When I calmed, my breathing hard and labored, I felt Zoya's breath clouding over my neck.

Without saying a thing, I wrapped my arms around her waist and pulled her close. Zoya's arms caged my head, and that's how we sat. We sat like this for a long time, just holding each other.

It was our good-bye.

My blood boiled when I tried to think of something I could do, but if I fought back I sentenced Zoya to death, and Inessa to a life of cruelty at the hands of the Master. But if I did nothing Mistress would drug Zoya and make my life twice as bad, forcing me to watch Zoya and my sister being raped by her sick guards.

"My mama used to say something to me all of the time, Valentin," Zoya spoke. I realized I'd been squeezing her to my body too tightly. Her small hands ran over my scarred shaven head, followed by a kiss. "She would say, *Change the things you can control, and let go of the things you cannot.*" On my hearing her words my eyes pricked and a burning feeling engulfed my throat.

"Zoya . . . ," I said her name, but I had nothing else to offer.

Zoya pulled back and covered my cheeks with her warm hands. As I met her big brown eyes, she said, "This is a hopeless situation. I know that." She sighed, and I could see her trying to be strong—her quivering lip betrayed her fear. "I have come to learn that I was born into a life of violence and crime. It seems it is a destiny from which neither of us can escape. Whatever happens next will happen. That is our life."

I shook my head and squeezed her hard. My cheek rested against her chest, and I said, "I hated Georgians, hated Georgian females in particular. But I can't hate you, Zoya. You're the only good I've ever known. You're the strongest person I've ever known." I sighed, and rearing back, I pressed a kiss over the place of her heart and said, "My little Georgian."

Zoya's breathing hitched in her chest, and she whispered, "Valentin."

She never got to say anything else. I never got to kiss her soft lips again, because as I held her close the door to the room opened and a Wraith blocked the entrance. I flipped Zoya from his view, showing the Wraith my back. A cold laugh came from his throat, and he ordered, "Get up! Mistress is ready for you."

I glanced down to Zoya, whom I had pushed against the corner of the wall, and with sad eyes she nodded her head. "Do not fight. I don't want to see you hurt again."

I closed my eyes, trying to cool my raging blood. When I opened them, I took a deep breath. Lifting Zoya in my arms, I picked the sweatshirt off the floor and pushed it over her naked body. "Put it on," I whispered. Zoya took the sweatshirt in her hands and quickly dressed. I zipped up the zipper and tucked my cock back in my pants.

Straightening, I turned to the Wraith guard, and he flicked his head for me to follow. Placing Zoya on the floor, I reached for her hand and wrapped her fingers in mine. I had stepped forward to move when the sight of her hand in mine pulled me to a stop. Zoya's free hand landed on my arm.

"Valentin?" she asked, her black eyebrows pulled down in question.

Lifting our joined hands, I brought the back of her hand to my lips and kissed the silky skin.

"Baby?" Zoya asked again, and my heart melted at that term of endearment coming from her lips.

I shook my head and fought back the image in my head.

"What?" Zoya pushed again.

"This," I said, and held up our joined hands. "We will never do this. We will never walk in the open air. Free. With our hands like this."

Zoya's face shone with sadness and her gaze dropped to our joined hands. "I used to watch people on the streets from my window and dream of the day I would do this with the man who would steal my heart." Zoya's lip hooked into a loving smile, and she asked, "You have dreamed of that, too?"

Staring at Zoya, memorizing every part of her face, I said, "Not until you."

Zoya had moved to kiss me on my lips when the Wraith guard reappeared in the doorway, crackling Taser in hand. "Move!"

Resisting the need to kill, I pulled Zoya behind me. We followed the shadow down the hallway and up some stairs. The Wraith opened a door and took us toward a room at the back of the mansion. When we walked through the door, my stomach fell. The room was dark but large. Sitting in the center of the room were two small beds with straps attached to the frames. And on the back wall was a stack of large screens.

Zoya's hand tightened in mine when the lowest screen showed Inessa. I stepped forward just as Mistress entered from a side door. Seeing her walk in, dressed all in black as always, her hair scraped back off her face, I whipped round to face her. "You bitch!" I snarled.

I glanced at the screen to see Inessa curled in the corner of a cell. Her arms were wrapped around her stomach, and sweat was dripping from her skin. She was rocking back and forth, crying out like she was in pain. And she was, but it was the need to be taken. It was the drug they had her on that made her need to be taken to calm the yearning. Only a male's seed could chemically soothe the ache.

Mistress moved to stand in front of the screens. Looking me straight in the eye, she said, "This has been 152's punishment since you decided to disobey orders." My jaw clenched so hard I feared it would snap. Mistress remained unmoved and added, "You knew the consequences, 194. You knew if you did not complete your hit you would cause 152 pain."

"Bitch!" I snapped again, feeling Zoya squeeze my hand in support.

Mistress smirked. "It's true: I am a bitch. Unapologetically."

I shook. I shook as I stared at Inessa writhing in pain. "Help her!" I commanded.

Mistress approached us. I saw the Wraith guards in the room

closing in, just in case I attacked. Mistress never even flinched. As she stood right before me, I pushed Zoya behind my back. Mistress reached out and ran her finger down my chest. "Are you asking me to send in one of my men to fuck 152? Is that what you are asking, 194? For your sister to be fucked?"

Red-hot pain flooded my body at the thought of my sister being taken like that, but I found myself saying, "Yes. Just put her out of her misery and take away her pain."

Mistress stared at me without expression, until she smiled and walked backward. "I don't think so, 194. In fact, I think I'll leave her downstairs screaming in pain for a while longer." She glanced over her shoulder at me and said, "In about an hour, if you listen hard enough, you should hear her agonized screams."

"Do it," I demanded. "Help her."

Mistress stopped at the screens, and taking out the remote from her pocket she turned on another screen. My heart fell, and I heard Zoya's quick inhale of breath when I saw it was Zoya and me in the chamber. It was Zoya in the cage, taking off her clothes as I stood before her holding the picana. My legs weakened as I watched myself under the influence of the serum collar. Zoya looked so afraid as she shivered in the cold room.

"You started off well, 194. When I watched you bring the Kostava back, I immediately recognized her face." Mistress flicked through scene after scene of me torturing Zoya, until she stopped at Zoya shackled against the wall. The kiss that I'd pressed on her lips.

Mistress turned and pointed at the screen. "And then you failed." She shook her head and laughed without humor. "All those years of training. All the years of my telling you the rules: Never feel sympathy for your victim. And never fall for one. Love has no place in a torturer's life. No place in a killer's heart."

I could see the fury in Mistress's eyes. Then the blood drained from my face when Zoya said quietly, "He's not a torturer. He's not a killer. He's Valentin Belrov. And he's a good man, despite your best efforts to take that goodness away."

My eyes closed at the sweet sound of those words from Zoya's lips. But they soon snapped open when I realized what she'd just done.

Mistress stood, frozen to the spot, glaring at Zoya. Everything else happened too quickly. Mistress nodded her head to her guard. The Wraith moved from behind us toward Zoya. Releasing Zoya's hand, I ran at the Wraith, only to feel a Taser's shock bolt through me from my neck. I boomed out a roar as the shock ran through me. But I kept running, until fire shot through my body from the back. I fell to the floor, hearing Zoya scream out.

I watched from the floor as the Wraith tied Zoya down to one of the beds.

I watched, unable to move, as they cuffed her to the frame, Mistress moving beside Zoya, ready to begin her torture.

My eyes closed as I fought for them to stay open, but as the darkness closed in I thought of the day Mistress had brought the torture to me. . . .

The lights in the dark room switched on, and I flinched at the brightness.

Blinking in my surroundings, I stared out of the metal bars of the cage to see if Mistress was coming back. I stared at the door to the back room, the room I feared most, but no one came through.

I pushed myself to sit up, glancing beside me to see 362 already with his back to wall, staring at the door, too. "They'll come," he said in Russian. "They always come."

I looked past 362 to 221. He was sitting in the center of the cage, his head down, long hair covering his face. He was like the living dead, obedient only to that prick of a man who was always with Mistress. He made 221 call him Master. They tried to make 362 do the same, but whatever drug they pumped into his body only made him obedient for a short period of time.

As I heard the sound of a lock turning, my attention was drawn to the door. My stomach sank when Mistress stepped through, her eyes immediately landing on me. Mistress nodded her head at the Wraith guard. The Wraith from the corner of the room came to my cage and opened the door.

"Out!" he ordered, and I stood on shaky feet.

I had walked only three steps when 362 said, "Hold on to your name and your memories. Do not let them erase them. No matter what they do."

Swallowing hard, I followed the Wraith guard to the door I most feared. I stopped in the doorway, but the Wraith shoved me forward. I stumbled into the room, hearing the door slam shut behind me. I straightened, and when I did the room came into focus.

My stomach fell, fear taking hold. Beds were in the center of the room, leather straps hanging from the frames. There were shackles on one of the walls, but on the other there was a metal pole, heavy chains hanging from the back.

Movement from the side caught my attention. I looked sideward, only to see Mistress and that man who tortured the twins. They were standing next to a long counter, its surface littered with needles and rows and rows of small bottles.

Mistress leaned in close to the man, and his eyes roved down my body. My skin shivered when it looked like he was sizing me up for something.

Mistress waved her hand, and a Wraith took hold of me, dragging me toward the metal pole. I tried to push back. I tried to fight, but the Wraith was too strong.

In minutes the Wraith had attached me to the pole, the heavy chains holding my feet to the floor and my body to the pole. No part of my body could move.

I breathed and breathed, trying to keep calm. All the time, I did what 362 had advised—I remembered. My name is Valentin Belrov. I have a sister called Inessa Belrova. She is being held captive. I have to set her free.

I repeated who I was and who I loved over and over, until I felt Mistress and her male friend standing before me.

As I opened my eyes, my focus immediately dropped to something in her hand. My nostrils flared when I saw what looked like a metal collar. I tried to move, I gave it everything I had, but I couldn't break free.

Mistress stepped closer and, catching my gaze, said, "If you want to save your sister, from now on you will do exactly what I say. You answer to me, and only me. I am your Mistress."

My eyes widened, and she asked, "Do you understand?"

Mistress raised the metal collar. "No," I bit out when I saw the inside. Sharp needles were all around the collar, small pellets filled with liquid lying underneath.

Mistress handed the collar to the male. The man approached, and without saying anything he opened the collar and brought it to my neck. I tensed, my eyes squeezing shut as I felt the tips of the needles pressing against my skin. I took in a deep breath, and as I did the man pushed the needles into my neck. I screamed out as the needles sank into my skin, the flesh of my throat on fire as I was pierced. My head fell forward as the pain became too much to bear. I heard the sound of metal on metal as the male locked the collar in place. The man stepped back, and when I rolled my eyes open Mistress was staring at my neck.

I felt warm trickles down my neck. I knew it was blood. The man said something to Mistress in Georgian. I could not understand.

He pointed to the back of the collar. Mistress nodded her head. The man walked back to the counter, but Mistress stayed close. Her hand gripped my jaw, and she pulled my head up to face her.

"194, if you want to save your sister, you will do everything I say, do you understand?"

I wanted to fight, but all I could see was Inessa waving at me as she entered the arch of the Blood Pit. Finding my voice, I rasped, "Yes."

Mistress's eyes lit with excitement, and reaching behind my collar she said, "I'm glad you understand, but I would have made you obey me regardless."

Mistress pressed something on the back of my collar. The collar suddenly tightened around my neck. The needles pushed farther into my skin. I screamed and screamed until no sound came from my lips.

I tried to breathe through the pain, but then I felt hot liquid injecting into my neck through the needles. At first the liquid felt strange, but as it began coursing through my blood it built up heat. As the seconds passed, the liquid turned into a roaring fire, flowing through my body, scorching me from the inside. As the fire burned, a thick fog began to fill my mind. Images and thoughts began to fall away. Suddenly 362's face was in my head, and remembering what he had said, I closed my eyes as the fire roared higher, and thought, My name is Valentin Belrov. I have a sister called Inessa Belrova. She is being held captive. I have to set her free. . . .

17

ZOYA

Valentin's large body jerked in spasms on the floor. I wanted nothing more than to be able to wrap my arms around him and keep him safe. I pulled at the straps tied around my wrists and ankles, but I couldn't get free.

I closed my eyes, and dark thoughts filled my mind. I pictured Valentin tied to a bed like this, being forced to wear the collar. I thought of the girl on the screen, Inessa, being forced to take the drugs that had her rocking in the corner, all for some man to fuck her and take away her pain. And I pictured Anri and Zaal. My big strong brothers, being tested on. Being the guineas pigs for these drugs. The successes, the failures—all the pain.

A gasp from the side pulled me from my thoughts, and I saw Valentin jerk into a sitting position. His head hung and I could see he was weak. His large arms hung at his sides as though he couldn't move. His beautiful eyes rolled as he fought for consciousness.

I wanted to cry for him, seeing this big man so weak and disorientated. But then the woman Valentin called Mistress ordered the Wraiths to move him. She had spoken to them in Georgian.

Two strong men dressed all in black picked Valentin up in their arms. Valentin's body sagged and his feet dragged across the floor as they moved him to what looked like a metal pole.

"Tie him up!" the woman ordered. The men attached him to the pole and wrapped heavy chains around his body. My chest constricted when they moved back and I knew he couldn't move.

As if sensing my despair, Valentin's eyes blinked, and blinked again, until I could see him returning to me. His blue eyes searched the room, until they found me. As soon as he saw me, his body fought to move and I could see the fury etched on his face.

His teeth clenched together as he fought the hold of the chains, but even his incredible strength couldn't move the heavy metal keeping him shackled.

"Zoya!" he shouted. My throat clogged at the pain and desperation in his voice.

"It's okay," I said back just as the woman moved from the counter along the wall.

Valentin's blazing eyes landed on her, and he hissed, "I'll fucking kill you."

Unaffected, the woman passed where he stood. She was heading in my direction. My blood cooled on seeing the severe expression on her face. Landing at my side, she pushed my hair from my forehead. She had blocked Valentin from my view, but I could hear the clashing of metal. I knew he was trying to get free.

I remained still, not wanting to give her the satisfaction of seeing my fear. As if knowing that was what I was doing, she smiled at me, before assuming a stern expression.

The woman looked at Valentin and began tracing the length of my body with her finger, over the sweatshirt that Valentin had made me wear.

I clasped my legs together, my muscles aching as I pulled at the ankle cuffs. The woman stopped. Retracing her path, she paused when her finger reached the top of the zip.

"No!" I heard Valentin snarl.

But the woman pulled the zipper, the large sweatshirt opening up, revealing my bare breasts and my bare body below. She pulled it down until the zip parted. The woman pushed the material aside, my skin goose-bumping as the cool air in the room hit my skin.

I turned my head from her when her finger touched my stomach and ran up until it reached my breast. Her long fingernails scraped over my nipples. I cried out in protest, my wrists becoming red as I tried to free my arms to push her away.

"Get the fuck off her!" I heard Valentin thunder out. The woman pulled back and looked to Valentin. "I can see why she caught your attention, 194. She is beautiful."

"Get off her," Valentin demanded, but this time the deep guttural threat evoked fear in me.

The woman didn't even flinch. The thrashing sounds of Valentin trying to get free increased, and my legs shook as I fought to keep my thighs together.

Then Valentin stopped moving altogether when the woman stood back and stared at my thighs. "Well, 194, it seems that you've already fucked her today."

"I'll kill you," Valentin promised again; because it was a promise, his words were thick with darkness and danger.

The woman shook her head and smiled. "You will not, 194. Because you will do anything you can to protect your little 152, and now your little Kostava whore."

The woman's finger stroked along the outside of my leg, and she said, "She'll make the perfect *mona.*" I closed my eyes at her words. Her words saying I would be a good slave. A sexual slave. Just like Inessa.

The woman moved away, and when she did I saw Valentin. His eyes were on me. When I captured his gaze, I mouthed, *I am okay. I am strong.*

But Valentin wasn't. His body was flushed and bleeding from where he had fought the chains. But what had my heart breaking were the tears cascading down his pale, scarred face, a striking visual contrast—emotion on his violent visage. His blue eyes were brimming with pain as he stared at me.

The woman stood right before him, and she lifted her hand to his chest, gathering the tears that were running down his skin. "194, I believe you may even love the Kostava whore. It has been many years since I have seen you cry."

Valentin never looked away from the woman, and I could see the reply to her comment in his eyes. My heart flooded with warmth when I saw the response loud and clear.

He loved me.

Opening my mouth, I made sure he was watching, and I mouthed back, *Ya tozhe tebya lyublyu.*

I love you, too.

I mouthed it in Russian so there would be no miscommunication.

Valentin's eyes closed at my words and I saw his body sag in defeat.

Suddenly a Wraith moved toward Valentin and the woman. He held something in his hand, and I shouted, "No!" when I saw it was a metal collar. A metal collar just like the one Valentin had ripped painfully from his neck.

The woman stayed silent as she lifted the collar to Valentin's neck. Valentin stayed silent as she lined up the needles with his healing wounds and pushed the sharp needles into his red, scarred skin. But Valentin's eyes stayed on mine. And my eyes stayed on his. There was strength when we endured this together.

The woman fastened the collar, and she moved her mouth to Valentin's ear, whispering loudly enough for me to hear, "You obey me, and only me, 194. You do anything I say. I own you."

Then I watched in horror as she pressed a button on the back of his collar. Valentin's eyes squeezed shut and his face turned bright red. The collar tightened against his neck, the veins and corded muscles protruding as the serum injected into his veins.

His teeth gritted together as his lips paled. Just as I thought he might collapse from the obvious pain, he thundered, "My name is Valentin Belrov. I have a sister called Inessa Belrova. I have a love called Zoya Kostava. They are being held captive. I have to set them free!"

My heart split in two as he choked out his new mantra, then his head fell forward. I waited with bated breath for him to move. Minutes and minutes passed by, until I saw a flicker of movement. His finger moved from underneath his chains. His body gradually began to wake, the blood running down his chest from the collar beginning to slow down.

My heart beat furiously in my chest when, as he lifted his head, I focused on his closed eyes. I heard my heavy anxious breathing echo in my ears; then it paused completely when Valentin's eyes snapped open.

My stomach dropped when two dark dilated eyes stared straight ahead. He was alive but not living.

The woman moved in front of him and asked, "What is your name?"

Without any bodily reaction, Valentin responded, "194."

I saw a victorious smile light up her face; then she asked, "Who do you obey?"

With the same vacant expression, Valentin replied, "Mistress."

The last of my hope drained out of my body. The Mistress snapped at her men to get Valentin down. Valentin stayed absolutely still, his empty gaze fixed straight ahead.

The heavy chains fell away, yet Valentin didn't move. The

woman stepped back until she was beside my bed, and she ordered, "194, come to me!"

Valentin walked forward, his body obeying the woman's command. When he halted before her and she looked down at me still strapped on the bed, my body washed with dread. "194," she said with a smile on her face, "capture Zaal Kostava. Return him to me within the day—dead or alive."

"Yes, Mistress," Valentin stated without question.

As I heard the sound of Valentin leaving to capture my brother, I was sure I would never be whole again.

I remained still and turned my head away from the woman in the room. A hand on my arm caused me to turn back. Strangely, I didn't feel pain. The woman had injected me with a serum that was like liquid fire flowing into my veins. I didn't react when she injected me with yet another syringe. And I didn't react as she picked up a third. Only at the fourth and fifth injection did I realize that she was trying to kill me.

The only time I reacted at all was when the woman bent down to my ear and whispered harshly, "This is for Levan Jakhua, Kostava whore. After tomorrow, there will be no more of your family left to plague the earth. After tomorrow, the love of my life can finally rest in peace—knowing the last of your poisonous hearts have stopped."

18

194

Capture and retrieve Kostava.

Capture and retrieve Kostava.

The van rocked from side to side as it took me to my hit. My hands reached out and held on to the bars of the cage, pulling at the metal, trying to release some of the rage deep inside.

Capture and retrieve Kostava rolled around my mind and as it did pictures of his face flashed behind my eyes. Tall, muscled, Georgian. Long hair. Green eyes.

Capture and retrieve Kostava.

I held my head when a bright pain slammed through my brain. It hit again and again, and a pair of brown eyes stuck in my mind. My body shivered when the eyes wouldn't move. My hands shook when the eyes told me I had to remember something. I tried and tried to remember the brown eyes; then Mistress's voice in my head screamed *"Capture Kostava!"* My blood boiled and the collar around my neck tightened.

Rage built in my veins, until it burned and burned, and I roared out in anger. My feet kicked at the cage, heavy boots the Wraith had made me wear slamming against the metal.

I struck the cage again and again until the van came to a stop.

I crouched in the cage needing to kill, ready to kill, whoever waited past that door. I waited and waited, until the van door opened and a Wraith snapped the lock off the cage.

Pushing on the metal door, I charged from the cage, snapping the neck of the Wraith, hissing at the sound of crunching bones.

Throwing the lifeless body to the ground, I jumped out of the van, the smell of salty air hitting my face. I looked left and right, then pulled the dark hood of my black sweatshirt over my head. Everywhere was dark and quiet.

I scanned the area, listening to the crash of waves behind me. Broken piers and dark sand sat on one side, old broken-down houses and empty shores sat on the other.

I broke into a run, keeping to the shadows. The cold wind whipped around me as I ran and I ran, my mind tracing the streets that would lead me to my hit. Store signs creaked as they swung in the wind. Boarded-up store windows were covered in graffiti.

I kept running, *capture Kostava, capture Kostava* still circling my mind. But something else tried to force its way in, making my hands ball in anger. Something else I was meant to remember.

But I couldn't remember. I couldn't remember. Suddenly my feet stumbled, lurching my body into a fallen brick wall. Brown eyes flooded my brain again. Brown eyes and soft lips mouthing, *Ya tozhe tebya lyublyu. I love you, too, I love you, too. . . .*

I bit back a roar as a female's face came into view, making me stumble again. I knew the face. I knew the face, but I couldn't remember why. *Kotyonok*, whispered in my head. Just as the fog seemed to clear, the collar tightened around my throat and a new wave of fire flooded through my veins, taking the face away.

My hand slammed on a house wall to my right. I fought to breathe through the pain. My legs kept running, Mistress's voice commanding me to capture and retrieve Zaal Kostava—dead or alive.

Darkness smothered my mind, leaving only one thought—*capture and retrieve Kostava.*

Sweat from my body dripped down my skin; then the darkness lifted again. My legs shook, something pushing Mistress from my mind.

My head switched back and forth, back and forth, between Mistress's voice and the female with the brown eyes telling me she loved me.

I had rounded a corner when suddenly the brownstone came into view. Lights were on inside, people moving past the windows. I halted, my breathing low and hard as I prepared for my kill. Lights turned the corner, and I ducked into an alley as a car moved past.

I blinked, and blinked again, as I saw a female in my head; she then appeared before me. I reached out, but my hands sliced through thin air, the female disappearing. I stumbled against a wall, my back hitting the hard brick. I shook my head and rubbed my eyes.

Capture and retrieve Kostava.

Capture and retrieve Kostava.

Mistress's voice always in my head forced me to stand straight. Forced me to obey her command. My eyes again concentrated on the brownstone, back on task. I moved to step forward, but that brown-eyed female in my head was there in front of me again. I could see her like she was real, dressed in black, holding a photograph in her hand. Suddenly she moved toward the house—I realized it was a memory trapped in my brain. I'd been here before. I'd watched this house before. I'd grabbed out to pull the female back and taken her to the torture chamber.

The female apparition looked so real to my eyes that I still reached out. As I did, my hand clutched at nothing but cold air, the female misting and fading into the background.

Clutching my head as a hot pain sliced through my skull, I hid back in the shadows. Sweat poured from my face; then I felt my collar tighten again. *No!* I thought, unable to take any more of the poison running through my veins.

Another surge of blazing heat surged through my veins. And I couldn't stand it. I couldn't stand it. But a clear command filtered through.

Capture and retrieve Kostava.

I scanned the street. Straight ahead I saw a man in black walking down an alley—the back entrance to the house.

Without making a sound, I crossed the dark street, snow crunching lightly beneath my feet. I pressed myself into the shadows and turned the corner into the alley. Four males stood there with guns. Guards.

Breathing deep, I rounded the corner and sneaked up to the first male. Snapping his neck, I dragged him backward into a garden, removing his gun from his jacket. I checked the model—silencer.

Good.

Jumping back into the alley, I held out the gun and fired three shots, each piercing the head of a guard. Throwing the gun to the ground, I climbed the wall of the house that held Kostava. A guard stood just below the wall. Jumping down to land at his back, I wrapped my arm around his neck and squeezed. The guard clawed at my arms, but with a twist of his neck he silently collapsed to the ground.

I had made to move toward the back door when the blinding pain came back. Dropping to my knees, I gripped my head. The pair of brown eyes flashed at me. I gasped for breath as the name *Kostava* again circled in my head.

I had to capture or kill Kostava, but I loved a Kostava, too? I didn't understand; my mind swam with dark fog. My skull ached, and pushing to my feet, I swayed. I hit the side of my head, my vision clearing to see stone steps that rose to the back door.

Kostava.

I silently ran up the steps. Seeing people sitting in a room through the glass, I scanned their faces. Three women, four men. Then my body cooled when it recognized Zaal Kostava as the one standing just beyond the door.

Sweat began to pour down my face, my skin too hot. My legs too weak. My mind too heavy. Just as my foot smashed through the door, the brown eyes filled my head. But this time they were crying; my heart ached in my chest. I wanted to hold her. I wanted her because she was *mine.*

I had to kill Kostava to get her back.

Plowing forward, I ran straight into Zaal Kostava just as he turned to look my way. I slammed into his body, bringing him to the floor. My fist flew into his face, my hard punches colliding with his jaw.

I heard women screaming. I heard men shouting orders. As I was about to deliver another blow, rage taking hold, I was flipped onto my back, a strong fist immediately striking my face. The hits rained down until I kicked out my legs. I moved to get to my feet, but the blinding pain came back. I clutched at my head; the pain ripped through my fucking skull. Then a face flashed in my head, but this time the face stayed.

"Valentin," she whispered softly, and I held out my hand for her to take.

"Zoya," I growled, trying to touch her face. *"Kotyonok,"* I whispered back, and I saw her smile.

Rough hands grabbed at my arms and pulled back my hood. I blinked at the flood of light. I looked up to see the bloodied face of Zaal Kostava staring back.

"Kostava," I slurred. "Zoya's brother."

"Zoya? My Zoya? Where's Zoya?" the man pushed before another man came into view.

I tried to meet their eyes, but my vision began to blur. "Capture or kill Kostava," I rasped, and pulled at my neck's metal collar. I pulled and pulled until I felt blood trickle down my neck. I couldn't remember why I needed this gone. I simply knew that I had to rip the collar off. Mistress's voice came to me once more, and I whispered, "Capture and retrieve—alive or dead."

Then my body failed to move and the room spun into a black hole.

I heard low voices in the background, but I couldn't open my eyes. My head felt heavy. My memory was shattered in pieces.

The voices came nearer, and when they did I heard they were speaking Russian.

Russian?

I hadn't heard Russian since I was in the orphanage.

Or since Zoya.

Zoya!

The thought of Zoya had my body arching, trying to get free, but my hands and feet were tied down.

I fought and fought, until I forced my eyes to open. My breath came out in short pants and my body was hot, sweat dripping down my face. My vision was blurred. I blinked until my eyes cleared. As clear vision returned, I found I was in a house, in what looked like a living room. I turned my head, trying to track the voices, but when I moved my neck pain seized my throat. I hissed at the pain, and anger asserted its grip.

I shook with the rage burning through my blood. I fought to remember what the hell had happened. Splintered memories floated to the surface—*Mistress finding us in the chamber, cages, being locked away, Tasers, Zoya being tied to a bed, Mistress tying me to a pole, attaching a collar, a command to kill . . .*

"Fuck!" I roared, and thrashed in the seat, desperate to get free. Feet came running into the room. I looked up to see a blond woman staring down at me. I opened my mouth to speak, but my throat was raw.

She ran out of the room. I heard voices, then several pairs of feet entering the room afterward. My hands had balled into fists when suddenly two men stood before me.

I traced the height of these males from their feet to their heads. I blinked, somehow knowing I'd seen them before. One man was blond with dark brown eyes. His stare was cold. He was built and looked like he could kill on the spot. But when I looked at the second male, my heart pounded.

Zaal Kostava.

"Kostava," I managed to rasp out. He was huge, bigger than I'd imagined. I saw his picture in my head, one that Mistress had trained me to memorize. He looked exactly the same. The only difference was his long hair, which was tied back.

Kostava's green eyes blazed with fury as he stared me down. His face was swollen and his lips were bloodied. I squeezed my eyes shut and remembered storming into the house but having no control of why I attacked. After that my memory was hazy. It never was; I remembered everything. But not this.

"Who are you working for?"

I opened my eyes, and the blond man was speaking to me in Russian.

"You're Russian?" I managed a reply. His head tilted to the side, and as he stared I asked, "Where am I?" My mind was too slow, information not coming to me fast enough.

"You tell me," the man bit back.

My focus drifted back to Kostava, and I spoke before I could stop myself. "I was sent for him."

I tried to catch the reason why in my head. Then I remembered Zoya on the bed. "Zoya," I gasped, trying to keep hold of the memory before it slipped away again.

This time Kostava slammed his hands on the arms of the chair I was in. "That's the third time you've said her name. Where is she?" His harsh words dripped with venom. But I was just as mad as him.

Zoya was *mine*.

I owned her.

I had to save her. A dark-haired female huddled in the corner of a cell was the next memory to slam into my mind. I choked on a scream but managed to roar out, "Inessa!"

Kostava stepped back. The male beside him grabbed the hand that was about to plow into my face. I pulled at the ties and demanded, "Untie me . . . have to save them." I inhaled and fought the razors slicing my throat apart, stealing my voice. "I have to save them. . . . From Mistress—"

Both males froze, then looked at each other. Bending down, the blond asked, "Who is Mistress?"

My teeth clenched as he questioned me rather than letting me go. Finally I calmed enough to snap, "The fucking . . . bitch Georgian . . . that controls me!"

"Georgian," the blond pushed as Kostava began to pace.

"Mistress Arziani," I replied, "the sister of the Master of the Blood Pit."

The blond man's eyes pulled down. When he stood, he asked, "Where did you get the number tattoo, 194?"

My muscles tensed, but I replied, "The Blood Pit. When the Night Wraiths stole me and my sister in the night and drove us to that hell."

"Explain," the blond pushed again.

Taking breath, I said, "I have to get back. I have to save them." Feeling the fog lifting from my head minute by minute, I could see Inessa and Zoya, both trapped with Mistress, and shouted, "You need to fucking let me go!"

The blond cracked his knuckles and said, "Not until we know who you are and why you tried to kill Zaal."

I dropped my head, and as I did I winced at the raw pain of my skin. The pain faded when I realized . . . "You removed the collar?"

Kostava stopped and looked down at me but otherwise gave nothing away. "The serum," I said. "Mistress gave me too much. Loaded the pellets with too much poison to ensure I got the kill. My head . . . ," I trailed off, wincing at the dull ache.

The blond informed me, "We removed it. The serum was an obedience drug. We have a male who has been studying it. He's developed a serum to counteract the effects. Sometimes it works; sometimes it doesn't. With you, we were fortunate. It brought you back fairly quickly." I stared at the blond; then I remembered something that Zoya had said: *My brother, Zaal Kostava, is marrying a Tolstaia. My brother, the* Lideri *of the Kostava Clan, is marrying into the Volkov Bratva.*

"The Bratva," I said quietly. "The Volkov Bratva."

The blond didn't look affected by what I had said, but he asked, "Who told you that?"

I flicked my eyes to Zaal and said, "Zoya. She said her brother was marrying a Tolstaia, a member of the Bratva. She said if we came to you, you would help us."

"Help you what?" the blond pushed.

"Kill my Mistress and rescue my sister."

"What's wrong with your sister?"

"Mistress has her drugged and captured. She's a *mona*—a sex slave. Mistress uses her to control me. She gives her to men to fuck, makes me watch, then promises that after my next hit she'll let me see her again. It never happens, but I can't leave her there alone. Mistress took her name, like she did mine, and also give her a number, 152."

Zaal Kostava suddenly went still. The blond Russian noticed and looked to him. "What?" he asked.

Zaal's jaw was clenched, but he dropped his head, his eyes darting from side to side like he was remembering something. "I think I know that number," he said quietly, then looked up, face paling. "Jakhua. Jakhua had a *mona,* a slave . . . 152, I think? I think he used her to advertise the Type B drug."

At his words all of the blood drained from my body and I said, "Master Jakhua? You knew Master Jakhua?"

Zaal this time replaced the blond Russian and said, "You knew him?"

My body stiffened, and I said, "He was my Mistress's lover. He was the bastard that gave me the collar when I was twelve. He designed it for me, for my Mistress, when I was training in the Blood Pit. He was developing the serum there, in the labs. He turned me into this. A torturer and killer." I smiled coldly, not even noticing Zaal too was lost in the memory. "But they never knew it only worked on me temporarily. I made them think I was completely under their control. But I remembered everything. I remembered everything, so when the day came I could get my revenge."

I panted, my muscles braced for that fight, when I noticed that the room had fallen silent. I lifted my head to see the blond Russian and Zaal Kostava completely frozen on the spot. "What?" I asked.

"Where is the Blood Pit? What is it?" the blond questioned urgently.

"Georgia. It's where the Arzianis bring all of the gulag champion fighters for the Ultimate Death Matches. It's where they train the fighters from kids, the *Ubitsy* and the *monebi*—the sex slaves—

before selling them on to the highest bidders, or keeping them in the pit for the gamblers' entertainment."

"Gulags?" the blond prompted, his voice now sharp and ice cold.

I nodded slowly. "The Arzianis run all the gulags around the world, and choose champions to bring to the Blood Pit for high-stakes gambling. They gamble on who will be the Blood Pit Champion."

I looked to Zaal and said, "Master Jakhua developed the serum there with my Mistress. It was where he did his experiments on his subjects."

This time it was Zaal's turn to embody death. His face contorted and he growled, "Experiments?"

Remembering the three of us boys in the cages as children, I said, "There was me in the cages, along with two brothers, for years. Twin brothers. But by the time I arrived, one was already lost to the serum. They'd already been there years. I spoke to the other twin, but he had already forgotten his name and who he was. He lived for the day he would kill Jakhua. He would sit and repeat Jakhua's name, trying not to forget. The serum didn't affect him like his brother. But it began to take his memories more and more each day. It wasn't enough; his mind never fully gave in. Jakhua eventually sent him away, leaving only his brother and me in the labs. When I was old enough, when I had finished my training, Master Arziani sent me out with his sister as his assassin." I lowered my head, flicking my chin at the names on my body. "Each tattoo is the name of my kill. Mistress and Master Arziani wanted their victims to see the names of people whose hearts I have stopped. They wanted me as their savage ugly beast."

Zaal looked pale and, towering over me, asked, "Do you remember the identity numbers of the twin boys in your cells?"

I frowned but nodded my head. "I remember it all," I said darkly. "The Blood Pit is ingrained in my fucking brain. Every part of it. From the day I arrived to the day I left." Zaal waited and I realized he wanted me to say the numbers. Sucking in a deep breath, pushing through the pain in my throat, I said, "362 and 221. They were Georgian. I knew nothing more than that. Neither did they."

I heard a gasp from behind me, but I couldn't see where it came from. It sounded female. Even if I could have turned, I wasn't sure I would have. Zaal Kostava's eyes burned with rage, and lifting his shirt, he threw it to the ground. He was panting hard and his muscles rippled with how tense his body had become.

My stomach fell when I stared at his chest. When I stared at his identity tattoo just like mine—221.

"You," I whispered, my heart thudding in my chest, my hands gripping the arms of the chair. "You, 221, are Zaal Kostava? You are Zoya's brother?"

Zaal nodded. It was obvious he couldn't speak. Suddenly the reason for his hit made sense. "It was you that killed Jakhua. That's why Mistress brought us to New York. That's why she wants you dead. In revenge for you killing her lover."

Zaal's eyes closed and he breathed deep. The blond next to him stepped forward and removed his shirt. My head fell forward when I saw the tattoo on his chest—818.

I had found males like me.

Beasts like me.

I eventually met his eyes, and he said, "Alaskan gulag champion. Taken at fourteen."

"Taken at twelve," I said after a few silent seconds, my voice breaking. "Taken from my orphanage in the middle of the night. Along with my sister and about twenty others."

Silence reigned until Kostava rasped, "Taken at eight. But made to watch my entire family killed first. Then grew lost to the serum until only months ago."

I studied his face, and I could now see the young 221 in his expression. And I could see Zoya. He was dark skinned and dark featured like my *kotyonok*—but for his green eyes. "Where's 362?" I asked.

Both men were silent, until Zaal simply said, "Dead."

My eyes closed, and I whispered, "It will kill her to know that."

"Who?" the blond pushed, his tone demanding.

"Zoya," I replied.

That seemed to kick-start Zaal, and he moved before me. "Where is she?"

"Mistress has her and my sister. I was ordered to take you weeks ago, but I couldn't get to you. You had too much protection. Mistress told me to take someone who knew you, if not you." I paused, then said, "I saw Zoya watching you from across the street. I saw a photograph she had in her hand of you. I took her. I needed a way in, and judged she could provide it."

Zaal flew forward and dug his fingers into my arms. "And what did you do to her? If you hurt her I'll kill you."

Shame ran through me, and I eventually said, "I fell in love with her, you Georgian prick. I fought the fucking serum that made me take her off the street, that made me obey anything that bitch Mistress wanted of me, and fell in love with the little Georgian." My eyes briefly closed at the pain of what Mistress had done to her.

Trying to hold back my rage, I explained, "Mistress found out and came for us both. She has her held captive. Mistress will kill Zoya if I don't come back with you. She wants you. This whole move to New York has been for you. You killed her lover—the man just as evil as her."

Zaal searched my eyes, then stood up. "How many males does she have with her, protecting her?"

"She keeps ten men in her mansion, and three bigger better-trained Night Wraiths around her at all times. Zoya and Inessa, my sister, will also be in the house."

"What are the Night Wraiths?" the blond asked.

Ice infused my blood. "The Wraiths are fucking made in hell. The Arzianis are not like other crime families. They're like an army, with Master Arziani as their general. They all dress in black uniforms, the symbol of two daggers crossing marked on all of their lapels. They have no souls. All of them—dead inside. They come for kids at night, blending into the shadows, and throw them into hell—the Blood Pit is hell on Earth. We called them Night Wraiths in the orphanage, as the children believed they were evil ghosts that came to take you to hell—the reality wasn't far off."

I shook my head, trying to chase those memories from my head before I exploded. But I looked to Zaal and said, "If I don't appear with you by the end of the day, Zoya and Inessa get shipped off to Georgia, to the Blood Pit. And they'll be used—a lot. They're both too beautiful to not gain Master's attentions."

Zaal was stone as I told him those words. His head fell slightly forward, and he whispered, "Zoya's beautiful?" His voice sounded like he'd swallowed razors. My stomach clenched. I could see the protectiveness, the sibling love, he had for Zoya, the same as I had for Inessa.

Feeling warmth fill my body just thinking of my female, I replied in a hushed voice, "So fucking beautiful. Long black hair, dark eyes, olive skin—she's stolen my dead heart."

Zaal looked to the blond and growled, "We're going in."

The blond man nodded his head, agreeing there was no other option; then he looked to me. "What's your name?"

My blood spiked with hope. I had hope for the first time in years that I'd free Inessa and I could save Zoya. "Valentin," I rasped, "Valentin Belrov."

The blond man signaled for someone to untie me. When the ties dropped away, I stood on shaking legs. I met the blond's eyes and he said, "I'm Luka Tolstoi, the *knyaz* of the Volkov Bratva."

My eyes widened and I instantly lowered my head. "I am the son of a crack whore, before I was this—the Arziani beast. But I am proud to fight beside you, *Knyaz*."

Luka nodded his head, looking every inch the Bratva prince, then pointed to Zaal. "My brother, Zaal Kostava, is the *Lideri* to the Kostava Clan of Tbilisi. They were the most powerful clan in Georgia until Jakhua massacred them. He's rebuilding his seat of power."

My stomach dropped, and my lips parted in shock. "Zoya is a Georgian underground *dis*?" Zaal gave me a stern curt nod in response, his eyes narrowing. My head dropped. Zoya was Georgian crime family royalty. Her brother was a crime boss who was marrying into the Bratva.

She would never be with me. Daughters of crime families only ever married well. To the people of Georgia, she may as well be a crowned *printsessa*.

"You remember the way back to your Mistress's house?" Zaal asked, pulling me from my thoughts.

"Yes," I replied, my body suddenly feeling drained, as I knew now that I could never be with Zoya when all of this was over. Knowing when the danger was no more, my *kotyonok* would realize the enormity of my sadistic acts—not all of them under the control of the serum.

"Good," Zaal said. "We need a map, and we need to call in our men." Luka moved forward and walked to another room. As I turned to go, Zaal's rigid hand landed on my arm. I glanced down at his fingers wrapped round my biceps, and my nostrils flared. No fucker touched me; I didn't care if he was the fucking king of the entire world.

Ignoring my glare, Zaal inched closer and said, "I do not know what happened between you and my sister. You say you love her; I am doubtful and questioning how that could be possible when you stole her in the night. I will follow you to retrieve your sister and mine, as I see the pain for your sibling in your eyes. But if I discover you have lied, or you hurt my Zoya in any way at all, regardless of our shared past I *will* kill you." Zaal leaned closer still, my body fighting the urge to attack. "You knew me as a boy. But I was a trained killer. *Am still* a trained killer. Remember that."

Zaal stepped away, and I said, "Georgian." Zaal stilled but did not look back. Teeth grinding, I said, "I too am a killer. I may not be crime ring royalty like every other fucker around here. Killing is what I do; it is the *only* thing I do." I paused, then added, "It is the only skill I possess. *You* remember that."

With tense shoulders, Zaal walked out of the room. When I turned to look behind me I saw two females in the doorway, staring at me, the blonde from before with cold eyes. When I lifted my chin at the Mafia *suki,* they left me alone in the room. A guard entered the doorway and pointed his gun in the direction Zaal and Luka went.

As I moved after the two men who had been incarcerated and tortured like me, I calculated I was down to my final hours in this life. Despite loving Zoya with such a fierceness I had no idea I possessed, the very moment her brother found out what I'd done to her he would slit my throat.

And that was okay.

As long as he rescued my sister and Zoya first, as long as he kept them safe.

Then this man-made ugly beast—194—could at last be put down.

19

VALENTIN

I sat in the back of the van the Night Wraith had brought me to Brooklyn in, flanked by Zaal and Luka. Their male guards followed behind in another van. The collar was back around my neck, but the needles were removed. We had to maintain the pretense that I continued to be under Mistress's control. I hated having this contraption around my neck. The heavy metal scraped against my new wounds. But with one thought of Zoya pinned on that bed, the pain faded to vapor.

We had sat and planned out our attack for hours. The Pakhan and another Bratva king joining us at the table. I had stared at Kirill Volkov as he listened to his *knyaz* plan this attack. I could see the pride in Kirill's eyes. The entire time my stomach had clenched. No one but Zoya had ever loved me like that. As a twelve-year-old child even I had heard of the Volkovs of Russia. Sitting at a table watching the legendary male let his *knyaz* handle business convinced me that the *knyaz* would probably not be the *knyaz* for very much longer.

Dawn was about to break, but the sky was still dark enough to approach the mansion undetected. The three of us sat silently in the van. The three of us were impatient for the van to arrive at our destination. Luka and Zaal had dressed all in black, Zaal refusing to wear a top, so Mistress would see his identity number straightaway. Luka dressed in dark clothes, the hood from his sweatshirt pulled over his head and bladed knuckle-dusters sitting ready on his hands.

Suddenly the van came to a stop. The van door opened and the three of us jumped out. Luka's head guard stood, gun already in hand. Luka's and Zaal's guards pulled up behind us. We were in the middle of the forest, just outside the mansion's grounds. Zaal stood before me and said, "Make it look believable."

Without hesitation I slammed my fist into Zaal's face, the huge man taking hit after hit. I struck him ten times until he was bloodied, his skin cracking open on his cheeks and forehead. The bruises and swellings would emerge soon. Mistress would be pleased that I had brought him pain.

Zaal wiped his bottom lip, glaring at me like he wanted to crack my skull. I strongly suspected that he knew I'd done something to his sister. I could see it in his suspicious eyes. He spat the blood from his mouth to the ground before turning and putting his wrists together. I bound them in rope. Zaal turned and silently waited for us to move. I nodded at Luka to let him know I was ready. He handed me a small white bottle.

"Put a few drops in your eyes; they'll dilate your pupils. We need that female in there to believe that the shit ton of serum she put in your collar still has you under its control. You fuck this up, everyone in there dies."

I ripped the bottle from his hands and put some of the liquid in my eyes. I did not need the prince of the Russians to tell me what would happen to the only two people I loved on this Earth. The drops' sting was immediate, but the fade was quick. I threw the bottle at Luka and without reacting, he said, "You have an hour to get to the mansion before we come in." He inched closer. "We'll kill everyone in there. Everyone but the two females you want to protect." He paused and, leaning in, said quietly, "Including anyone who betrays us."

I got his warning, but I stepped back and confirmed, "Understood."

We set off deeper into the forest. Walking ahead of Zaal, Luka followed close behind me, never letting me out of his sight. We never spoke as we trudged through the trees. When we crossed the boundaries of the estate, I took hold of Zaal by the wrists and began dragging him until we reached the lawn.

The Wraiths immediately flooded outside but hung back, guns raised, as I passed them without a word. They knew to expect me. I never failed. This was like any other retrieval.

I dragged Zaal forward as I entered the back door of the mansion. I felt Zaal tense as the door closed behind us. I knew it was because he was about to see his sister, Zoya. I could only imagine what I'd be like if I saw my sister again after all of these years.

My heart started pumping in relief, because I *would* see her again today. If this plan worked, I would see her again within the hour.

We walked down the hallway toward the room Mistress always stayed in—the one where she had drugged Zoya and me. As we reached the door, I kicked it open and threw Zaal inside. Zaal stumbled into the room. When I heard an immediate roar pull from his throat, I reached out and took him again in my grip.

Zaal's body shook. I kept my eyes forward, fighting the urge to look at what he was seeing. I couldn't, though. I, under the influence of the serum, would never look. My heart beat fast, knowing Zoya must still be on the table where Mistress had strapped her down. Fear mixed with rage when I wondered if the evil bitch had killed my *kotyonok*. If Mistress had beat her or tortured her in some way.

Mistress suddenly appeared from the back room and her heels

clapped on the hard floor. I fought back a wince at that sound. I *hated* that sound. My blood rushed through my veins at the thought that her life would soon be mine. That I would soon see her blood. That I could soon torture her.

Mistress stopped before us, and I saw her eyes light up with excitement. "Well done, 194," Mistress praised, and ran her hand over my scarred cheek. I fought with everything I had not to break her wrist. Her free hand reached out and she touched Zaal's chest, her skin flushing in anger and her lips thinning.

"Get the fuck off me," Zaal threatened, the anger he felt toward this female showing in his deep voice.

Mistress pulled back her hand and smiled. "Levan said you were big and strong, but I never knew you looked like this. And susceptible to the serum, too? You were a dream for my love, weren't you, 221? Until you killed him like the Kostava dog you are." Zaal's body shook harder as she called him by his number. I pulled on his roped hands warning him to keep his shit together. Suddenly I heard three small raps on the wall of the hallway—the sign that the Bratva had moved in. I knew Zaal had heard it too, when he froze and his skin rose in temperature.

Out of sight from the Mistress, I discreetly untied Zaal's bonds until his hands were free. Mistress stepped back. I tracked the path of the Wraiths in the room. I pressed my finger into the left side of Zaal's back twice, telling him to take the two Wraiths to the left. I would take the one to the right.

Then Mistress would be mine.

A loud noise sounded from outside—the distraction. Like lambs to slaughter, the Wraiths moved to see what the noise was. As they did, Zaal and I launched forward, blood about to be spilled.

I turned to face the Wraith on my right, but just as I did I saw Zaal pull out two black sais from his pants. He spun them in his hands as he charged at the first Wraith. The Wraith raised his gun, the second guard beginning to fire shots. But their aim was off at the sight of a feral Zaal running for them. The spikes of his sais sliced into their flesh.

A bullet flew past my ear as I ran at the Wraith guard to my right. I heard the hallway door burst open and feet enter the room. Luka and his men had arrived.

The Wraith cocked his gun ready to shoot, but as he did I slammed my body into his, my hands twisting his head until his neck snapped. I launched to my feet, but as I did my eyes landed on the small bed to my right. My stomach sank, and my heart almost stopped, as I saw my Zoya lying still in the bed. Her skin was pale and for a moment I thought that Mistress had taken her from me. I moved closer and touched her hand. Her skin was cold, her lips were a pale shade of blue but, thankfully, I noticed the slight rising and falling of her chest.

Relief flooded my body. Leaning forward, I kissed her lips. Breaking from the kiss, I quickly untied her freezing hands and moved my mouth to her ear. *"Kotyonok,"* I whispered. Tears pricked my eyes at how bruised and vulnerable she appeared. "I'm back. And I have Zaal with me. Your brother is here, to take you home. You're finally safe."

I felt someone behind me. Possessiveness kicking in, I turned in a crouching position ready to strike, to kill. I saw it was Zaal.

He didn't even react to my threat; instead his haunted eyes stared down at his sister. My heart squeezed at the look of sheer horror on his face. I straightened and stepped to the side.

"Is she dead?" he asked, his voice betraying his fear.

"No," I said, "she's breathing. I think Mistress has drugged her." I pointed to the needle marks on her arm. And hell, they were all over.

A long exhale escaped Zaal's mouth. Pointing to a Bratva *byki,* he ordered, "Go find me a blanket and bring it back *now*!" He pushed past me and covered Zoya's body with my sweatshirt, which hung limply at her sides.

I watched, wanting to care for Zoya. I wanted to push the Georgian out of the way, to keep his hands off my female. But I forced myself back.

I stood, frozen, watching him press a kiss to her forehead. Then as a surge of rage swept through me I looked for Mistress.

When I scanned the room, it was Luka who had Mistress in his grip. He waited for me, expectation in his eyes.

Mistress's eyes were fixed on me. I smiled coldly. For the first time in my life I saw real fear in their depths.

My feet slowly carried me forward. As they did, I said darkly, "I have been waiting for this day since the night you came into the orphanage and ripped the children from their beds." Her cheeks paled, but I didn't stop there. "I have been waiting for this day since the night you took my sister from my arms and beat me on the floor. Since you took my only family away and turned her into a fuck puppet for your sadistic pleasure." I reached Luka and Mistress. Lifting my hand, I ran it through her hair. I took the clip from the back and wrapped my fists in the dry lengths. Wrenching her head back, my cock hardening at the cry coming from her lips, I closed in and said, "I have been waiting for this since the day you slashed my face and head, making the fucking scarred ugly beast I am today. And since you tied that collar around my neck and forced me to kill day in and day out."

Tightening my fists in her hair, I finished, "Since the day you forced me to fuck your desert of a cunt."

Releasing her hair, I paced before her, losing my shit. I stilled and closed my eyes, then inhaled a long deep breath. Getting my rage under control, I opened my eyes and looked directly at Luka.

"Tie her to the metal post. Wrap those chains around her so she can't move." Luka wrenched her back toward that post, but I shouted, "Wait!" Luka stilled. Mistress looked at me in fear. Staring into her poisonous fucking gaze, I ordered coldly, "Strip."

Mistress's chin kicked up. I heard the men murmuring around me. Turning to face them, I said, "This is about to get a whole lot worse. Leave now if you can't stand the screams of a female."

The males stared at me with wide eyes, yet none of them moved.

Good little Mafia soldiers, I thought. My narrowed eyes caught sight of Zaal holding Zoya in his arms, her slim body wrapped in a blanket. The sight of my little Georgian looking so pale and unmoving made my inner fire roar.

Facing Mistress again, I watched Luka release her arms and I ordered more loudly, "Strip, bitch!"

Keeping that fucking ugly old face stern, Mistress did not lower her eyes as she divested herself of her jacket and then her black dress. Of course she didn't have underwear on; she was probably counting on raping Zaal when she got her claws into him, too.

Her clothes fell in a heap on the floor. Her fucking repulsive body was revealed for all to see. Unable to stand the sight of her bare flesh, I flicked my chin at Luka. "I'll be right back; there's someone who deserves to see her suffer."

Turning on my heel, without looking at any of the guards, I tore through the house. I ran down to the basement, the long hallway with lots of doors leading off to isolated rooms. I threw open the doors one by one, empty room after empty room. My eyebrows furrowed when there was no trace of Inessa.

As I sprinted back up the stairs, my blood ran like lava through my body. I searched every floor, every door, every closet, everywhere, but Inessa was nowhere to be found. Seeing the Mafia guards near the exit, I asked, "Are there any buildings out back?"

One of them nodded. "Two small storage sheds."

Hope sparked in my chest, then quickly faded when I asked, "Did you find anyone in them?"

"No, sir," one of the guards replied.

Real fear sprouted within me, and feeling the panic I harbored inside coming to the surface, I smashed through the door to the room, immediately finding Mistress on the metal pole. "You!" I spat right in her face.

Mistress's lips twitched, fighting a smile, and I just knew. I knew the bitch had sent Inessa away.

"You bitch!" I snarled. I threw my head back and thundered out a tortured cry. Unable to contain my anger, I walked to the nearest bed and flipped it on its side, roaring out my rage with every new step. I tore the fucking room apart, the Mafia guards staying well clear.

After I sent my fist into the wall, I turned. My eyes locked on to her plaited leather whip, the one she liked to carry around with her. Grasping it tightly, I walked to where she was tied up. Luka had wrapped the chains around her shoulders and hips, leaving plenty of flesh for me to rip to shreds.

Hands shaking, I went to swing the whip when it suddenly froze in my hand. Mistress was looking at me proudly. She stared at me like I was the greatest creation. Then it hit me: even as she faced her own death, pride shone in her face at the monster she'd created.

Her perfect killing machine.

Her perfect torturer . . . her prized bringer of death.

My heart pounded hard, the whip tightening in my grip. I wanted to kill her slowly and painfully. I wanted her to suffer, yet I wanted no part of her pride.

I stepped closer, and closer still, until I dropped the whip to the floor, watching Mistress's face fall, too.

Leaning close, I stopped just before her face. Her dark eyes watched me, and grimacing she spat, "You were always a failure. Even now, given the moment you've waited for all your pathetic life, you're going to fail again!"

"Where is she?" I demanded, ignoring Mistress's taunts. The look of victory flashed across her ugly face.

"Back with Master," she muttered happily.

My heart sank. I asked, "When?"

Mistress's eyes seared mine. Any laughter, any happiness at sending my sister away, fell from Mistress's face as she bit out, "When you fell for the Georgian Kostava whore. When you stopped doing as I ordered and began fucking her instead, holding her in your arms and calling her your *kitten*." Her lip curled in disgust and she spat, "I trained you to be an unfeeling killer. A torturer, an evil beast. And you failed. You've *failed*. You made a fool of *me*. So I did what you feared most—I sent scared little 152 to the Blood Pit, to be schooled, to be owned by Master in every possible way!" Her dark eyes narrowed until they became slits. "You knew the rules, 194. You broke them. I followed through on the punishment." Her head cocked to the side. "Tell me, was the taste of your little Georgian's pussy worth losing your sister for?"

I heard the sound of raw fury from behind me. I knew it came from Zaal. My skin burned with the need to bring this bitch down. Mistress's face never flinched.

The room was quiet, my anger too strong, until Zaal said, "I need to get Zoya home and to a doctor. If you are coming, just fucking kill her."

My head whipped to Zaal and the still and pale Zoya in his arms. Urgency took hold. I turned back to Mistress.

Without even looking in her eyes, I lifted my hand and in one quick move snapped her neck. I turned, only catching her body slumping forward in my peripheral vision.

I was a monster, she had that right, but I would no longer be the monster she wanted me to be.

I suddenly fell forward, my body leaning on my fists as I fought to breathe. My body sweated and shook with the reality hitting home—she was dead. Our torturer, mine and Inessa's captor, was *dead.*

Then pain filled every cell of my body as I thought of my sister. Adrenaline surged through my body. But I staggered to my feet, only to see Luka and his guards staring at me. I glanced behind to see Zaal staring at me too, his green eyes tracking my every move. And I saw my Zoya in his arms.

Luka moved forward, reaching out his hand, but I snarled, "No!" and wrenched my arm free. Running to the wall of screens. My hands searched the counter until I found the remote control Mistress always used. Panting for breath, I randomly hit at the buttons until the screens turned on. I searched for Inessa. Then on the far right screen I saw her huddled in the corner of a cage, writhing on the floor with her hands between her legs, her dark hair damp as the pain took its hold. Then a male walked into the room, and I shook my head. "No," I hissed under my breath.

"Master," I whispered, and watched as he approached my sister. Inessa's naked body arched on the floor, and Master dropped before her, crawling over her body. I watched, helpless, as he spread her legs and in one hard thrust slammed himself into her.

Inessa screamed out in relief. I had to avert my eyes. Emptiness and failure spread through my heart. Inessa was already in Georgia. She was already back in the Blood Pit.

My head stayed bowed until I heard the sound of my voice coming from one of the screens, followed by the crackle of my picana and a scream from her throat. *"Tell me your name."* My voice sounded cold and unfeeling.

My heart tore when I heard Zoya's timid voice reply, *"Elene Melua. Kazreti, Georgia."*

I heard Zaal. I heard his heavy uncontrolled breathing from behind me. His strong arm hooked around my neck. Zaal Kostava,

Lideri of the Kostava Clan, promised, "I am going to kill you, you lying fuck!"

I didn't fight back. As Zaal threw me to the ground and straddled my chest, I searched for my Zoya. Luka Tolstoi stood in the corner with her in his arms and watched with seething eyes as Zaal began to punch my face. Blood filled my mouth, but I didn't feel the pain.

"You fucking hurt *her*!" Zaal roared, and tore at the flesh of my chest with the tip of his sai. As I never took my eyes off Zoya in Tolstoi's arms, my body began to turn cold. I vaguely saw someone pull Kostava from my body, but by that point it was too late.

Darkness closed in; the last thing I saw was Zoya's limp arm hanging loose from the blanket.

And I smiled.

I smiled knowing she was safe.

Knowing that she was back where she belonged—with her family and her blood.

But as I stared at her hand I wished I could hold it in mine.

Hold her hand as I finally passed.

Just one last time.

20

ZOYA

I woke, an incredible heat setting my body alight. Deep confusion and a thick fog clogged my mind. My heart raced as I tried to think where I was. Opening my eyes, I was met with near darkness; the only illumination came from a lightly draped window at the far side of the room.

I tried to push myself from the plush soft bed in which I lay, but as I did my teeth gritted together at the aching in my limbs. I exhaled a long breath through my nostrils as I racked my brain. Where was I? What had happened? No matter how hard I tried, the fog wouldn't clear.

Panting through my discomfort, I managed to slide to the end of the bed and swing my feet over the side. Hardwood floor; I jumped at the cold feeling. My hair hung over my shoulders and I ran my fingers through the silky strands. I frowned. My hair smelled of coconut. It was soft to the touch like it had been washed and carefully dried.

As I stared down at my body, I saw I was dressed in a long black nightdress. I couldn't remember if this was mine, but as my hands felt the silk I knew it was expensive. Somehow I knew it wasn't mine.

Needing to find out where I was, I pushed myself to stand up. As I scanned the room, I walked toward the window. I stayed to the side of the large pane but took a peek through the drape to see a busy street below me. I was up high; the building I was in stood tall compared to its surroundings.

Dropping the drape, I stood back. In front of me, across the room, was a door, light spilling out underneath.

My feet moved me across the hardwood floor. I opened the door, making sure I did it silently. A large ornate hallway lay beyond the door. I stepped out, immediately searching left to right.

I listened for any sign of life; to my left I heard the murmur of low voices. Running my fingers through my hair to calm my nerves, I slowly walked forward, my eyes widening at the tall ceilings and old pictures hanging on the walls.

My skin crawled at the unfamiliarity of such richness. I pushed my mind again to remember something, an ache at the back of my head telling me that I had to remember something important. But no matter how hard I tried, nothing sprang into my mind.

I reached a room; the door was open and voices came through. My heart initially raced when I realized the people were speaking Russian. Fear spiked down my spine, and I spun on my heel to flee, but I heard a deep voice that froze me mid-motion.

My head cocked to the side to listen harder. The voice was speaking in Russian, but it held an accent, an accent that sounded familiar to me. I couldn't place the person, but instinct and a lightness in my heart prompted me to walk to the doorway.

I peered down at my hand, only to see it shaking. Tears pricked in my eyes, and I squeezed them shut, unsure why I was overcome with such emotion. The voices grew louder, many people contributing to the conversation. On a deep inhale, I edged through the door. This room was massive, dripping with expensive decoration. I padded silently along the floor, until the room turned to feature a living area. I stopped dead when I saw four people sitting on couches—the source of the conversation. All seemed young. One couch faced a huge roaring fireplace; a large blond man with his arm around a brown-haired woman sat on its plush cushions. My pulse quickened, but no recognition came.

I couldn't move. I couldn't move when my eyes fell upon the couple with their backs to me. A blond woman rested her head on an olive-skinned man's arm. His large back was covered in a white T-shirt the material of which was severely tested by his muscles. His black hair was tied back in a messy bun at the top of his head. For some reason my lungs ceased to function as I stared at him.

My body was rooted to the spot. I feared I would never be able to move. Perhaps sensing me, the blond woman leaning on the dark man turned her head. Brown eyes collided with mine. She froze. I stared at her and she stared at me. Something inside of me cooled as her lips parted. I couldn't remember why, but something inside told me I was not meant to like her. My mind was filled with a thick fog. I was struggling to organize my thoughts, to put anything into the correct place.

The man beside her turned to the blonde. The blonde, seeing him move, laid her hand on his arm. The man stared at her, his sharply defined profile coming into view. But he didn't look back toward me. The blond woman rubbed at his arm and his back stiffened. His head fell forward and his hands ran through his hair. I watched his every movement; the burning in my chest increased, nerves racked my body, as I waited for him to look my way.

I blew out a shaky breath, but that was cut off when the man suddenly launched to his feet. My eyes widened at his sheer height and massive build. His hands opened and closed at his sides. Then, as if in slow motion, he turned. I watched with bated breath as he finally faced me.

His eyes were down, long black lashes pressed to his cheek. On another breath, his eyes fluttered open, his bright green gaze immediately slamming into mine.

The reaction was instant. The recognition was immediate, penetrating through the fog. Images flashed before my eyes at the sight of that powerful green gaze; it flicked by, like a show reel of my youth—*my little legs running in the field through high grass, two boys chasing me. A green-eyed boy scooping me into his arms, me laughing as I kissed him on the cheek and pointed at three moles on the side of his left cheek. Two boys, identical looks but for their different-colored eyes. Two boys lying by the river, laughing and smiling with me tucked safely by their side. A green-eyed boy kissing me on my cheek good night and telling me that he loved me . . .*

As I gasped, my trembling hand flew to my mouth. Tears built in my eyes and began pouring down my cheeks. My hand fell away at the sight of this man, once my best friend in the entire world, my protector, looking so fierce and strong, no longer a young boy.

I breathed, fighting to gain my voice, and whispered, "*Sykhaara* . . ."

The stern expression on his face fell into one of returned love. The aching in my legs was instantly forgotten as I ran forward to throw myself into his embrace.

My arms wrapped around his thick neck, and I sobbed when I felt familiar arms holding me around my waist. The world around us fell away as I sobbed and sobbed, tucking my face into his neck. Zaal's face tucked into my neck, and I could feel tears tracking down the skin on my back.

"Zoya," his deep voice murmured. Squeezing me tighter, he said, "I thought you'd died. I thought I'd lost you, too."

We stayed like that for what could have been hours, but eventually I pulled back and with blurred swollen eyes I looked up to his face. Lifting my shaking hand, I brought my finger to his left cheek and ran the pad over his moles. Smiling, I whispered, "One, two, three . . ."

The pain showed in Zaal's face and his eyes closed as he tried to breathe. Understanding he was finding this as difficult as I was to cope with, I got to my tiptoes and pulled the band from the top of his hair. I smiled widely as his long black hair came tumbling down.

I stepped back as his hair fell over his shoulders to land against his chest. I took the strands in my fingers and met his amused face. "You still have the long hair?" I said in awe, too overcome that my *sykhaara* was standing before me after all this time.

"Like the Georgian warriors of old," he replied.

Pain sliced through my heart as he repeated Grandmama's words. With a shaking voice, I offered a compliment: "Grandmama would be happy to see you like this."

The tears fell silently down Zaal's cheeks and he made no move to wipe them away. His eyes were staring at every part of me; then I saw his nostrils flare and a choked sound came from his throat when he stared at my shoulders.

I turned away, staring into the large flames of the fire when I felt his finger run over my bullet scar. "I watched you die," he said quietly, devastation in his tone. "Those bastards held me back as you called my name, begging me to save you. Your eyes were on mine as they shot you, and I couldn't save you."

I laid my hand over his on my shoulder and faced him again. "You and Anri were boys. What could you have done against all those men?"

My eyes widened at the sudden mention of Anri. I quickly scanned the room. I saw the woman and man from the couch watching me, smiling, and I saw the blond woman sitting behind Zaal on the couch. Her face was wet with streams of tears, too.

My attention stayed on her for a lot longer than the others, but she didn't say anything to me, barely reacted to my attention. I couldn't remember if I knew her. I couldn't place her face in my mind.

When I looked back to Zaal, I asked, "Where's Anri? Where's my brother?" My stomach roiled, as I was eager to see him again soon. Zaal's expression fell, as did my cracking heart.

Stumbling back, I shook my head and whispered, "No. . . ." My head shook again and again, and my hand flew to my mouth. "Don't tell me," I said through my thick throat. "Please, tell me he's alive."

Zaal turned away and I saw his shoulders shaking. When he faced me again, I knew. The desperately sad expression on his face told me everything I needed to know. My legs too weak to take the news, I collapsed to the floor.

Cries racked my body as it felt like someone was twisting my heart and lungs in their tight grip. Strong arms suddenly wrapped around me, a large body pulling me to his chest. I fell into his hold, and his familiar scent took me back to when we were children. Minutes and minutes passed by. I cried until I was sure I couldn't cry any more.

Obviously hearing I had calmed down, Zaal pressed a kiss on my head and said, "I have missed you, Zoya. I still have you. We still have each other."

I gripped him tightly and whispered, "I missed you too, *sykhaara*."

I took courage from his hold. Eventually I pulled back, my cheeks flushed, feeling the eyes of strangers watching me.

When I looked at Zaal's face, I said, "You look just like Papa, *sykhaara*. You've grown to be handsome, just like him."

Zaal's lip hooked into a proud smirk. When I touched his long hair, I then touched mine. "We have the same hair now," I remarked.

A gruff laugh burst from Zaal's lips. I laughed, too. He nodded his head, "Your hair is longer than mine. At last."

I shook my head, remembering my annoyance as a child that my brothers had longer hair than I. I quickly sobered as I saw Zaal's scarred and tattooed arms. "You look so different, *sykhaara,* yet exactly the same, if such a thing is possible."

Zaal's head dropped, and he admitted, "I'm not the brother you remember, Zoya." I lifted his chin, my stomach turning when I examined his beaten face.

His eyes met mine and I replied, "And I am not the same sister you knew, either." I sighed and said, "After everything that we have been through, how could we be?"

Silence hung heavily between us. The climbing flames of the fire caught my attention; then I asked, "How did Anri die and you survive?"

The tension crackled between us. Zaal said, "Jakhua tested his drugs on us, drugs he created for obedience—"

"I know about the drugs," I said, then frowned when I tried to remember why I knew about the drugs.

"The drugs," Zaal continued, making me refocus on him, "the drugs worked on me immediately. They took away my memories"—Zaal sighed—"and even my recognition of Anri."

"No!" I exclaimed, trying to imagine my twin brothers as strangers. It was impossible. They were always together.

"Almost as soon as Jakhua killed our family and took us into captivity, I no longer knew Anri. I was rescued from Jakhua last year and discovered Anri had been taken from me as the drugs failed to work on him. He was used in underground death-match rings."

I felt nauseous listening to the story of their lives. It was surreal. "Death matches?" I asked, "Did he die in a death match?"

Zaal nodded his head, and his gaze flicked to the other man in the room. Suddenly, as if my brother reminded me we had an audience, I looked at the other people.

Zaal's hand tightened on mine, and in a low voice I asked,

"Where are we? My mind . . . nothing is too clear. I'm finding it hard to gather my memories and thoughts."

"It's the drugs, Zoya. They take a while to wear off." I was about to question Zaal on what he was talking of, but Zaal shifted to his feet and he offered me his hand before I could.

With another nervous glance at the strangers, I placed my hand in his and let him pull me to my feet. Zaal put his arms around my shoulders, protectively pulling me to his side. I kept my eyes to the floor; too many years locked away in isolation had made me feel uncomfortable in the headlights of their intense stares.

"Zoya," Zaal said carefully, "I was rescued early this year by Luka." Zaal's hand pointed to the blond man. I flicked my eyes to look at him, and when I did he nodded his head. I nodded back and then looked at the woman beside him. She was beautiful, all long brown hair and bright blue eyes. She too nodded her head and smiled.

Zaal took a deep breath and next turned to the blond woman on the couch. Zaal held out his hand and the blond woman threaded her fingers in his. She got to her feet and smiled at me. She held out her hand, but something made me stop.

Zaal stiffened at my hesitation, and a pain sliced through my head. I shifted from under his arm. Suddenly he stood before me, holding me up. "Zoya?" he pushed. "Do you still feel sick?"

I looked up in confusion. "Sick? I'm sick?"

"You have been sick for the last few days. We have cared for you, brought you through the worst of it."

I tried to remember something from the last few days, but there was nothing. My mind was empty. As I smelled the coconut scent on my hair, it suddenly made sense—someone had cleaned me.

Zaal was patiently waiting for me as I racked my brain. I worked on gaining composure, trying not to panic at the fact that I couldn't remember anything, I replayed Zaal telling me I had been sick. Then I frowned. It occurred to me that Zaal was speaking to me in Georgian again. When he had introduced me to these people he had spoken in Russian. Another flash of pain cut through me. I staggered back to the fireplace, the warmth of the flames helping me refocus. They helped clear the fog.

Blinking fast, I looked to Zaal and the others. I spoke in our native tongue, "You introduced them to me in Russian." I knew why, but I needed to make sure I was correct, that the information Avto had told me a while ago was correct.

"Zoya," Zaal said calmly. I could tell by the tone of his voice and the apprehension on his face that he was nervous.

Pressing my hands to my throbbing temples, I shook my head. Zaal pulled the blonde closer to his side, and an image of a photograph came to mind. Zaal with this woman, laughing and happy.

"Zoya, you need to understand that Luka rescued me. He too was taken captive as a child, like Anri and me. He . . . he knew Anri, he was his best friend. They were made to fight for their lives in the death-match clubs. From teens."

I stared at the blond man who nodded his head. "You speak Georgian?" I asked him in my native tongue.

"Yes," he replied. "My gulag's owners were Georgian; most of the fighters were Georgian. I learned to speak it by listening to them." He swallowed. "And through Anri; he taught me how to survive."

I looked to my brother again, and he was twitching on his feet; the blond woman soothingly rubbed his chest. She loved him. I could see it in her eyes. And Zaal's. I could see the fierceness of his love for her in his eyes, too.

"Tell me from your lips," I said, injecting a little more power into my voice. "I need to hear it from you. Just to be sure I have all the facts."

Zaal lifted his chin and said, "Her name is Talia Tolstaia, Zoya."

My eyes closed as I heard this, the instant feel of betrayal hitting me deeply. I remembered that I'd known this.

I remembered not knowing what to think of this news then, too.

Zaal stepped forward, but I held out my hand for him to halt. "Stop!" I urged, needing some space, some time, to process the information. He did; he stopped dead in his tracks. My hands shook as a flashback of my papa telling us how the Tolstois, Volkovs, and Durovs ruined our lives. How they were our family's enemies.

And Avto . . . *Avto? Where is Avto?* I shook my head, trying to focus, remembering him telling me that the Volkov Bratva were to blame for Jakhua turning against our family.

A sudden mixture of betrayal and hot anger flowed in my veins. I had been taught that my family . . . my family was massacred because of these people.

"How could you?" I found myself asking Zaal before my eyes eventually found my brother. Pain and shame seemed to flash across his face before his expression changed to one of protectiveness of the Tolstaia.

"Zoya," he said calmly, "they saved my life. Luka found out I was alive and saved me from Jakhua. He risked his life and those of his men to come and take me from *him.* He did it out of honor to Anri." He hugged Talia closer, then continued, "I almost died from the drugs, but Talia cared for me. She cared for me and we eventually fell in love."

I shook my head. I looked to the blond man and then to the brown-haired woman. "And their surnames?" I directed my question at Zaal.

"I'm Luka Tolstoi, and this is my wife, Kisa Tolstaia." I felt sick as *Luka* replied in perfect Georgian again. His wife glanced to him; then facing me, she said, "My maiden name was Kisa Volkova, Zoya. I'm the Kirill Volkov's, the Bratva Pakhan's, daughter."

My hand rose to the side of my head, the dull ache inside growing unbearable. I didn't know if it was from the sickness I apparently had or the fact that all I had been raised to believe was now standing on its head.

Zaal moved to come to me. But I found myself whispering, "You betrayed your family." I glared at Talia, standing by his side, a Russian enemy. I added, "Avto, my guardian, told me it was their fault that our family was massacred. They are the reason Jakhua turned his back on us and sought revenge."

Zaal's face contorted with anger, and he bit, "That isn't true. There are things you do not know, Zoya."

I stared at my brother and shook my head. With a trembling voice, I said, "I feel like a stranger to you right now. I don't know what to believe. My head is full. . . . I don't know what's correct."

Zaal's face blanched. I felt a stab of regret in my stomach at the effect my response had on him. But I was confused. They were the Kostavas' enemies. I'd been brought up to despise them.

The blond woman by his side stepped forward and said, "Our family histories are bad, the worst. But that is not where we stand now. We have moved past it. We have to, Zoya. We cannot live with pain and hatred anymore."

My eyes narrowed on this blond woman, and I found myself laughing incredulously. "I was shot and almost died, trapped underneath my dead family, feeling their flesh turn cold as their blood seeped into my skin. My twin brothers were stolen and tested upon like animals. I have just found out my much-loved elder brother Anri died in an underground death match, and I have been in hiding for twenty years to escape our enemies who were still hunting me when my body wasn't found!"

My anger wrapped around me, and I added in a cold voice, "I was eventually told Zaal had survived after I'd long given up hope that anyone else in my family was alive. For the first time ever, I no longer felt alone in the world, only to seek him out and be kidnapped and tortured for days—"

My words cut off when the last of the heaviness finally cleared and a pair of blue eyes engulfed my mind. Shaved black hair and maps of raised scars on a roughly handsome face. The most prominent scar stretched from his temple to his chest. A face like that nightmare should have brought fear; instead it brought me peace. It brought me warmth.

My heart beat wildly as the events of recent weeks came flooding back with the force of a tidal wave: the Mistress, the collar being reattached to Valentin's neck, the Mistress ordering him to kill Zaal . . . then she brought the drugs to me. She'd wanted me to die through the drugs.

I snapped my eyes to my arms; needle marks were still prominent on my skin. "Valentin." I whispered the scarred man's name aloud and ice ran down my spine.

I confronted Zaal and demanded, "Where's Valentin?" My body began to shake at not having him by my side. I fired off questions: "Did he survive? Did she kill him?"

Zaal's hands fisted at his sides, but he refused to speak.

"He died?" I whispered. A new kind of heartbreak shattered in my chest. The kind that was impossible to endure.

"He's alive," Luka Tolstoi informed me, drawing my attention to him.

"Where is he?" I demanded. "I have to see him. Is he okay?"

Luka glanced to Zaal. I followed his lead to stare at my brother. His huge body was radiating red-hot rage. "He tortured you," Zaal said coldly. "He hurt you."

"Yes," I replied. "The woman forced him to wear a collar that made him hurt me. But we fell in love despite our awful situation. We fell in love and he tried to save me." I narrowed my eyes. "He tried to save you, too. He's a killer, one that never fails, and he was sent for you. His love for me stopped him from carrying out the hit on you, didn't it?" I could feel that was the truth.

"You fell in love with your captor?" Zaal snarled. "He tortured you and you fell in love? The male is evil, Zoya, too far gone. You can see the killer in his eyes. And you fell in love? Do you hear how messed up that sounds?"

I stepped up to my brother, his Russian fiancée moving aside. Meeting my brother's huge chest, I peered up and said, "Do not judge me. You do not know how it is between us. You do not know me, Zaal. You do not know me as I am now, and you do not know Valentin. You do not know what that woman did to him and his sister."

"His sister has been taken. The woman who was his captor sent her to her brother in Georgia. The Blood Pit." Talia spoke from Zaal's side. Tears dropped down my face on my hearing this information.

"Does Valentin know?" I asked Zaal, not Talia, my heart tearing at the thought of Valentin alone, no one to comfort him, to hold him, to share his pain. Inessa being gone would destroy him. My chest constricted at the sheer amount of pain he must be in.

"Take me to him," I whispered, unable to speak out with all of this confusion in my heart.

"He's in our cells," Talia answered again. My eyes met my brother's. My stare burned through him. I was talking to *him*.

"Cells?" I questioned coldly.

Zaal raised his chin. "I saw the video of him hurting you at the Mistress's mansion. I saw him hurting you, torturing you, making you scream. Fuck, Zoya! He was breaking you!"

Realization hit. "You harmed him. You punished him for hurting me." Zaal's silence told me all I needed to know. "Take me to him!" I commanded. Zaal remained unmoving. A twinge of nostalgia twisted in my stomach. *This* Zaal I knew. The one fiercely protective of his little sister. The big brother who would never let me be harmed.

My Georgian warrior.

I held his stare, refusing to back down. Zaal never moved.

Surprising me, Luka's wife moved behind me and, with her hand on my shoulder, quietly said, "I'll take Zoya to Valentin."

Her husband frowned at her, but she waved her hand in dismissal. She addressed Talia. "Tal, get Zoya some of your clothes—jeans, sweater, boots. They should fit well enough." Talia looked at me with sad eyes. She seemed to want to say something to me, but she held back and quickly left the room. Part of me felt guilty seeing the desperation written on her pretty face, but I just couldn't handle all this right now.

Kisa moved beside me and said, "Let's go to the guest room, Zoya. My car will take us to Valentin, after you dress."

Thankful for someone taking the lead, I followed her out of the room. Zaal took hold of my arm as I passed. "Zoya," he whispered brokenly, almost breaking my resolve. "*Please . . .*"

Almost.

Confused to hell with my current reality, with the stream of revelations, I sighed and pulled my arm free. "I dreamed what this day would be like since I woke up, age five, alone and scared in Georgia. Avto was by my side telling me everyone I loved was gone." I fought back the sting in my chest at the memory and said, "What was said earlier was right, Zaal. You're not the brother *I* remember, and I'm not the sister *you* remember. Maybe I was naive to believe that after all these years we could be anything other than strangers." I walked off before I broke down into his familiar arms. I winced when I heard him calling my name. I didn't turn around. I couldn't.

I just needed to see Valentin.

Talia passed Kisa and me in the hallway. She stopped and stated, "I've left the clothes on your bed, Zoya. It's cold, so I've put a coat out for you."

I kept walking, unable to talk to the woman right now. The pain was too much. This was all too overwhelming. I heard her sigh in defeat and enter the room where I'd left my brother. I almost stopped and ran back, freely forgiving him for finding love with the enemy. Because he had found love after all the pain. But a stubbornness and a sense of family pride kept my feet moving. *It is peculiar,* I thought. I had spent my entire life waiting to run into his arms, but now the opportunity presented itself I found myself running away.

It seemed that this answered prayer came with consequences.

My heart pined to see Valentin, so I dressed quickly. Kisa silently led me to a waiting car. The driver didn't speak, clearly knowing where to go. The silence was heavy in the secure and private backseat. I glanced to the woman beside me and saw her hands gently running over her raised stomach.

She smiled when she saw me watching her hands. "It's strange, but I can't stop touching it."

Her kind voice set me at ease, and I found myself asking, "How far along are you?"

"Six months," she said. I could hear the excitement in her voice.

I turned to look out of the window, envious that this woman was so content with her life. Then Kisa said, "I understand why you're angry, Zoya." I stiffened, not wanting to hear it, but she pressed on, "I really do. I would never dare patronize or fail to see why you are so angry with Zaal. With Talia. With us all." I tensed, but she continued, "Our families have had a horrid past; there's no shying away from this fact. I get that you're still living it, every single day."

I looked at Kisa, not knowing what to say. Thankfully, all I saw was openness and understanding in her eyes. Leaning forward, she shifted her body toward me. "I was there when Talia told us she was in love with Zaal. And it wasn't easy for her, either. She loved her *babushka* very much, and believe me, Talia hated your father for ordering the death of her *dedushka*. His widow was the woman Talia deemed to be her best friend. A woman she had not long lost.

"She fought her attraction to Zaal out of respect for her deceased family, but in the end, neither of them could fight their love. Zaal warred over his family's—*your family's*—memory and honor. But he was so alone, so confused, and very much in love with a forbidden woman. It wasn't easy for anyone. Even my father-in-law, at first, could not bring himself to welcome your brother into the family—for exactly the same reason you refuse to accept Talia. But he has warmed to your brother, immensely. He now believes that it is not fair to continue to hold a grudge against the son of the wronged man. Or vice versa, as I'm sure you view it."

"Right now, I find I can't move past it," I admitted after quiet seconds of reflection. My throat thickened, and I said, "It's my *family*. The family I never got to know because they were taken from me. Brutally. And the worst thing is, I remember it all. I may have been young, but I remember it all. The smell of the blood, the stench of burning from the bullets cutting through flesh. Zaal was my hero. I cannot help but feel betrayed."

Kisa cautiously reached out to lay her hand in mine. "Zoya, Talia is my best friend, and one of the best people I know. She loves Zaal with a fierceness I didn't believe possible in my friend. And I also have come to know Zaal—the Zaal as he is *now*. He is quiet and reserved; he barely speaks. I know this is because he lives every day with the same sorrow and pain you do." She squeezed my hand. "For your family. For not remembering his twin . . . for losing the little sister he talks of at every opportunity."

My eyes filled with tears and I rasped, "He does?"

Kisa smiled softly and she nodded her head. "I feel I know you already, even though we have just met."

Her sentiment warmed my heart. "I'm not sure I can move past it. How do I move past him marrying the enemy? How can I move past him imprisoning the man I love?"

Kisa shrugged. "You forgive, Zoya."

"That easily?"

Kisa sighed. "Believe me, Zoya, my life, Talia's life, has been filled with heartache too, through people similar to those that took Zaal and your family away from you. One day I will tell you about it. But I found that if I did not forgive the past I wasted the new chance at life I have been awarded with *lyubov moya*." Her eyes met mine. "The new chance we all have been given. You survived. Zaal survived. And you have both found your way to each other, right now, here in Brooklyn, far from your native land. I refuse to believe it is mere coincidence."

I had taken a long deep breath, absorbing what she had said, when she added, "I'll stop talking now, but I want you to know one thing. I was there when Zaal got news of you. That you were alive. It was as though the heaviest of burdens had been lifted from his shoulders. Before the news of your survival he would get lost in his head. Talia was the only person who could lead him out of the darkness. I always felt so sad for him.

"Then when we discovered you had been taken he changed. Gone was the quiet reserved giant, and born was a fierce leader. He gathered your people, those protecting you here in New York, and asked them to pledge their loyalty." Kisa paused, then said emphatically, "Zoya, he took on the mantle of *Lideri* to your people for one reason only—to bring you home. Because you *are* home.

"Zaal had refused the title of *Lideri* until that day. Knowing you were out there somewhere, *alive,* awoke something within him. If you want us, Zoya, *we* are your *family*. And we will love you as hard as we do each other."

I couldn't speak. I couldn't respond to what she had said. All I could imagine was Zaal standing in front of our people, tall and strong, leading them on his own. It was always meant to be both Anri and Zaal standing there, leading our people side by side, but Zaal had taken on the role of *Lideri,* by himself, for me.

Just like my Zaal of old would have done.

My head flopped back against the leather seat, and I closed my eyes. In my mind I saw how lovingly he looked at Talia. How Talia defended him when I was angry. And I knew Kisa was right. Talia loved him deeply despite him being a Kostava.

My anger washed away. I felt tired. Tired of harboring hate. Tired of pain and heartache. And I so wanted to see Valentin's face. I wanted my beautiful monster.

As the streets passed by in a blur, I smiled to myself at Kisa's hand still lying on top of mine. Inhaling, I asked quietly, "You are to be the Pakhan's wife one day, aren't you? Luka, he will be the Bratva boss?"

Kisa's fingers twitched as she said, "Yes. Someday."

I smiled wider this time. "You'll be a good leader to your people, Kisa. Someone to look up to and admire. Someone to confide in and trust. A strong woman for other wives to emulate."

A breath hitched in Kisa's chest. I slowly rolled my head against the headrest to face her. Her shocked pretty face was locked on mine, and her eyes glistened in the glow of passing streetlights.

"Thank you," she whispered, sincerity lacing her sweet tone.

Looking out of the window once more, I sighed. "It's true. You are exactly what a pakhan's wife should be. Luka should be very proud to have you by his side."

"He is," she confirmed, and I heard the love for her husband clearly in her voice, "as I am of him. So very proud."

Nothing else was said for the rest of the journey.

But her hand remained holding mine.

21

ZOYA

"This is the place?"

I stared at what looked like a run-down gym. Kisa nodded. "'The Dungeon.' I'm the manager. Come."

We entered via the private back door. Kisa led me downstairs until we came to a vast gym. Cages and training equipment of all descriptions covered the floor and walls. My eyes narrowed as I inspected the equipment. I swallowed hard.

Kisa must have seen my reaction, and explained, "We run a death-match enterprise. The men are mostly volunteers, or prisoners—rapists, murderers. Men that don't belong in the streets."

I stared at the bloodstained floors, the weapons on the walls, and I felt overwhelmed. I didn't know life at all.

At least this life.

I had a feeling this would change very soon.

Kisa headed for the back of the gym. We walked past locker rooms and stopped at a barred metal door. A large man stood there, clearly guarding the entrance.

"Pavel, let us in, please?" Kisa asked. The man, Pavel, pulled out a ring of keys and opened the heavy door.

As a dank, dimly lit stone hallway revealed itself, I felt the name the Dungeon was appropriate. The lights randomly hanging from the ceilings were straight out of a gothic novel. Kisa led me down the hallway, then down some steps until we reached the mouth of a short hallway.

Pausing on the final step, she turned to me and said, "Zoya. You must understand this. Zaal saw the screens in the Mistress's mansion. He watched Valentin torturing you and he snapped. Luka told me you were cold and pale in his arms. Zaal couldn't contain his anger. He'd just gotten you back. You were unresponsive. Then he saw footage of you being tortured."

My heart beat with a fierce rhythm, because I did understand. With mounting trepidation, I inquired, "What has he done to Valentin?"

Kisa paled. "He hurt him, Zoya. Badly. As close as he could to like for like." Kisa winced. "Valentin has been down here for days. You should prepare yourself."

For a moment I closed my eyes. My heart pained for my lost man. "Why did no one help him?"

"Because Zaal commanded that Valentin be left to him, and him alone." I frowned. Kisa laid her hand upon my arm. "Zoya, Zaal is in the Volkovs' inner circle. The Bratva have always had three men leading. There's always the Pakhan in the head seat, of course. But historically, there have been three, or even four, Bratva kings to rule the Red Brotherhood. It's stronger that way. Luka is *knyaz*. Before Zaal became the Georgian *Lideri,* Luka had chosen Zaal to be at his side, as one of the future kings."

A strong sense of pride filled my chest when I heard this information. "So—"

"So Zaal ordered Valentin to be left solely to him. And as he is a man in the inner circle, that's precisely what has happened. No one would dare challenge a command that comes directly from him."

Licking my lips, the cold air bringing a chill to my skin, I whispered nervously, "I need to see Valentin."

Kisa handed me the ring of keys the guard had held and said, "He is in the cell at the end. There are no windows. Zaal cut the lights near his cell. There is a light switch outside of the cell. You'll need it to see. This place is aptly named 'the Darkness.' It is designed for torture and extreme punishment of enemies, nothing else."

I swallowed again. With a shaking hand, I took the keys from Kisa. As she turned to walk away, she instructed, "There are four guards in this building. I will tell them you're down here and that you're not to be disturbed. Ask Pavel if you need anything. He'll get whatever you ask for."

Kisa started to climb the stairs. I felt the need to ask, "Why are you helping me? Valentin *did* torture me. Shouldn't you be warning me off, too?"

Kisa glanced back, her face sympathetic. "Let's just say that I fell for a man I shouldn't have, either. Turns out he was the *right* man for me all along. Turns out he was, he *is,* my soul mate." She nudged her chin in the direction of the cells. "You will know soon enough if you truly love that man down there, or if that obsession was prompted by your capture and eagerness to be free." She shrugged. "Who are we to tell you what's in your heart, no matter how extreme the circumstances in which you two met?"

"Thank you," I said quietly after several seconds of not being able to respond.

"You're welcome, sweetie," Kisa replied with a smile. She left me alone. I turned to face the hallway.

My hands shook, rattling the metal keys, as I walked down the dimly lit hallway. Open cells with thick iron bars surrounded me on both sides. My footsteps echoed loudly on the hard stone floor, but I forced myself to keep moving. I had to reach the cell at the end of the hallway. When I reached the large isolated cell at the end, I could see nothing inside. The ceiling lights were out.

Valentin had been kept in total darkness for days.

Pulse pounding, I hurried the rest of the way, blind in the darkness. I pushed my hands out, feeling in front of me until I reached a hard slick wall. My fingers searched until they landed on the switch. I flicked it on—another dull light fighting a losing battle to illuminate the darkness. I blinked, adjusting my eyes to see in the poor light. When I glanced through the steel bars, I sank to my knees.

Valentin.

Valentin was shackled to the wall, his face and body bloodied and beaten. My stomach lurched when I saw deep gashes across his stomach and chest.

He'd lost weight. His head was hanging low on his slumped body. His arms were holding him up and his feet were dragging on the stone floor.

I retched. The sight of this man so broken tore my heart. Spurred into action, I checked the lock of the door and sought to find the right key from the bundle in my hand. It took me five tries to find the right one. As the cell door swung open, I ran in. Valentin didn't move. He didn't lift his head.

My hands were trembling at the sight of him hanging from the wall. I had to look away from his broken body to stop myself from collapsing. Instead I focused on the cuffs around his wrists. I stared at the small lock and searched for the key that would fit. My fingers were clumsy, but I caught sight of a tiny key. It had to be the one.

Holding the key, I edged closer. Inhaling sharply, I whispered, "Valentin?"

A soft moan drifted from Valentin's mouth at the sound of my voice. I saw his fingers flinch. The coil in my chest began to unwind as he fought to lift his head.

I unlocked the cuff on his right hand. As soon as the cuff parted, his body lurched forward. Valentin's large body now hung on the strength of one arm.

I tried to push him up, but his huge frame and height defeated me. I moved to the other cuff and unlocked it. As soon as the metal cuff came apart, Valentin fell facedown on the hard stone floor.

I had to glance away to regain my composure. He was naked. Every inch of his body was bruised, bloodied, or swollen. Zaal had punished him severely.

Half of me was angry at my brother, but the other half understood. I had been unconscious for days, unable to understand or articulate what this Russian man had come to mean to me.

Everything, I thought. *This man had become my everything.*

Spurred back to action, I bent down. I shucked off the coat Talia had given me, ignoring the severe cold in this dank sparse space. Valentin wasn't moving. He lay in a heap on the floor, his arms twisted in the awkward position in which he had fallen.

Rubbing my hands together to generate some heat, I placed them on his side and pushed his body until he lay on his back.

A low stuttered groan came from Valentin's bruised lips. I winced at the sight of his body. My breathing paused when I caught his eyes moving behind swollen eyelids.

"Valentin," I whispered. "Are you okay?"

Valentin tried to move, tried to put his hands on the floor, but when his hands found purchase he was too weak to move.

"No, don't," I soothed, and inched closer. Valentin seemed to relax, his body calming and his breathing evening out. His fingers twitched. When I saw his hand twitch, I realized he was trying to hold my hand. My stomach turned, as I was reassured that he wanted me to hold him.

After everything Valentin still wanted me close.

I carefully laid my palm against his, my fingers featherlight against his. I didn't want to hurt him.

I ran my free hand over his forehead and brought my face close to his. "It's okay, Valentin. I'm here now."

At my words, Valentin squeezed my hand. It was light, barely a squeeze at all, but I could feel his relief that I was here, that he was no longer alone.

My heart ached at the thought of him in this cell, being tortured. I knew this was a strange thought, considering what he'd done to me, but I felt it all the same. He wasn't Valentin then; he was desperately trying to be the hero to his sister—which made him every inch a hero to me.

My eyes roved down his injured body. Unable to suppress the sentiment on the tip of my tongue, I whispered, "I love you."

Valentin's hand tightened on mine. I stared at his bruised hand and how it looked against my skin. Shivers ran over my body at the feel of someone watching me. I glanced up. Staring at me, tired but bright, were Valentin's crystal blue eyes. His dark eyebrows made him appear as severe as always, as did his many facial scars. But those eyes were as soft as a cloud as they gazed upon me.

"Hey," I said, and moved to hover over his face. His hand kept hold of mine. As I felt the warmth from his broken body, my eyes began to fill with tears. His eyes searched mine.

They moved down to search my body. I assured, "I am fine." I knew he was checking that I was okay. His eyebrows pulled down slightly, letting me know he didn't believe me.

Swallowing, I explained, "She drugged me, Valentin. I have been sick for days, but I have no memory. I didn't even remember you until my mind cleared and your eyes flashed in my mind." Tears built, but I blinked them away. "I am so sorry that you're hurt. What Zaal has done to you . . . ," I trailed off.

My head lowered until I laid my cheek against his chest.

"Was . . . deserved."

I stilled when he croaked out his response. I moved to look up but felt his hand gently press my head, and I melted further into his chest at his touch.

I pressed a kiss to his skin and confessed, "Even though I don't remember anything, I feel that I have missed you."

"Zoya," Valentin rasped, and I heard his heart beat louder in his chest.

Zaal's warning about my closeness to Valentin sprang to mind. Coldness filled my body at the thought that I wanted Valentin simply because he had been my captor.

"What?" Valentin asked.

Raising my head to look down at him, I hesitated, then eventually admitted, "Zaal doesn't understand how I can want you. He thinks it's wrong"—I paused and swallowed—"because you hurt me."

Valentin closed his eyes. When they reopened, they were radiating regret. "He's right," Valentin confirmed after a long silence.

I shook my head. He squeezed my hand. "No," I argued. "I'm not some victim who has a strange obsession with their abuser. You are not evil. You were doing what you could to save your sister." I pointed to Valentin's broken body. "Zaal has just done the same." I huffed out a single humorless laugh. "It is gallant in a way. It was cruelty born from the duty of love."

I had run my hand over Valentin's head when his watery gaze looked up at me. He licked across his spilt lips and whispered, "Mistress sent her away."

I froze, then blew out a deep exhale. "I know, baby."

Valentin's eyes squeezed shut, and I could see him fighting for control of his emotions. His entire life had been about saving his sister—his childhood, his teens, his adult life. And he believed he had failed.

Seeing him so upset provided another facet to this kaleidoscope of a man. I had seen him vicious. I had seen him cruel and cold, and I had seen him loving and kind. Now I was seeing him crushed and broken.

I was witnessing him feeling completely alone.

Gripping him tighter, I promised, "We'll get her back, Valentin. Somehow, we'll get her back."

He watched me and confessed, "I don't know what to do."

My heart broke for how lost and young he sounded. "I know," I rasped. "But there will be a way. We will work something out."

He deserved to hear it would all work out, even though deep down I wasn't sure.

Valentin stared after that. He stared at me like I was an angel. Smoothing the back of my hand down his troubled face, I said, "You have me, Valentin. I am not going anywhere. I'm here for you, with you . . . in love with you."

"Kotyonok," he whispered, his sweet name for me warming me to my core. "You're mine? You belong to me?"

Smiling through the emotions wrapping me in their hold, I nodded my head. "Yes. I am yours."

Valentin tried to move but winced as a pain shot through him. Leaning away, I rolled up the sleeves of my sweater and said, "I'll be right back. I'm going to clean you up. I'm going to make the pain go away."

Valentin gripped my hand, but when I smiled and nodded my head he let me go. I rushed out of the cell and up the stairs. The man Kisa had called Pavel was at the top. Straightening my shoulders, I ordered, "I need the heat turned on downstairs. And I need a list of other things sent down immediately!"

Pavel nodded his head without expression and minutes later

brought down what I had asked for. I sat beside Valentin on the floor. "Thank you," I said to Pavel, taking the supplies and feeling warmth from the heating vent raising the temperature of the cell.

As he was about to leave, I called, "Pavel?" He turned. "Can you bring down one of the gym mats I saw upstairs and some linen?"

He frowned at my request, but as I set to cleaning Valentin he brought them down. He soon left us alone.

I cleaned Valentin until I could see his beautiful fair skin once again. Zaal had cut him with something. I realized as I cleaned and poured peroxide on the slashes that I had no idea what Zaal was capable of. I loved him unconditionally. He was my brother. But, like Valentin and, I suspected, like Luka, Zaal was a trained killer.

Two monsters whom I loved.

As I pressed the last of the bandages and sterile strips on Valentin's wounds, I pushed the supplies aside. Taking the gym mat, I pulled it to the corner of the room and dressed it in the linen Pavel had found. He had brought brand-new pillows and a comforter down. I suspected this had something to do with Kisa.

Once a pallet had been made, I turned to see Valentin getting to his feet. His legs shook with the effort. He swayed, and as he did I ran to help him balance, then led him to the bed.

He lay down, and I pulled the comforter over his body. I tucked him in and noticed his broad chest was rising up and down. His glittering blue eyes were on me. Wondering what was wrong, I slid beside him on the mat, sharing his pillow. I took his hand, pressing a kiss to his fingers, and asked, "What is it?"

His beautifully scarred face was conflicted, flushed and warm to the touch. The silence lasted so long I didn't think he would speak. Then he did. "I've slept in a cage so long, that I don't remember ever sleeping on something soft." My heart sank and my throat clogged up. "I don't remember ever having a comforter." Valentin paused and, inching his head closer, he said, "And I know, memories or not, that no one has ever tucked me in. No one has ever cared about me enough to do that."

"Valentin—" I said, my voice weak and hoarse.

Valentin cut in, "I have always been alone. My mama was always on drugs until she overdosed and died. And Inessa, Inessa has been on the drugs so long, she has little or no memory of me. I am alone. Always have been."

"You were alone," I pushed. "You *were* alone. Now you have *me*."

Valentin's chin dropped and he said, "I have nothing to offer you, *kotyonok*. I am nothing; you are a born *printsessa*."

I shook my head. "You are wrong, Valentin." I saw his mouth open to argue; then I said, "Maybe once I was somebody, a *mafiya printsessa,* if you want to call me that. But I am like you. I'm without parents. I have no power, no status, nothing. I am no *printsessa*. I am *nothing, too*."

Valentin studied my face. As he shifted closer, his bare chest pressed against mine. His touch sent shivers to my core and stole my breath. Valentin turned his cheek and kissed my lower neck. My eyes fluttered closed, and he whispered, "You are not nothing. You are everything to me. You are my *printsessa;* my little Georgian *printsessa*."

"You have stolen my breath," I whispered.

Valentin rolled until half of his chest hovered over mine. Looking me straight in the eye, his long scar bright now that he was clean, he whispered back, "You have stolen my heart."

My heart swelled and I smiled. Placing my hand on his cheek, my thumb tracing the scar that was imprinted in my soul, I said, "Then we both are *vory serdtsa;* we are both thieves of the heart."

Valentin growled at my words and crushed his mouth to mine. My blood burned with the desire to be with him again, but when he stiffened at the pain our contact caused I broke away. Valentin's gaze blazed with anger. Pushing him to his back, I laid my cheek on his chest and wrapped my arms around his waist.

"Shh," I soothed, and let my fingers drift over the muscles on his stomach. "I'm not going anywhere. We'll sleep and make love when you heal."

Valentin held me as close as his injuries would allow. Breathing in the scent of my hair, he said, "You cannot stay down here. You cannot stay in these cells. You deserve more."

Clutching him tighter, I responded, "I stay where you stay. And right now we are in the cells. I'm with you. That's all that counts."

Valentin said nothing else. After a long time as we lay in each other's arms, Valentin reluctantly took some pills to help him sleep and heal. We fell asleep wrapped in each other's arms.

I was in a cell, in a dungeon, in a corner of hell itself.

And I couldn't imagine anywhere else I'd rather be.

I blinked, and blinked again, as I tried to focus on what looked like a dark figure sitting just outside the cell. My heart kicked into a sprint as I wondered who it was. As if sensing my rising fear, Valentin held me closer, but the sleeping pills he had taken kept him locked in deep slumber.

I stared and I stared trying to make out a face. Then the shadow shifted position, the dim light revealing who it was.

"Zaal?" I whispered. I could not move from my side of the makeshift bed. Valentin's arm was wrapped around my waist. Even in sleep, he wasn't letting me go.

"It's me." Zaal's deep quiet voice echoed off the walls.

My heart warmed on my hearing his voice. Having him close again after all these years. But there was an awkwardness, too.

"I can barely see you," I said, squinting my eyes to bring him into focus.

"I didn't want you to know I was here," he revealed. His voice was sad in tone. I knew it was because I had hurt him.

"Come closer, *sykhaara,*" I instructed softly.

Zaal paused, but I saw his legs move. My brother rose to his impressive height and slowly moved closer to the bars of the cell. Zaal stepped into the light. I couldn't help but smile at his long hair that hung over his shoulders. He was wearing all black—black shirt and black jeans. I smiled wider knowing that Zaal had become the man my father dreamed he would be. My throat clogged with emotion when I imagined a replica of him standing by his side. Together, my brothers would have been a force to be reckoned with.

Zaal's head was down as he loomed beyond the bars.

"Why were you hiding, *sykhaara*?"

His shoulders dropped and he ran his hand through his long hair. "I didn't think you'd want to see me. But I needed to know you were safe. I needed to make sure you were okay."

In an act of possession, I ran my hand over Valentin's arm around my waist and tucked myself farther against his chest. Valentin never stirred, but I heard a soft sigh escape his lips and blow against my hair.

I smiled a whisper of a smile and lifted his hand to kiss his warm clean skin. A sound from beyond the cell pulled my attention, and when I glanced up I saw Zaal had sat down on the floor, right in the center of the doorway. He leaned against the rigid bars, his torso facing mine.

I stared at my brother. He had his legs bent and his strong arms leaning on his elbows. His head was down, and my heart sank with disappointment at how awkward our meeting had been.

Keeping hold of Valentin's hand for strength, I admitted, "I did not imagine that our reunion would be so strained."

Zaal tensed. I watched as his head dropped farther forward. Inhaling deeply, he agreed, "Neither did I."

He didn't add anything else. In this reserved persona I saw the Zaal of old. Anri had always been the joker, the louder of the two. He would speak for Zaal, Zaal—quiet, timid, but just as strong—stood at Anri's side. It seemed all the years spent apart had not changed the fact that Zaal was happy to let others speak while he sat back and watched the world from afar.

I pictured him laughing with Talia and wondered if she was louder in personality. I hoped so. Zaal needed someone vibrant in his life. He was never happy being alone.

Sighing, I ran my hand down my face and said, "I dreamed what meeting you again would be like." I huffed a laugh and admitted, "I fear I may have placed too much expectation on that dream. The reality of seeing you again is so different."

Zaal tensed. His head moved as if my words had struck a sensitive chord. Panicking, I proclaimed, "I love you, *sykhaara.* This has never changed. And I am so unbelievably happy you are here. You're my big brother and I have you back. I have family again." I laughed, gentler this time, and said, "You know you were always my favorite. You were my hero and my heart. That is unchanged. In fact, seeing you again has only strengthened that love."

Zaal kept his head down, and I pleaded, "Please look at me, *sykhaara.*"

Zaal raised his head. His bright green gaze met mine. Just as I thought he would not speak again, he rasped brokenly, "I watched you die. I watched you all die. I see it so clearly now—the screams, the blood, all of it." He tapped his head. "But the drugs stole that from me for many years. They made it all go away. Jakhua made me his dog. I killed him for that, but worse, he stole my memories of you, of Anri, of all the family." His face contorted. "I am still missing some years. Some things I can't remember, but I always remembered you." Zaal lifted his hand to touch his three moles. His eyes warmed as he did, and I whispered, "One, two, three."

Zaal slowly nodded his head and his thick lips hooked into a shy smile. It quickly dropped, but he confessed, "The memories came back quickly, but so did the pain. I relived everything over and over again, and it's been killing me, Zoya." He clenched his hands, then added, "It killed me remembering you the most, reaching out your little arms for me to take. Screaming for me to save you. It kept me awake every night." He shook his head in disbelief. "And now you're here. Before me. But older and different. A woman. A strong woman." Zaal smiled. "You think Papa would have been proud of me. I know he would have been proud of you. What you've been through . . ."

His eyes fell on Valentin's arms holding me possessively, and I said, "He's not leaving me. I'm not leaving him. I love him."

Zaal sighed and dropped his head again. "He hurt you, Zoya. I saw it. And I fucking broke. I don't know if I can get past it. You fell for your torturer."

I held Valentin tighter and glanced behind me to see his scarred face relaxed in sleep. The face I once thought of as monstrous I now only saw as beautiful. Leaning in, I kissed the long scar on his cheek and said, "I love him. I know how it looks, but you only saw glimpses of him on the drugs, or fighting for his sister." With a final stroke of his cheek, I turned back to Zaal. "You would have done the same. Tell me, if Jakhua had me locked away and on the Type B drug, if you had to watch me get raped by men but were promised that if you just killed one more hit I would be free, would you have done whatever he would have asked?"

Zaal's jaw clenched, and he said darkly, "I wouldn't have had a choice if I was on the drugs."

"So was Valentin."

"Not all the time," Zaal argued.

"And if that was you, what would you have done?"

Zaal's silence told me I'd finally gotten through. Shaking my head, I said, "I do not want to argue, *sykhaara.* But I won't give him up. Our lives have been so hard. I have forever dreamed of finding my true love. I never imagined it would be through this dark path, but I find myself here and happy. I find myself in love with *this* man."

Zaal stared at Valentin's hand in mine. I brought it to lie under my cheek and proclaimed, "Zaal, I shall make you a deal."

Zaal frowned. A ghost of a humored smile spread on his lips. He waited for me to speak. Hope stirred in my heart. "Kisa and I spoke at length. She helped me see things clearly. I"—I coughed, finding the next sentence difficult—"I would like to know Talia. I would like to know your love, because she is yours." I forced to the side the pain of who her family was, and I continued, "She is your present and your future. As sad as it makes me, I am your *past.*" Making sure Zaal's eyes were fixed on mine, I said, "We knew each other as children, Zaal, when life was simple and easy. I would very much like to know you *now.*" I fought the thickness from my throat. "I would very much like you to be my best friend again."

"I want that too, so much," Zaal admitted hoarsely.

I smiled on noticing the tension leave his shoulders. "But you have to accept Valentin. He is mine; I am his. That's how it will be. You do not know what he has been through, though if you took the time to speak to him you might find you are not so dissimilar."

Zaal glanced away but curtly nodded his head. "I asked him to speak to me over the past three days. I asked him to explain everything to me, but he wouldn't. He just kept telling me you were better off without him, that he was your Tbilisi monster in the woods. That there was no *good* in his heart, like you thought there was."

Tears fell down my cheeks on my hearing that Valentin had said such sad things. "He has lost his sister, Zaal." I pointed at Zaal, then to myself. "Just like you had lost me. He is broken." Zaal remained still, unmoving, and I added quietly, "But I think *I* can heal him. I think *I* can give him something he has never had before."

"What's that?" Zaal asked huskily.

"Love. Affection. A safe place. Someone who actually cares for him." I blushed and said, "The way he watched me as I cleaned him and tucked him in bed, it makes me want to hold him and never ever let go. He calls himself an ugly scarred beast, but I also see the beautiful man beneath. Even if you don't, he's there. And he's the other half of my soul. Whether it is rational or not. Whether it's wrong or not."

Zaal was quiet for many minutes, then nodded his head. "I *will* get to know him and *I will* accept him. We were all fucked up by those people. But now he is out, and he is strong. And if Luka and I are any indication, he will find it hard adjusting to life outside." Zaal patted his chest. "As your brother, I will help him adjust."

My cheeks were wet with gratitude. Gently moving out of Valentin's embrace, I stood up from the mat and walked to Zaal. Zaal got to his feet and stood anxiously before me. A wave of shattering emotion, mainly gratitude, washed over me. Needing my big brother, I launched forward and wrapped my arms around his waist. Zaal held me close, and I warmed knowing this was the reunion we should have had. This was Zoya holding her Zaal—like it always should have been.

I held him for what felt like an age. Drawing back, I reached up to hold his head and pulled him down. I pressed a kiss on his forehead and brushed my thumb over his moles. Catching the instant smile on his face I declared, "I love you, Zaal. You are my blood. My heart. My big warrior brother."

"I love you, Zoya." Zaal pulled back and nervously said, "Talia is upstairs. We are never apart. She does for me what you do for Valentin. She cares for me. She loved me when I could not remember what love was." My heart squeezed and I immediately regretted my earlier reaction. I hadn't let myself see it or maybe I simply didn't acknowledge that he was damaged, too. Right now, hearing him talk of Talia as though she was his lifeline, I could detect the vulnerability in his voice. He *was* just like Valentin: a killer, a monster that deep down simply wanted to be loved.

Zaal shifted on his feet and muttered, "Would you . . . could you—"

"Meet her properly?" I interrupted.

Zaal's eyes were wide with apprehension. "Yes," I replied.

Zaal sharply exhaled and said, "If you give her a chance, you will love her. And"—he paused—"and she wants to know you, too. She's been upset since you left."

Shame flowed in my blood and I pointed to the stairs. "Then let's go. I want to be back in case Valentin wakes up."

Zaal led the way. When he opened the door to the gym, I heard a female voice ask, "How is she, baby? Would she speak to you? Are you okay?"

Before Zaal could reply, I walked through the door, to see her arms around his neck. Talia's brown eyes landed on me and I walked to her side. Talia broke from Zaal and stood proudly at his side.

I could see the confidence she clearly had in the way she stood. And to my shame, I could also see how much she wanted to know me. Talia glanced to Zaal, whose face still betrayed his apprehension.

I made myself store away my conditioned reaction to her being a Tolstaia. Instead I offered my hand. Talia's shocked face fixed on my hand, but, slowly, she threaded her hand through mine.

"Talia," I greeted, and cleared my throat. "It's nice to meet you. I apologize for my reaction to you this morning." I looked at Zaal to see his pride for me on his face, and that look, that look from my big brother, forced the last fragment of our family's historic betrayal in my heart to fade away.

"Zoya," Talia said in response. She looked like she wanted to say more. Instead she wrapped her arms around me and pulled me close. I was surprised at first, but when I saw Zaal laugh at his fiancée's embrace—*he laughed*—I let it happen. As Talia went to move away, a simple "Thank you" drifted past my ear.

She was thanking me for making him happy.

I smiled at Talia and Zaal. As he put his hand around her shoulders, Talia said, "Thank you for coming to see me."

I had turned to go back downstairs when Zaal asked, "Where are you going?"

I froze. "Back to Valentin. He remains here; therefore so do I. I'm staying with him; he's my heart, Zaal." I flicked a look at Zaal and said, "He's badly injured, *sykhaara:* he needs to heal. And he's alone. He needs me."

I had set off for the stairs when I heard: "You'll both come with us. There's no way I'm having my sister-in-law and her boyfriend sleeping in this place, in 'the Darkness,' for Christ sakes. You'll come home with us; we have plenty of room. And you'll stay for however long you wish."

I had opened my mouth to respond when Zaal caught Pavel's eye. Zaal flicked his head and said, "Help me get Valentin into the car; we're taking him to my home." Before I could argue, Zaal had walked down the stairs, Pavel and some other guards following immediately behind.

As I watched Valentin go I felt my heart swell. Suddenly Talia was beside me, and she laid a hand on my shoulder. "You have completed him, Zoya. By returning, you have healed the last crack in his heart."

Without looking at her, I said, "Not as much as you do. I may have only been five when we parted, but I know my brother, and you have saved him. I didn't need to be here to know what you've done for him."

Talia was silent: then she whispered, "It's because I love him more than myself. More than life."

I hid a happy smile. Shrugging, I replied, "Then no matter what has happened between our families in the past, this allows us to forgive, forget, and rebuild."

"It does?" Talia asked with a relieved sigh.

"It does."

Then we all went home.

22

ZOYA

A week came and went, days spent lying beside Valentin in bed. With each day he grew stronger. He didn't speak often. I could tell that his mind would wander to dark places—he had so many to choose from that I was never quite sure which occupied his mind. But the times he held me close, the times he curled me against his body and pulled me hard against his chest as though I might leave if he didn't keep me close, I knew he was thinking of his sister.

He would kiss me and touch me, but never sexually. I wasn't sure if it was due to his injuries or something more sinister. He caressed me as though he was savoring every part of me—committing me to memory, as he had said to me in the chamber. It sent fear down my spine, because to me it felt like our situation was temporary—like he feared that one day we must say good-bye.

When I woke each day, it was to find him watching me, body tensed like he was preparing for me to say or do something—I didn't know what. When I asked him if he was okay, he would pull me close and simply say, "Yes."

But there was something.

Zaal and Talia left us alone, but I had begun to spend time with them, little by little. And Zaal was right, I really liked Talia, and I loved how deeply she loved my brother.

One day later that week, I walked into our suite's bedroom and found the bed was empty. I frowned. Valentin did not seem to be strong enough to be out of bed when I checked in on him this morning. I placed my coffee on the table and headed for the bathroom. As I approached I heard the sound of the running shower.

Silently I pushed the door open and tiptoed inside. Valentin's sweatpants were in a heap on the floor. When I looked at the glass cubicle, I saw his large body standing motionless under the hot spray.

Steam billowed in the room, fogging up the large mirror on the wall. Even though the steam was thick I could see Valentin's head was down, the fast spray caressing his skull.

Without thinking I stripped off my clothes, dropping them on the floor over his. The steam clung to my skin. Eyes fixed on Valentin, I quietly opened the shower door and slipped inside. The door closed behind me. In his numb state Valentin didn't even register that I was behind him.

I lifted my hands to touch Valentin's broad tattooed scarred back. Valentin jumped when my hands touched his skin, and his head whipped back to look at me. His eyes were pained yet soft as they met mine. His head turned forward, and I pressed my mouth to his wet skin, peppering kisses along his wide shoulders.

Valentin's skin tasted sweet against my mouth. Continuing my exploration, I moved around his body until I was standing in front of him. Valentin's head was downcast, but that didn't stop me kissing his chest, over the black tattooed identity number.

His breathing increased as I sucked and lapped at his skin. Too much time had passed since we'd made love. And we were out of the chamber and free. We were free to make love without the fear of being caught or hurt.

Just us.

Joined.

In love.

My hands ran over Valentin's pectorals and as they ghosted over his skin I felt moisture pool at my core. My hands dropped down to Valentin's ripped torso, until they moved to his length—his length was hard, awaiting my attention.

I rolled my lips and glanced to his face, but Valentin's head was still down. His eyes were squeezed shut and his nostrils were flared. His full lips were thin and pursed. His muscles felt like stone under my touch.

I couldn't understand what was wrong. I knew if I asked him he wouldn't answer me. Whatever was troubling him was buried deep inside.

Needing him to snap out of this numbness, I wrapped my hand around his hardness and began stroking it up and down. Slowly at first, but harder and faster when no reaction was forthcoming.

"Valentin," I whispered as my mouth found his nipple and licked over the flesh. I moaned at the taste and closeness of this dominant man. I squeezed my thighs together as the pressure at my center began to ache.

Valentin's breathing labored at my attention. Just when I feared nothing would happen, Valentin suddenly reached forward. Hard and powerful hands picked me up and Valentin's hard body slammed me against the wall. My head threw back as his mouth kissed my neck, and I cried out as his chest pushed against my breasts. My fingers clutched at his bulging back, and when his length slipped to run through my folds my fingernails pushed through his skin.

Valentin snapped.

Suddenly pulling himself from his numbness, Valentin roared out long and loud and hitched up my legs. My back slid up the wet tiles of the shower. Before I could draw breath, Valentin slammed into my channel. I cried out, a mixture of shock and intense pleasure from the fullness of Valentine inside me. He did not pause for me to adjust to his size. Instead he tucked his head in the crook between my neck and shoulder, and began thrusting hard and fast. I gripped on to his shoulders as he possessed and dominated me. I submitted, wholeheartedly and with complete abandon. It was quick, the quickest I had ever felt the oncoming climax. As if sensing I was about to burst apart, Valentin pounded into me with an incredible force, my mouth dropping open and a scream pouring out into the steamy air as my climax took me by surprise.

Behind my eyes, bright lights blinded me and my body convulsed at the all-consuming pleasure surging through my body. My core clenched Valentin's length, and with a loud cry Valentin slammed into me one last time. Every muscle in Valentin's body stiffened and his grip on my legs was iron tight. His seed was warm as it poured into me. Our breathing, in the aftermath, was heavy.

My head, now limp, fell to lie on Valentin's shoulder. I smiled, feeling weightless and loved.

This was what I craved from Valentin. His strong and unyielding presence. After a lifetime of feeling unsafe, his presence brought with it a sense of protection and possession.

I breathed in the hot air that filled every inch of the cubicle. After minutes suspended in the same position, Valentin pulled out from within me and brought me to my feet. My cheek was pressed against his torso, and I leaned against his strongly built frame.

Valentin tensed when I lifted my head. When I looked up into his eyes, they were wide and braced, as though I was about to react. As if I were about to say something that would crush his soul.

Nervousness trickled into my body. Lifting my hands to pull his head down to me, I asked, "Talk to me. Tell me what's wrong. Your eyes, your beautiful eyes, are wide and filled with apprehension, but I don't know why. You need to talk to me, Valentin. I love you. Please let me in."

Valentin expelled a rough breath. Seeming full of frustration, he turned on his heel and pushed out of the shower. He left the bathroom without drying off or taking a towel. Wanting this resolved now, I followed.

My skin shivered as my nakedness hit the cooler air of the bedroom. But I ignored it. My eyes fixed on Valentin, who was sitting on the end of the bed. He head was in his hands, his knuckles white and his muscles flinching.

I approached slowly and spoke. "Valentin—"

"How is it that you're with me?" Valentin interrupted. I stilled, shocked and confused by his very direct question.

"How is it that I'm with you?" I asked gently, not wanting to upset him more.

Valentin lifted his head and his tortured blue eyes bored into mine. My heart sank when I saw real doubt etched on his face. He really meant this. He meant every single word. He couldn't understand why I was here with him.

"Valentin," I spoke, "I love you. Surely that is reason enough?"

Valentin looked down at his hands, his palms upturned. He glared at his hands and said, "I hurt you. I caused you pain. I made you scream. How can you love me? Lots of time has gone past, and I keep waiting, I keep waiting for you to realize that you thought you loved me, because I had captured you and made you bend to my will. Every day when you wake, I wait for you to see the real monster lying in your bed. I wait for you to tell me to leave, disgusted by what I've done to you."

My mouth dropped open hearing such rawness, the sheer pain in his voice. "I won't," I assured.

But Valentin got to his feet and shook his head. "You will. I took your innocence and made you mine. You said it yourself; I am a thief of hearts. I stole your first kiss with these lips. I stole your virgin barrier. And I took you, possessed you, made you mine. And

I did that. I did that without your permission. I took it. And foolishly, you fell in love with me, the fucking ugly beast."

Anger stirred within me. Stepping forward, I pointed at his chest, and I shouted, "I may have fallen for you, *beast or not*, but never call me foolish! I may have been untouched, but I was anything but innocent. I wanted *you*. Despite how fucked-up it sounds, I wanted to feel your hand caress me when I was shackled to that wall. Not at first; at first you terrified me. Of course I feared you, but when I saw the real you emerge through my pleasure, I craved you. I wanted you to take me."

"That's fucked up, Zoya," he stated plainly.

"Then it's fucked up. I don't care."

Valentin's lips pulled over his teeth and he stepped forward to meet me. His huge frame towered over me. The scowl on his scarred and stern face should have induced fear. But for me, it didn't.

Valentin peered down at me and, grabbing my hand, he brought it to his face. He ran my fingers over his deep scars—on his cheeks, on and over his eyes, down the side of his lips, and down to his chest. I watched my roving hand, but Valentin stopped, too many scars on his skin to pick one out.

He guided my palm to stop on his ruined face and asked, "How can you want this?" There was no longer any anger in his voice; instead his shoulders had slumped and his expression pleaded with me for an answer.

I couldn't give one. His face was beautiful to me. Scarred, ruined, or not.

"I have looked in the mirror since we have been free. The drugs have finally gone from my body, allowing me a clarity I've never had before. And I can see me. I can see the man I've become. The man that fucking evil bitch turned me into. A monster to look at, and the things I've done . . ." I shook my head, but Valentin put his fingers over my lips to silence me. "*Kotyonok,* I *am* your Tbilisi monster. I stole you like the monster stole the children. I hurt you just like the monster hurt them. Only you can't see it."

His piercing blue eyes—the only part of his face untouched—searched mine. I knew he was waiting for the penny to drop. He was waiting for me to realize I didn't want him.

He'd never been wanted.

Only this time he was, and he didn't know how to deal with it.

Removing Valentin's fingers from my lips, I clutched them in my hand and said, "You're right." I watched as his face paled with devastation as soon as those words left my lips. Feeling his pain in my heart, I stepped even closer, until our chests touched, and continued, "You are the Tbilisi monster, Valentin. You stole me. You hurt me. You brought me pain." Valentin had stilled, but with a tilted head and an expression of pure love I added, "But from the minute I heard the story I had an obsession with that monster. And when all the children were running away from the dangerous monster in the woods, I would instead stand at the edge of the line of trees, searching through the darkness of the forest, trying to bring him home, so he would not be alone, so he would never again be alone."

Valentin's expression caused my heart to crack. I knew the regret for what he'd done to me was taking its hold.

"I can't make love," he abruptly whispered. "I can only fuck, brutal and hard. It's all I've ever known." He stepped back as if his very presence would wound me.

I followed this movement. "That's fine, because *I* can make love to you."

His head shook in protest. "I'm not soft or kind or loving, or—"

"That's fine, because I am all of these things and, besides, *I love you. You,* not someone you think I should have."

Valentin groaned as though he couldn't cope with my words. His hands lifted to grip the sides of his head. "I'm fucked up. The

Mistress fucked me up. I'll cause you pain even when I want to make love." He paused, and with lost eyes he said, "And I look like this; I'm designed to scare everyone I meet. I was never meant to be loved."

Closing in until we shared the same air, I reached down and took hold of his length, and I said, "And all that is fine, because I love you unconditionally, and I will not break. You can be who you need to be with *me*. You can dominate me, possess me, and own me. Because I want *you* and accept whatever that comes with. I want to love you and want you to love me back, so that we both are never again alone."

"Zoya," Valentin whispered painfully, but this time I heard a hint of acceptance in his tone. His length hardened at my touch.

Flesh to flesh, I moved my mouth below his ear and said, "I am going to make love to you now. I am going to take the lead and show you with my body just how I feel for you, in my heart."

Valentin's forehead fell onto my shoulder, and he admitted in a hushed voice, "I'm not only scarred on the outside, *kotyonok;* I'm scarred on the inside: my mind, my heart, and my soul."

I fought back tears and the raw emotion of his confession. Turning my head until my lips met his long scar, I pressed them against the raised skin and said, "And I will find those scars as beautiful as I do these."

A strangled moan fell from Valentin's lips. As it did, I pushed him down on the bed, my hands on his chest.

Valentin lay back on the mattress. Wet and ready, needing to physically express my love, I straddled Valentin's thighs and crushed my lips against his.

As soon as I tasted him in my mouth, I rolled my wet center along his length, slow and controlled, lovingly, not rushed. Valentin wrapped his arms around my waist. Following my lead, he lazily massaged his tongue against mine. I was breathless from the slow intensity of this moment. Needing more, needing to show him just how much he was wanted, I lifted my thighs and, with my hand, placed his hardness at my entrance.

I pushed down, the tip of his length breaching my channel. Pausing, I caged in Valentin's head with my arms and licked along the seam of his lips with my tongue. Valentin tried to take control and pushed me down on his length, but I shook my head, and whispered, "Just feel. Let me go slow."

A low growl built in his chest, but his hands loosened and with a painstaking yet delicious slowness I pushed down on his length, taking him into my body inch by inch.

Valentin threw his head back, his eyes closed and his mouth opened at the intensity of the feeling. "I love you," I confessed quietly as I took him all in and he filled me so full.

I smoothed my hands down to his shoulders. Using his strength, I pushed up until only the tip of him was still inside me, before pushing back down on a long hungry groan.

I rose and fell, rose and fell, until a light sheen had built on our skin. Valentin's eyes were leaden and filled with love as he allowed me to take control. His heart beat like a drum in his chest, and his warm minty breath released in short ragged pants.

As I felt my body beginning to tingle, both of our moans grew in volume and speed. I rolled my hips back and forth, my clit dragging against his hard muscles.

"Valentin," I whispered so it was barely audible, "I'm close, baby. I'm so close."

Valentin opened his mouth, but his voice hitched in his throat. I knew that was a sign he was close; with that his length seemed to expand within my channel, its girth pushing against something inside me that made me see stars.

I increased my speed, my arms locking behind Valentin's thick neck. I moaned; he groaned. I built us higher and higher. Valentin's fingers suddenly tightened on my legs, and stilling, his face showed his pleasure as he poured himself into my channel with a long loud cry. At his release, I lost control. Unable to hold back any longer, I felt myself slip over the edge, light and shivers accosting my body as a blazing heat engulfed me from within.

My heart beat in rhythm with his. I slumped against his chest, replete and happy. I was happy. With Valentin, I was completely happy and content. My whole life my soul had yearned for something I couldn't comprehend, but it was this. It was sharing itself with my true Russian love.

My beautiful monster.

My heart.

Valentin's arms never released from mine, nor mine his. Eventually, I pulled back my head, only for Valentin to crush his lips to mine in a quick searing kiss.

Breaking the kiss, he searched my eyes and said, "I love you, *kotyonok*. So much."

Smiling wide, I peppered kisses all across his face and said, "I love you, too."

Valentin sighed and rolled us back onto the bed. We stayed joined, until Valentin withdrew from inside me and pulled me to his chest. I sprawled across his torso. Keeping tight hold of me, he asked, "So you are mine? Now and forever, mine?"

My heart swelled and a peace rippled through me. "Yes," I said without a hint of doubt, "I'm yours. I belong to you. You possess and own me. As I do you."

Valentin squeezed me hard. When I looked up, he was smiling. I lost my breath at the sight. He wasn't the monster he believed himself to be; he was simply my Valentin. A fellow thief of hearts.

I had closed my eyes, content with where I was, when Valentin suddenly asked, "What now, Zoya? What happens now that we are free? I never thought ahead this far, and now we're here, I have no idea what happens next."

My eyes opened and I moved to lean on Valentin's chest. Meeting his eyes, I confessed, "I don't know, baby, but whatever happens, we'll do it together."

He nodded, deep in thought, and I knew he was thinking of Inessa. Kissing his sternum, I laid my head back down against his chest. As I drifted off to sleep, I felt Valentin's hand trace down my spine, and he whispered to himself, "No longer alone. I'll never be alone ever again."

My lips pulled into a small satisfied smile.

Then I drifted off to sleep.

In love.

Nightmare-free.

And heart claimed.

23

LUKA

Two weeks later . . .

Kirill stood up from the dining room table now that everyone had finished their meal. He walked from the room to my father's office. My father, Zaal, and I got up from our seats to follow.

I glanced back to the table and saw Valentin watching us go. He never spoke during these dinners, but then neither did Zoya. They ate and answered questions when asked, but dinner with the Bratva seemed to put them both out of their depth. I remembered how that felt, to be new to this "normal" life. To no longer be locked away like a fucking animal or, in Zoya's case, like a target. Shit, Zaal was still finding it difficult, but at least he had Talia. Zoya and Valentin both seemed lost, but then, the way they never let go of each other's hands, they now had each other.

That was everything in this life.

Zaal was coming around to Valentin. Slowly, but he was trying. Zoya was trying with the family too, spending time with Talia when she could, allowing my sister to burrow into her life, like Talia did with everyone she met.

But Kisa? My heart squeezed when I thought of how she'd

stepped up to bring Zoya into our lives. And I could see that Zoya adored her. But that was how my wife was.

Kirill's face had lit up with interest when he had officially met Valentin. The massive man had walked into my parents' house with his shaven head and scarred face, the inch-thick permanent red scar of the collar wrapping around his neck. I knew what the Pakhan was seeing—a monster of a Russian. Trained to kill, an expert in torture, and, through Zoya, tied to our family. Valentin was a Pakhan's wet dream. The things he could do, and the way he was built and looked scary enough for our enemies to drop in submission at his feet.

My mama's eyes had widened as Valentin walked into the room for the first time two weeks ago. He looked like something from a horror movie when compared to Zoya's pretty face, his hand locked tightly in hers. But my mama had pulled herself together and hugged him to her chest. He had been welcomed straight into the fold.

Someone cleared his throat. When I looked up, my father was at the door. He waved his hand for me to come inside. I entered the office and took my place on the other side of the desk from Kirill, who poured us each a drink.

Sitting back in his seat, Kirill said, "So, Arziani . . ." He paused and took a sip of his premium vodka. I stilled, desperate to know what our insiders, what Zaal's insiders, had managed to find out.

Kirill shook his head. For the first time ever, I saw a hint of worry in his stern face. My stomach tightened at this glimpse of concern. Kirill feared nothing and no one; he was so confident in our Bratva that it was borderline arrogance.

As he placed his glass on the table, his face morphed with anger. Clearing his throat, he said, "The Arzianis are an underground Georgian enterprise. But unlike anything I've heard of before. From what I can tell, Arziani runs his empire—because it is an international empire—like a new Stalin. His men are organized and military grade."

Kirill reached into his pocket and threw a silver pin on the desk. I leaned forward, seeing an emblem of two swords, one lying over the other. Kirill pointed to the pin. "Their emblem. They wear it on their black uniforms."

Zaal glanced to me. I could see the rage on his face, too. These bastards had him in their hold as a child. He wanted them dead and gone.

"To my knowledge, there are hundreds of these men all over the world. They live in secret. The very fact that they've managed to keep off our radar tells us everything we need to know about them—they're good. Dangerous. Nothing like we've ever seen before. They don't operate like a crime family, or any made men that we see in this life. They're their own entity."

We were all silent as we soaked up this information. My father sat forward and picked up the emblem. He ran his thumb over the swords and asked, "And how do we know of them now?"

Kirill pointed to Zaal. Zaal shifted on his seat. "One of my men has a cousin in Georgia that began worrying about one of his family members. He was sneaking off in the middle of the night. His father followed him one time. He said the boy was attending a rally. A Night Wraith rally, as they're known. He said at the end of the rally his son pledged something to the male standing on a raised stage. His father questioned him about it when he got home. But the next day his son had vanished. He hasn't been seen since." Zaal met all of our eyes and explained, "They believe he was recruited by these Wraiths, and taken away to work for them."

"The Blood Pit," I said knowingly.

Zaal nodded his head. "I think so. That and the gulags, and any other routes they run."

"Shit," my father said, speaking for us all. "Are they a threat to us?" my father asked. I whipped my head round to look directly at him. My father met my furious eyes and paled. "Luka—"

"They deserve to die, threat or not," I said coldly, my hands almost snapping the wooden arms of the chair. "They fucking forced me to fight. They took my memories with their drugs and they raped me. Over and over again, for years." I fought to breathe, then growled, "Threat or not, I get near them and I'll tear them apart."

I felt Zaal radiating fury on his seat and he added, "And whatever's left will be mine."

My father's eyes widened and he flitted his worried gaze between me and Zaal. "Luka—"

"We've heard rumors that they intend to come to New York." My blood went from warm to scalding hot in an instant as Kirill moved the conversation on.

"Coming to New York?" I questioned darkly.

Kirill shifted to rest his elbows on his desk and said, "To establish a gulag. The Georgian scum intend to bring a death-match ring to *my* city, on *my* turf, and they plan to do it under *my* nose."

"They come and they'll ignite a war," my father said coolly, but as I looked to his face I could see he was anything but calm.

"Unless we kill them first," I offered. Kirill smiled at me with his coldest smile and nodded his head.

"Unless we kill them first," Kirill echoed.

The room fell silent again. Kirill leaned back on his seat. "We have found out that Abram Durov was being paid off by a Georgian organization. At the time of his death, it was assumed it was a private business, because it wasn't attached to any crime family. Now"—Kirill's sharp face darkened—"now we know that he was paid off by the Arzianis. Paid off to keep them from our knowledge." Kirill faced me. "Kept close so when the day came he had an out for the things his psycho of a son did to this brotherhood."

"Me," I stated. "He kept them close so he could send me away after Alik killed Rodian."

The Pakhan's face was like stone, and he sat before me as Kirill "the Silencer" Volkov. This was the man who ran the most successful crime ring in the world.

"How do we find out more about them?" my father said. Zaal leaned forward and pointed to the door.

"He's sitting around the dining table," he said, and pulled all of our attention. Zaal's jaw clenched and he said, "Valentin. He knows about the Night Wraiths. The Mistress was Arziani's sister. Unlike me, the drugs only worked temporarily on him, so he watched them. Studied them. He remembers everything."

"What do you mean, 'remembers everything'?" Kirill asked. That glint of excitement was back in his eyes when anyone spoke of Valentin.

"Everything," Zaal pushed. "Names, ages, maps, locations, number of men our enemies have, weapons they use, schedules—*everything*. It's all so strange to me, but he remembers details about everything he has experienced, has happened, in his life."

Kirill smiled and said, "An eidetic memory." Kirill faced my father. "A trained killer and assassin, an expert in torture, and he remembers everything he sees and hears. Including the Arziani Blood Pit."

"But more than that," I added. All eyes fell on me. I sat back in my seat and said, "They have his sister. The Master, Arziani, has an obsession with Valentin's sister. She's on the drug they use for their sex slaves and trafficked females." I stared at the door of the office, like I was looking straight at Valentin. "Valentin will do anything to get her back."

"A vicious assassin who will do anything to get his sister back?" Kirill's skin flushed with the prospect of having someone as lethal as Valentin as a member of our inner circle. Kirill faced Zaal. "How loyal is he to your sister? We need this man. If we bring him in without a trial period, he could betray us."

Zaal shook his head. "She is for him. He's not leaving her. They are forever."

"And he's Russian," my father added. "He knows of us. He respected us when he found out who we were."

"And he needs a purpose. If he is to survive in this new life, he needs to do what he does best—kill. It's what he's been made into and there's no going back." I met Zaal's eyes and said, "For any of us who have known that life."

Kirill's hands steepled. After several seconds of thought, he ordered, "Bring him in!"

Rising from my chair, I walked outside to find Valentin standing at the window of the dining room, staring outside. When I walked in, his scarred face turned toward me. I nudged my head. Valentin's eyes narrowed.

"Come," I said.

I saw Zoya stand up from the table and ask, "Where are you taking him?"

"The Pakhan wants to see him."

Zoya's eyes were suspicious. I glanced to Kisa, and when she saw me I nodded my head. Kisa rose from her seat. Placing her hand on Zoya's arm she said, "He'll be fine, Zoya. Let him go in; you sit with us." Zoya stared at me in suspicion. I knew she didn't entirely trust our family yet, but she would in time.

Valentin leaned in to speak into Zoya's ear. Her shoulders sagged at whatever he said; then Valentin lifted her chin and kissed her on her lips. It still looked strange, a man so raw and ravaged with scars acting so soft with his pretty female.

He broke away and without looking back followed me. We entered the office. As we did, I watched his assessing eyes drinking in the room—committing everything to memory.

Kirill stood. As he did, Valentin tensed. "Valentin," Kirill greeted, and pointed at a spare seat next to Zaal. "Take a seat."

Valentin's arms were crossed over his chest, but under the Pakhan's stare he walked to the seat. He sat down and Zaal nodded his head. I sat down, too. Kirill poured Valentin a drink.

Kirill pushed the vodka to Valentin and said, "The Arzianis are planning to set up a gulag here in New York." The air in the room thickened as soon as Kirill mentioned the Arzianis to Valentin. Kirill's face hardened. "We can't allow that to happen."

"What do you need to know?" Valentin said, the hatred that he felt for the Georgian organization clear in his deep voice.

"Everything," Kirill replied. "Everything *you* know."

"I know a lot," Valentin informed.

Kirill's face spread into a wide smile. "Even better."

Valentin shifted on his seat and said, "I'll tell you anything you need to know, but on one condition."

Kirill cocked his head to the side, and I knew he was taken aback by Valentin's disrespectful response. You didn't negotiate with the Pakhan; you did what he said without conditions.

Kirill laughed and said, "You have balls, Valentin. But"—Kirill leaned back—"I'm listening."

Valentin's jaw tensed and he said, "I want my sister back. I want your word that we'll get my sister back. Whatever the cost."

Kirill nodded and asked, "What else?"

Fury spread across Valentin's hard face and he growled, "That I get to kill as many of the Wraiths that I can lay my hands on. However it needs to be done. Torture, stealth, or out-and-out war, just let me tear them all apart for everything they've done. I'll be the most effective killer you'll ever have. Trust me on that."

Blood rushed through me at the excitement in Valentin's voice. His tone and message were contagious. I saw Zaal nodding his head; he too wanted a share of the kills. Kirill stared at the three of us all sitting beside one another and his face lit with pride. He slowly nodded his head. Moving around his desk, he held his hand out to Valentin. Valentin took his hand, kissed the back, and brought it to his head.

Now he was pledged to the Volkov Red King.

Kirill stepped back, folded his arms, and said, "We will gather what we know from Valentin, then wait."

My skin pricked with shivers. With a wave of his hand the meeting was over. My father stood and said, "Come. Let's go and drink. I need one."

One by one we filed from the office into the living room. Kisa stood up as I came in. Wrapping my hands around her waist, I pulled her close.

"Everything okay?" she asked as she melted into my body.

Pulling her back, I placed my hand on her rounded stomach and said, "Perfect."

Kisa smiled and hugged me again. Over my wife's head, I met the gazes of Zaal and then Valentin. They were looking at me as they held their females tightly in their arms.

I could see the hunger for revenge burning in their eyes, the thirst for the kill. I could feel the heat rushing through my body, as I anticipated the fight that lay ahead, knowing they would be feeling this way, too.

The Arzianis were the head of the snake that controlled everything we three had been through.

A head that I planned to rip off.

These men were my brothers in arms.

And we were fucking going to war, for the prisoners yet to be freed.

EPILOGUE: VALENTIN

One month later . . .

"Are you ready, baby?" Zoya asked as she came into our living room. I got up from the couch and took her in my arms. Zoya's head looked around the room and she smiled in satisfaction.

"It feels strange to have a home of our own," she said happily.

I tracked the small room with my own eyes and felt something ache in my chest. "I've never had a home before." Zoya's arms tightened around my waist. She didn't say anything in response, but I knew she understood.

Kirill and Ivan, along with Luka and Zaal, had gifted us this house. They wanted to give us a larger house, one worthy of a member of the Bratva, but Zoya and I preferred something small. We were both so lost living here on the outside. We wanted to be on our own, in a place big enough just for her and me. And Zoya wanted to be among her people. Avto and his wife only living two doors down.

Zoya pulled back and moved to the closet to get our coats. She slipped hers on. I couldn't help but smile as her face became lost in the fur hood around her neck.

She was so beautiful. Every inch the Kostava *printsessa*.

I was busy staring at my Zoya when she turned and smiled. Taking my coat off the hook, she brought it to me and kissed me on the lips. I groaned against her mouth, my hands lifting to cup her face. I pushed her back until she hit the wall, but Zoya wrenched her head to the side and gasped for breath. "Valentin, I need a break. We've been in bed all day, and I want to go outside."

My nose ran over her cheek and down her neck. I felt her shiver beneath my touch. "I can't get enough of you," I said, and pushed my groin against her.

Zoya laughed and pushed on my chest. "I know, baby, but I want to take a walk with you. I want us to go outside. We need to." She reached down and took hold of my hand. She brought it to her lips and said, "With your hand in mine. Free, like other couples. We're no longer prisoners trapped indoors. We finally get to go outside."

My eyes blazed as I watched her press kiss after kiss on the back of my hand. A hungry growl rumbled in my chest. Reaching down to the coat that had fallen to the floor, Zoya picked it up and pushed it in to my chest.

"Put it on," she said playfully.

Taking the damn coat, I pushed it on and followed Zoya to the door. I pulled on a heavy woolen hat and pulled the hood of the coat to cover my face.

Zoya opened the door, but when she caught sight of me behind she pushed it back shut. I frowned, wondering what she was doing. Then she reached up and pushed my hood down. I swallowed hard at that look on her face, the one I couldn't believe she ever cast on me. The one that told me she loved me.

The one that told me I owned her soul.

Zoya pushed the hat off my shaven head and kissed along the scars on my cheek. As she pulled back, her gaze bored into mine. "Do not hide away from me," she said.

I pushed my fingers into her hair and said, "I'm not hiding from you. You see me. I could never hide from you, *kotyonok.*"

Zoya sighed and said, "Then don't hide from everyone out there, either." She pointed out of the door. My stomach clenched at the thought of going outside. I had barely been outside in the daylight since becoming a free male. I never went out during the day. I had seen the reaction of the Volkovs and Tolstois when they met me. I saw the way the guards stared at my face. Unlike Luka and Zaal, I couldn't hide the scars of my past with clothes. I wore them for everyone to see. The few people we had come into contact with had cowered away at one look. The people who lived close by always gave me a wide berth.

Zoya had made me promise to walk through Brighton Beach with her today. She was sick of being inside. She wanted to show her people we were together. She was sick of hiding us from the world.

Zoya threw the hat to the floor and said, "It's not cold enough to wear that. And there is no need to hide your face."

"They'll stare," I replied, feeling pathetic for even caring.

Zoya's face softened and she whispered, "Then let them stare."

Zoya's fingers squeezed mine and she opened the door. I pulled up the collar as high as it would go and stepped out into the daylight.

The bright winter sun was blinding. I wanted to lift my face and feel its warmth. But when I scanned the area I could see the Kostavas' Georgian people who lived around us beginning to stare. Their heir was making her first appearance.

I kept my head down when Zoya pressed against my side, lifting my arm to wrap around her shoulders. I pulled her close. With her shorter height, she fit perfectly.

Zoya's warm breath ghosted over my skin, and she whispered, "They are staring at me more than you. Most of my people, they have not seen me since I was five."

I nodded my head, but I saw the looks the people were giving us as we walked on. The Georgians were opening the doors of their houses, running out on the street to kiss Zoya's hand, and greeted her with, *"K'alishvili."* Happiness at her survival showed on their faces.

Then they looked at me and the blood drained from their cheeks. I tried to pull my arm away from Zoya's shoulders as she smiled and greeted her people in return. But Zoya gripped my hand tightly, forcing me to stand beside her. Forcing her people to see that I was hers. Introducing me as her male.

My heart swelled knowing she wanted me this much. I would never understand it, but I would never refuse it, either.

The farther we walked toward the beach and the pier, the more the Georgians came out to see her. I watched in awe as the people kissed her hand or waved at her from afar. She *was* a *printsessa*. They were overwhelmed that she had survived, and Zoya thanked her people for their love and support.

Children came out with their mothers, Zoya stopping to stroke their faces. I watched, starving for breath, seeing Zoya with the babies. An image sprang into my mind—Zoya holding our child in her arms. A peace drifted through my body at the thought.

As we continued our walk, I stored the image at the back of my mind, not wanting to lose the happiness I felt when I pictured it.

We had crossed the road that led to the pier when a little girl called out, *"K'alishvili!"* The little girl shouted again and ran across the road holding a red flower in her hand.

She stopped before us and held her flower up for Zoya to take. Zoya smiled at the little dark-haired girl and bent down to take the flower. "Thank you," Zoya said, and the little girl nodded her head shyly.

Then the little girl looked up at me and her mouth dropped open. I tucked my head farther into my collar to not scare her anymore just as the little girl asked Zoya, "Is he a monster, *K'alishvili*?"

My stomach fell and I saw Zoya tense. "No, baby," Zoya replied softly. "He's a warrior, big and strong. He has fought his whole life and sometimes got hurt. That's why he wears scars. They show how brave he has been." Zoya glanced up to me. My muscles tensed at the look of pure love written on her face, at the words coming from her mouth.

Turning back to the little girl, she said, "Valentin has moved to this area with me so he can protect us all and keep us safe. You see how big and strong he is?" The little girl nodded, her brown eyes wide. "Well, that's so he can fight off the bad people."

"Like the scary monsters that live under my bed? Those bad people?"

Zoya laughed and nodded her head. "Yes, just like those. And Valentin always wins, because he has a pure heart."

The little girl looked up at me again, but this time in awe, this time seeing someone else other than a monster.

All because of my Zoya.

The little girl gave me a huge smile, then turned round and ran across the road to her waiting mother.

As Zoya stood, she threaded her hand in mine, and silently led us down the pier. The old wood of the floorboards creaked under my weight. The sound of the waves crashing against the shore grew louder. We reached the end of the pier and gazed out to sea.

I closed my eyes, feeling Zoya's hand in mine. As soon as I was met with darkness, images of my sister infiltrated my mind. The dread that always accompanied them took hold. I slowly breathed in the salty air, pushing the dread aside. We *were* going to get her back. She just had to hold on a while longer. And she would. Inessa was strong.

Opening my eyes, I looked down at Zoya, who was staring out to sea. Inessa was strong, just like my little Georgian *kotyonok*.

As if feeling my stare, Zoya glanced up at me and smiled. My heart almost cracked. When her hand tightened in mine, I looked at her hand and remembered savoring that moment in the chamber, convinced that I would never be able to hold her hand again.

"What are you thinking about?" Zoya inquired.

Pulling her into my chest, I pushed back her long windblown hair from her face and said, "You." I lifted our joined hands. "Us, like this. Out here. Free."

Zoya laid her head on my chest, and I held her close. "Those people . . ." I trailed off and shook my head. "The way they treat you. You *are* their *printsessa*."

"No," she argued, but I shook my head in disagreement. She was. She was beautiful, she was loved, and best of all, she was *mine*.

Zoya lifted her head. With those huge dark eyes, she stared up at me with nothing but love. Reaching up her hands, she pulled back the collar of my coat and smiled. "That's better. Now I can see you."

Leaning down, I pressed a kiss to her lips and tilted my head toward the sun. The warm rays immediately heated my face. I smiled.

Here I was, my hand in Zoya's, sun on my face, and free.

I was *happy*.

I never imagined I could be happy. But it was Zoya. It was all Zoya. My *kotyonok,* the thief of my heart, my little Georgian.

Here I was, the monster that she saved.

The one she searched the dark woods for.

The one she believed deserved to be loved.

152

The Blood Pit

Georgia

As Master left my room, his release calming the fire inside, my eyes drifted shut. Images of a little girl with an older boy suddenly filled my head. My heart beat fast as I saw the boy holding a trembling girl in his arms.

"I am scared," the little girl said.

"Don't be scared," the little boy replied. "I'll never let anything bad happen to you."

I felt the little girl calm and hold out her finger. "Big Brother Promise?" she asked with such trust and hope.

The boy smiled, his handsome face bright with love. He wrapped his finger around the little girl's and said, "Big Brother Promise."

As the memory faded in my mind, now alone in my cell, I opened my eyes to see my hand held up, my finger curled in the air with that promise. Tears ran down my face. Just as the fog in my mind began to thicken again, I stared at my finger, and whispered, "I'm holding on, Valentin. I promise I'm still holding on. . . ."